PENGUIN CLASSICS

THE MAYOR OF CASTERBRIDGE

THOMAS HARDY was born in a cottage in Higher Bockhampton, near Dorchester, on 2 June 1840. He was educated locally and at sixteen was articled to a Dorchester architect, John Hicks. In 1862 he moved to London and found employment with another architect, Arthur Blomfield. He now began to write poetry and published an essay. By 1867 he had returned to Dorset to work as Hicks's assistant and began his first (unpublished) novel, *The Poor Man and the Lady*.

On an architectural visit to St Juliot in Cornwall in 1870 he met his first wife, Emma Gifford. Before their marriage in 1874 he had published four novels and was earning his living as a writer. More novels followed and in 1878 the Hardys moved from Dorset to the London literary scene. But in 1885, after building his house at Max Gate near Dorchester, Hardy again returned to Dorset. He then produced most of his major novels: *The Mayor of Casterbridge* (1886), *The Woodlanders* (1887), *Tess of the d'Urbervilles* (1891), *The Pursuit of the Well-Beloved* (1892) and *Jude the Obscure* (1895). Amidst the controversy caused by *Jude the Obscure*, he turned to the poetry he had been writing all his life. In the next thirty years he published over nine hundred poems and his epic drama in verse, *The Dynasts*.

After a long and bitter estrangement, Emma Hardy died at Max Gate in 1912. Paradoxically, the event triggered some of Hardy's finest love poetry. In 1914, however, he married Florence Dugdale, a close friend for several years. In 1910 he had been awarded the Order of Merit and was recognized, even revered, as the major literary figure of the time. He died on 11 January 1928. His ashes were buried in Westminster Abbey and his heart at Stinsford in Dorset.

KEITH WILSON is Professor and Chair of English at the University of Ottawa. Educated at the City of London School, Magdalene College, Cambridge, and Queen's University, Ontario, he has published widely on nineteenth- and twentieth-century British literature. Among his work on Hardy is *Thomas Hardy on Stage* (1995), a study of Hardy's plays, dramatic adaptations of his own fiction and relationship with the theatre.

PATRICIA INGHAM is General Editor of all Hardy's fiction in the Penguin Classics Edition. She is a Fellow of St Anne's College, Reader in English and *The Times* Lecturer in English Language, Oxford University. She has written extensively on the Victorian novel and on Hardy in particular. Her most recent publications include *Dickens, Women and Language* (1992) and *The Language of Gender and Class: Transformation in the Victorian Novel* (1996). She has also edited Elizabeth Gaskell's *North and South* and Thomas Hardy's *The Pursuit of the Well-Beloved and The Well-Beloved* for Penguin Classics.

THOMAS HARDY

The Mayor of Casterbridge

THE LIFE AND DEATH
OF A MAN OF CHARACTER

Edited with an introduction and notes by
KEITH WILSON

PENGUIN BOOKS

PENGUIN BOOKS

Published by the Penguin Group
Penguin Books Ltd, 27 Wrights Lane, London w8 5tz, England
Penguin Books USA Inc., 375 Hudson Street, New York, New York 10014, USA
Penguin Books Australia Ltd, Ringwood, Victoria, Australia
Penguin Books Canada Ltd, 10 Alcorn Avenue, Toronto, Ontario, Canada m4v 3b2
Penguin Books (NZ) Ltd, 182–190 Wairau Road, Auckland 10, New Zealand

Penguin Books Ltd, Registered Offices: Harmondsworth, Middlesex, England

First published 1886
This edition published in Penguin Classics 1997
3 5 7 9 10 8 6 4 2

Editorial matter copyright © Keith Wilson, 1997
All rights reserved

The moral right of the editor has been asserted

Set in 10/12.5pt Monotype Baskerville
Typeset by Rowland Phototypesetting Ltd, Bury St Edmunds, Suffolk
Printed in England by Clays Ltd, St Ives plc

CONTENTS

ACKNOWLEDGEMENTS

I would like to thank the staffs of the following institutions for help or access to material in their possession: Beinecke Library, Yale University; Buswell Memorial Library, Wheaton College; Colby College Library; Dorset County Museum, especially its Curator, Mr R. M. de Peyer; Houghton Library, Harvard University; McMaster University Library; Morisset Library, University of Ottawa, in particular Grace Welch and Gilbert Desgranges-Adam of its map department and the staff at Interlibrary Loan; University of New Brunswick Library.

My thanks also to Patricia Ingham, who has been an exemplary General Editor, there when needed but never obtrusive. My colleagues Ina Ferris, April London, and David Shore read the Introduction with even greater care than I had anticipated they would when I asked them to, and I am very grateful for their valuable suggestions. Leslie Reid knows considerably more about print plates than I do, and gave helpful advice on the illustrations.

My sons Neil and James as yet know little about introductions, plates, or even Thomas Hardy. But I thank them for their understanding when I was preoccupied with Casterbridge and the delight of their company when I was not.

This edition uses, with one exception, the first edition in *volume* form of each of Hardy's novels and therefore offers something not generally available. Their dates range from 1871 to 1897. The purpose behind this choice is to present each novel as the creation of its own period and without revisions of later times, since these versions have an integrity and value of their own. The outline of textual history that follows is designed to expand on this statement.

All of Hardy's fourteen novels, except *Jude the Obscure* (1895) which first appeared as a volume in the Wessex Novels, were published individually as he wrote them (from 1871 onwards). Apart from *Desperate Remedies* (1871) and *Under the Greenwood Tree* (1872), all were published first as serials in periodicals, where they were subjected to varying degrees of editorial interference and censorship. *Desperate Remedies* and *Under the Greenwood Tree* appeared directly in volume form from Tinsley Brothers. By 1895 ten more novels had been published in volumes by six different publishers.

By 1895 Hardy was sufficiently well established to negotiate with Osgood, McIlvaine a collected edition of all earlier novels and short-story collections plus the volume edition of *Jude the Obscure*. *The Well-Beloved* (radically changed from its serialized version) was added in 1897, completing the appearance of all Hardy's novels in volume form. Significantly this collection was called the 'Wessex Novels' and contained a map of 'The Wessex of the Novels' and authorial prefaces, as well as frontispieces by Macbeth-Raeburn of a scene from the novel sketched 'on the spot'. The texts were heavily revised by Hardy, amongst other things, in relation to topography to strengthen the 'Wessex' element so as to suggest that this half-real half-imagined location had been coherently conceived from the beginning, though of course he knew that this was not so. In practice 'Wessex' had an uncertain and ambiguous development in the earlier editions. To trace the growth of Wessex in the novels as they appeared it is necessary to read them in their original pre-1895 form. For the 1895–6 edition represents a substantial layer of reworking.

Similarly in the last fully revised and collected edition of 1912–13, the Wessex Edition, further alterations were made to topographical detail and photographs of Dorset were included. In the more open climate of opinion then prevailing, sexual and religious references were sometimes (though not always) made bolder. In both collected editions there were also many changes of other kinds. In addition novels and short-story volumes were grouped thematically as 'Novels of Character and Environment', 'Romances and Fantasies' and 'Novels of Ingenuity' in a way suggesting a unifying master plan underlying all texts. A few revisions were made for the Mellstock Edition of 1919–20, but to only some texts.

It is various versions of the 1912–13 edition which are generally available today, incorporating these layers of alteration and shaped in part by the critical climate when the alterations were made. Therefore the present edition offers the texts as Hardy's readers first encountered them, in a form of which he in general approved, the version that his early critics reacted to. It reveals Hardy as he first dawned upon the public and shows how his writing (including the creation of Wessex) developed, partly in response to differing climates of opinion in the 1870s, 1880s and early 1890s. In keeping with these general aims, the edition will reproduce all contemporary illustrations where the originals were line drawings. In addition for all texts which were illustrated, individual volumes will provide an appendix discussing the artist and the illustrations.

The exception to the use of the first volume editions is *Far from the Madding Crowd*, for which Hardy's holograph manuscript will be used. That edition will demonstrate in detail just how the text is 'the creation of its own period': by relating the manuscript to the serial version and to the first volume edition. The heavy editorial censoring by Leslie Stephen for the serial and the subsequent revision for the volume provide an extreme example of the processes that in many cases precede and produce the first book versions. In addition, the complete serial version (1892) of *The Well-Beloved* will be printed alongside the volume edition, since it is arguably a different novel from the latter.

To complete the picture of how the texts developed later, editors trace in their Notes on the History of the Text the major changes in 1895–6 and 1912–13. They quote significant alterations in their explanatory notes and include the authorial prefaces of 1895–6 and 1912–13. They also indicate something of the pre-history of the texts in manuscripts where these are available. The editing of the short stories will be separately dealt with in the two volumes containing them.

Patricia Ingham
St Anne's College, Oxford

1840 2 June: Thomas Hardy born, Higher Bockhampton, Dorset, eldest child of a builder, Thomas Hardy, and Jemima Hand, who had been married for less than six months. Younger siblings: Mary, Henry, Katharine (Kate), to whom he remained close.

1848–56 Schooling in Dorset.

1856 Hardy watched the hanging of Martha Browne for the murder of her husband. (Thought to be remembered in the death of Tess Durbeyfield.)

1856–60 Articled to Dorchester architect, John Hicks; later his assistant.

late 1850s Important friendship with Horace Moule (eight years older, middle class and well educated), who became his intellectual mentor and encouraged his self-education.

1862 London architect, Arthur Blomfield, employed him as a draughtsman. Self-education continued.

1867 Returned to Dorset as a jobbing architect. He worked for Hicks on church restoration.

1868 Completed his first novel *The Poor Man and the Lady* but it was rejected for publication (see 1878).

1869 Worked for the architect Crickmay in Weymouth, again on church restoration.

1870 After many youthful infatuations thought to be referred to in early poems, met his first wife, Emma Lavinia Gifford, on a professional visit to St Juliot in north Cornwall.

1871 *Desperate Remedies* published in volume form by Tinsley Brothers.

1872 *Under the Greenwood Tree* published in volume form by Tinsley Brothers.

1873 *A Pair of Blue Eyes* (previously serialized in *Tinsleys' Magazine*). Horace Moule committed suicide.

1874 *Far from the Madding Crowd* (previously serialized in the *Cornhill Magazine*). Hardy married Emma and set up house in London

(Surbiton). They had no children, to Hardy's regret; and she never got on with his family.

1875   The Hardys returned to Dorset (Swanage).

1876   *The Hand of Ethelberta* (previously serialized in the *Cornhill Magazine*).

1878   *The Return of the Native* (previously serialized in *Belgravia*). The Hardys moved back to London (Tooting). Serialized version of part of first unpublished novel appeared in *Harper's Weekly* in New York as *An Indiscretion in the Life of an Heiress*. It was never included in his collected works.

1880   *The Trumpet-Major* (previously serialized in *Good Words*). Hardy ill for many months.

1881   *A Laodicean* (previously serialized in *Harper's New Monthly Magazine*). The Hardys returned to Dorset.

1882   *Two on a Tower* (previously serialized in the *Atlantic Monthly*).

1885   The Hardys moved for the last time to a house, Max Gate, outside Dorchester, designed by Hardy and built by his brother.

1886   *The Mayor of Casterbridge* (previously serialized in the *Graphic*).

1887   *The Woodlanders* (previously serialized in *Macmillan's Magazine*).

1888   *Wessex Tales*.

1891   *A Group of Noble Dames* (tales). *Tess of the d'Urbervilles* (previously serialized in censored form in the *Graphic*). It simultaneously enhanced his reputation as a novelist and caused a scandal because of its advanced views on sexual conduct.

1892   Hardy's father, Thomas, died. Serialized version of *The Well-Beloved*, entitled *The Pursuit of the Well-Beloved*, in the *Illustrated London News*. Growing estrangement from Emma.

1892–3   *Our Exploits at West Poley*, a long tale for boys, published in an American periodical, the *Household*.

1893   Met Florence Henniker, one of several society women with whom he had intense friendships. Collaborated with her on *The Spectre of the Real* (published 1894).

1894   *Life's Little Ironies* (tales).

1895   *Jude the Obscure*, a savage attack on marriage which worsened relations with Emma. Serialized previously in *Harper's New Monthly Magazine*. It received both eulogistic and vitriolic reviews. The latter were a factor in his ceasing to write novels.

1895–6 First Collected Edition of novels: Wessex Novels (16 volumes), published by Osgood, McIlvaine. This included the first book edition of *Jude the Obscure*.

1897 *The Well-Beloved* (rewritten) published as a book; added to the Wessex Novels as vol. XVII. From now on he published only the poetry he had been writing since the 1860s. **No more novels**.

1898 *Wessex Poems and Other Verses*. Hardy and Emma continued to live at Max Gate but were now estranged and 'kept separate'.

1901 *Poems of the Past and the Present*.

1902 Macmillan became his publishers.

1904 Part 1 of *The Dynasts* (epic-drama in verse on Napoleon). Hardy's mother, Jemima, 'the single most important influence in his life', died.

1905 Met Florence Emily Dugdale, his future second wife, then aged 26. Soon a friend and secretary.

1906 Part 2 of *The Dynasts*.

1908 Part 3 of *The Dynasts*.

1909 *Time's Laughingstocks and Other Verses*.

1910 Awarded Order of Merit, having previously refused a knighthood.

1912–13 Major collected edition of novels and verse, revised by Hardy: The Wessex Edition (24 volumes). 27 November: Emma died still estranged. This triggered the writing of Hardy's finest love-lyrics about their early time in Cornwall.

1913 *A Changed Man and Other Tales*.

1914 10 February: married Florence Dugdale (already hurt by his poetic reaction to Emma's death). *Satires of Circumstance. The Dynasts: Prologue and Epilogue*.

1915 Mary, Hardy's sister, died. His distant young cousin, Frank, killed at Gallipoli.

1916 *Selected Poems*.

1917 *Moments of Vision and Miscellaneous Verses*.

1919–20 Mellstock Edition of novels and verse (37 volumes).

1922 *Late Lyrics and Earlier with Many Other Verses*.

1923 *The Famous Tragedy of the Queen of Cornwall* (drama).

1924 Dramatized *Tess* performed at Dorchester. Hardy infatuated with the local woman, Gertrude Bugler, who played Tess.

1925 *Human Shows, Far Phantasies, Songs and Trifles.*

1928 Hardy died on 11 January. His heart was buried in Emma's grave at Stinsford, his ashes in Westminster Abbey. *Winter Words in various moods and metres* published posthumously. Hardy's brother, Henry, died.

1928–30 Hardy's autobiography published (on his instructions) under his second wife's name.

1937 Florence Hardy (his second wife) died.

1940 Hardy's last sibling, Kate, died.

PLACE NAMES

Hardy's name	*Real name*
Anglebury	Wareham
Budmouth	Weymouth
Casterbridge	Dorchester
Dummerford	Fordington
Havenpool	Poole
Hintock	Imaginary village in the Melbury, Evershot, Hermitage area
Kingsbere	Bere Regis
Melchester	Salisbury
Mellstock	Stinsford, including Lower and Higher Bockhampton
Overcombe	Suggested by Sutton-Poyntz, but relocated
Port-Bredy (Breedy)	Bridport
Sherton-Abbas	Sherborne
Shottsford	Blandford Forum
Stickleford	Tincleton
Weatherbury	Puddletown
Weydon Priors	Weyhill

This map is from the Wessex Novels Edition, 1895–6

River Ceme

C A S T E R B R I D G E   M O O R

To Mellstock
and Weatherbury

River Froom

Ten
Hatches

Priory

Grey's
Bridge

1

2

Bull Stake
Square

Swan Bridge

6

New Walk

Top
o' Town

3   4 5

High East Street

High West Street

8   7

9

Mixen Lane

10

Gallows Hill

Old (West) Walk

Back Street

r

Chestnut (South) Walk

Bowling Walk

C A S T E R B R I D G E   M O O R

To Anglebury

Maumbury
Rings

1. Hangman's Cottage   6. King of Prussia
2. Jail   7. High Street Hall
3. St. Peter's Church   8. Town Pump
4. Town Hall   9. Stag
5. Golden Crown   10. Henchard's House

To Budmouth

Casterbridge

LIST OF ILLUSTRATIONS

N.B. The captions attached to the illustrations are those that appeared in the original serial publication in the *Graphic*. The episode to which Plate XVI relates was excised from the end of Chapter XXXV. For the episode pictured in Plate XX, see Appendix I.

The publication in 1886 of *The Mayor of Casterbridge: The Life and Death of a Man of Character* marked the beginning of what was to be the richest period in Thomas Hardy's twenty-five-year career as a novelist. The fulfilment of the great tragic novels – *The Woodlanders* (1887), *Tess of the d'Urbervilles* (1891) and *Jude the Obscure* (1895) – would not in the mid-1880s have seemed predictable from the tenor and quality of Hardy's most recent work. While some short stories had appeared in periodicals, his last full novel, *Two on a Tower* (1882), had been published more than three years earlier, a mere eleven months after the appearance of the ill-starred *A Laodicean* (1881), much of which was dictated by the ailing Hardy to his wife from what looked for a while like being his deathbed. Between them these two minor novels displayed an unpromising pre-occupation with romance in highish society, an emphasis which may have suggested a return to the laboured social and class preoccupations of his first unpublished novel *The Poor Man and the Lady* (written in 1867), the early *Desperate Remedies* (1871) and *A Pair of Blue Eyes* (1873), and his 'comedy in chapters' *The Hand of Ethelberta* (1876). It could equally have seemed an advance into more contemporary class concerns: the social paradoxes attendant upon the emergence of a modern professional and scientific meritocracy. But whether *A Laodicean* and *Two on a Tower* invited a look backwards or forwards, they would certainly have suggested a movement away from the pastoral rusticity of *Under the Greenwood Tree* (1872) and *Far from the Madding Crowd* (1874), the louring existential drama of *The Return of the Native* (1878), or the regional history of *The Trumpet-Major* (1880). The *Saturday Review*'s notice of *Two on a Tower* identified and censured this apparent tendency, complaining that *A Laodicean* 'can hardly have been thought an improvement on the previous works . . . and, unfortunately, it is not easy to think that *Two on a Tower* is much of an improvement on *A Laodicean*' (18 November 1882; reprinted in R. G. Cox, (ed.), *Thomas Hardy: The Critical Heritage* (London: Routledge

& Kegan Paul), p. 97). While contemporary reviewers often advanced what now seem eccentric judgements on Hardy's novels, time has done little to promote either novel to a higher echelon of his fiction. Anyone hazarding in 1885 an opinion on his past achievements and future prospects might have been forgiven for predicting that a novelist to whom posterity would accord an honourable if modest place in the history of nineteenth-century fiction had already produced his best work.

And then came the remarkable achievement of *The Mayor of Caster-bridge*. It came at a time when, as he entered his mid-forties, Hardy's life was taking a decided turn back towards its Dorset roots. The need to convalesce from his extended 1880–81 illness had encouraged the Hardys' relocation in June 1881 from London, where they had lived for the previous three years, to Wimborne. Exactly two years later they moved from Wimborne to the centre of Dorchester, taking up residence in Shire-Hall Place, where *The Mayor of Casterbridge* was written: a diary entry for 17 April 1885 notes: 'Wrote the last page of "*The Mayor of Casterbridge*", begun at least a year ago, and frequently interrupted in the writing of each part' (*Life and Work*, p. 177). Here they were to stay for another two years before a final move into Max Gate, the Hardy-designed house on the edge of Dorchester, built by his father and brother, in which he was to live for the rest of his life. The move was a return home both literally and imaginatively, and one attended with residual doubts. On 31 December 1885, after six months in Max Gate and with the first instalment of *The Mayor of Casterbridge* due to appear in the *Graphic* in just two days, Hardy mused: 'This evening, the end of the old year 1885 finds me sadder than many previous New Year's eves have done. Whether building this house at Max Gate was a wise expenditure of energy is one doubt, which, if resolved in the negative, is depressing enough. And there are others' (*Life and Work*, pp. 182–3).

At this remove it is pointless to speculate about the extent to which these doubts may have included uncertainties about his own marital situation, and presumptuous to draw any conclusions about that situation's influence on the choice of domestic disharmony, stylized into the notorious wife-sale, as originating plot moment in *The Mayor of Casterbridge*. More reliable is the evidence that the return to Dorset, and particularly Dorchester, helped re-confirm Wessex as the most fertile imaginative ground for Hardy. Renewed daily familiarity would logically have suggested Dorchester, fictionalized into Casterbridge, as a centre for the most topographically cohesive (in both inner imaginative coherence and relationship of setting to original) of all his major works.

The Return of the Native had been the last novel so intimately connected in its location – the heathland adjacent to his Bockhampton birthplace – with Hardy's own personal past. In that book, the native in question, Clym Yeobright, turns his back on the bubble reputation floated by the cosmopolitan sophistications of Paris in order to seek, with disastrous consequences, a renewed relationship with origin. *The Mayor of Casterbridge* rings pointed changes on this situation. Michael Henchard begins and ends the novel away from Casterbridge and in virtual anonymity – his origins unexplained, his death a self-willed annihilation – and achieves renown only *in* his association with Casterbridge. The Casterbridge Henchard, seen only after ascent to the mayoralty, is defined by social position, his municipal office providing the book's eponymous title. While Yeobright courts regional obscurity in the service of good works, despite the fact that his cosmopolitan allure comprises most of his appeal to the woman he has married, Henchard is a Casterbridge-made public man. But his very status contributes to his downfall: only a public figure would be vulnerable to the court-room revelations of Mrs Goodenough or the community lampooning of the skimmity-ride. In their opposed but complementary ways, both Yeobright and Henchard offer bleak versions of the uneasy relationship between celebrity and obscurity, centre and margin. Between them they reflect what may have been contradictory impulses in Hardy himself, who had good reason to ponder both the familial and personal costs of being a public figure and the possible career implications of a return from London, the social and cultural centre of the English-speaking world, to permanent residence a few miles from his childhood home. There is suggestive irony in the fact that Hardy was sworn in as a Dorchester magistrate, the civic responsibility that brings so humiliatingly to light the discrepancy between Henchard's present social position and past history, while working on the early stages of his Casterbridge novel.

Although *The Mayor of Casterbridge* may invite speculation about the now-famous Hardy's own ambivalent relationship with a community in which he had once been merely an apprentice architect, whose modest professional expectations even then were already moving him away from his origins in a Bockhampton cottage, any similarity between Michael Henchard and his creator ends with their shared local celebrity. Henchard is the first Hardy character so completely to dominate the novel in which he appears, and only Tess and Jude are protagonists of comparable, although very differently figured, psychological power. In Henchard's case, the self-destructive nature of that power – source of the fury that causes him to lash out against both himself and those who stand closest to him – expresses itself in terms that for a later age, more familiar with the easy jargon of psychiatric diagnosis, bear the clear stamp of manic depression. His emotional collapse is what initially attracts Lucetta's attention, suggesting that she is drawn towards the vulnerability that is so near allied to aggression. In the serial versions of the novel, their Jersey meeting takes place when she rescues Henchard from drowning, but revision transformed this into an illness in which 'I sank into one of those gloomy fits I sometimes suffer from . . . when the world seems to have the blackness of hell, and, like Job, I could curse the day that gave me birth' (Chapter XII). Lucetta's 'pity' nurses Henchard out of this state, just as his own self-pity recurrently plunges him back into it. While he ascribes these fits to 'the loneliness of my domestic life', the opening chapter, when he still has the company of wife and child, suggests a constitutional rather than situational cause for his gloom. Because of Henchard's taciturnity, Susan 'walked the highway alone, save for the child she bore', as her husband proclaims in 'the turn and plant of each foot . . . a dogged and cynical indifference, personal to himself.'

Henchard's self-destructive darkness strikes only by fits, leaving him susceptible in less overcast phases of his emotional life to guilt, affectional impulse, self-sacrifice, and generosity. Either greater self-control or greater ruthlessness might be his saving. The lack of self-control leads to the wife-sale, the rejection of Farfrae and subsequent verbal and physical attacks on him, the attempt to blackmail Lucetta into marriage, the toying with her reputation by reading Farfrae extracts from her old love-letters, and the lying to Newson about Elizabeth-Jane's supposed death. The lack of ruthlessness leads to the decision to re-marry Susan, the public acknowledgement of the truth of Mrs Goodenough's court-room revelation, his exemplary conduct at the bankruptcy proceedings, and the inability to carry to a conclusion his impulses to harm Farfrae and Lucetta. He is a man whose governing inclinations are tragically at war with each other: generosity with meagre calculation, altruism with self-pity, hatred with love, civic responsibility with fecklessness. To the extent that there is a 'real' Michael Henchard, he is a compound of antithetical terms and, as Dr Jekyll, the even more tortured protagonist of a novel published in the same year as *The Mayor of Casterbridge*, came to say of his own double nature, 'if I could rightly be said to be either, it was only because I was radically both' (Robert Louis Stevenson, 'Henry Jekyll's Full Statement of the Case', *The Strange Case of Dr. Jekyll and Mr. Hyde*).

Apart from being made privy to the wife-sale, we know nothing of Henchard's pre-Casterbridge life, except for one telling fact: he once had a brother, who died. A key part of Farfrae's uncanny appeal for Henchard lies in his possession of facial features similar to those of the dead brother, whose loss still haunts Henchard. Elizabeth-Jane herself notes the quasi-fraternal terms of their relationship, Henchard laying 'his arm familiarly on his manager's shoulder, as if Farfrae were a younger brother, bearing so heavily that his slight figure bent under the weight' (Chapter XIV). The division within him is thus externalized in the equally antithetical terms of his relationship with the young stranger, in which love mystified into blood-brotherhood and hatred verging on the homicidal compete for dominance. Despite the recurrent critical tendency to read Henchard and Farfrae as existing in simple opposition – Henchard embodying tradition, superstition, passion, body, the spoken word, instinct and community, Farfrae figuring modernity, science, reason, mind, the written word, calculation, and society – Henchard's extreme responses to Farfrae are clearly at some level the expression of *self*-love and *self*-loathing, with Farfrae standing for the dead other self of a lost brother.

This is made explicit in the tendency of both extremities of response to have more profound effects on Henchard himself than on Farfrae. The love, expressed in the domineering tones that distinguish all Henchard's emotive impulses, is associated not only with the lost brother but also with the salvation of his own reputation by Farfrae's method for recovering grown wheat. The hatred is expressed in acts of aggression which unfailingly rebound on the aggressor: the raining-out of the celebration that Henchard establishes in competition with Farfrae's (Chapter XVI); the public cursing of Farfrae (Chapter XXXIII), whose terms ('And the next age his hated name/Shall utterly deface') are fulfilled against Henchard himself in the self-erasing '& that no man remember me' of his will; the wrestling bout in which honour demands that Henchard first disable himself before attempting to destroy Farfrae (Chapter XXXVIII). On the only occasion he actually does significant damage to Farfrae, when his careless return of Lucetta's love-letters results ultimately in her death, it is damage brought about by thoughtlessness and the interference of malign external agency rather than by his own design. And even then he arguably does more damage to himself than to the resilient Farfrae, who soon takes consolation in having 'exchanged a looming misery for a simple sorrow' since 'it was hard to believe that life with her would have been productive of further happiness' (Chapter XLII).

The reflexive nature of Henchard's responses to Farfrae is, of course, most fully acted out in the mirrored paths of their careers. Not only does Farfrae become Henchard, by taking possession of his business, prospective wife, domestic furnishings, house and municipal office, but Henchard becomes Farfrae, contemplating emigration, resisting pressing invitation to take lodgings in his would-be patron's house, and finally capitulating and accepting employment with him. As Henchard observes bitterly to Jopp, 'Surely he'll buy my body and soul likewise' (Chapter XXXII). While the Faustian echoes may dominate here, particularly given the earlier specific association of Henchard with Faust (see Chapter XVII, n. 5), Farfrae seems, one would have thought even to Henchard himself, somewhat miscast in the role of Lucifer. But if, as Henchard's own Casterbridge experience would suggest, position and possessions are the making of the man, Farfrae's appropriations make him and Henchard increasingly difficult to distinguish from each other.

This pattern of doubling that at once makes Henchard himself so fundamentally divided and externalizes that self-fracture in the fraternal relationship with Farfrae, runs through all the characterization, generating a novel of unusually elaborate psychological inversions, anticipatory of similar complexities in *The Woodlanders*, *Tess*, and *Jude*. In March 1886, as the serialization of *The Mayor of Casterbridge* continued in the *Graphic*, Hardy made a diary note that speaks to techniques of characterization foreshadowed in his most recent novel: 'Novel-writing as an art cannot go backward. Having reached the analytic stage it must transcend it by going still further in the same direction. Why not by rendering as visible essences, spectres, &c. the abstract thoughts of the analytic school' (*Life and Work*, p. 183). This is not to suggest that *The Mayor of Casterbridge* substitutes spectral presences for real characters. But it does align contradictory human propensities, both within and between characters, in ways that destabilize character consistency and place emphasis as much on protean human responses as on the particular character who happens at any given time to be manifesting them.

For example, essential to the plot complications is another lost sibling, Henchard's actual daughter, who, though dead in infancy, fundamentally influences Elizabeth-Jane's fate. Without her knowledge, her relationship with Henchard is governed by his progressively bifurcated sense of her identity: on the one hand as the daughter he effectively sold along with his wife and believes himself to have bought back, on the other as an alien intruder who has appropriated that daughter's place. She becomes the means of introducing Henchard, however inadequately, to the relativizing of absolute notions of identity, her ministrations after the skimmity-ride encouraging him to develop again 'the dream of a future lit by her filial presence' (Chapter XLI), despite his awareness of the lack of biological relationship between them. His 'greedy exclusiveness' and fear of losing her prevents this leading to equal flexibility in his glossing of paternal identity, with the result that he immediately sends Newson packing with the lie of Elizabeth-Jane's death. But the final bestowal of affection on the rejected stepdaughter with whom he has no actual blood-ties is the reversed analogue of his earlier attachment to Farfrae, the quasi-brother he comes to hate. The apparently oppositional exclusiveness of love and dislike, premised upon absolutist notions of identity and its obligations, is challenged in the instability of the uncompromising Henchard's own erratic teetering between such attitudinal extremes.

The eventual marriage between Elizabeth-Jane and Farfrae sanctifies the possibilities of compromise between the kind of antithetical terms whose irreconcilability, in their undiluted forms, destroys the absolutist Henchard. The rejected early love becomes Farfrae's less glamorous and idealized, but finally more satisfactory, second wife. Elizabeth-Jane's blood-father, who once proved his paternal affection by the eccentric course of desertion and feigned death, discusses the economics of wedding celebration with the thrifty groom and, after demonstrating his frenzied terpsichorean joy at the happy event, departs again to the comfortingly unfamilial solitude of his Budmouth lodgings. And Elizabeth-Jane herself, as the 'sparkling emotions of her early married life cohered into an equable serenity', comes to reflect that 'the doubtful honour of a brief transit through a sorry world hardly called for effusiveness, even when the path was suddenly irradiated at some half-way point by daybeams rich as hers' (Chapter XLV). The mood is one of qualified contentment not passional extremity, generated by the capacity to strike an unspectacular balance between calculation and generosity, solipsism and altruism, business, pleasure and the sheer grind of existence. It defines a context that finally has no place for a Michael Henchard.

The doubling, at times tripling and quadrupling, patterns extend far beyond Henchard's and Elizabeth-Jane's lost brother and sister, forming themselves into a dense web comprising the plot's immanent design. All six of the major characters are implicated in the process, their identities constantly being reshaped as a function of changing relationship with others. At the centre of all the interconnected threads is Henchard.

Farfrae may be the brother Henchard lost, returned to replace him as corn factor and mayor, but he also both plays a filial role in relation to Henchard and shares his spousal connection to Lucetta. Their relationship is further complicated by Farfrae's recurrent figuring as mentor, and hence surrogate paternal figure, to Henchard, to whom he offers advice not only on professional matters but also on the confusions of his private life.

Newson, in turn, has been for many years – at least until the unconvincingly well-intentioned desertion and feigned death – the husband Henchard might have been, returned after Susan's death to replace him as father to Elizabeth-Jane. As well as sharing Henchard's spousal and paternal relationships to Susan and Elizabeth-Jane, he displays a number of his less edifying characteristics, in addition to the most obvious: their shared and extremely questionable understanding of the responsibilities marriage and fatherhood carry. He enables marital irregularity by buying where Henchard sells; he contributes to major private and public discord by helping fund the skimmity-ride, which given his own domestic arrangements and Mixen Lane's doorstep sex-trade is as hypocritical as it is heartless; he shares Henchard's egregious and self-excusing condescension to Susan's supposed simplemindedness; and he is finally so taken by the 'joke' played upon him by Henchard in lying about Elizabeth-Jane's 'death' as to regard the whole episode 'as much my fault as his' (Chapter XLIII). But at the same time, he shares certain character traits with Farfrae: restraint and calculation in emotion, caution in financial dealings, contentment with his own company. This 'eclipsing personage' who 'out-Farfraed Farfrae in saltatory intensity' at the wedding celebration (Chapter XLIV), just as Farfrae has out-Hencharded Henchard in corn-dealing, municipal politics and marriageability, is also, like both Farfrae and Henchard, an opportunistic itinerant, the only one of the three actually to have fulfilled intentions to emigrate.

The patterning between the women is similarly convoluted. After the death of Susan, Elizabeth-Jane finds a surrogate mother-figure in Lucetta, in some degree through Lucetta's vestigial relationship with Henchard, but more particularly through her quasi-adoption of Elizabeth-Jane in the latter's movement from Henchard's house to High Street Hall. Lucetta is also figured as Elizabeth-Jane's sisterly double, most specifically when Elizabeth-Jane first sees her, standing by Susan's grave: '[t]he personage was in mourning like herself, was about her age and size, and might have been her wraith or double, but for the fact that it was a lady much more beautifully dressed than she' (Chapter XX). But after becoming Lucetta's companion, Elizabeth-Jane herself increasingly plays a quasi-maternal role *vis-à-vis* the older woman. Like

Henchard consulting Farfrae, Lucetta seeks, albeit with unconvincing dissimulation as if on behalf of a friend, Elizabeth-Jane's advice on her responsibilities to her former lover and the enduring power of her own beauty, so that 'Elizabeth, though the younger, had come to play the part of experienced sage in these discussions' (Chapter XXIV). This refiguring of relational terms is all the more pronounced in the serial version of the novel, and given a remarkably physical application. During the exchange with the escaped bull, Lucetta is reduced to immediate hysteria while Elizabeth-Jane grabs the leading-stick to restrain the bull for what she thinks is long enough for Lucetta to make her escape to the top of a clover stack (Chapter XXIX). Lucetta's confusion prevents the fulfilment of Elizabeth-Jane's plans, and Henchard duly arrives to complete the rescue. But here, as in her later taking command of a desperate situation by rushing in to close window and shutters in a fruitless attempt to protect Lucetta from sight of the skimmity-ride (Chapter XXXIX), Elizabeth-Jane shows a presence of mind that defines her as the dominant force, whatever her social inferiority, in her dealings with Lucetta. She also, of course, shares Lucetta's spousal relationship to Farfrae, giving her effectively a fourfold identity *vis-à-vis* Lucetta – sister, daughter, mother and rival – to match Farfrae's similar fourfold identity – brother, son, father and rival – *vis-à-vis* Henchard.

Lucetta, in turn, is not only one of Farfrae's two wives but also one of Henchard's, literally so in the novel's earliest version, where Henchard, assuming Susan is dead, actually marries her. She unintentionally acts out the association with Susan in one of the novel's most striking mirror scenes: her Casterbridge Ring supplication to Henchard for the return of her love-letters (Chapter XXXV). The deliberate attempt to impair her own beauty succeeds so well that Henchard takes pity on her after being reminded of his previous meeting at the same place with the returned Susan. Again, the serial version increases the resonance of these echoes. Enlisting the help of a local chemist to employ 'disfiguring ointments of various kinds', Lucetta appears to Henchard a 'poor, withered, worn-out woman' (Chapter XXXV), linguistically a revenant of Susan, the 'poor fragile woman', termed 'The Ghost', whose attractions for Henchard had appeared so puzzling to local gossip (Chapter XIII). The serial version underlines the association still further by having

Farfrae come upon Lucetta and Henchard at the Ring, causing Henchard to draw 'Lucetta's arm through his own to lend a delusive aspect to the rendezvous he had been surprised in'. Farfrae fails to recognize Lucetta, and after his departure she rushes home, restores herself to beauty, and joins her unsuspecting husband, who conjectures that 'poor Henchard is going to console himself by speculating in a wife once more. I met him courting just now' (Chapter XXXV). And Susan and Lucetta are associated not only in their maternal/quasi-maternal relationships with Elizabeth-Jane and their marital/quasi-marital relationships with Henchard but also in their respective marriages to Newson and Farfrae, the two outsider figures who enter Henchard's life at his request and devastatingly disrupt it.

With protean relationships relativizing identity this completely, Hardy is already working with novelistic characterization in ways that anticipate the refining of human response into emblematic terms in *The Dynasts* (published originally in three volumes, 1904, 1906, 1908). In this vast epic-drama of the Napoleonic War, Hardy created as choric comment-ators a group of cumbersome 'Phantom Intelligences', who look down and comment on European history as it unfolds over ten years, from the weeks before Trafalgar to the Battle of Waterloo. These Intelligences represent little more than the refinement of human attitude and response, for good and ill, into 'visible essences': the Spirit of the Years, the Spirit of the Pities, the Spirits Sinister and Ironic, and the Spirit of Rumour. These figures translate into fuller modes of abstraction a tendency already evident in the doublings and self-divisions of the inhabitants of Casterbridge.

At different times, all the major characters reveal a capacity, worthy of the Spirit of the Years at his most deterministic, of responding to experience as the working-out of inevitable courses uninfluenceable by individual attempts to redirect them. The Henchard who consults the weather-prophet or interprets another double – the discarded effigy of himself at Ten-Hatches – as a sign (Chapters XXVI and XLI); the Farfrae who reads the meeting with Henchard and consequent job offer as 'destiny' and 'fate' (Chapter IX) and his own ascent to the mayoralty as evidence of being 'ruled by the powers above us' (Chapter XXXIV); the Susan whose countenance 'deems anything possible at the hands of Time and Chance, except, perhaps, fair-play' (Chapter I) or who responds to Henchard's threats to sell her 'in the resigned tones of a fatalist' (Chapter II); the Lucetta who responds to the skimmity-ride with the accurate prediction that it will kill her (Chapter XXXIX) – all offer themselves as hostages to a fortune analogous in its workings to the Immanent Will of *The Dynasts*, glossed by the Spirit of the Years as a force 'Which thinking on, yet weighing not Its thought,/Unchecks Its clock-like laws' (*The Dynasts*, Part First, Fore Scene). But equally meliorative impulses reflective of the Spirit of the Pities are shown by the Henchard who takes pity on Lucetta and who cannot act out his intention of wrestling Farfrae to his death, or the Farfrae who refuses his first customer because he is a client of Henchard's, takes pity on his bankrupt patron, buys in his furniture, gives him employment, and sets him up in his own seed-shop.

Nor are these impulses separable in the composite body of Casterbridge humanity from those of the Spirits Sinister and Ironic, which could stand as the presiding geniuses of Mixen Lane and such worshippers at its 'church', Saint Peter's Finger inn, as Nance Mockridge, Mother Cuxsom, Mrs Goodenough and Jopp. They are also the spirits who govern Henchard's own sardonic flirtations with cruelty, and influence Newson's unfortunate meddlings in the human tragi-comedy. And the Spirit of Rumour, the relentless force that makes events while claiming only to record them and combines the chaos of disparate contingencies into mythic design, controls community response to all the major and minor sensations that ruffle the even surface of Casterbridge life: the initiatory saga of the spoiled bread; the attraction and later antipathy between the mayor and the young Scottish stranger; the mayor's baffling marriage to a lacklustre widow; the death of the mayor's wife; the drunken vagrant's startling revelations about his past; the marriage between Farfrae and the new tenant of High Street Hall; the insult to royalty perpetrated by the ex-mayor; the discovery that the new mayor's wife once knew the old mayor better than she should have; the skimmity-ride; another mayoral wife's death; Farfrae's remarriage shortly after the return of his new wife's long-lost father; and the disappearance and death of the disgraced former mayor.

Casterbridge is an ideal landscape to frame and witness these dramas.

For all its symmetry and enclosure, a tree-bound squareness 'compact as a box of dominoes' (Chapter IV), Casterbridge itself has no more singular and consistent an identity than any individual inhabitant. Just as characters tend to the composite and paradoxical in their embodiment of protean human responses, so 'Casterbridge was the complement of the rural life around; not its urban opposite' (Chapter IX). Its rural/urban duality is recurrently evoked as its most distinctive characteristic, productive of the kind of environmental ironies that have sheep-stealers hearing their sentences 'to the tune of Baa, that floated in at the window from the remainder of the flock browsing hard by' or a town-jail execution viewed from a meadow 'out of which the cows had been temporarily driven to give the spectators room' (Chapter XIV). But the complementary forces which Casterbridge brings into relationship are not just simple antitheses like nature and society, innocence and corruption, unconsciousness and tragic awareness. For the colours of each inhere in rather than merely coexisting with the other. Like the topography of Casterbridge as viewed by 'birds of the more soaring kind' (Chapter IV) – granted a view of the whole suggestively similar to that enjoyed by the 'Overworld' of *The Dynasts* – disparate components of the scene coalesce into the fissured clarity of mosaic-work, whose fractured parts require distance to yield up the illusion of design.

The conceptual complexity of *The Mayor of Casterbridge*'s use of setting can be seen at its subtlest in relation to the building that sits at the literal centre of the town, despite its possession of 'the characteristics of a country mansion – birds'-nests in its chimneys, damp nooks where fungi grew, and irregularities of surface direct from Nature's trowel' (Chapter XXI). High Street Hall, the vantage-point from which Lucetta and Elizabeth-Jane survey the to-ings and fro-ings of Casterbridge mercantile life (on which the socio-political successes of both Henchard and Farfrae are founded), grants the perspectival distance that allows the marketplace, 'the node of all orbits', to function as 'the regulation Open Place in spectacular dramas, where the incidents that occur always happen to bear on the lives of the adjoining residents' (Chapter XXIV). In this respect, High Street Hall is disengaged from the world it overlooks. But in its own internal paradoxes Lucetta's house also embodies the contradictions of identity inherent in both the community as a whole and its individual members. Its façade is a monument to Palladian symmetry: dignified, public, reasonable, impressive. Its rear, however, gives access to one of the town's hidden alleys, through whose concealed mazes surreptitious and criminal activities – illicit assignations, infanticide, and, of course, the rapid dispersals essential to such riotous assemblies as skimmity-rides – can proceed at will. It is a context of shadow, subterfuge and gothic grotesquerie. If the window overlooking the public daytime space of the market defines one principle, the 'queer old door' with the leprotic or syphilitic leer on its disease-chipped keystone mask defines the private night-time complement. Like Henchard and Lucetta, the eminent public figures with the hidden private pasts, or Newson, the well-intentioned rescuer of an ill-used wife, who leads his family to think him dead and funds the cruel skimmity-ride, or Farfrae, who brings tears to his listener's eyes with sentimental songs about the homeland from which he has deliberately exiled himself, or even Elizabeth-Jane, the ministering angel whose 'craving for correctness' is 'almost vicious' (Chapter XXX), High Street Hall is in its own mixed identity a site of paradox that draws together disparate human impulses and helps turn their chaos into design.

High Street Hall's moralized spatial contradictions are matched by temporal equivalents. Farfrae first enters the house, having been given Henchard's permission to court the non-daughter he now regards as an encumbrance, during Candlemas Fair. In Elizabeth-Jane's absence, flirtatious exchanges between him and Lucetta immediately begin (Chapter XXIII). Like the call to business that terminates this scene by drawing Farfrae back into the market, the agricultural hiring they view together through the windows is specifically rendered as inimical to love: economic circumstance is forcing a young farm worker, for the sake of his age-bowed father, to take employment at a farm many miles away from his sweetheart. In helping establish his claim on Lucetta's affections by himself hiring both men, Farfrae momentarily reconciles economics and romance. The calendar ratifies this symbiosis of contraries. In Casterbridge, Candlemas Fair with its yearly labour commitments is held on Old Candlemas Day, 14 February, which also happens to be St. Valentine's Day. While the association is not specifically mentioned, the ironic conflation of the opposed imperatives of economic survival and romance would not have been unintended by Hardy, who in *Far from the Madding Crowd* had already used the playful flirtatiousness sanctioned by Valentine's Day as the inception of the Bathsheba – Boldwood tragedy of misalliance. If Farfrae's Valentine's Day ministration to young love ironically counterpoints the early stages of his own involvement with Lucetta, the form it takes – the hiring of a promising young man whose eminent employability is the only thing that stands between his father's waning skills and final defeat in the battle of life – offers its own comment on the inevitable outcome of the unwise and unnecessary generational rivalry Henchard has precipitated with another promising young man *he* once employed.

High Street Hall, in physical nature and location, thus integrates the contending human forces it embodies and witnesses. Its referential density encapsulates the immense subtlety, greater in its range and relevance to character and situation than that manifested in any of his earlier novels, with which Hardy uses physical context in *The Mayor of Casterbridge*. As Michael Millgate has suggested, it was in this novel 'that Hardy achieved a full realisation of the Wessex concept, a realisation which depended on the establishment of Casterbridge itself . . . as the central point, the economic, administrative, and social capital, of a whole region' (Millgate, pp. 235–6). Hardy's fluctuating sense of the most efficacious way of doing this is reflected in the uncertainty that took him from manuscript use of real Dorchester place names, such as the King's Arms, Three Mariners and Antelope inns, to fictitious equivalents – the Golden Crown, the King of Prussia and the Stag – and back again. But equally impressive is the imaginative conviction with which Casterbridge is made to speak as much to existential as to social situation, in the process revealing why England's greatest regional novelist can stake convincing claim to being its greatest tragic novelist too. High Street Hall sits, a monument to threateningly suggestive contradictions, at Casterbridge's centre, surrounded by a town whose tree-lined walks bestow a superficial formal symmetry on the rectangular whole as authoritatively as a Palladian façade does on a rectangular part. But the town itself is also irregularly enclosed by isolated, and isolating, sites of threat that transcend, while encompassing, the terms of mere social circumstance.

The Ring is at first prosaically defined as 'the local name of one of the finest Roman amphitheatres, if not the very finest, remaining in Britain' (Chapter XI). But narratorial elaboration on its grotesque and melancholic associations obliterates such bland guide-book perfunctoriness. Standing near Casterbridge's south-western exit, it has a past that drew inhabitants together primarily at times of collective, officially sanctioned barbarity, while its superstition-enshrouded present repels community pastimes and romantic intimacies alike, leaving it unused for anything except joyless clandestine meetings. To the south-east is Mixen Lane, very much used but primarily as 'the hiding-place of those who were in distress, and in debt, and trouble of every kind' (Chapter XXXVI). Approached, usually at night and with the obliquity of the shiftless and criminal, it is the town's blighted slum, a 'mildewed leaf in the sturdy and flourishing Casterbridge plant'. More isolated, if also more exposed, is Grey's Bridge at the town's eastern exit. This, the more distant of the two bridges at the lower end of Casterbridge that are the haunt of the town's social failures, is frequented by unfortunates of the Henchard class, whose self-consciousness causes them to shun public scrutiny, and whose despair leads them on occasion to choose, as Henchard himself almost does at nearby Ten Hatches, the ultimate isolation and unconsciousness afforded by suicide. The town's 'north-eastern limits' are bounded by what Hardy designates 'the Schwarzwasser of Casterbridge' (Chapter XIX): the slow, dark waters running through the area to which Henchard resorts after reading Susan's letter, with its devastating revelations about Elizabeth-Jane's actual paternity. 'These precincts embodied the mournful phases of Casterbridge life', and include a ruined Franciscan priory, its mill – 'the water of which roared down a back-hatch like the voice of desolation' – the town gaol with its public gallows, and the cottage in which, as a tenant of Jopp, Henchard takes up residence after his bankruptcy. And almost surrounding the whole is 'Casterbridge Moor' (in later editions 'Durnover'), whose main textual associations are with the poachers, indistinguishable from the gamekeepers some of them once were, who stealthily cross it *en route* to the imperfect sanctuary of Mixen Lane.

Hardy's use of locations such as these contributes to the status of *The Mayor of Casterbridge* as one of his major tragic novels, whose story, while convincingly evocative of life in south-west England in the mid-nineteenth century, is even more concerned with the universal human predicament of being the only species possessed of rational or moral consciousness in a world governed by nothing much more meaningful than chance. As the early poem 'Hap' (*Wessex Poems* [1898]) – published a dozen years after but written twenty years before *The Mayor of Caster-bridge* – declares, the unsympathetic machinations of a hostile divinity would be preferable to the operation of mere 'Crass Casualty'. The novel's sites of failure and despair are locales whose bleakness, like that embodied in the blighted mental extremity of the Renaissance tragic hero or the melancholia of Romantic *Weltschmerz*, anticipates the waste-land of Modernist alienation. Visited primarily by the threatened, the corrupted, the desolate, and the tormented, they attract the two extremes of human awareness: the supremely unconscious, who have barely lifted themselves above the level of animals in anything other than a wilful capacity for brutality, and the supremely conscious, who are tortured by the lack of correspondence between the world as it is and the world as it should be. If the lowest denizens of Mixen Lane exemplify the former, Michael Henchard embodies the latter. He is the figure who carries the greatest burden of disabling consciousness in this novel, and arguably (with the possible exception of Jude Fawley) in any Hardy novel. He stands, along with Job whom he himself invokes or Lear whom criticism routinely invokes on his behalf, as the type of the exceptional human who experiences, recognizes and accepts the inevit-ability of suffering. Mixen Lane is home to many a 'poor, bare, forked animal' – the 'unaccommodated man' of *King Lear* (III. iv). Only Hen-chard fully recognizes the extent to which he is such a creature. He conveys that recognition in the last exchange recorded between him and Abel Whittle, another brother figure to the Henchard who on his departure from Casterbridge has identified himself with Cain, who goes 'alone as I deserve – an outcast and a vagabond' (Chapter XLIII). He transposes on to Whittle, the Abel ministering to a Cain who in this recension kills himself rather than his brother, words that echo Lear's self-judging 'I am a very foolish, fond old man' (IV. vii): 'What, Whittle . . . and can ye really be such a poor fond fool as to care for such a wretch as I!' (Chapter XLV).

Hence the importance of the textual revision that has Lucetta rescuing him, at least temporarily, from despair, a quality of consciousness, rather than from drowning, an unfortunate by-product of mere accident. Farfrae, or for that matter the least thoughtful inhabitant of Mixen Lane, could suffer drowning, but Henchard's affliction – while engendered by that most distinctively human of attributes, knowledge – is of a kind unknown to the callow Farfrae. As Henchard tells him of the fits 'when the world seems to have the blackness of hell, and, like Job, I could curse the day that gave me birth', Farfrae's only response is 'Ah, now, I never feel like it' (Chapter XII), which surely competes for rhetorical inadequacy with his response to Abel Whittle's extended account of Henchard's harrowing last days and death: '"Dear me – is it so!" said Farfrae' (Chapter XLV).

At the most literal level, Henchard is obviously possessed of one piece of knowledge unshared by anyone else in Casterbridge, at least until Susan's arrival: only he knows what happened eighteen years ago at Weydon-Priors fair. But more fundamentally, he is the character most troubled by the antithetical relationship of human thought and feeling to each other, and to what actually happens in the world. Even when what happens *is* a direct fulfilment of avowed purpose – Henchard says he wants to sell his wife and Newson walks in and buys her, Henchard says that Farfrae will be leaving his employ and Farfrae leaves, Henchard tells Newson that Elizabeth-Jane is dead and Newson believes him – the outcome observes the letter but belies the spirit of the intent. The rational and passional sides of Henchard's consciousness are at once divided against each other and inseparable. To a less self-questioning sensibility, like that of Farfrae, this would be no problem: the sentimentalist and the man of business manage to coexist in relative harmony, untroubled by guilt, doubt or mutual antipathy. To Henchard, part of the price of being conscious is the almost suicidal need to seek the relief of unconsciousness, both in himself and, as his will attests, of himself in others.

'Consciousness' is a key term for Hardy, for reasons endemic to his subjectivist and associational presuppositions about the relationship between the individual and the world. Nowhere is its primacy revealed with greater poignancy, and, given subsequent events, more ironic consequences, than in Angel Clare's ruminations on his responsibilities to Tess Durbeyfield, the vulnerable dairymaid whose affections he is aware of having aroused. He is also aware that 'Tess was no insignificant creature to toy with and dismiss; but a woman living her precious life – a life which, to herself who endured or enjoyed it, possessed as great a dimension as the life of the mightiest to himself. . . . This consciousness upon which he had intruded was the single opportunity of existence ever vouchsafed to Tess by an unsympathetic First Cause – her all; her every and only chance, (*Tess of the d'Urbervilles*, Chapter xxv). For all its totality, it is also a chance which to Hardy, as to Henchard or Tess, often seems as much of a curse as a blessing.

A telling emendation in a poem whose entire subject is the burden of human consciousness helps clarify Henchard's malaise. In 'Before Life and After' (*Time's Laughingstocks* [1909]), Hardy speculates on the possible desirability of unconsciousness, given that 'Before the birth of consciousness,/ . . . all went well.' As in Henchard's depressive states, consciousness is figured here as a 'disease', and Hardy identifies the point at which 'the disease of feeling germed' as a kind of fall into tragic awareness. In manuscript, this phrase originally read 'the disease of thought engermed', superficially a quite different, not to say contradictory, emphasis. The change was almost certainly made to accord with metrical rather than semantic imperatives. No doubt having decided that 'engermed' sounded a little too tortured, even for his developed appetite for word coinage, Hardy dropped the obtrusive first syllable and found himself in need of another to carry its metrical weight: hence the monosyllabic 'thought' became the disyllabic 'feeling'. But what the change does suggest is that for Hardy's purposes, the two were effectively interchangeable, since both are equally expressive – indeed, perhaps so expressive *only* in their conflation – of the distinctively human quality of apprehension about which he was writing: 'consciousness'.

Certainly for Henchard thought and feeling, however often they may seem at war with each other, are inextricably entwined, and totally disabling in their effect on his response to circumstance. They are burdens by which Farfrae or Newson seem almost entirely untroubled and that Henchard himself becomes increasingly desperate to unshoulder. He casts a final vote for unconsciousness, effected by virtual suicide in the face of emotional trauma: as Abel Whittle explains, 'he couldn't eat – no, no appetite at all – and he got weaker; and to-day he died' (Chapter XLV). In trying also to effect unconsciousness of himself in others, by the self-obliterating directive 'that no man remember me', Henchard anticipates a similar impulse in his spiritual successor, Jude Fawley, whose final words are an extended quotation from *Job* that includes the terrible self-annihilating verse: '*Let the day perish wherein I was born, and the night in which it was said, There is a man child conceived*' (*Jude the Obscure*, VI, xi).

But perhaps he also anticipates a more modern, and markedly less heroic, recognition of the consolations of nescience. Thirty years after the publication of *The Mayor of Casterbridge*, Hardy transcribed into the second of his literary notebooks two extended quotations from an unidentified poem. The extracts were not taken directly from the poem itself, but from an anthology with the dauntingly ambitious title *From Shakespeare to O. Henry*. The poet's name is, however, given: it is T. S. Eliot, who is glossed by Hardy as 'a poet of the vers-libre school' (Item 2443: *Literary Notebooks*, 2, pp. 226–7). The extracts come from 'The Love Song of J. Alfred Prufrock' (ll. 99–110, 120–31), and they bracket a section that is not quoted: the lines in which Prufrock confesses to not being Prince Hamlet, but rather 'an attendant lord . . . almost ridiculous – Almost, at times, the Fool' (ll. 112, 118–19). These Shakespearian echoes (overtly of *Hamlet*, less obtrusively of *King Lear*) in a poem that Hardy may well never have read in its entirety, offer suggestive comment on those final exchanges between Whittle and Henchard, in which a troubled consciousness considerably more daring than Prufrock's comes to a recognition of its close alliance to folly.

But perhaps even more resonant is another Prufrockian self-characterization excluded from Hardy's quotations: 'I should have been a pair of ragged claws/ Scuttling across the floors of silent seas' (ll. 73–4). Prufrock's desire for a state of unconsciousness as complete as can be reconciled with vital signs, which are reduced to the purely reflexive movements of disembodied pincers, indicates something of his need to escape the impotent self-awareness that consciousness brings. That it should be expressed in the first published poem of a 27-year-old writer who was about to become one of the most distinctive voices of literary modernism may also suggest something of Hardy's own legacy to modernism. Given the overwhelming burdens borne by Michael Henchard, Tess Durbeyfield, and Jude Fawley, whose son 'Little Father Time' takes his route to unconsciousness in childhood as an almost clinical demonstration of 'the coming universal wish not to live' (*Jude the Obscure*, VI.ii), it was perhaps inevitable that, ten years after publication of *The Mayor of Casterbridge*, Hardy would take his own vows of novelistic silence and begin the new thirty-year career that would establish him as the twentieth century's first major English poet.

The Mayor of Casterbridge has been well served by both the quantity and quality of commentary it has elicited. The two dominant strands in this criticism are evoked in the title of Laurence Lerner's useful student introduction, *Thomas Hardy's 'The Mayor of Casterbridge': Tragedy or Social History* (London: Sussex University Press, 1975). For some years another slim volume, Douglas Brown's *Thomas Hardy: The Mayor of Casterbridge* (London: Edward Arnold, 1962) was the main exemplar of the sociological approach, seeing the novel as essentially a conflict between the old and new social orders embodied respectively in Michael Henchard and Donald Farfrae. J. C. Maxwell offered a corrective to Brown's view in 'The Sociological Approach to *The Mayor of Casterbridge*', in *Imagined Worlds: Essays on Some English Novels and Novelists in Honour of John Butt*, ed. Maynard Mack and Ian Gregor (London: Methuen, 1968), pp. 225–36. Merryn Williams, *Thomas Hardy and Rural England* (London: Macmillan, 1972), locates Hardy's work against the particulars of nineteenth-century rural circumstance. More precisely grounded in the social and intellectual milieu specific to Hardy himself is the relevant chapter in Michael Millgate, *Thomas Hardy: His Career as a Novelist* (London: Bodley Head, 1971; rev. ed. Basingstoke: Macmillan, 1994), still the most valuable single introduction to Hardy's fiction. Peter Widdowson, *Hardy in History: A Study in Literary Sociology* (London: Routledge, 1989) is a more theoretically based discussion of the place of Hardy the man and 'Hardy' the text in socio-cultural history, and includes a discussion of the televisual Mayor of Casterbridge.

Two excellent studies of Hardy and tragedy are Dale Kramer, *Thomas Hardy: The Forms of Tragedy* (London: Macmillan, 1975) and Jeannette King, *Tragedy in the Victorian Novel: Theory and Practice in the Novels of George Eliot, Thomas Hardy, and Henry James* (Cambridge: Cambridge University Press, 1978). D. A. Dike's 'A Modern Oedipus: *The Mayor of Casterbridge*', *Essays in Criticism* 2 (1952), 169–79 and John Paterson's '*The Mayor of*

Casterbridge as Tragedy', *Victorian Studies* 3 (1959), 151–72 have held up well over the years. The special Hardy issue of *Studies in the Novel* 4 (1972) contains two useful discussions: Duane D. Edwards, '*The Mayor of Casterbridge* as Aeschylean Tragedy', 608–18, and Lawrence J. Starzyk, 'Hardy's *Mayor*: The Antitraditional Basis of Tragedy', 592–607. This line of inquiry is still flourishing, as evidenced in Michael Valdez Moses, 'Agon in the Marketplace: *The Mayor of Casterbridge* as Bourgeois Tragedy', *South Atlantic Quarterly* 87 (1988), 219–51.

Perhaps not surprisingly in the light of the text's own Novalis-inspired invitation to associate Character and Fate, analysis of Henchard's character often attempts to share responsibility for his fate between sociology, tragedy, and personality. Two such syntheses are Jean Brooks, '*The Mayor of Casterbridge*: A Novel of Character and Environment', in her *Thomas Hardy: The Poetic Structure* (London: Elek, 1971), pp. 196–215, and Robert C. Schweik, 'Character and Fate in Hardy's *The Mayor of Casterbridge*', *Nineteenth Century Fiction* 21 (1966), 249–62.

Feminist readings are increasingly providing some of the most vigorous analysis of Henchard's situation and psychology. Elaine Showalter's 'The Unmanning of the Mayor of Casterbridge', in Dale Kramer, ed., *Critical Approaches to the Fiction of Thomas Hardy* (London: Macmillan, 1979), pp. 99–115, and Marjorie Garson's '*The Mayor of Casterbridge*: The Bounds of Propriety', in her *Hardy's Fables of Integrity: Woman, Body, Text* (Oxford: Clarendon Press, 1991), pp. 94–129, are particularly subtle.

For many years, biographical scholarship on Hardy advanced with the help, or perhaps in the shadow, of his disguised autobiography, published under the name of Florence Emily Hardy, his second wife, in two volumes: *The Early Life of Thomas Hardy* (London: Macmillan, 1928) and *The Later Years of Thomas Hardy* (London: Macmillan, 1930). This is now available in a form that restores Hardy's original intentions for it before the excisions made by Florence and her advisers. Edited by Michael Millgate, it is published as *The Life and Work of Thomas Hardy* (London: Macmillan, 1985). Millgate is also the author of what is by far the most reliable and meticulously researched biography: *Thomas Hardy: A Biography* (Oxford: Oxford University Press, 1982). Complementing these are the seven volumes of *Collected Letters*, ed. Michael Millgate and Richard Little Purdy (Oxford: Clarendon Press, 1978–88).

Information about relevant published Hardy notebooks and about material on the textual evolution of *The Mayor of Casterbridge* can be found in the Notes and in A Note on the Text respectively. The standard bibliography on Hardy's own works is Richard Little Purdy, *Thomas Hardy: A Bibliographical Study* (Oxford: Clarendon Press, 1954, 1968). For a sampling of reviews contemporaneous with the first publication of Hardy's works, see R. G. Cox, ed., *Thomas Hardy: The Critical Heritage* (London: Routledge & Kegan Paul, 1970).

This edition of *The Mayor of Casterbridge* is based upon the text of the first English edition in book form, published in two volumes by Smith, Elder on 10 May 1886. The novel that English readers then saw, and with minor changes continued to see in the single-volume edition issued by Sampson Low in 1887, differed substantially from the first American book edition, published at the end of May 1886 by Henry Holt in his Leisure Hour series. Both, in turn, differed from the English and American serials (themselves showing minor variations between each other, primarily as a result of space constraints in the American version), published simultaneously in the *Graphic* and *Harper's Weekly* between 2 January and 15 May 1886. One distinction between the two earliest book versions was particularly striking. It was not until 1895, when Osgood, McIlvaine published *The Mayor of Casterbridge* as the third volume in their collected Wessex Novels edition, that Hardy restored in England the longer penultimate chapter that had appeared in both the serial and the American edition. The text of the later stages of this chapter, taken for the sake of period consistency from the American first edition rather than the later collected editions, is reprinted here as Appendix I.

In its original and final forms, but not in the early English editions, Chapter XLIV has Henchard return to Casterbridge for Elizabeth-Jane's marriage. Because of his lie to Newson about her death, she speaks harshly to him and is apparently in the process of rejecting him. In the face of her distress, and without attempting to exculpate himself, he immediately makes his final departure from Casterbridge. The deleted section contains one of Hardy's most poignant images. Henchard brings with him a wedding gift, a caged goldfinch, and having left the cage under a bush in the garden 'to lessen the awkwardness of his arrival', he leaves without remembering to present it. Some days later Elizabeth-Jane discovers the bird starved to death and is told by a servant of its connection with Henchard. It is this discovery which resolves her to track him down.

The retention of this longer chapter in the American edition was the result of accident rather than design. By 11 May 1886, Holt had received Hardy's revisions for only the first forty chapters.[1] The threat of possible pirated editions precluded further delay in preparing the authorized edition, but there is every reason to suppose that had Hardy got revised copy to Holt in time, the American version would have been similarly modified. Hardy probably deleted Henchard's return as part of the general streamlining that took place between serial and book. He was later to assert that *The Mayor of Casterbridge* was more damaged than any of his other novels by the demands of serialization, the need 'to get an incident into almost every week's part causing him in his own judgment to add events to the narrative somewhat too freely' (*Life and Work*, p. 185). Part of this sensed superfluity of event may well have been the need, created by Henchard's return for the wedding, to have him depart from Casterbridge a second time, which Hardy identified as a weakness to the same 'good judges across the Atlantic' who persuaded him to restore the goldfinch episode.[2] But as significant in the decision may have been the desire to cast Elizabeth-Jane in a less unflattering light than her recent conduct and final rejection of Henchard had allowed. For in the serial and American book versions, Elizabeth-Jane, already aware of Newson's survival, has been meeting him for some months without Henchard's knowledge. The excision of both this and her harsh response to the returned Henchard absolves her not only of deception but also of any responsibility for his death.

Hardy made another important change in these last chapters for the first English book appearance, and this one he retained in subsequent editions. Originally Chapter XLII contained a scene in which Henchard observes, through a telescope, Elizabeth-Jane and Farfrae meeting and kissing on the Budmouth Road (see Chapter XLII, n. 7). Hardy deleted this from the English edition, but incorporated elements of the scene into Chapter XLIII. When Henchard looks through the telescope he sees instead the returning Newson (see Chapter XLIII, n. 3). Elizabeth-Jane subsequently tells him that she has received a mysterious letter from someone who wishes to meet her on the Budmouth Road. Thus it is only with the first English edition that Henchard's motivation for leaving Casterbridge becomes primarily the inevitable revelation consequent upon Newson's return, not as before a desire to remove himself before the imminent marriage of Elizabeth-Jane and Farfrae.

While the English first edition thus departed significantly in its later stages from the serial and the American first edition, the most important changes for the first forty chapters were substantially incorporated into the American edition.[3] They did much to remedy Hardy's concern with the over-eventfulness of the serial plot. Henchard and Lucetta have no longer married on the assumption that Susan is dead, and Farfrae is no longer used as a messenger to intercept Lucetta at Budmouth with news of Susan's return (Chapter XII, nn. 8 and 12). No longer does Lucetta meet Susan while killing time between coaches in Casterbridge, nor does Henchard use Elizabeth-Jane as an intermediary in his first attempt to return Lucetta's letters (Chapter XVIII, n. 6). As a consequence no longer do the letters take a convoluted passage from Elizabeth-Jane to Farfrae to a coach-guard and back to Farfrae again, who having failed to get them delivered to Lucetta also fails to return them to Henchard, not wanting to disturb him on the morning of Susan's death. The removal of this implausible array of foiled good intentions also obviates the need for Farfrae himself absent-mindedly to have held on to them, through two house-removals, so that Henchard can reclaim them much later (Chapter XXXIV, n. 2). Nor does Farfrae come upon Lucetta and Henchard during their meeting at the Ring, an almost comically gratuitous ironic encounter that necessitates her playing the role of the new woman in Henchard's life to avoid being recognized by her husband, the new man in her own life (Chapter XXXV, n. 6).

Hardy's concern to correct what he saw as serial-generated blemishes may indicate that his early prediction to Leslie Stephen, during the monthly appearances of *Far from the Madding Crowd* in *Cornhill*, had come to pass: content in 1874 'merely to be considered a good hand at a serial', by 1886 he was much more of 'a stickler for the proper artistic balance of the completed work' (*Letters*, I, 28). But the fact that *The Mayor of Casterbridge* originally took the form that it did is also indication that the requirements of a serial had over the years been well learned by Hardy. The manuscript's completion as early as 17 April 1885 (*Life and Work*, p. 177) meant that, as with his other work for the *Graphic* but unlike his usual situation with periodical publication, he was not working against relentless deadlines imposed by the need to complete later stages of a novel while earlier chapters were already appearing.[4] Whatever doubts he may subsequently have expressed about the serial version, Hardy shaped its more strained plot moments in full awareness of what he was doing and with plenty of time to modify anything about which he had second thoughts.

The surviving manuscript reveals some of the second thoughts he had at earlier stages of composition. It is, unfortunately, incomplete, lacking 108 pages entirely and with five others reduced to fragments. The excisions were almost certainly made by Hardy himself, before he presented the manuscript to the Dorset County Museum in November 1911, and were probably of sections copied out by his wife, Emma.[5] But the surviving portion, 374 pages in all, shows many modifications. They include the changing of Henchard's name from 'Giles' to 'James' to the final 'Michael' and his trade from 'woodman' to 'sawyer' to 'stone mason' to 'trusser'. The initially anonymous young Scotsman evolves from 'Alan Stansbie' to 'Donald Farfrae', 'Dawson' becomes 'Newson', and 'Kezia Littlechild' is changed to 'Nance Mockridge'. The naming of Abel Whittle seems to have proved particularly troublesome: 'Lackday', 'Lackstraw', 'Small', 'Smallbone' and 'John Wringbone' were all considered as alternatives. The marriage of Susan and Henchard was originally to have lasted five years and generated two daughters, one of whom was to stay with her father after the wife-sale – a strange impromptu arrangement which would have resulted in Susan looking almost as cavalier in her attitude to parental responsibility as Henchard himself. The relationship of Lucetta and Henchard was at first more overtly sexual and unredeemed by marriage, which was presumably introduced into the later development of the manuscript specifically with a view to the demands of serial publication: hence Hardy's alacrity in dispensing with the marriage in the book revision, although his circumspection in dealing with the degree of physical intimacy in the relationship endured until 1895.

Some minor alterations in phrasing were made for Sampson Low's cheap 1887 edition, including the deletion at the beginning of Chapter XV (see nn. 2 and 3) of comments about the unresponsiveness of Casterbridge young men to Elizabeth-Jane. Briefer but more devastating in effect was the addition to the final chapter of one of Farfrae's most telling, if unwitting, self-indictments: the observation that to extend the search for Henchard overnight would 'make a hole in a sovereign' (see Chapter XLV, n. 9).

The reintroduction of Henchard's return to Casterbridge for the 1895–6 Osgood, McIlvaine Wessex Novels edition was the most prominent of a large number of modifications. The authenticity of Farfrae's dialect was improved, Hardy having benefited from the advice of his Scottish friend Sir George Douglas. This formed part of a more general relaxation into greater colloquialism, with the Dorset 'v' substituted for 'f' (e.g. 'volks' for 'folks') and 'z' for 's' (e.g. 'zee' for 'see'). Overblown phrasing was deflated: Henchard's 'enable us to retain' became 'help us to keep' (Chapter XII, n. 13), and Solomon Longways' 'deprive life of fourpence' became 'rob life o' fourpence' (Chapter XVIII, n. 7). In general, contractions were used more liberally. Henchard's expletives, however, were expanded from discreet initial letters to full transcriptions, and greater frankness was also used both in defining the nature of the Lucetta–Henchard relationship and in less veiled references to Lucetta's pregnancy at the time of the skimmity-ride (Chapters XII, n. 11, and XL, nn. 4 and 7). It was also with this edition that actual Dorchester inn names were restored, the fictitious St Jude's Church became the actual St Peter's, and High Street Hall became High-Place Hall. Wessex locations generally were made more consistent with those in other novels, and even the name of a minor character was modified to avoid an apparent discrepancy with a namesake in *Under the Greenwood Tree* (see Chapter XIII, n. 3). Hardy also added a Preface for the first time (see Appendix II).

Relatively few changes were made for the 1912–13 Wessex Edition, most of them little more than minor refinements in phrasing, many a continuation of the tendency towards greater colloquialism in dialogue instituted in 1895. The time scheme is slightly modified. Henchard's abstention from alcohol now lasts twenty-one years rather than twenty (Chapter II, n. 5), he tells Farfrae that he 'lost' his wife nineteen years earlier rather than eighteen (Chapter XII, n. 4), and he returns to

Weydon-Priors twenty-five years after the wife-sale rather than twenty-two or twenty-three (Chapter XLIV, n. 1). The addition of three elegiac footnotes (Chapters IV and IX) attests to both the effect of time's passage on Casterbridge and the increasing prominence of Hardy's invitations to readers to associate his imaginative setting with the actual townscape of Dorchester. These revisions for the Wessex Edition were the last of any substance, modifications for the de luxe Mellstock Edition (1919–20) being limited to little more than typographical correction.

PUNCTUATION

Punctuation-theory having become a somewhat contentious topic in editorial circles, the decision made for this edition – namely to use the accidentals (punctuation, paragraphing, etc.) as well as the substantives (the words) of the Smith, Elder first edition – perhaps needs some comment.[6] In part the decision was based on the editorial policy for the whole Penguin Classics edition: to offer the texts 'as Hardy's readers first encountered them', which encounter included in the case of *The Mayor of Casterbridge* engagement with a relatively consistent Smith, Elder house-style for punctuation. This decision was further advised by the incompleteness of the obvious alternative contender, the manuscript. Use of its punctuation would therefore have necessitated, for the missing sections, incorporation of the punctuation from the relevant parts of an early published version, either the *Graphic* serialization or the Smith, Elder first edition itself. It was therefore more logical to use for the whole what would in any case have been adopted for the missing part.

That having been said, it is important to acknowledge that Hardy's punctuation practice in the manuscript is significantly different from that of the first edition. In many ways it is much less consistent. In the broadest terms, comma use is considerably lighter, as is generally the case with Hardy's manuscripts. While this may, on occasion, have signified deliberate emphasis, which compositorial normalization risked obliterating, more frequently it suggests mere casualness. Lucetta's letter to Henchard upon her arrival to live in Casterbridge provides a representative example. In manuscript one of its sentences reads, 'As however I did not know how you were situated, or what had happened since our separation I decided to come and establish myself here before communicating with you' (Chapter XXII). The decision, made in every edition published in Hardy's lifetime, to place commas around 'however' and to add another after 'separation' is surely the right one, on grounds of both grammar and cadence. Comparable examples of problematic manuscript comma use abound, and semicolons fare little better. A sentence in the next chapter reads in manuscript 'and the son had a sweetheart on his present farm; who stood by, waiting the issue with pale lips'. Again, no edition that Hardy had any hand in felt bound by this eccentricity: all replaced the semicolon after 'farm' with a comma. On the same page, another errant semicolon before a capitalized 'Oh' was replaced by either a full stop or an exclamation mark.

Thus the manuscript evidence suggests that while some deliberate emphases may have been lost to a compositor's standardization, in numerous other instances Hardy's punctuation was at this stage somewhat casual – far too casual to allow an editor to place consistent reliance on the firmness of its intentions. Rather than deferring to the manuscript's questionable and incomplete authority, this Penguin edition privileges the punctuation consistency of the first book edition proof-read by Hardy himself.

Notes

1. See Seth Weiner, 'Thomas Hardy and His First American Publisher: A Chapter from the Henry Holt Archives', *Princeton University Library Chronicle*, 39 (1978), 134–57.
2. See Hardy's Preface (Appendix II) and Carl J. Weber, *Hardy of Wessex: His Life and Literary Career*, rev. edn (London: Routledge & Kegan Paul, 1965), pp. 152–3.
3. More than 500 revisions were made in the first forty chapters for the first English and American book editions, with another 250 changes made in these chapters in the English edition (see Simon Gatrell, *Hardy the Creator: A Textual Biography* [Oxford: Clarendon Press, 1988], p. 80). For the fullest discussions of the novel's textual evolution, see Mary Ellen Chase, *Thomas Hardy from Serial to Novel* (Minneapolis: University of Minnesota Press, 1927; reprinted New York:

Russell & Russell, 1964), pp. 15–65; Dieter Riesner, 'Kuntsprosa in der Werkstatt: Hardy's *The Mayor of Casterbridge* 1884–1912', *Festschrift für Walter Hübner*, ed. Dieter Riesner and Helmut Gneuss (Berlin: Erich Schmidt, 1964), pp. 267–326; and Christine Winfield, 'The Manuscript of Hardy's *Mayor of Casterbridge*', *Papers of the Bibliographical Society of America*, 67 (1973), 33–58. The most authoritative critical edition of the 1912 Wessex Edition of *The Mayor of Casterbridge* is that prepared by Dale Kramer (Oxford, 1987). Kramer's implication that the Holt American edition is the first is made on the strength of its not having undergone, by an accident of geographical circumstance, the fuller revisions Hardy made for the Smith, Elder English edition, which was published before the American edition.

4. For a full discussion of Hardy's relationship with the *Graphic*, see Gatrell, *Hardy the Creator*, pp. 71–96.

5. See Gatrell, *Hardy the Creator*, p. 48.

6. Readers interested in the debate as it relates specifically to editorial practice in Hardy scholarship are referred to Gatrell, *Hardy the Creator*, pp. 209–22, and his 'Hardy, House-Style, and the Aesthetics of Punctuation', in Anne Smith, ed., *The Novels of Thomas Hardy* (London: Vision Press, 1979), pp. 169–92; Michael Millgate, 'The Making and Unmaking of Hardy's Wessex Edition', in Jane Millgate, ed., *Editing Nineteenth-Century Fiction* (New York: Garland, 1978), pp. 61–82; and Robert Schweik and Michael Piret, 'Editing Hardy', *Browning Institute Studies*, 9 (1981), 15–41.

THE

MAYOR OF CASTERBRIDGE:

THE LIFE AND DEATH OF A
MAN OF CHARACTER.

BY

THOMAS HARDY,

AUTHOR OF

"FAR FROM THE MADDING CROWD," "A PAIR OF BLUE EYES," ETC.

IN TWO VOLUMES.

VOL. I.

LONDON:

SMITH, ELDER & CO., 15 WATERLOO PLACE.

1886.

CHAPTER I

One evening of late summer, before the present century had reached
its thirtieth year, a young man and woman, the latter carrying a child,
were approaching the large village of Weydon-Priors[1] on foot. They
were plainly but not ill clad, though the thick hoar of dust which had
accumulated on their shoes and garments from an obviously long
journey lent a disadvantageous shabbiness to their appearance just now.

The man was of fine figure, swarthy, and stern in aspect; and he
showed in profile a facial angle so slightly inclined as to be almost
perpendicular. He wore a short jacket of brown corduroy, newer than
the remainder of his suit, which was a fustian waistcoat with white horn
buttons, breeches of the same, tanned leggings, and a straw hat overlaid
with black glazed canvas. At his back he carried by a looped strap a
rush basket, from which protruded at one end the crutch of a hay-knife,
a wimble for hay-bonds being also visible in the aperture.[2] His measured
springless walk was the walk of the skilled countryman as distinct from
the desultory shamble of the general labourer; while in the turn and
plant of each foot there was, further, a dogged and cynical indifference,
personal to himself, showing itself even in the regularly interchanging
fustian folds, now in the left leg, now in the right, as he paced along.

What was really peculiar, however, in this couple's progress, and
would have attracted the attention of any casual observer otherwise
disposed to overlook them, was the perfect silence they preserved. They
walked side by side in such a way as to suggest afar off the low, easy,
confidential chat of people full of reciprocity; but on closer view it could
be discerned that the man was reading, or pretending to read, a
ballad-sheet which he kept before his eyes with some difficulty by the
hand that was passed through the basket-strap. Whether this apparent
cause were the real cause, or whether it were an assumed one to escape
an intercourse that would have been irksome to him, nobody but himself
could have said precisely; but his taciturnity was unbroken, and the

3

woman enjoyed no society whatever from his presence. Virtually she walked the highway alone, save for the child she bore. Sometimes the man's bent elbow almost touched her shoulder, for she kept as close to his side as was possible without actual contact; but she seemed to have no idea of taking his arm, nor he of offering it; and far from exhibiting surprise at his ignoring silence she appeared to receive it as a natural thing. If any word at all was uttered by the little group it was an occasional whisper of the woman to the child – a tiny girl in short clothes and blue boots of knitted yarn – and the murmured babble of the child in reply.

The chief – almost the only – attraction of the young woman's face was its mobility. When she looked down sideways to the girl she became pretty, and even handsome, particularly that in the action her features caught slantwise the rays of the strongly coloured sun, which made transparencies of her eyelids and nostrils, and set fire on her lips. When she plodded on in the shade of the hedge, silently thinking, she had the hard, half-apathetic expression of one who deems anything possible at the hands of Time and Chance, except, perhaps, fair-play. The first phase was the work of Nature, the second probably of civilization.

That the man and woman were husband and wife, and the parents of the girl in arms, there could be little doubt. No other than such relationship would have accounted for the atmosphere of domesticity[3] which the trio carried along with them like a nimbus as they moved down the road.

The wife mostly kept her eyes fixed ahead, though with little interest – the scene for that matter being one that might have been matched at almost any spot in any county in England at this time of the year: a road neither straight nor crooked, neither level nor hilly, bordered by hedges, trees, and other vegetation, which had entered the blackened-green stage of colour that the doomed leaves pass through on their way to dingy, and yellow, and red. The grassy margin of the bank, and the nearest hedgerow boughs, were powdered by the dust that had been stirred over them by hasty vehicles, the same dust as it lay on the road deadening their footfalls like a carpet; and this, with the aforesaid total absence of conversation, allowed every extraneous sound to be heard.

For a long time there was none, beyond the voice of a weak bird

4

singing a trite old evening song that might doubtless have been heard
on the hill at the same hour, and with the self-same trills, quavers, and
breves, at any sunset of that season for centuries untold. But as they
approached the village sundry distant shouts and rattles reached their
ears from some elevated spot in that direction, as yet screened from
view by foliage. When the outlying houses of Weydon-Priors could just
be descried, the family group was met by a turnip-hoer with his hoe on
his shoulder, and his dinner-bag suspended from it. The reader promptly
glanced up.

"Any trade doing here?" he asked phlegmatically, designating
the village in his van by a wave of the broadsheet. And thinking the
labourer did not understand him, he added, "Anything in the hay-
trussing line?"

The turnip-hoer had already begun shaking his head. "Why, save
the man, what wisdom's in fashion that 'a should come to Weydon for
a job of that sort this time o' year?"

"Then is there any house to let – a little small new cottage just a
builded, or such like?" asked the other.

The pessimist still maintained a negative: "Pulling down is more the
nater of Weydon. There were five houses cleared away last year, and
three this; and the fokes nowhere to go – no, not so much as a thatched
hurdle; that's the way o' Weydon-Priors."

The hay-trusser, which he obviously was, nodded with some supercili-
ousness. Looking towards the village, he continued, "There is something
going on here, however, is there not?"

"Ay. 'Tis Fair-Day. Though what you hear now is little more than
the clatter and scurry of getting away the money o' children and fools,
for the real business is done earlier than this. I've been working within
sound o't all day, but I didn't go up – not I. 'Twas no business of mine."

The trusser and his family proceeded on their way, and soon entered
the Fair-field, which showed standing-places and pens where many
hundreds of horses and sheep had been exhibited and sold in the
forenoon, but were now in great part taken away. At present, as their
informant had observed, but little real business remained on hand, the
chief being the sale by auction of a few inferior animals, that could not
otherwise be disposed of, and had been absolutely refused by the better

PLATE I

'"Haytrussing — ?" said the turnip-hoer, who had already begun shaking his head.
"O no."'

class of traders, who came and went early. Yet the crowd was denser now than during the morning hours, the frivolous contingent of visitors, including journeymen out for a holiday, a stray soldier or two home on furlough, village shopkeepers, and the like, having latterly flocked in; persons whose activities found a congenial field among the peep-shows, toy-stands, wax-works, inspired monsters, disinterested medical men who travelled for the public good, thimble-riggers, nick-nack vendors, and readers of Fate.

Neither of our pedestrians had much heart for these things, and they looked around for a refreshment tent among the many which dotted the down. Two, which stood nearest to them in the ochreous haze of expiring sunlight, seemed almost equally inviting. One was formed of new, milk-hued canvas, and bore red flags on its summit; it announced "Good Home-brewed Beer, Ale, and Cyder." The other was less new; a little iron stovepipe came out of it at the back, and in front appeared the placard, "Good Furmity Sold Hear." The man mentally weighed the two inscriptions, and inclined to the former tent.

"No – no – the other one," said the woman. "I always like furmity; and so does Elizabeth-Jane; and so will you. It is nourishing after a long hard day."

"I've never tasted it," said the man. However, he gave way to her representations, and they entered the furmity-booth forthwith.

A rather numerous company appeared within, seated at the long narrow tables that ran down the tent on each side. At the upper end stood a stove, containing a charcoal fire, over which hung a large three-legged crock, sufficiently polished round the rim to show that it was made of bell-metal. A haggish creature of about fifty presided, in a white apron, which, as it threw an air of respectability over her as far as it extended, was made so wide as to reach nearly round her waist. She slowly stirred the contents of the pot. The dull scrape of her large spoon was audible throughout the tent as she thus kept from burning the mixture of corn in the grain, milk, raisins, currants, and what not that composes the antiquated slop in which she dealt. Vessels holding the separate ingredients stood on a white-clothed table of boards and trestles close by.

The young man and woman ordered a basin each of the mixture, steaming hot, and sat down to consume it at leisure. This was very well so far, for furmity, as the woman had said, was nourishing, and as proper a food as could be obtained within the four seas; though, to those not accustomed to it, the grains of wheat, swollen as large as lemon-pips, which floated on its surface might have a deterrent effect at first.

But there was more in that tent than met the cursory glance; and the man, with the instinct of a perverse character, scented it quickly. After a mincing attack on his bowl, he watched the hag's proceedings from the corner of his eye, and saw the game she played. He winked to her, and passed up his basin in reply to her nod; when she took a bottle from under the table, slily measured out a quantity of its contents, and tipped the same into the man's furmity. The liquor poured in was rum. The man as slily sent back money in payment.

He found the concoction, thus strongly laced, much more to his satisfaction than it had been in its natural state. His wife had observed the proceeding with much uneasiness, but he persuaded her to have hers laced also, and she agreed to a milder allowance after some misgiving.

The man finished his basin, and called for another, the rum being signalled for in yet stronger proportion. The effect of it was soon apparent in his manner, and his wife but too sadly perceived that in strenuously steering off the rocks of the licensed liquor-tent she had only got into Maelstrom depths[4] here amongst the smugglers.

The child began to prattle impatiently, and the wife more than once said to her husband, "Michael, how about our lodging? You know we may have trouble in getting it if we don't go soon."

But he turned a deaf ear to these bird-like chirpings. He talked loud to the company. The child's black eyes, after slow, round, ruminating gazes at the candles when they were lighted, fell together; then they opened, then shut again, and she slept.

At the end of the first basin the man had risen to serenity. At the second he was jovial; at the third argumentative. At the fourth, the points signified by the shape of his face, the occasional clench of his mouth, and the fiery spark of his dark eye, began to tell in his conduct; he was overbearing – even brilliantly quarrelsome.

The conversation took a high turn, as it often does on such occasions. The ruin of good men by bad wives, and, more particularly, the frustration of many a promising youth's high aims and hopes, and the extinction of his energies, by an early imprudent marriage, was the theme.

"I did for myself that way thoroughly," said the trusser, with a contemplative bitterness that was well-nigh resentful. "I married at eighteen, like a fool that I was; and this is the consequence o't." He pointed at himself and family with a wave of the hand intended to bring out the penuriousness of the exhibition.

The young woman his wife, who seemed accustomed to such remarks, acted as if she did not hear them, and continued her intermittent private words on tender trifles to the sleeping and waking child, who was just big enough to be placed for a moment on the bench beside her when she wished to ease her arms. The man continued:

"I haven't more than fifteen shillings in the world, and yet I am a good experienced hand in my line. I'd challenge England to beat me in the fodder business; and if I were a free man again I'd be worth a thousand pound before I'd done o't. But a fellow never knows these little things till all chance of acting upon 'em is past."

The auctioneer selling the old horses in the field outside could be heard saying, "Now this is the last lot – now who'll take the last lot for a song? Shall I say forty shillings? 'Tis a very promising brood-mare, a trifle over five years old, and nothing the matter with the hoss at all, except that she's a little holler in the back and had her left eye knocked out by the kick of another, her own sister, coming along the road."

"For my part I don't see why men who have got wives, and don't want 'em, shouldn't get rid of 'em as these gipsy fellows do their old horses," said the man in the tent. "Why shouldn't they put 'em up and sell 'em by auction to men who are in want of such articles? Hey? Why, begad, I'd sell mine this minute, if anybody would buy her!"

"There's them that would do that," some of the guests replied, looking at the woman, who was by no means ill-favoured.

"True," said a smoking gentleman, whose coat had the fine polish about the collar, elbows, seams, and shoulder-blades that long-continued friction with oily surfaces will produce, and which is usually more desired on furniture than on clothes. From his appearance he had possibly been in former time groom or coachman to some neighbouring county family. "I've had my breedings in as good circles, I may say, as any man," he added, "and I know true cultivation, or nobody do; and I can declare she's got it – in the bone, mind ye, I say – as much as any female in the fair – though it may want a little bringing out." Then, crossing his legs, he resumed his pipe with a nicely adjusted gaze at a point in the air.

The fuddled young husband stared for a few seconds at this unexpected praise of his wife, half in doubt of the wisdom of his own attitude towards the possessor of such qualities. But he speedily lapsed into his former conviction, and said harshly:

"Well, then, now is your chance; I am open to an offer for this gem of creation."

She turned to her husband and murmured, "Michael, you have talked this nonsense in public places before. A joke is a joke, but you may make it once too often, mind!"

"I know I've said it before; I meant it. All I want is a buyer."

At the moment a swallow, one among the last of the season, which had by chance found its way through an opening into the upper part of the tent, flew to and fro in quick curves above their heads, causing all eyes to follow it absently. In watching the bird till it made its escape the assembled company neglected to respond to the workman's offer, and the subject dropped.

But a quarter of an hour later the man, who had gone on lacing his furmity more and more heavily, though he was either so strong-minded or such an intrepid toper that he still appeared fairly sober, recurred to the old strain, as in a musical fantasy the instrument fetches up the original theme. "Here – I am waiting to know about this offer of mine. The woman is no good to me. Who'll have her?"

The company had by this time decidedly degenerated, and the renewed inquiry was received with a laugh of appreciation. The woman whispered; she was imploring and anxious: "Come, come, it is getting dark, and this nonsense won't do. If you don't come along I shall go without you. Come!"

She waited and waited; yet he did not move. In ten minutes the man broke in upon the desultory conversation of the furmity drinkers with, "I asked this question, and nobody answered to 't. Will any Jack Rag or Tom Straw[5] among ye buy my goods?"

The woman's manner changed, and her face assumed the grim shape and colour of which mention has been made.

"Mike, Mike," said she; "this is getting serious. Oh – too serious!"

"Will anybody buy her?" said the man.

"I wish somebody would," said she firmly. "Her present owner is not at all to her liking!"

"Nor you to mine," said he. "So we are agreed about that. Gentlemen, you hear? It's an agreement to part. She shall take the girl[6] if she wants to, and go her ways. I'll take my tools, and go my ways. 'Tis simple as Scripture history.[7] Now then, stand up, Susan, and show yourself."

"Don't, my chiel," whispered a buxom staylace dealer in voluminous petticoats, who sat near the woman; "yer good man don't know what he's saying."

The woman, however, did stand up. "Now, who's auctioneer?" cried the hay-trusser.

"I be," promptly answered a short man, with a nose resembling a copper knob, a damp voice, and eyes like button-holes. "Who'll make an offer for this lady?"

The woman looked on the ground, as if she maintained her position by a supreme effort of will.

"Five shillings," said some one, at which there was a laugh.

"No insults," said the husband. "Who'll say a guinea?"

Nobody answered; and the female dealer in staylaces interposed.

"Behave yerself moral, good man, for Heaven's love! Ah, what a cruelty is the poor soul married to! Bed and board is dear at some figures, 'pon my 'vation 'tis!"

"Set it higher, auctioneer," said the trusser.[8]

"Two guineas!" said the auctioneer; and no one replied.

"If they don't take her for that, in ten seconds they'll have to give more," said the husband. "Very well. Now, auctioneer, add another."

"Three guineas – going for three guineas!" said the rheumy man.

"No bid?" said the husband. "Good Lord, why she's cost me fifty times the money, if a penny. Go on."

"Four guineas!" cried the auctioneer.

"I'll tell ye what – I won't sell her for less than five," said the husband, bringing down his fist so that the basins danced. "I'll sell her for five guineas to any man that will pay me the money, and treat her well; and he shall have her for ever, and never hear aught o' me. But she sha'n't go for less. Now then – five guineas – and she's yours. Susan, you agree?"

She bowed her head with absolute indifference.

"Five guineas," said the auctioneer, "or she'll be withdrawn. Do anybody give it? The last time. Yes or no?"

"Yes," said a loud voice from the doorway.

All eyes were turned. Standing in the triangular opening which formed the door of the tent was a sailor, who, unobserved by the rest, had arrived there within the last two or three minutes. A dead silence followed his affirmation.

"You say you do?" asked the husband, staring at him.

"I say so," replied the sailor.

"Saying is one thing, and paying is another. Where's the money?"

The sailor hesitated a moment, looked anew at the woman, came in, unfolded a crisp piece of paper,[9] and threw it down upon the table-cloth. It was a Bank-of-England note for five pounds. Upon the face of this he chinked down the shillings severally – one, two, three, four, five.

The sight of real money in full amount, in answer to a challenge for the same till then deemed slightly hypothetical, had a great effect upon the spectators. Their eyes became riveted upon the faces of the chief actors, and then upon the note, as it lay, weighted by the shillings, on the table.

Up to this moment it could not positively have been asserted that the man, in spite of his tantalizing declaration, was really in earnest. The spectators had, indeed, taken the proceedings throughout as a piece of mirthful irony carried to extremes; and had assumed that, being out of work, he was, as a consequence, out of temper with the world, and society, and his nearest kin. But with the demand and response of real cash the jovial frivolity of the scene departed. A lurid colour seemed to fill the tent, and change the aspect of all therein. The mirth-wrinkles left the listeners' faces, and they waited with parting lips.

"Now," said the woman, breaking the silence, so that her low dry voice sounded quite loud, "before you go further, Michael,[10] listen to me. If you touch that money, I and this girl go with the man. Mind, it is a joke no longer."

"A joke? – Of course it is not a joke!" shouted her husband, his resentment rising at her suggestion. "I take the money: the sailor takes you. That's plain enough. It has been done elsewhere – and why not here?"[11]

"'Tis quite on the understanding that the young woman is willing," said the sailor, blandly. "I wouldn't hurt her feelings for the world."

"Faith, nor I," said her husband. "But she is willing, provided she can have the child. She said so only the other day when I talked o't!"

"That you swear?" said the sailor to her.

"I do," said she, after glancing at her husband's face and seeing no repentance there.

"Very well, she shall have the child, and the bargain's complete," said the trusser. He took the sailor's note and deliberately folded it, and put it with the shillings in a high remote pocket with an air of finality.

The sailor looked at the woman and smiled. "Come along!" he said, kindly. "The little one, too – the more the merrier!" She paused for an instant, with a close glance at him. Then dropping her eyes again, and saying nothing, she took up the child and followed him as he made towards the door. On reaching it, she turned, and pulling off her wedding-ring flung it across the room[12] in the hay-trusser's face.

"Mike," she said, "I've lived with thee a couple[13] of years and had nothing but temper! Now I'm no more to you; I'll try my luck elsewhere. 'Twill be better for me and the child, both.[14] So good-bye."

Seizing the sailor's arm with her right hand, and mounting the little girl on her left, she went out of the tent, sobbing bitterly, and apparently without a thought that she was not strictly bound to go with the man who had paid for her.[15]

A stolid look of concern filled the husband's face, as if, after all, he had not quite anticipated this ending; and some of the guests laughed.

"Is she gone?" he said.

"Faith, ay; she gone clane enough," said some rustics near the door.

He rose and walked to the entrance with the careful tread of one conscious of his alcoholic load. Some others followed, and they stood looking into the twilight. The difference between the peacefulness of inferior nature and the wilful hostilities of mankind was very apparent at this place. In contrast with the harshness of the act just ended within the tent was the sight of several horses crossing their necks and rubbing each other lovingly as they waited in patience to be harnessed for the homeward journey. Outside the fair, in the valleys and woods, all was quiet. The sun had recently set, and the west heaven was hung with rosy cloud, which seemed permanent, yet slowly changed. To watch it was like looking at some grand feat of stagery from a darkened auditorium. In presence of this scene, after the other, there was a natural instinct to abjure man as the blot on an otherwise kindly universe; till it was remembered that all terrestrial conditions were intermittent, and that mankind might some night be innocently sleeping when these quiet objects were raging loud.

"Where do the sailor live?" asked a spectator, when they had vainly gazed around.

"God knows that," replied the man who had seen high life. "He's without doubt a stranger here."

"He came in about five minutes ago," said the furmity woman, joining the rest with her hands on her hips. "And then 'a stepped back, and then 'a looked in again. I'm not a penny the better for him."

"Serves the husband well be-right," said the staylace vendor. "A comely respectable body like her – what can a man want more? I glory in the woman's sperrit. I'd ha' done it myself – od send if I wouldn't, if a husband had behaved so to me! I'd go, and 'a might call, and call, till his keacorn was raw; but I'd never come back – no, not till the great trumpet,[16] would I."

"Well, the woman will be better off," said another of a more deliberative turn. "For seafaring naters be very good shelter for shorn lambs, and the man do seem to have plenty of money, which is what she's not been used to lately, by all showings."

"Mark me – I'll not go after her!"[17] said the trusser, returning doggedly

14

to his seat. "Let her go. If she's up to such vagaries she must suffer for 'em. She'd no business to take the maid – 'tis my maid; and if it were the doing again she shouldn't have her!"

Perhaps from some little sense of having countenanced an indefensible proceeding, perhaps because it was late, the customers thinned away from the tent shortly after this episode. The man stretched his elbows forward on the table, leant his face upon his arms, and soon began to snore. The furmity-seller decided to close for the night, and after seeing the rum-bottles, milk, corn, raisins, &c., that remained on hand, loaded into the cart, came to where the man reclined. She shook him; but could not wake him. As the tent was not to be struck that night, the fair continuing for two or three days, she decided to let the sleeper, who was obviously no tramp, stay where he was, and his basket with him. Extinguishing the last candle, and lowering the flap of the tent, she left it, and drove away.

CHAPTER II

The morning sun was streaming through the crevices of the canvas when the man awoke. A warm glow pervaded the whole atmosphere of the marquee, and a single big blue fly buzzed musically round and round it. Besides the buzz of the fly there was not a sound. He looked about – at the benches – at the table supported by trestles – at his basket of tools – at the stove where the furmity had been boiled – at the empty basins – at some shed grains of wheat – at the corks which dotted the grassy floor. Among the odds and ends he discerned a little shining object, and picked it up. It was his wife's ring.

A confused picture of the events of the previous evening seemed to come back to him, and he thrust his hand into his coat pocket. A rustling revealed the sailor's bank-note thrust carelessly in.

This second verification of his dim memories was enough; he knew now they were not dreams. He remained seated, looking on the ground for some time. "I must get out of this as soon as I can," he said deliberately at last, with the air of one who could not catch his thoughts without pronouncing them. "She's gone – to be sure she is – gone with that sailor who bought her, and little Elizabeth-Jane. We walked here, and I had the furmity, and rum in it – and sold her. Yes, that's what's happened, and here am I. Now, what am I to do – am I sober enough to walk, I wonder?" He stood up, found that he was in fairly good condition for progress, unencumbered. Next he shouldered his tool basket, and found he could carry it. Then lifting the tent door he emerged into the open air.

Here the man looked around with gloomy curiosity. The freshness of the September morning inspired and braced him as he stood. He and his family had been weary when they arrived the night before, and they had observed but little of the place; so that he now beheld it as a new thing. It exhibited itself as the top of an open down, bounded on one extreme by a plantation, and approached by a winding road. At the bottom stood the village which lent its name to the upland, and the annual fair that was held thereon. The spot stretched downward into valleys, and onward to other uplands, dotted with barrows, and trenched with the remains of prehistoric forts. The whole scene lay under the rays of a newly risen sun, which had not as yet dried a single blade of the heavily dewed grass, whereon the shadows of the yellow and red vans were projected far away, those thrown by the felloe of each wheel being elongated in shape to the orbit of a comet. All the gipsies and showmen who had remained on the ground lay snug within their carts and tents, or wrapped in horse-cloths under them, and were silent and still as death, with the exception of an occasional snore that revealed their presence. But the Seven Sleepers[1] had a dog; and dogs of the mysterious breeds that vagrants own, that are as much like cats as dogs, and as much like foxes as cats, also lay about here. A little one started up under one of the carts, barked as a matter of principle, and quickly lay down again. He was the only positive spectator of the hay-trusser's exit from the Weydon fairfield.

This seemed to accord with his desire. He went on in silent thought, unheeding the yellow-hammers which flitted about the hedges with straws in their bills, the crowns of the mushrooms, and the tinkling of local sheep-bells, whose wearers had had the good fortune not to be included in the fair. When he reached a lane, a good mile from the scene of the previous evening, the man pitched his basket, and leant upon a gate. A difficult problem or two occupied his mind.

"Did I tell my name to anybody last night, or didn't I tell my name?" he said to himself; and at last concluded that he did not. His general demeanour was enough to show how he was surprised and nettled that his wife had taken him so literally – as much could be seen in his face, and in the way he nibbled a straw which he pulled from the hedge. He knew that she must have been somewhat excited to do this; moreover, she must have believed in the binding force of the transaction. On this latter point he felt quite certain, knowing her freedom from levity of character, and the extreme simplicity of her intellect.[2] There may have been a little recklessness beneath her ordinary placidity.[3] On a previous occasion when he had declared during a fuddle that he would dispose of her as he had done, she had declared that she should not hear him say that many times more before it happened, in the resigned tones of a fatalist. . . . . "Yet she knows I am not in my senses when I do that!" he exclaimed. "Well, I must walk about till I find her. . . . . Seize her, why didn't she know better than bring me into this disgrace!" he roared out. "She wasn't queer if I was. 'Tis like Susan to show such idiotic simplicity. Meek – that meekness has done me more harm than the bitterest temper!"

When he was calmer, he returned to his original conviction that he must somehow find her and his little Elizabeth-Jane, and put up with the shame as best he could. It was of his own making, and he ought to bear it. But first he resolved to register an oath, a greater oath than he had ever sworn before: and to do it properly he required a fit place and imagery; for there was something fetichistic[4] in this man's beliefs.

He shouldered his basket and moved on, casting his eyes inquisitively round upon the landscape as he walked, and at the distance of three or four miles perceived the roofs of a village and the tower of a church. He instantly made towards the latter object. The village was quite still, it being that motionless hour of rustic daily life which fills the interval between the departure of the field labourers to their work, and the rising of their wives and daughters to prepare the breakfast for their return. Hence he reached the church without observation, and the door being only latched he entered. The hay-trusser deposited his basket by the font, went up the nave till he reached the altar-rails, and opening the gate entered the sacrarium, where he seemed to feel a sense of the strangeness for a moment, then knelt upon the foot-pace. Dropping his head upon the clamped book which lay on the Communion table, he said aloud:

"I, Michael Henchard, on this morning of the sixteenth of September, do take an oath here in this solemn place that I will avoid all strong liquors for the space of twenty[5] years to come, being a year for every year that I have lived. And this I swear upon the Book before me; and may I be stricken dumb, blind, and helpless if I break this my oath."

When he had said it and kissed the big book, the hay-trusser arose, and seemed relieved at having made a start in a new direction. While standing in the porch a moment, he saw a thick jet of wood-smoke suddenly start up from the red chimney of a cottage near, and knew that the occupant had just lit her fire. He went round to the door, and the housewife agreed to prepare him some breakfast for a trifling payment, which was done. Then he started on the search for his wife and child.

The tantalizing[6] nature of the undertaking became apparent soon enough. Though he examined and inquired, and walked hither and thither day after day, no such characters as those he described had anywhere been seen since the evening of the fair. To add to the difficulty he could gain no sound of the sailor's name. As money was short with him he decided, after some hesitation, to spend the sailor's money in the prosecution of this search; but it was equally in vain. The truth was that a certain shyness of revealing his conduct prevented Michael Henchard from following up the investigation with the loud hue-and-cry such a pursuit demanded to render it effectual; and it was probably for this reason that he obtained no clue, though everything was done by him that did not involve an explanation of the circumstances under which he had lost her.

Weeks counted up to months and still he searched on, maintaining himself by small jobs of work in the intervals. By this time he had arrived at a western seaport, and there he derived intelligence that persons answering somewhat to his description had emigrated a little time before. Then he said he would search no longer, and that he would go and settle in the district which he had had for some time in his mind. Next day he started, journeying southward,[7] and did not pause till he reached the town of Casterbridge, more than a hundred miles off.[8]

CHAPTER III

The high road into the village of Weydon-Priors was again carpeted with dust. The trees had put on as of yore their aspect of dingy green, and where the Henchard family of three had once walked along, two persons not unconnected with that family walked now.

The scene in its broad aspect had so much of its previous character, even to the voices and rattle from the neighbouring village down, that it might for that matter have been the afternoon following the previously recorded episode. Change was only to be observed in details; but here it was obvious that a long procession of years had passed by. One of the two who walked the road was she who had figured as the young wife of Henchard on the previous occasion; now her face had lost much of its rotundity; her skin had undergone a textural change; and though her hair had not lost colour, it was considerably thinner than heretofore. She was dressed in the mourning clothes of a widow. Her companion, also in black, appeared as a well-formed young woman of eighteen,[1] completely possessed of that ephemeral precious essence, youth, which is itself beauty, irrespective of complexion or contour.

A glance was sufficient to inform the eye that this was Susan Henchard's grown-up daughter. While life's middle summer had set its hardening mark on the mother's face, her former spring-like specialities were transferred so dexterously by Time to the second figure, her child, that the absence of certain facts within her mother's knowledge from the girl's mind would have seemed for the moment, to one reflecting on those facts, to be a curious imperfection in Nature's powers of continuity.

They walked with joined hands, and it could be perceived that this was the act of simple affection. The daughter carried in her outer hand a withy basket of old-fashioned make; the mother a blue bundle, which contrasted oddly with her black stuff gown.

Reaching the outskirts of the village they pursued the same track as formerly, and ascended to the fair. Here, too, it was evident that the years had told. Certain mechanical improvements might have been noticed in the roundabouts and highfliers, machines for testing rustic strength and weight, and in the erections devoted to shooting for nuts. But the real business of the fair had considerably dwindled. The new periodical great markets of neighbouring towns were beginning to interfere seriously with the trade carried on here for centuries. The pens for sheep, the tie-ropes for horses, were about half as long as they had been. The stalls of tailors, hosiers, coopers, linen-drapers, and other such trades had almost disappeared, and the vehicles were far less numerous. The mother and daughter threaded the crowd for some little distance, and then stood still.

"Why did we hinder our time by coming in here? I thought you wished to get onward?" said the maiden.

"Yes, my dear Elizabeth-Jane," explained the other. "But I had a fancy for looking up here."

"Why?"

"It was here I first met with Newson – on such a day as this."

"First met with father here? Yes, you have told me so before. And now he's drowned and gone from us!" As she spoke the girl drew a card from her pocket and looked at it with a sigh. It was edged with black, and inscribed within a design resembling a mural tablet were the words, "In affectionate memory of Richard Newson, mariner, who was unfortunately lost at sea, in the month of November,[2] 184—, aged 41 years."

"And it was here," continued her mother, with more hesitation, "that I last saw the relative we are going to look for – Mr. Michael Henchard."

"What is his exact relation to us, mother? I have never clearly had it told me."

"He is, or was – for he may be dead – a relation by marriage," said her mother, deliberately.

"That's exactly what you have said a score of times before!" replied the young woman, looking about her inattentively. "He's not a near relation, I suppose?"

"Not by any means."

"He was a hay-trusser, wasn't he, when you last heard of him?"

"He was."

"I suppose he never knew me?"[3] the girl innocently continued.

Mrs. Henchard paused for a moment, and answered uneasily, "Of course not, Elizabeth-Jane. But come this way." She moved on to another part of the field.

"It is not much use inquiring here for anybody, I should think," the daughter observed, as she gazed round about. "People at fairs change like the leaves of trees; and I dare say you are the only one here to-day who was here all those years ago."

"I am not so sure of that," said Mrs. Newson, as she now called herself,[4] keenly eyeing something under a green bank a little way off. "See there."

The daughter looked in the direction signified. The object pointed out was a tripod of sticks stuck into the earth, from which hung a three-legged crock, kept hot by a smouldering wood fire beneath. Over the pot stooped an old woman, haggard, wrinkled, and almost in rags. She stirred the contents of the pot with a large spoon, and occasionally croaked in a broken voice, "Good furmity sold here!"

It was indeed the former mistress of the furmity-tent – once thriving, cleanly, white-aproned, and chinking with money – now tentless, dirty, owning no tables or benches, and having scarce any customers except two small whitey-brown boys, who came up and asked for "A ha'p'orth please – good measure," which she served in a couple of chipped yellow basins of commonest clay.

"She was here at that time," resumed Mrs. Newson, making a step as if to draw nearer.

"Don't speak to her – it isn't respectable!" urged the other.

"I will just say a word – you, Elizabeth-Jane, can stay here."

The girl was not loth, and turned to some stalls of coloured prints while her mother went forward. The old woman begged for the latter's custom as soon as she saw her, and responded to Mrs. Henchard-Newson's request for a pennyworth with more alacrity than she had shown in selling sixpennyworths in her younger days. When the *soi-disant* widow had taken the basin of thin poor slop that stood for the rich concoction of the former time, the hag opened a little basket behind the fire, and, looking up slyly, whispered, "Just a thought o' rum in it? – smuggled, you know – say two penn'orth – 'twill make it slip down like cordial."

Her customer smiled bitterly at this survival of the old trick, and shook her head with a meaning the old woman was far from translating. She pretended to eat a little of the furmity with the leaden spoon offered, and as she did so said blandly to the hag, "You've seen better days?"

"Ah, ma'am – well ye may say it!" responded the old woman, opening the sluices of her heart forthwith. "I've stood in this fair-ground, maid, wife, and widow, these nine-and-thirty year, and in that time have known what it was to do business with the richest stomachs in the land! Ma'am, you'd hardly believe that I was once the owner of a great pavilion-tent that was the attraction of the fair. Nobody could come, nobody could go, without having a dish of Mrs. Goodenough's furmity. I knew the clergy's taste, the dandy gent's taste; I knew the town's taste, the country's taste. I even knowed the taste of the coarse shameless[5] females. But seize my life[6] – the world's no memory; straightforward dealings don't bring profit – 'tis the sly and the underhand that get on in these times!"

Mrs. Newson glanced round – her daughter was still bending over the distant stalls. "Can you call to mind," she said cautiously to the old woman, "the sale of a wife by her husband in your tent eighteen years ago to-day?"

The hag reflected, and half shook her head. "If it had been a big thing I should have minded it in a moment," she said. "I can mind every serious fight o' married parties, every murder, every manslaughter, even every pocket-picking – leastwise large ones – that 't has been my lot to witness. But a selling? Was it done quiet-like?"

"Well, yes. I think so."

The furmity-woman half shook her head again. "And yet," she said,

PLATE II

'The hag opened a little basket behind the fire, and, looking up slily,
whispered, "Just a thought o' rum in it?"'

"I do. At any rate I can mind a man doing something o' the sort – a man in a cord jacket, with a basket of tools; but, Lord bless ye, we don't gie it head-room, we don't, such as that. The only reason why I can mind the man is that he came back here to the next year's fair, and told me quite private-like that if a woman ever asked for him I was to say he had gone to – where? – Casterbridge – yes – to Casterbridge, said he. But, Lord's my life, I shouldn't ha' thought of it again!"

Mrs. Newson would have rewarded the old woman as far as her small means afforded, had she not discreetly borne in mind that it was by that unscrupulous person's liquor her husband had been degraded. She briefly thanked her informant, and rejoined Elizabeth, who greeted her with, "Mother, do let's go on – it was hardly respectable for you to buy refreshments there. I see none but the lowest do."

"I have learned what I wanted, however," said her mother, quietly. "The last time our relative visited this fair he said he was living at Casterbridge. It is a long, long way from here, and it was many years ago that he said it; but there I think we'll go."

With this they descended out of the fair, and went onward to the village, where they obtained a night's lodging.

CHAPTER IV

Henchard's wife acted for the best, but she had involved herself in difficulties. A hundred times she had been upon the point of telling her daughter, Elizabeth-Jane, the true story of her life, the tragical crisis of which had been the transaction at Weydon Fair, when she was not much older than the girl now beside her. But she had refrained. An innocent maiden had thus grown up in the belief that the relations between the genial sailor and her mother were the ordinary ones that they had always appeared to be. The risk of endangering a child's strong affection by disturbing ideas which had grown with her growth was to

Mrs. Henchard too fearful a thing to contemplate. It had seemed, indeed, folly to think of making Elizabeth-Jane wise.[1]

But Susan Henchard's fear of losing her dearly loved daughter's heart by a revelation had little to do with any sense of wrongdoing on her own part. Her simplicity[2] – the original ground of Henchard's contempt for her – had allowed her to live on in the conviction that Newson had acquired a real and binding right[3] to her by his purchase – though the exact bearings and legal limits of that right were vague. It may seem strange to sophisticated minds that a sane young matron could believe in the validity of such a transfer; and were there not numerous other instances of the same belief the thing might scarcely be credited. But she was by no means the first or last peasant woman who had religiously adhered to her purchaser, as too many rural records show.[4]

The history of Susan Henchard's adventures in the interim can be told in two or three sentences. Absolutely helpless, she had been taken off to Canada, where they had lived several years without any great worldly success, though she worked as hard as any woman could to keep their cottage cheerful and well-provided. When Elizabeth-Jane was about twelve years old the three returned to England, and settled at Falmouth, where Newson made a living for a few years as boatman and general handy shoreman.

He then engaged in the Newfoundland trade, and it was during this period that Susan had an awakening. A friend to whom she confided her history ridiculed her belief and position; and all was over with her peace of mind. When Newson came home at the end of one winter he saw that the delusion he had so carefully sustained had vanished for ever.

There was then a time of sadness.[5] Newson left home again on the Newfoundland trade when the season came round. The news of his loss at sea a little later on solved a problem which had become torture to her meek conscience. She saw him no more.

Of Henchard they heard nothing. To the liege subjects of Labour, England is a continent,[6] and a mile a geographical degree.

Elizabeth-Jane developed early into womanliness. One day, a month or so after receiving intelligence of Newson's death off the Bank of Newfoundland, when the girl was about eighteen, she was sitting on a willow chair in the cottage they still occupied, working twine nets for the fishermen. Her mother was in a back corner of the same room, engaged in the same labour; and dropping the heavy wood needle she was filling, she surveyed her daughter thoughtfully. The sun shone in at the door upon the young woman's head and hair, which was worn loose, so that the rays streamed into its depths as into a hazel copse. Her face, though somewhat wan and incomplete, possessed the raw materials of beauty in a promising degree. There was an under-handsomeness in it, struggling to reveal itself through the provisional curves of immaturity, and the casual disfigurements that resulted from the straitened circumstances of their lives. She was handsome in the bone, hardly as yet handsome in the flesh. She possibly might never be fully handsome, unless the carking accidents of her daily existence could be evaded before the mobile parts of her countenance had settled to their final mould.

The sight of the girl made her mother sad – not vaguely, but by logical inference. They both were still in that strait-waistcoat of poverty from which she had tried so many times to be delivered for the girl's sake. The woman had long perceived how zealously and constantly the young mind of her companion was struggling for enlargement; and yet now, in her eighteenth year, it still remained but little unfolded. The desire – sober and repressed – of Elizabeth-Jane's heart was indeed to see, to hear, and to understand.[7] How could she become a woman of wider knowledge, higher repute – "better," as she termed it: – this was her constant inquiry of her mother. She sought further into things than other girls in her position ever did, and her mother groaned as she felt she could not aid in the search.

The sailor was now lost to them;[8] and Susan's staunch, religious adherence to him as her husband,[9] till her views had been disturbed by enlightenment, was demanded no more. She asked herself whether the present moment, now that she was a free woman again, were not as opportune a one as she would find, in a world where everything had been so inopportune, for making a desperate effort to advance Elizabeth. To pocket her pride and search for the first husband seemed, wisely or not, the best initiatory step. He had possibly drunk himself into his tomb. But he might, on the other hand, have had too much sense to do so; for in her time with him he had been given to bouts only, and was not a habitual drunkard.

At any rate the propriety of returning to him, if he lived, was unquestionable. The awkwardness of searching for him lay in enlightening Elizabeth, a proceeding which her mother could not endure to contemplate. She finally resolved to undertake the search without confiding to the girl her former relations with Henchard, leaving it to him if they found him to take what steps he might choose to that end. This will account for their conversation at the fair, and the half-informed state in which Elizabeth was led onward.

In this attitude they proceeded on their journey, trusting solely to the dim light afforded of Henchard's whereabouts by the furmity-woman. The strictest economy was indispensable. Sometimes they might have been seen on foot, sometimes on farmers' waggons, sometimes in carriers' vans; and thus they drew near to Casterbridge. Elizabeth-Jane discovered to her alarm that her mother's health was not what it once had been, and there was ever and anon in her talk that renunciatory tone which showed that, but for the girl, she would not be very sorry to quit a life she was growing thoroughly weary of.

It was on a Friday evening, near the middle of September, and just before dusk, that they reached the summit of a hill within a mile of the place they sought. There were no hedges to the highway here, and they mounted upon the green turf and sat down.[10] The spot commanded a full view of the town and its environs.

"What an old-fashioned place it seems to be!" said Elizabeth-Jane, while her silent mother mused on other things than topography. "It is huddled all together; and it is shut in by a square wall of trees, like a plot of garden ground by a box-edging."

Its squareness was, indeed, the characteristic which most struck the eye in this antiquated borough, the borough of Casterbridge – at that time, recent as it was, untouched by the faintest sprinkle of modernism. It was compact as a box of dominoes. It had no suburbs – in the ordinary sense. Country and town met at a mathematical line.

To birds of the more soaring kind Casterbridge must have appeared on this fine evening as a mosaic-work of subdued reds, browns, greys, and crystals, held together by a rectangular frame of deep green. To the level eye of humanity it stood as an indistinct mass behind a dense stockade of limes and chestnuts, set in the midst of miles of rotund down and concave field. The mass became gradually dissected by the vision into towers, gables, chimneys, and casements, the highest glazings shining bleared and bloodshot with the coppery fire they caught from the belt of sunlit cloud in the west.

From the centre of each side of this treebound square ran avenues east, west, and south into the wide expanse of corn-land and combe to the distance of a mile or so, after which the highway was bare. It was one of these avenues that the pedestrians had entered. Before they had risen to proceed two men passed by, engaged in argumentative conversation.

"Why, surely," said Elizabeth, as they receded; "those men mentioned the name of Henchard in their talk – the name of our relative?"

"I thought so too," said Mrs. Newson (as she may be called for the present).[11]

"That seems a hint to us that he is still here."

"Yes."

"Shall I run after them, and ask them about him—"

"No, no, no! Not for the world just yet. He may be in the workhouse or in the stocks for all we know."

"Dear me – why should you think that, mother?"

"'Twas just something to say – that's all. But we must make private inquiries."

Having sufficiently rested, they proceeded on their way. The dense trees of the avenue rendered the road dark as a tunnel, though the corn-land on each side was still under a faint daylight; in other words, they passed down a midnight between two gloamings. The features of the town had a keen interest for Elizabeth's mother now that the human side came to the fore. As soon as they approached the margin they could see that the stockade of gnarled trees which framed in Casterbridge was itself an avenue, standing on a low green bank or escarpment, with a ditch yet visible without. Within the avenue and bank was a wall more or less discontinuous, and within the wall were packed the abodes of the burghers.

Though the two women did not know it, these external features were but the ancient defences of the town, planted as a promenade.

The lamplights now glimmered through the engirdling trees, conveying a sense of great snugness and comfort inside, and rendering at the same time the unlighted country without strangely solitary and vacant in aspect, considering its nearness to life. The difference between burgh and champaign was increased, too, by sounds which now reached them above others – the notes of a brass band. The travellers wandered down the High Street, where there were timber houses with overhanging stories, whose small-paned lattices were screened by dimity curtains on a drawing-string, and under whose barge-boards old cobwebs waved in the breeze. There were houses of brick-nogging, which derived their chief support from those adjoining. There were slate roofs patched with tiles, and tile roofs patched with slate, with occasionally a roof of thatch.[12]

The agricultural and pastoral character of the people upon whom the town depended for its existence was shown by the class of objects displayed in the shop-windows. Scythes, reap-hooks, sheep-shears, bill-hooks, spades, mattocks, and hoes at the ironmonger's; beehives, butter-firkins, churns, milking-stools and pails, hay-rakes, field-flagons, and seed-lips at the cooper's; cart-ropes and plough-harness at the saddler's; corn-drills and winnowing-machines[13] at the wheelwright's and machinist's; horse-embrocations at the chemist's; at the glover's and leather-cutter's hedging-gloves, thatcher's knee-caps, ploughman's leggings, villager's pattens and clogs.

They came to a grizzled church, whose massive square tower rose unbroken into the darkening sky, the lower parts being illuminated by the nearest lamps sufficiently to show how completely the mortar from the joints of the stonework had been nibbled out by time and weather, which had planted in the crevices thus made little tufts of stonecrop and grass almost as far up as the very battlements. From this tower the clock struck eight, and thereupon a bell began to toll with a peremptory clang. The curfew[14] was still rung in Casterbridge, and it was utilized by the inhabitants as a signal for shutting their shops. No sooner did the deep notes of the bell throb between the house-fronts than a clatter of shutters arose through the whole length of the High Street. In a few minutes business at Casterbridge was ended for the day.

Other clocks struck eight from time to time – one gloomily from the gaol, another from the gable of an almshouse, with a preparative creak of machinery, more audible than the note of the bell; a row of tall, varnished case-clocks from the interior of a watch-maker's shop joined in one after another just as the shutters were enclosing them, like a row of actors delivering their final speeches before the fall of the curtain; then chimes were heard stammering out the Sicilian Mariners' Hymn;[15] so that chronologists of the advanced school were appreciably on their way to the next hour before the whole business of the old one was satisfactorily wound up.

In an open space before the church walked a woman with her gown-sleeves rolled up so high that the edge of her under-linen was visible, and her skirt tucked up through her pocket-hole. She carried a loaf under her arm, from which she was pulling pieces of bread, and handing them to some other women who walked with her; which pieces they nibbled critically. The sight reminded Mrs. Henchard-Newson and her daughter that they had an appetite; and they inquired of the woman for the nearest baker's.

"Ye may as well look for manna-food[16] as good bread in Casterbridge just now," she said, after directing them. "They can blare their trumpets and thump their drums, and have their roaring dinners" – waving her hand towards a point further down the street, where the brass band could be seen standing in front of an illuminated building – "but we must needs be put-to for want of a wholesome crust. There's less good bread than good beer in Casterbridge now."

"And less good beer than swipes," said a man with his hands in his pockets.

"How does it happen there's no good bread?" asked Mrs. Henchard.

"Oh, 'tis the corn-factor – he's the man that our millers and bakers all deal wi', and he has sold 'em grown wheat,[17] which they didn't know was grown, so they say, till the dough ran all over the ovens like quicksilver; so that the loaves be as flat as toads, and like suet pudden inside. I've been a wife, and I've been a mother, and I never see such unprincipled bread in Casterbridge as this before—But you must be a real stranger here not to know what's made all the poor folks plim like blowed blathers this week?"

"I am," said Elizabeth's mother, shyly.

Not wishing to be observed further till she knew more of her future in this place, she withdrew with her daughter from the speaker's side. Getting a couple of biscuits at the shop indicated, as a temporary substitute for a meal, they next bent their steps instinctively to where the music was playing.

CHAPTER V

A few score yards brought them to the spot where the town band was now shaking the window-panes with the strains of "The Roast Beef of Old England."[1]

The building before whose doors they had pitched their music-stands was the chief hotel in Casterbridge – namely, The Golden Crown.[2] A spacious bow-window projected into the street over the main portico, and from the open sashes came the babble of voices, the jingle of glasses, and the drawing of corks. The blinds, moreover, being left unclosed, the whole interior of this room could be surveyed from the top of a flight of steps opposite, for which reason a knot of idlers had gathered there.

"We might, perhaps, after all, make a few inquiries about – our relation, Mr. Henchard," whispered Mrs. Newson, who, since her entry into Casterbridge, had seemed strangely weak and agitated. "And this, I think, would be a good place for trying it – just to ask, you know, how he stands in the town – if he is here, as I think he must be. You, Elizabeth-Jane, had better be the one to do it. I'm too worn out to do anything – pull down your fall first."

She sat down upon the lowest step, and Elizabeth-Jane obeyed her directions and stood among the idlers.

"What's going on to-night?" asked the girl, after singling out an old man, and standing by him long enough to acquire a neighbourly right of converse.

"Well, ye must be a stranger sure," said the old man, without taking

31

his eyes from the window. "Why, 'tis a great public dinner of the gentle-people and such like leading folk – wi' the Mayor in the chair. As we plainer fellows baint invited, they leave the winder-shutters open that we may get jest a sense o't out here. If you mount the steps you can see 'em. That's Mr. Henchard, the Mayor, at the end of the table, a facing ye; and that's the Council-men right and left. . . . . Ah, lots of them when they begun life were no more than I be now!"

"Henchard?" said Elizabeth-Jane, surprised, but by no means suspecting the whole force of the revelation. She ascended among the other persons to the space at the top of the steps.

Her mother, though her head was bowed, had already caught from the window tones that strangely riveted her attention, before the old man's words, "Mr. Henchard, the Mayor," reached her ears. She arose, and ascended in her daughter's rear as soon as she could do so without showing exceptional eagerness.

The interior of the hotel dining-room was spread out before her, with its tables, and glass, and plate, and inmates. Facing the window, in the chair of dignity, sat a man approaching forty[3] years of age; of heavy frame, large features, and commanding voice; his general build being rather coarse than compact. He had a rich complexion, which verged on swarthiness, a flashing black eye, and dark, bushy brows and hair. When he indulged in an occasional loud laugh at some remark among the guests his large mouth parted so far back as to show to the rays of the chandelier a full score or more of the two-and-thirty sound white teeth that he obviously still could boast of.

That laugh was not encouraging to strangers; and hence it may have been well that it was rarely heard. Many theories might have been built upon it. It fell in well with conjectures of a temperament which would have no pity for weakness, but would be ready to yield ungrudging admiration to greatness and strength. Its producer's personal goodness, if he had any, would be of a very fitful cast – an occasional almost oppressive generosity rather than a mild and constant kindness.

Susan Henchard's[4] husband – in law, at least – sat before them, matured in shape, stiffened in line, exaggerated in traits; disciplined, thought-marked – in a word, older. Elizabeth, encumbered with no recollections as her mother was, regarded him with nothing more than the keen curiosity and interest which the discovery of such unexpected social standing in the long-sought relative naturally begot. He was dressed in an old-fashioned evening suit, an expanse of frilled shirt showing on his broad breast; jewelled studs; and a heavy gold chain. Three glasses stood at his right hand; but, to his wife's surprise, the two for wine were empty, while the third, a tumbler, was half full of water.

When last she had seen him he was sitting in a light fustian jacket, corduroy waistcoat and breeches, and tanned leather leggings, with a basin of hot furmity before him. Time, the magician, had wrought much here. Watching him, and thus thinking of past days, she became so moved that she shrank back against the jamb of the deep doorway to which the steps gave access, the shadow from it conveniently hiding her features. She forgot her daughter, till a touch from Elizabeth-Jane aroused her. "Have you seen him, mother?" whispered the girl.

"Yes, yes," answered her companion hastily. "I have seen him, and it is enough for me! Now I only want to go – pass away – die."

"Why – O what?" She drew closer, and whispered in her mother's ear, "Does he seem to you not likely to befriend us? I thought he looked a generous man. What a gentleman he is, isn't he? and how his diamond studs shine! How strange that you should have said he might be in the stocks or in the workhouse, or dead! Did ever anything go more by contraries! Why do you feel so afraid of him? I am not at all; I'll call upon him – he can but say he don't own such remote kin."

"I don't know at all – I can't tell what to set about. I feel so down."

"Don't be that, mother, now we have got here and all! Rest there where you be a little while – I will look on and find out more about him."

"I don't think I can ever meet Mr. Henchard. He is not how I thought he would be – he overpowers me. I don't wish to see him any more."

"But wait a little time and consider."

Elizabeth-Jane had never been so much interested in anything in her life as in their present position, partly from the natural elation she felt at discovering herself akin to a coach;[5] and she gazed again at the scene. The younger guests were talking and eating with animation; their elders were searching for tit-bits, and sniffing and grunting over their plates like sows nuzzling for acorns. Three drinks seemed to be sacred to the company – port, sherry, and rum; outside which old-established trinity few or no palates ranged.

A row of ancient rummers with ground figures on their sides, and each primed with a spoon, was now placed down the table, and these were promptly filled with grog at such high temperatures as to raise serious considerations for the articles exposed to its vapours. But Eliza-beth-Jane noticed that, though this filling went on with great promptness up and down the table, nobody filled the Mayor's glass, who still drank large quantities of water from the tumbler behind the clump of crystal vessels intended for wine and spirits.

"They don't fill Mr. Henchard's wine-glasses," she ventured to say to her elbow acquaintance, the old man.

"Oh no; don't ye know him to be the celebrated abstaining worthy of that name? He scorns all tempting liquors; never touches nothing. Oh yes, he've strong qualities that way. I have heard tell that he sware a gospel oath in bygone times, and has bode by it ever since. So they don't press him, knowing it would be unbecoming in the face of that; for yer gospel oath is a serious thing."

Another elderly man, hearing this discourse, now joined in by inquir-ing, "How much longer have he got to suffer from it, Solomon Longways?"

"Another two year, they say. I don't know the why and the wherefore of his fixing such a time, for 'a never has told anybody. But 'tis exactly two calendar years longer, they say. A powerful mind to hold out so long!"

"True. . . . . But there's great strength in hope. Knowing that in four-and-twenty months' time ye'll be out of your bondage, and able to make up for all you've suffered, by partaking without stint; why, it keeps a man up, no doubt."

"No doubt, Christopher Coney, no doubt. And 'a must need such reflections – a lonely widow man," said Longways.

"When did he lose his wife?" asked Elizabeth.

"I never knowed her. 'Twas afore he came to Casterbridge," Solomon Longways replied, with terminative emphasis, as if the fact of his ignorance of Mrs. Henchard were sufficient to deprive her history of all interest. "But I know that 'a's a banded teetotaller,[6] and that if any of his men be ever so little overtook by a drop, he's down upon 'em as stern as the Lord upon the jovial Jews."[7]

"Has he many men, then?" said Elizabeth-Jane.

"Many? Why, my good maid, he's the powerfullest member of the town council, and quite a principal man in the country round besides. He and Casterbridge bank-folk are sworn brothers.[8] Never a big dealing in wheat, barley, oats, hay, roots, and such-like in this county but Henchard's got a hand in it. Ay, and he'll go into other things, too; and that's where he makes his mistake. He worked his way up from nothing when 'a came here; and now he's a pillar of the town. Not but what he's been shook a little to-year about this bad corn he has supplied in his contracts. I've seen the sun rise over Casterbridge Moor[9] these nine-and-sixty year, and though Mr. Henchard has never cussed me unfairly ever since I've worked for'n, seeing I be but a little small man, and though 'tis not my interest to spak against him,[10] I must say that I have never before tasted such rough bread as hev been made from Henchard's wheat lately. 'Tis that growed out that ye could a'most call it malt, and there's a list at bottom o' the loaf as thick as the sole of one's shoe."

The band now struck up another melody, and by the time it was ended the dinner was over, and speeches began to be made. The evening being calm, and the windows still open, these orations could be distinctly heard. Henchard's voice arose above the rest; he was telling a story of his hay-dealing experiences, in which he had outwitted a sharper who had been bent upon outwitting him.[11]

"Ha-ha-ha!" responded his audience at the upshot of the story; and hilarity was general till a new voice arose with, "This is all very well; but how about the bad bread?"

It came from the lower end of the table, where there sat a group of minor tradesmen who, although part of the company, appeared to be a little below the social level of the others; and who seemed to nourish a certain independence of opinion, and carry on discussions not quite in harmony with those at the head; just as the west end of a church is sometimes persistently found to sing out of time and tune with the leading spirits in the chancel.

This interruption about the bad bread afforded infinite satisfaction to the loungers outside, several of whom were in the mood which finds its pleasure in others' discomfiture; and hence they echoed pretty freely, "Hey! How about the bad bread, Mr. Mayor?" Moreover, feeling none of the restraints of those who shared the feast, they could afford to add, "You rather ought to tell the story o' that, sir!"

The interruption was sufficient to compel the Mayor to notice it.

"Well, I admit that the wheat turned out badly," he said. "But I was taken in in buying it as much as the bakers who bought it o' me."

"And the poor folk who had to eat it whether or no," said the inharmonious man outside the window.

Henchard's face darkened. There was temper under the thin bland surface – the temper which, artificially intensified, had banished a wife nearly a score of years before.

"You must make allowances for the accidents of a large business," he said. "You must bear in mind that the weather just at the harvest of that corn was worse than we have known it for years. However, I have mended my arrangements on account o't. Since I have found my business too large to be well looked after by myself alone, I have advertised for a thorough good man as manager of the corn department. When I've got him you will find these mistakes will no longer occur – matters will be better looked into."

"But what are you going to do to repay us for the past?" inquired the man who had before spoken, and who seemed to be a baker or miller. "Will you replace the grown flour we've still got by sound grain?"

Henchard's face had grown[12] still more stern at these interruptions, and he drank from his tumbler of water as if to calm himself or gain time. Instead of vouchsafing a direct reply he stiffly observed:

"If anybody will tell me how to turn grown wheat into wholesome wheat, I'll take it back with pleasure. But it can't be done."

Henchard was not to be drawn again. Having said this he sat down.

CHAPTER VI

Now the group outside the window had within the last few minutes been reinforced by new arrivals, some of them respectable shopkeepers and their assistants, who had come out for a whiff of air after putting up the shutters for the night; some of them of a lower class. Distinct from either there appeared a stranger – a young man of remarkably pleasant aspect, who carried in his hand a carpet-bag of the smart floral pattern prevalent in such articles at that time.

He was fair and ruddy,[1] bright-eyed, and slight in build. He might possibly have passed by without stopping at all, or at most for half a minute to glance in at the scene, had not his advent coincided with the discussion on corn and bread; in which event this history had never been enacted. But the subject seemed to arrest him, and he whispered some inquiries of the other bystanders, and remained listening.

When he heard Henchard's closing words, "It can't be done," he smiled, impulsively drew out his pocket-book, and wrote down a few words by the aid of the light in the window. He tore out the leaf, folded and directed it, and seemed about to throw it in through the open sash upon the dining-table, but, on second thoughts, edged himself through the loiterers, till he reached the door of the hotel, where one of the waiters who had been serving inside was now idly leaning against the door-post.

"Give this to the Mayor at once," he said, handing in his hasty note.

Elizabeth-Jane had seen his movements and heard the words, which attracted her both by their subject and by their accent – a strange one for those parts. It was quaint and northerly.

The waiter took the note, while the young stranger continued:

"And can ye tell me of a respectable hotel that's a little more moderate than this?"

The waiter glanced indifferently up and down the street.

"They say the King of Prussia,[2] just below here, is a very good place," he languidly answered; "but I have never stayed there myself."

The Scotchman, as he seemed to be, thanked him, and strolled on in the direction of the King of Prussia aforesaid, apparently more concerned about the question of an inn than about the fate of his note, now that the momentary impulse of writing it was over. While he was disappearing slowly down the street the waiter left the door, and Elizabeth-Jane saw with some interest the note brought into the dining-room and handed to the Mayor.

Henchard looked at it carelessly, unfolded it with one hand, and glanced it through. Thereupon it was curious to note an unexpected effect. The nettled, clouded aspect which had held possession of his face since the subject of his corn-dealings had been broached, changed itself into one of arrested attention. He read the note slowly, and fell into thought, not moody, but fitfully intense, as that of a man who has been captured by an idea.

By this time toasts and speeches had given place to songs, the wheat subject being quite forgotten. Men were putting their heads together in twos and threes, telling good stories, with pantomimic laughter which reached convulsive grimace. Some were beginning to look as if they did not know how they had come there, what they had come for, or how they were going to get home again; and provisionally sat on with a dazed smile. Square-built men showed a tendency to become hunchbacks, men with a dignified presence lost it in a curious obliquity of figure, in which their features grew disarranged and one-sided; whilst the heads of a few who had dined with extreme thoroughness were somehow sinking into their shoulders, the corners of their mouth and eyes being bent upwards by the subsidence. Only Henchard did not conform to these flexuous changes; he remained stately and vertical, silently thinking.

The clock struck nine; Elizabeth-Jane turned to her companion. "The evening is drawing on, mother," she said. "What do you propose to do?"

She was surprised to find how irresolute her mother had become. "We must get a place to lie down in," she murmured, "I have seen – Mr. Henchard; and that's all I wanted to do."

"That's enough for to-night at any rate," Elizabeth-Jane replied soothingly. "We can think to-morrow what is best to do about him. The question now is – is it not? – how shall we find a lodging?"

As her mother did not reply, Elizabeth-Jane's mind reverted to the words of the waiter, that the King of Prussia was an inn of moderate charges. A recommendation good for one person was probably good for another. "Let's go where the young man has gone to," she said. "He is respectable. What do you say?"

Her mother assented, and down the street they went.

In the meantime the Mayor's thoughtfulness, engendered by the note as stated, continued to hold him in abstraction; till, whispering to his neighbour to take his place, he found opportunity to leave the chair. This was just after the departure of his wife and Elizabeth.

Outside the door of the assembly-room he saw the waiter, and beckoning to him, asked who brought the note which had been handed in a quarter of an hour before.

"A young man, sir – a sort of traveller. He was a Scotchman seemingly."

"Did he say how he had got it?"

"He wrote it himself, sir, as he stood outside the window."

"Oh – wrote it himself. . . . . Is the young man in the hotel?"

"No, sir. He went to the King o' Prussia, I believe."

The Mayor walked up and down the vestibule of the hotel with his hands under his coat-tails, as if he were merely seeking a cooler atmosphere than that of the room he had quitted. But there could be no doubt that he was in reality still possessed to the full by the new idea, whatever that might be. At length, he went back to the door of the dining-room, paused, and found that the songs, toasts, and conversation were proceeding quite satisfactorily without his presence. The corporation, private residents, and major and minor tradesmen had, in fact, gone in for comforting beverages to such an extent, that they had quite forgotten, not only the Mayor, but all those vast political, religious, and social differences which they felt necessary to maintain in the daytime, and which separated them like iron grills. Seeing this, the Mayor took his hat, and, when the waiter had helped him on with a thin holland overcoat, went out and stood under the portico.

Very few persons were now in the street; and his eyes, by a sort of attraction, turned and dwelt upon a spot about a hundred yards further down. It was the house to which the writer of the note had gone – the King of Prussia – whose two prominent gables, bow-window, and passage-light could be seen from where he stood. Having kept his eyes on it for a while, he strolled in that direction.

This immutable[3] house of accommodation for man and beast was built of mellow sandstone, with mullioned windows of the same material, now markedly out of perpendicular from the settlement of foundations. The bow-window projecting into the street, whose interior was so popular among the frequenters of the inn, was closed with shutters, in each of which appeared a heart-shaped aperture, somewhat more attenuated in the right and left ventricles than is seen in Nature. Inside these illuminated holes, at a distance of about three inches, were ranged at this hour, as every passer knew, the ruddy polls of Billy Wills the glazier, Smart the shoemaker, Buzzford the general dealer, and others of that set,[4] each with his yard of clay.

A four-centred Tudor arch was over the entrance, and over the arch the signboard, now visible in the rays of an opposite lamp. Hereon, the King, who had been represented by the artist as a person of two dimensions only – in other words, flat as a shadow – was seated on a war-horse in a paralyzed prance. Being on the sunny side of the street, both he and his charger[5] had suffered largely from warping, splitting, fading, and shrinkage, so that he was but a half invisible film upon the reality of the grain, and knots, and nails, which composed the signboard. As a matter of fact, this state of things was not so much owing to Stannidge the landlord's neglect, as from the lack of a painter in Casterbridge who would undertake to reproduce the uniform of a man so traditional.

A long, narrow, dimly-lit passage gave access to the inn, within which passage the horses going to their stalls at the back, and the coming and departing human guests, rubbed shoulders indiscriminately, the latter running no slight risk of having their toes trodden upon by the animals. The good stabling and the good ale of the King of Prussia, though somewhat difficult to reach on account of there being but this narrow way to both, were nevertheless perseveringly sought out by the sagacious old heads who knew what was what in Casterbridge.

Henchard stood without the inn for a few instants; then, lowering the dignity of his presence as much as possible by buttoning the brown-holland coat over his shirt-front, and in other ways toning himself down to his ordinary everyday appearance, he entered the inn door.

CHAPTER VII

Elizabeth-Jane and her mother had arrived some twenty minutes earlier. Outside the house they had stood and considered whether even this homely place, though recommended as moderate, might not be too serious in its prices for their light pockets. Finally, however, they had found courage to enter, and duly met Stannidge, the landlord; a silent man, who drew and carried frothing measures to this room and to that, shoulder to shoulder with his waiting-maids – a stately slowness, however, entering into his ministrations by contrast with theirs, as became one whose service was somewhat optional. It would have been altogether optional but for the orders of the landlady, a person who sat in the bar, corporeally motionless, but with a flitting eye and quick ear, with which she observed and heard through the open door and hatchway the pressing needs of customers whom her husband overlooked though close at hand. Elizabeth and her mother were passively accepted as sojourners, and shown to a small bedroom under one of the gables, where they sat down.

The principle of the inn seemed to be to compensate for the antique awkwardness, crookedness, and obscurity of the passages, floors and ceilings,[1] by quantities of clean linen spread about everywhere, and this had a dazzling effect upon the travellers.

"'Tis too good for us – we can't meet it!" said the elder woman, looking round the apartment with misgiving as soon as they were left alone.

"I fear it is, too," said Elizabeth. "But we must be respectable."

"We must pay our way even before we must be respectable," replied her mother. "Mr. Henchard is too high for us to make ourselves known to him, I much fear; so we've only our own pockets to depend on."

"I know what I'll do," said Elizabeth-Jane, after an interval of waiting, during which their needs seemed quite forgotten under the press of business below. And leaving the room, she descended the stairs and penetrated to the bar.

If there was one good thing more than another which characterized this single-hearted girl, it was a willingness to sacrifice her personal comfort and dignity to the common weal.

"As you seem busy here to-night, and mother's not well off, might I take out part of our accommodation by helping?" she asked of the landlady.

The latter, who remained as fixed in the arm-chair as if she had been melted into it when in a liquid state, and could not now be unstuck, looked the girl up and down inquiringly, with her hands on the chair-arms. Such arrangements as the one Elizabeth proposed were not uncommon in country villages; but, though Casterbridge was old-fashioned, the custom was well-nigh obsolete here. The mistress of the house, however, was an easy woman to strangers, and she made no objection. Thereupon Elizabeth, being instructed by nods and motions from the taciturn landlord as to where she could find the different things, trotted up and down stairs with materials for her own and her parent's meal.

While she was doing this, the wood partition in the centre of the house thrilled to its centre with the tugging of a bell-pull upstairs. A bell below tinkled a note that was feebler in sound than the twanging of wires and cranks that had produced it.

"'Tis the Scotch gentleman," said the landlady omnisciently; and, turning her eyes to Elizabeth: "Now then, can you go and see if his supper is on the tray? If it is, you can take it up to him. The front room over this."

Elizabeth-Jane, though hungry, willingly postponed serving herself a while, and applied to the cook in the kitchen, whence she brought forth the tray of supper viands, and proceeded with it upstairs to the apartment indicated. The accommodation of the King of Prussia was far from spacious, despite the fair area of ground it covered. The room demanded by intrusive beams and rafters, partitions, passages, staircases, disused ovens, settles, and four-posters, left comparatively small quarters for human beings. Moreover, this being at a time before home-brewing was abandoned by the smaller victuallers, and a house in which the twelve-bushel strength[2] was still religiously adhered to by the landlord in his ale, the quality of the liquor was the chief attraction of the premises, so that everything had to make way for utensils and operations in connection therewith. Thus Elizabeth found that the Scotchman was located in a room quite close to the small one that had been allotted to herself and her mother.

When she entered nobody was present but the young man himself – the same whom she had seen lingering without the windows of the Golden Crown Hotel. He was now idly reading a copy of the local paper, and was hardly conscious of her entry, so that she looked at him quite coolly, and saw how his forehead shone where the light caught it, and how nicely his hair was cut, and the sort of velvet-pile or down that was on the skin at the back of his neck, and how his cheek was so truly curved as to be part of a globe, and how clearly drawn were the lids and lashes which hid his bent eyes.

She set down the tray, spread his supper, and went away without a word. On her arrival below, the landlady, who was as kind as she was fat and lazy, saw that Elizabeth-Jane was rather tired, though in her earnestness to be useful she was waiving her own needs altogether. Mrs. Stannidge thereupon said, with a considerate peremptoriness, that she and her mother had better take their own suppers if they meant to have any.

Elizabeth fetched their simple provisions, as she had fetched the Scotchman's, and went up to the little chamber where she had left her mother, noiselessly pushing open the door with the edge of the tray. To her surprise her mother, instead of being reclined on the bed where she had left her, was in an erect position, with lips parted. At Elizabeth's entry she lifted her finger.

The meaning of this was soon apparent. The room allotted to the two women had at at one time served as a dressing-room to the Scotchman's chamber, as was evidenced by signs of a door of communication between them – now screwed up and pasted over with the wall paper. But, as is frequently the case with hotels of far higher pretensions than the King of Prussia, every word spoken in either of these rooms was distinctly audible in the other. Such sounds came through now.

Thus silently conjured, Elizabeth deposited the tray, and her mother whispered as she drew near, "'Tis he."

"Who?" said the girl.

"The Mayor."

The tremors in Susan Henchard's tone might have led any person but one so perfectly unsuspicious of the truth as the girl was, to surmise some closer connection than the admitted simple kinship as a means of accounting for them.

Two men were indeed talking in the adjoining chamber, the young Scotchman and Henchard, who, having entered the inn while Elizabeth-Jane was in the kitchen waiting for the supper, had been deferentially conducted upstairs by host Stannidge himself. The girl noiselessly laid out their little meal, and beckoned to her mother to join her, which Mrs. Henchard mechanically did, her attention being fixed on the conversation through the door.

"I merely strolled in on my way home to ask you a question about something that has excited my curiosity," said the Mayor, with careless geniality. "But I see you have not finished supper."

"Ay, but I will have done in a few minutes! Ye needn't go, sir. Take a seat. I've almost done, and it makes no difference at all."

Henchard seemed to take the seat offered, and in a moment he resumed: "Well, first I should ask, did you write this?" A rustling of paper followed.

"Yes, I did," said the Scotchman.

"Then," said Henchard, "I am under the impression that we have met by accident while waiting for the morning to keep an appointment with each other? My name is Henchard; ha'n't you replied to an advertisement for a corn-factor's manager that I put into the paper – ha'n't you come here to see me about it?"

"No," said the Scotchman, with some surprise.

"Surely you are the man," went on Henchard, insistingly, "who arranged to come and see me? Joshua, Joshua, Jipp – Jopp – what was his name?"

44

PLATE III

'Her mother whispered as she drew near, "'Tis he."'

"No, indeed?" said the young man. "My name is Donald Farfrae.[3] It is true I am in the corern trade – but I have replied to no advarrtisment, and arranged to see no one. I am on my way to Bristol – from there to the other side of the warrld to try my fortune in the great wheat-growing districts of the West? I have some inventions useful to the trade, and there is no scope for developing them heere."

"To America – well, well," said Henchard, in a tone of disappointment, so strong as to make itself felt like a damp atmosphere. "And yet I could have sworn you were the man!"

The Scotchman murmured another negative, and there was a silence, till Henchard resumed: "Then I am truly and sincerely obliged to you for the few words you wrote on that paper."

"It was nothing."

"Well, it has a great importance for me just now. This row about my grown wheat, which I declare to heaven I didn't know to be bad till the people came complaining, has put me to my wits' end. I've some hundreds of quarters of it on hand; and if your renovating process will make it wholesome, why you can see what a quag 'twould get me out of. I saw in a moment there might be truth in it. But I should like to have it proved; and of course you don't care to tell the steps of the process sufficiently for me to do that, without my paying ye well for't first."

The young man reflected a moment or two. "I don't know that I have any objection," he said. "I'm going to another country, and curing bad corn is not the line I'll take up there. Yes, I'll tell ye the whole of it – you'll make more of it here than I will in a foreign country. Just look here a minute, sir. I can show ye by a sample in my carpet-bag."

The click of a lock followed, and there was a sifting and rustling; then a discussion about so many ounces to the bushel, and drying, and refrigerating, and so on.

"These few grains will be sufficient to show ye with," came in the young fellow's voice; and after a pause, during which some operation seemed to be intently watched by them both, he exclaimed, "There, now do you taste that."

"It's complete! – quite restored, or – well – nearly."

"Quite enough restored to make good seconds out of it," said the

Scotchman. "To fetch it back entirely is impossible; Nature won't stand so much as that, but here you go a great way towards it. Well, sir, that's the process; I don't value it, for it can be but of little use in countries where the weather is more settled than in ours; and I'll be only too glad if it's of service to you."

"But, hearken to me," pleaded Henchard. "My business, you know, is in corn and in hay, but I was brought up as a hay-trusser simply, and hay is what I understand best, though I now do more in corn than in the other. If you'll accept the situation, you shall manage the corn branch entirely, and receive a commission in addition to salary."

"It is liberal – very liberal; but no, no – I cannet!" the young man still replied, with some distress in his accents.

"So be it!" said Henchard conclusively. "Now – to change the subject – one good turn deserves another; don't stay to finish that miserable supper. Come to my house; I can find something better for ye than cold ham and ale."

Donald Farfrae was grateful – said he feared he must decline – that he wished to leave early next day.

"Very well," said Henchard quickly, "please yourself. But I tell you, young man, if this holds good for the bulk, as it has done for the sample, you have saved my credit, stranger though you be. What shall I pay you for this knowledge?"

"Nothing at all, nothing at all. It may not prove necessary to ye to use it often, and I don't value it at all. I thought I might just as well let ye know, as you were in a difficulty, and they were harrd upon ye."

Henchard paused. "I sha'n't soon forget this," he said. "And from a stranger! . . . I couldn't believe you were not the man I had engaged! Says I to myself, 'He knows who I am, and recommends himself by this stroke.' And yet it turns out, after all, that you are not the man who answered my advertisement, but a stranger!"

"Ay, ay; 'tis so," said the young man.

Henchard again suspended his words, and then his voice came thoughtfully: "Your forehead, Farfrae, is something like my poor brother's – now dead and gone; and the nose, too, isn't unlike his. You must be, what – five foot nine, I reckon? I am six foot one and a half out of my shoes. But what of that? In my business, 'tis true that strength

47

and bustle build up a firm. But judgment and knowledge are what keep it established. Unluckily, I am bad at science, Farfrae; bad at figures – a rule o' thumb sort of man. You are just the reverse – I can see that. I have been looking for such as you these two year, and yet you are not for me. Well, before I go, let me ask this: Though you are not the young man I thought you were, what's the difference? Can't ye stay just the same? Have you really made up your mind about this American notion? I won't mince matters. I feel you would be invaluable to me – that needn't be said – and if you will stay and be my manager I will make it worth your while."

"My plans are fixed," said the young man in negative tones, "I have formed a scheme, and there can be no more words about it. But will you not drink with me, sir? I find this Casterbridge ale warreming to the stomach – ay, as Presbyterian cream."[4]

"No, no; I fain would, but I can't," said Henchard gravely, the scraping of his chair informing the listeners that he was rising to leave. "When I was a young man I went in for that sort of thing too strong – far too strong – and was well-nigh ruined by it! I did a deed on account of it which I shall be ashamed of to my dying day. It made such an impression on me that I swore, there and then, that I'd drink nothing stronger than tea for as many years as I was old that day. I have kept my oath; and though, Farfrae, I am sometimes that dry in the dog days that I could drink a quarter-barrel to the pitching,[5] I think o' my oath, and touch no strong drink at all."

"I won't press ye, sir – I won't press ye. I respect your vow."

"Well, I shall get a manager somewhere, no doubt," said Henchard, with strong feeling in his tones. "But it will be long before I see one that would suit me so well!"

The young man appeared much moved by Henchard's warm convictions of his value. He was silent till they reached the door. "I wish I could stay – sincerely wish it," he replied. "But no – it cannet be! it cannet! I want to see the warrld."

48

CHAPTER VIII

Thus they parted; and Elizabeth-Jane and her mother remained each in her thoughts over their meal, the mother's face being strangely bright since Henchard's avowal of shame for a past action. The quivering of the partition to its core presently denoted that Donald Farfrae had again rung his bell, no doubt to have his supper removed; for humming a tune, and walking up and down, he seemed to be attracted by the lively bursts of conversation and melody from the general company below. He sauntered out upon the landing, and descended the staircase.

When Elizabeth-Jane had carried down his supper tray, and also that used by her mother and herself, she found the bustle of serving to be at its height below, as it always was at this hour. The young woman shrank from having anything to do with the ground-floor serving, and crept silently about observing the scene – so new to her, fresh from the seclusion of a sea-side cottage. In the general parlour, which was large, she remarked the two or three dozen strong-backed chairs that stood round against the wall, each fitted with its genial occupant – the sanded floor – the black settle which, projecting endwise from the wall within the door, permitted Elizabeth to be a spectator of all that went on, without herself being particularly seen.

The young Scotchman had just joined the guests. These, in addition to the respectable master-tradesmen occupying the seats of privilege in the bow-window and its neighbourhood, included an inferior set at the unlighted end, whose seats were mere benches against the wall, and who drank from cups instead of from glasses. Among the latter she noticed some of those personages who had stood outside the windows of the Golden Crown.

Behind their backs was a small window, with a wheel ventilator in one of the panes, which would suddenly start off spinning with a jingling sound, as suddenly stop, and as suddenly start again.

While thus furtively making her survey, the opening words of a song greeted her ears from behind the settle, in a melody and accent of peculiar charm. There had been some singing before she came down; and now the Scotchman had made himself so soon at home that, at the request of some of the master-tradesmen, he too was favouring the room with a song.

Elizabeth-Jane was fond of music; she could not help pausing to listen; and the longer she listened, the more she was enraptured. She had never heard any singing like this; and it was evident that the majority of the audience had not heard such frequently, for they were attentive to a much greater degree than ordinary. They neither whispered, nor drank, nor dipped their pipe-stems in their ale to moisten them, nor pushed the mug to their neighbours. The singer himself grew emotional, till she could imagine a tear in his eye as the words went on: –

> "It's hame and it's hame, hame fain would I be,
> O hame, hame, hame to my ain countree!
> There's an eye that ever weeps, and a fair face will be fain,
> As I pass through Annan Water with my bonnie bands again;
> When the flower is in the bud, and the leaf upon the tree,
> The lark shall sing me hame to my ain countree!"[1]

There was a burst of applause; and a deep silence which was even more eloquent than the applause. It was of such a kind that the snapping of a pipe-stem too long for him by old Solomon Longways, who was one of those gathered at the shady end of the room, seemed a harsh and irreverent act. Then the ventilator in the window-pane spasmodically started off for a new spin, and the pathos of Donald's song was temporarily effaced.

"'Twas not amiss – not at all amiss!" muttered Christopher Coney, who was also present. And removing his pipe a finger's-breadth from his lips, he said aloud, "Draw on with the next verse, young gentleman, please."

"Yes. Let's have it again, stranger," said the glazier, a stout, bucket-headed man, with a white apron rolled up round his waist. "Folks don't lift up their hearts like that in this part of the world." And turning aside he said in undertones, "Who is the young man? – Scotch, d'ye say?"

"Yes, straight from the mountains of Scotland, I believe," replied Coney.

Young Farfrae repeated the last verse. It was plain that nothing so pathetic had been heard at the King of Prussia for a considerable time. The difference of accent, the excitability of the singer, the intense local feeling, and the seriousness with which he worked himself up to a climax, surprised this set of worthies, who were only too prone to shut up their emotions with caustic words.

"Danged if our country down here is worth singing about like that!" continued the glazier, as the Scotchman again melodised with a dying fall "my ain countree!" "When you take away from among us the fools and the rogues, and the lammigers, and the wanton hussies and the slatterns, and such like, there's cust few left to ornament a song with in Casterbridge, or the country round."

"True," said Buzzford, the dealer, looking at the grain of the table. "Casterbridge is a old, hoary place o' wickedness, by all account. 'Tis recorded in history that we rebelled against the King one or two hundred years ago, in the time of the Romans, and that lots of us was hanged on Gallows Hill, and quartered, and our different jints sent about the country like butcher's meat; and for my part I can well believe it."[2]

"What did ye come away from yer own country for, young maister, if ye be so wownded about it?" inquired Christopher Coney, from the background, with the tone of a man who preferred the original subject. "Faith, it wasn't worth your while on our account, for as Maister Billy Wills says, we be bruckle folk here – the best o' us hardly honest sometimes, what with hard winters, and so many mouths to fill, and Goda'mighty sending his little taties so terrible small to fill 'em with. We don't think about flowers and fair faces, not we – except in the shape o' cauliflowers and pigs' chaps."

"But, no?" said Donald Farfrae, gazing round into their faces with earnest concern, "the best of ye hardly honest – not surely? None of ye has been stealing what didn't belong to him?"

"No, no. God forbid!" said Solomon Longways. "That's only his random way o' speaking. 'A was always such a man of under-thoughts." (And reprovingly towards Christopher): "Don't ye be so over-familiar

PLATE IV

*'Young Farfrae repeated the last verse. It was plain that nothing so pathetic
had been heard at the King of Prussia for a considerable time.'*

with a gentleman that ye know nothing of – and that's travelled a'most from the North Pole."

Christopher Coney was silenced, and as he could get no public sympathy he mumbled his feelings to himself: "Be dazed, if I loved my country half as well as the young feller do, I'd live by claning my neighbour's pigsties afore I'd go away! For my part I've no more love for my country than I have for Botany Bay."[3]

"Come," said Longways; "let the young man draw onward with his ballet, or we shall be here all night."

"That's all of it," said the singer, apologetically.

"Soul of my body, then we'll have another!" said the general dealer.

"Can you turn a strain to the ladies, sir?" inquired a fat woman with a figured purple apron, the waist-string of which was overhung so far by her sides as to be invisible.

"Let him breathe – let him breathe, Mother Cuxsom. He hain't got his second wind yet," said the master glazier.

"Oh, yes, but I have!" exclaimed the young man; and he at once rendered "Oh Nannie"[4] with faultless modulations, and another or two of the like sentiment, winding up at their earnest request with "Auld Lang Syne."

By this time he had completely taken possession of the hearts of the King of Prussia's inmates, including even old Coney. Notwithstanding an occasional oddity which awoke their sense of the ludicrous for the moment, they began to view him through a golden haze which the tone of his mind seemed to raise around him. Casterbridge had sentiment – Casterbridge had romance; but this stranger's sentiment was of differing quality. Or rather, perhaps, the difference was mainly superficial; he was to them like the poet of a new school who takes his contemporaries by storm; who is not really new, but is the first to articulate what all his listeners have felt, though but dumbly till then.

The silent landlord came and leant over the settle while the young man sang; and even Mrs. Stannidge managed to unstick herself from the framework of her chair in the bar, and get as far as the door-post, which movement she accomplished by rolling herself round, as a cask is trundled on the chine by a drayman without losing the perpendicular.

"And are you going to bide in Casterbridge, sir?" she asked.

"Ah – no!" said the Scotchman, with melancholy fatality in his voice, "I'm only passing thirrough. I am on my way to Bristol, and thence to foreign parts."

"We be truly sorry to hear it," said Solomon Longways. "We can ill afford to lose tuneful wynd-pipes like yours when they fall among us. And verily, to mak' acquaintance with a man a come from so far, from the land o' perpetual snow as we may say, where wolves and wild boars and other dangerous animalcules be as common as blackbirds hereabout – why, 'tis a thing we can't do every day; and there's good sound information for bide-at-homes like we when such a man opens his mouth."

"Nay, but ye mistake my country," said the young man, looking round upon them with tragic fixity;[5] till his eye lighted up and his cheek kindled with a sudden enthusiasm to right their errors. "There are not perpetual snow and wolves at all in it! – except snow in winter, and – well – a little in summer just sometimes, and a 'gaberlunzie' or two stalking about here and there, if ye may call them dangerous. Oh, but men, you should take a summer jarreny to Edinboro', and Arthur's Seat,[6] and all around, and then go on to the Lochs, and all the Highland scenery – in May and June – and you would never say 'tis the land of wolves and perpetual snow!"

"Of course not – it stands to reason," said Buzzford. "'Tis barren ignorance that leads to such words. He's a simple home-spun man, that never was fit for good company – think nothing of him, sir."

"And do ye carry your flock bed, and your quilt, and your crock, and your bit of chiney; or do ye go in bare bones, as I may say?" inquired Christopher Coney.

"I've sent on my luggage – though it isn't much; for the voyage is long." Donald's eyes dropped into a remote gaze as he added: "But I said to myself, 'Never a one of the prizes of life will I come by unless I undertake it!' and I decided to go."

A general sense of regret, in which Elizabeth-Jane shared not least, made itself apparent in the company. As she looked at Farfrae from the back of the settle she decided that his statements showed him to be no less thoughtful than his fascinating melodies revealed him to be cordial and impassioned. She admired the serious light in which he looked at serious things. He had seen no jest in ambiguities and roguery, as the Casterbridge toss-pots had done; and rightly not – there was none. She disliked those wretched humours of Christopher Coney and his tribe; and he did not appreciate them. He seemed to feel exactly as she felt about life and its surroundings – that they were a tragical, rather than a comical, thing; that though one could be gay on occasion, moments of gaiety were interludes, and no part of the actual drama. It was extraordinary how similar their views were.

Though it was still early, the young Scotchman expressed his wish to retire, whereupon the landlady whispered to Elizabeth to run upstairs and turn down his bed. She took a candlestick and proceeded on her mission, which was the act of a few moments only. When, candle in hand, she reached the top of the stairs on her way down again, Mr. Farfrae was at the foot coming up. She could not very well retreat; they met and passed in the turn of the staircase.

She must have appeared interesting in some way – notwithstanding her plain dress – or rather, possibly, in consequence of it, for she was a girl characterized by earnestness and soberness of mien, with which simple drapery accorded well. Her face flushed, too, at the slight awkwardness of the meeting, and she passed him with her eyes bent on the candle-flame that she carried just below her nose. Thus it happened that when confronting her he smiled; and then, with the manner of a temporarily light-hearted man, who has started himself on a flight of song whose momentum he cannot readily check, he softly tuned an old ditty that she seemed to suggest:

> "As I came in by my bower door,
>   As day was waxin' wearie,
> O wha came tripping down the stair
>   But bonnie Peg my dearie."[7]

Elizabeth-Jane, rather disconcerted, hastened on; and the Scotchman's voice died away, humming more of the same within the closed door of his room.

Here the scene and sentiment ended for the present. When, soon after, the girl rejoined her mother, the latter was still in thought – on quite another matter than a young man's song.

"We've made a mistake," she whispered (that the Scotchman might not overhear). "On no account ought ye to have helped serve here to-night. Not because of ourselves, but for the sake of *him*. If he should befriend us, and take us up, and then find out what you did when staying here, 'twould grieve and wound his natural pride as Mayor of the town."

Elizabeth, who would perhaps have been more alarmed at this than her mother had she known the real relationship, was not much disturbed about it as things stood. Her "he" was another man than her poor mother's. "For myself," she said, "I didn't at all mind waiting a little upon him. He's so respectable, and educated – far above the rest of 'em in the inn. They thought him very simple not to know their grim broad way of talking about themselves here. But of course he didn't know – he was too refined in his mind to know such things!" Thus she earnestly pleaded.

Meanwhile, the "he" of her mother was not so far away as even they thought. After leaving the King of Prussia he had sauntered up and down the empty High Street, passing and repassing the inn in his promenade. When the Scotchman sang, his voice had reached Henchard's ears through the heart-shaped holes in the window-shutters, and had led him to pause outside them a long while.

"To be sure, to be sure, how that fellow does draw me!" he had said to himself. "I suppose 'tis because I'm so lonely. I'd have given him a third share to have stayed!"

CHAPTER IX

When Elizabeth-Jane opened the hinged casement next morning the mellow air brought in the feel of imminent autumn almost as distinctly as if she had been in the remotest hamlet. Casterbridge was the complement of the rural life around; not its urban opposite. Bees and butterflies in the corn-fields at the top of the town, who desired to get to the meads at the bottom, took no circuitous course, but flew straight down High Street without any apparent consciousness that they were traversing strange latitudes. And in autumn airy spheres of thistledown floated into the same street, lodged upon the shop-fronts, blew into drains; and innumerable tawny and yellow leaves skimmed along the pavement, and stole through people's doorways into their passages with a hesitating scratch on the floor, like the skirts of timid visitors.

Hearing voices, one of which was close at hand, she withdrew her head, and glanced from behind the window-curtains. Mr. Henchard – now habited no longer as a great personage, but as a thriving man of business – was pausing on his way up the middle of the street, and the Scotchman was looking from the window adjoining her own. Henchard, it appeared, had gone a little way past the inn before he had noticed his acquaintance of the previous evening. He came back a few steps, Donald Farfrae opening the window further.

"And you are off soon, I suppose?" said Henchard upwards.

"Yes – almost this moment, sir," said the other. "Maybe I'll walk on till the coach overtakes me."

"Which way?"

"The way ye are going."

"Then shall we walk together to the top o' town?"

"If ye'll wait a minute," said the Scotchman.

In a few minutes the latter emerged, bag in hand. Henchard looked at the bag as at an enemy. It showed there was no mistake about the young man's departure. "Ah, my lad," he said; "you should have been a wise man, and have stayed with me."

"Yes, yes – it might have been wiser," said Donald, looking microscopically at the houses that were farthest off. "It is only telling ye the truth when I say my plans are vague."

They had by this time passed on from the precincts of the inn, and Elizabeth-Jane heard no more. She saw that they continued in conversation, Henchard turning to the other occasionally, and emphasizing some remark with a gesture. Thus they passed the Golden Crown Hotel, the Market House, the churchyard wall,[1] ascending to the upper end of the long street till they were small as two grains of corn;[2] when they bent suddenly to the right into the Bristol Road, and were out of view.

"He was a good man – and he's gone," she said to herself. "I was nothing to him, and there was no reason why he should have wished me good-bye."

The simple thought, with its latent sense of slight, had moulded itself out of the following little fact: when the Scotchman came out at the door he had by accident glanced up at her; and then he had looked away again without nodding, or smiling, or saying a word.

"You are still thinking, mother," she said when she turned inwards.

"Yes; I am thinking of Mr. Henchard's sudden liking for that young man. He was always so. Now surely, if he takes so warmly to people who are not related to him at all, may he not take as warmly to his own kin?"

While they debated this question a procession of five large waggons went past, laden with hay up to the bedroom windows. They came in from the country, and the steaming horses had probably been travelling a great part of the night. To the shaft of each hung a little board on which was painted in white letters, "Henchard, corn-factor and hay-merchant." The spectacle renewed his wife's conviction that, for her daughter's sake, she should strain a point to rejoin him.

The discussion was continued during breakfast, and the end of it was that Mrs. Henchard decided, for good or for ill, to send Elizabeth-Jane with a message to Henchard, to the effect that his relative Susan, a sailor's widow, was in the town; leaving it to him to say whether or not he would recognize her. What had brought her to this determination were chiefly two things. He had been described as a lonely widower; and he had expressed shame for a past transaction of his life. There was promise in both.

"If he says no," she enjoined, as Elizabeth-Jane stood, bonnet on, ready to depart; "if he thinks it does not become the good position he has reached to in the town, to own – to let us call on him as – his distant kinsfolk, say, 'Then, sir, we would rather not intrude; we will leave Casterbridge as quietly as we have come, and go back to our own country.' . . . I almost feel that I would rather he did say so, as I have not seen him for so many years, and we are so – little allied to him!"

"And if he says yes?" inquired the more sanguine one.

"In that case," answered Mrs. Henchard cautiously, "ask him to write me a note, saying when and how he will see us – or *me*."

Elizabeth-Jane went a few steps towards the landing. "And tell him," continued her mother, "that I fully know I have no claim upon him – that I am glad to find he is thriving; that I hope his life may be long and happy – there, go." Thus with a half-hearted willingness, a smothered reluctance, did the poor forgiving woman start her unconscious daughter on this errand.

It was about ten o'clock, and market-day, when Elizabeth paced up the High Street, in no great hurry; for to herself her position was only that of a poor relation deputed to hunt up a rich one. The front doors of the private houses were mostly left open at this warm autumn time, no thought of umbrella stealers disturbing the minds of the placid burgesses. Hence, through the long, straight entrance passages thus unclosed could be seen, as through tunnels, the mossy gardens at the back, glowing with nasturtiums, fuchsias, scarlet geraniums, "bloody warriors," snapdragons, and dahlias, this floral blaze being backed by crusted grey stone-work remaining from a yet remoter Casterbridge than the venerable one visible in the street. The old-fashioned fronts of these houses, which had older than old-fashioned backs, rose sheer from the pavement, into which the bow-windows protruded like bastions, necessitating a pleasing *chassez-déchassez* movement to the time-pressed pedestrian at every few yards. He was bound also to evolve other Terpsichorean figures in respect of door-steps, scrapers, cellar-hatches, church buttresses, and the overhanging angles of walls which, originally unobtrusive, had become bow-legged and knock-kneed.

In addition to these fixed obstacles which spoke so cheerfully of individual unrestraint as to boundaries, movables occupied the path and roadway to a perplexing extent. First the vans of the carriers in and out of Casterbridge, who hailed from Mellstock, Weatherbury, Hintock,[3] Sherton-Abbas, Stickleford, Overcombe, and many other villages round. Their owners were numerous enough to be regarded as a tribe, and had almost distinctiveness enough to be regarded as a race. Their vans had just arrived, and were drawn up on each side of the street in close file, so as to form at places a wall between the pavement and the roadway. Next every shop pitched out half its contents upon trestles and boxes on the kerb, extending the display each week a little farther and farther into the roadway, despite the expostulations of the two feeble old constables, until there remained but a tortuous defile for carriages down the centre of the street, which afforded fine opportunities for showing skill with the reins. Over the pavement on the sunny side of the way hung shop-blinds so constructed as to give the passenger's hat a smart buffet off his head as from the unseen hands of Cranstoun's Goblin Page,[4] celebrated in romantic lore.

Horses for sale were tied in rows, their fore-legs on the pavement, their hind-legs in the street, in which position they occasionally nipped little boys by the shoulder who were passing to school. And any inviting recess in front of a house that had been modestly kept back from the general line was utilized by pig-dealers as a pen for their stock.[5]

The yeomen, farmers, dairymen, and townsfolk, who came to transact business in these ancient streets, spoke in other ways than by articulation. Not to hear the words of your interlocutor in metropolitan centres is to know nothing of his meaning. Here the face, the arms, the hat, the stick, the body throughout spoke equally with the tongue. To express satisfaction the Casterbridge market-man added to his utterance a broadening of the cheeks, a crevicing of the eyes, a throwing back of the shoulders, which was intelligible from the other end of the street. If he wondered, though all Henchard's carts and waggons were rattling past him, you knew it from perceiving the inside of his crimson mouth, and a target-like circling of his eyes. Deliberation caused sundry attacks on the moss of adjoining walls with the end of his stick, a change of his hat from the horizontal to the less so; a sense of tediousness announced itself in a lowering of the person by spreading the knees to a lozenge-shaped aperture, and contorting the arms. Chicanery, subterfuge, had hardly a place in the streets of this honest borough to all appearance; and it was said that the lawyers in the Court House hard by occasionally threw in strong arguments for the other side out of pure generosity (though apparently by mischance) when advancing their own.

Thus Casterbridge was in most respects but the pole, focus, or nerve-knot of the surrounding country life; differing from the many manufacturing towns which are as foreign bodies set down, like boulders on a plain, in a green world with which they have nothing in common. Casterbridge lived by agriculture at one remove further from the fountain-head than the adjoining villagers – no more. The townsfolk understood every fluctuation in the rustic's condition, for it affected their receipts as much as the labourer's; they entered into the troubles and joys which moved the aristocratic families ten miles round – for the same reason. And even at the dinner-parties of the professional families the subjects of discussion were corn, cattle-disease, sowing and reaping, fencing and planting; while politics were viewed by them less from their own standpoint of burgesses with rights and privileges than from the standpoint of their county neighbours.

All the venerable contrivances and confusions which delighted the eye by their quaintness, and in a measure reasonableness, in this rare old market-town, were metropolitan novelties to the unpractised eyes of Elizabeth-Jane, fresh from netting fish-seines in a sea-side cottage. Very little inquiry was necessary to guide her footsteps. Henchard's house was one of the best, fronted with murrey-coloured old brick.[6] The front door was open, and, as in other houses, she could see through the passage to the end of the garden – nearly a quarter of a mile off.

Mr. Henchard was not in the house, but in the store-yard. She was conducted into the mossy garden, and through a side-door in the wall, which was studded with rusty nails speaking of generations of fruit-trees that had been trained there. The door opened upon the yard, and here she was left to find him as she could. It was a place flanked by hay-barns, into which tons of fodder, all in trusses, were being packed from the waggons she had seen pass the inn that morning. On other sides of the yard were wooden granaries on stone staddles, to which access was given by Flemish ladders,[7] and a store-house several floors high. Wherever the doors of these places were open, a closely packed throng of bursting wheat-sacks could be seen standing, with the air of awaiting a famine that would not come.

She wandered about this place, uncomfortably conscious of the impending interview, till she was quite weary of searching; she ventured to inquire of a boy in what quarter of the labyrinth Mr. Henchard could be found. He directed her to an office which she had not seen before, and knocking at the door she was answered by a cry of "Come in."

Elizabeth turned the handle; and there stood before her, bending over some sample-bags on a table, not the corn-merchant, but the young Scotchman Mr. Farfrae – in the act of pouring some grains of wheat from one hand to the other. His hat hung on a peg behind him, and the roses of his carpet-bag glowed from the corner of the room.

Having toned her feelings and arranged words on her lip for Mr. Henchard, and for him alone, she was for the moment confounded.

"Yes, what is it?" said the Scotchman, like a man who permanently ruled there.

She said she wanted to see Mr. Henchard.

"Ah, yes; will ye wait a minute? He's engaged just now," said the young man, apparently not recognizing her as the girl at the inn. He handed her a chair, bade her sit down, and turned to his sample-bags again. While Elizabeth-Jane sits waiting in great amaze at the young man's presence we may briefly explain how he came there.

When the two new acquaintances had passed out of sight that morning towards the Bath-and-Bristol road they went on silently, except for a few commonplaces, till they had gone down an avenue on the town walls called the New Walk,[8] leading to an angle where the North and West escarpments met. From this high corner of the square earthworks a vast extent of country could be seen. A footpath ran steeply down the green slope, conducting from the shady promenade on the walls to a road at the bottom of the scarp. It was by this path the Scotchman had to descend.

"Well, here's success to ye," said Henchard, holding out his right hand and leaning with his left upon the wicket which protected the descent. In the act there was the inelegance of one whose feelings are nipped and wishes defeated. "I shall often think of this time, and of how you came at the very moment to throw a light upon my difficulty."

Still holding the young man's hand he paused, and then added deliberately: "Now I am not the man to let a cause be lost for want of a word. And before ye are gone for ever I'll speak. Once more, will ye stay? There it is, flat and plain. You can see that it isn't all selfishness that makes me press 'ee; for my business is not quite so scientific as to require an intellect entirely out of the common. Others would do for the place without doubt. Some selfishness perhaps there is, but there is more; it isn't vor me to repeat what. Come, bide with me – and nâme your own terms. I'll agree to 'em willingly and 'ithout a word of gainsaying; for, hang it, Farfrae, I like thee well!"[9]

The young man's hand remained steady in Henchard's for a moment or two. He looked over the fertile country that stretched beneath them, then backward along the shaded walk reaching to the top of the town. His face flushed.

"I didn't expect such as this – I did not!" he said. "Surely there's destiny in it? Should a man turrun against fate?[10] No; I'll not go to America; I'll stay and be your man!"

His hand, which had lain lifeless in Henchard's, returned the latter's grasp.

"Done," said Henchard.

"Done," said Donald Farfrae.

The face of Mr. Henchard beamed forth a satisfaction that was almost fierce in its strength. "Now you are my friend!" he exclaimed. "Come back to my house; let's clinch it at once by clear terms, so as to be comfortable in our minds." Farfrae caught up his bag and retraced the North-West Avenue in Henchard's company as he had come. Henchard was all confidence now.

"I am the most distant fellow in the world when I don't care for a man," he said. "But when a man takes my fancy he takes it strong. Now I am sure you can eat another breakfast. You couldn't have eaten much so early even if they had anything at that place to gie thee, which they hadn't; so come to my house and we will have a solid, staunch tuck-in, and settle terms in black-and-white if you like; though my word's my bond. I can always make a good meal in the morning. I've got a splendid cold pigeon-pie going just now. You can have some home-brew if you want to, you know."

"It is too early in the morning for that," said Farfrae with a smile.

"Well, of course I didn't know. I don't drink it because of my oath; but I am obliged to brew for my work-people."

Thus talking they returned, and entered Henchard's premises by the back way or traffic-entrance. Here the matter was settled over the breakfast, at which Henchard heaped the young Scotchman's plate to a prodigal fulness. He would not rest satisfied till Farfrae had written for his luggage from Bristol, and despatched the letter to the post-office. When it was done this man of strong impulses declared that his new friend should take up his abode in his house – at least till some suitable lodgings could be found.

He then took Farfrae round and showed him the place, and the stores of grain, and other stock; and finally entered the offices where the younger of them had[11] already been discovered by Elizabeth.

CHAPTER X

While she still sat under the Scotchman's eyes a man came up to the door, reaching it as Henchard opened the door of the inner office to admit Elizabeth. The new-comer stepped forward like the quicker cripple at Bethesda,[1] and entered in her stead. She could hear his words to Henchard: "Joshua Jopp, sir – by appointment – the new manager."

"The new manager! – he's in his office," said Henchard bluntly.

"In his office!" said the man with a stultified air.

"I mentioned Thursday," said Henchard; "and as you did not keep your appointment, I have engaged another manager. At first I thought he must be you. Do you think I can wait when business is in question?"

"You said Thursday or Saturday, sir," said the new-comer, pulling out a letter.

"Well, you are too late," said the corn-factor. "I can say no more."

"You as good as engaged me," murmured the man.

"Subject to an interview," said Henchard. "I am sorry for you – very sorry indeed. But it can't be helped."

There was no more to be said, and the man came out, encountering Elizabeth-Jane in his passage. She could see that his mouth twitched with anger, and that bitter disappointment was written in his face everywhere.

Elizabeth-Jane now entered, and stood before the master of the premises.[2] His dark pupils – which always seemed to have a red spark of light in them, though this could hardly be a physical fact – turned indifferently round under his dark brows until they rested on her figure. "Now then, what is it, my young woman?" he said blandly.

"Can I speak to you – not on business, sir?" said she.

"Yes – I suppose." He looked at her more thoughtfully.

"I am sent to tell you, sir," she innocently went on, "that a distant relative of yours by marriage, Susan Newson, a sailor's widow, is in the town; and to ask whether you would wish to see her."

The rich *rouge-et-noir* of his countenance underwent a slight change. "Oh – Susan is – still alive?" he asked with difficulty.

"Yes, sir."

"Are you her daughter?"

"Yes, sir – her only daughter."

"What – do you call yourself – your Christian name?"

"Elizabeth-Jane, sir."

"Newson?"

"Elizabeth-Jane Newson."

This at once suggested to Henchard that the transaction of his early married life at Weydon Fair was unrecorded in the family history. It was more than he could have expected. His wife had behaved kindly to him in return for his unkindness, and had never proclaimed her wrong to her child or to the world.

"I am – a good deal interested in your news," he said. "And as this is not a matter of business, but pleasure, suppose we go indoors."

It was with a gentle delicacy of manner, surprising to Elizabeth, that he showed her out of the office, and through the outer room, where Donald Farfrae was overhauling bins and samples with the inquiring inspection of a beginner in charge. Henchard preceded her through the door in the wall to the suddenly changed scene of the garden and flowers, and onward into the house. The dining-room to which he introduced her still exhibited the remnants of the lavish breakfast laid for Farfrae. It was furnished to profusion with heavy mahogany furniture of the deepest red-Spanish hues. Pembroke tables,[3] with leaves hanging so low that they well-nigh touched the floor, stood against the walls on legs and feet shaped like those of an elephant, and on one lay three huge folio volumes – a family Bible, a "Josephus,"[4] and a "Whole Duty of Man."[5] In the chimney corner was a fire-grate with a fluted semi-circular back, having urns and festoons cast in relief thereon; and the chairs were of the kind which, since that day, has cast lustre upon the names of Chippendale and Sheraton,[6] though, in point of fact, their patterns may have been such as those illustrious carpenters never saw or heard of.

"Sit down – Elizabeth-Jane – sit down," he said, with a shake in his voice as he uttered her name; and sitting down himself he allowed his hands to hang between his knees, while he looked upon the carpet. "Your mother, then, is quite well?"

"She is rather worn out, sir, with travelling."

"A sailor's widow – when did he die?"

"Father was lost last spring."[7]

Henchard winced at the word "father," thus applied. "Do you and she come from abroad – America or Australia?" he asked.

"No. We have been in England some years. I was twelve when we came here from Canada."

"Ah; exactly." By such conversation he discovered the circumstances which had enveloped his wife and her child in such total obscurity that he had long ago believed them to be in their graves. These things being clear, he returned to the present. "And where is your mother staying?"

"At the King o' Prussia."

"And you are her daughter Elizabeth-Jane," repeated Henchard. He arose, came close to her, and glanced in her face. "I think," he said, suddenly turning away with a wet eye, "you shall take a note from me to your mother. I should like to see her. . . . She is not left very well off by her late husband?" His eye fell on Elizabeth's clothes, which, though a respectable suit of black, and her very best, were decidedly old-fashioned, even to Casterbridge eyes.

"Not very well," she said, glad that he had divined this without her being obliged to express it.

He sat down at the table and wrote a few lines; next taking from his pocket-book a five-pound note, which he put in the envelope with the letter, adding to it, as by an afterthought, five shillings. Sealing the whole up carefully, he directed it to "Mrs. Newson, King of Prussia Inn," and handed the packet to Elizabeth.

"Deliver it to her personally, please," said Henchard. "Well, I am glad to see you here, Elizabeth-Jane – very glad. We must have a long talk together – but not just now."

He took her hand at parting, and held it so warmly that she, who had known so little friendship, was much affected, and tears rose to her aërial-grey eyes. The instant that she was gone Henchard's state showed itself more distinctly; having shut the door, he sat in his dining-room stiffly erect, gazing at the opposite wall as if he read his history there.

"Begad!" he suddenly exclaimed, jumping up. "I didn't think of that. Perhaps these are impostors – and Susan and the child dead after all!"

However, a something in Elizabeth-Jane soon assured him that, as regarded her, at least, there could be little doubt. And a few hours would settle the question of her mother's identity; for he had arranged in his note to see her that evening.

"It never rains but it pours!" said Henchard. His keenly excited interest in his new friend the Scotchman was now eclipsed by this event; and Donald Farfrae saw so little of him during the rest of the day that he wondered at the suddenness of his employer's moods.

In the meantime Elizabeth had reached the inn. Her mother, instead of taking the note with the curiosity of a poor woman expecting assistance, was much moved at sight of it. She did not read it at once, asking Elizabeth to describe her reception, and the very words Mr. Henchard used. Elizabeth's back was turned when her mother opened the letter. It ran thus: –

"Meet me at eight o'clock this evening, if you can, at the Ring on the Budmouth road. The place is easy to find. I can say no more now. The news upsets me almost. The girl seems to be in ignorance. Keep her so till I have seen you.

"M. H."

He said nothing about the enclosure of five guineas. The amount was significant; it may tacitly have said to her that he bought her back again. She waited restlessly for the close of the day, telling Elizabeth-Jane that she was invited to see Mr. Henchard; that she would go alone. But she said nothing to show that the place of meeting was not at his house, nor did she hand the note to Elizabeth.

CHAPTER XI

The Ring at Casterbridge[1] was merely the local name of one of the finest Roman Amphitheatres, if not the very finest, remaining in Britain.

Casterbridge announced old Rome in every street, alley, and precinct. It looked Roman, bespoke the art of Rome, concealed dead men of Rome. It was impossible to dig more than a foot or two deep about the town fields and gardens without coming upon some tall soldier or other of the Empire, who had lain there in his silent unobtrusive rest for a space of fifteen hundred years. He was mostly found lying on his side, in an oval scoop in the chalk, like a chicken in its shell; his knees drawn up to his chest; sometimes with the remains of his spear against his arm; a fibula or brooch of bronze on his breast or forehead; an urn at his knees, a jar at his breast, a bottle at his mouth; and mystified conjecture pouring down upon him from the eyes of Casterbridge street-boys and men, who had turned a moment to gaze at the familiar spectacle as they passed by.[2]

Imaginative inhabitants, who would have felt an unpleasantness at the discovery of a comparatively modern skeleton in their gardens, were quite unmoved by these hoary shapes. They had lived so long ago, their time was so unlike the present, their hopes and motives were so widely removed from ours, that between them and the living there seemed to stretch a gulf too wide for even a spirit to pass.

The Amphitheatre was a huge circular enclosure,[3] with a notch at opposite extremities of its diameter north and south. From its sloping internal form it might have been called the spittoon of the Jötuns. It was to Casterbridge what the ruined Coliseum is to modern Rome, and was nearly of the same magnitude.[4] The dusk of evening was the proper hour at which a true impression of this suggestive place could be received. Standing in the middle of the arena at that time there by degrees became apparent its real vastness, which a cursory view from the summit at noon-day was apt to obscure. Melancholy, impressive, lonely, yet accessible from every part of the town, the historic circle was the frequent spot for appointments of a furtive kind. Intrigues were arranged there; tentative meetings were there experimented after divisions and feuds. But one kind of appointment – in itself the most common of any – seldom had place in the Amphitheatre: that of happy lovers.

Why, seeing that it was pre-eminently an airy, accessible, and interesting spot for assignations, the cheerfullest form of those occurrences never took kindly to the soil of the ruin would be a curious inquiry. Perhaps it was because its associations had about them something sinister. Its history proved that. Apart from the sanguinary nature of the games originally played therein, such incidents attached to its past as these: that for scores of years the town-gallows had stood at one corner: that in 1705 a woman who had murdered her husband was half-strangled and then burnt there in the presence of ten thousand spectators. Tradition reports that at a certain stage of the burning her heart burst and leapt out of her body to the terror of them all, and that not one of those ten thousand people ever cared particularly for hot roast after that.[5] In addition to these old tragedies pugilistic encounters almost to the death had come off down to recent dates in that secluded arena, entirely invisible to the outside world, save by climbing to the top of the enclosure, which few townspeople in the daily round of their lives ever took the trouble to do. So that, though close to the turnpike-road, crimes might be perpetrated there unseen at mid-day.

Some boys had latterly tried to impart gaiety to the ruin by using the central arena as a cricket-ground. But the game usually languished, for the aforesaid reason – that of the dismal privacy which the earthen circle enforced, shutting out every appreciative passer's vision, every commendatory remark from outsiders – everything, except the sky; and to play at games in such circumstances was like acting to an empty house. Possibly, too, the boys were timid, for some old people said that at certain moments in the summer time, in broad daylight, persons sitting with a book, or dozing in the arena, had, on lifting their eyes, beheld the slopes lined with a gazing legion of Hadrian's soldiery[6] as if watching the gladiatorial combat; and had heard the roar of their excited voices; that the scene would remain but a moment, like a lightning flash, and then disappear.

It was related that there still remained under the south entrance arched cells for the reception of the wild animals and athletes who took part in the games. The arena was still smooth and circular, as if used for its original purpose not so very long ago. The sloping pathways by which spectators had ascended to their seats were pathways yet. But the whole was grown over with grass, which now, at the end of summer, was bearded with withered bents that formed waves under the brush of the wind, returning to the attentive ear Æolian modulations,[7] and detaining for moments the flying globes of thistledown.

Henchard had chosen this spot as being the safest from observation which he could think of for meeting his long-lost wife, and at the same time as one easily to be found by a stranger after nightfall. As Mayor of the town, with a reputation to keep up, he could not invite her to come to his house till some definite course had been decided on.

Just before eight he approached the deserted earthwork, and entered by the south path which descended over the *débris* of the former dens. In a few moments he could discern a female figure creeping in by the great north gap, or public gateway. They met in the middle of the arena. Neither spoke just at first – there was no necessity for speech – and the poor woman leant against Henchard, who supported her in his arms.

"I don't drink," he said in a low, halting, apologetic voice. "You hear, Susan? – I don't drink now – I haven't since that night." Those were his first words.

He felt her bow her head in acknowledgment that she understood. After a minute or two he again began:

"If I had known you were living, Susan! But there was every reason to suppose you and the child were dead and gone. I took every possible step to find you – travelled – advertised. My opinion at last was that

PLATE V

"'I don't drink now — I haven't since that night.'"

you had started for some colony with that man, and had been drowned on your voyage out. Why did you keep silent like this?"

"Oh, Michael, because of him – what other reason could there be? I thought I owed him faithfulness to the end of one of our lives – foolishly I believed there was something solemn and binding in the bargain; I thought that even in honour I dared not desert him when he had paid so much for me in good faith. I meet you now only as his widow – I consider myself that, and that I have no claim upon you. Had he not died, I should never have come – never. Of that you may be sure."

"Tut-tut! How could you be so simple?"

"I don't know. Yet it would have been very wicked – if I had not thought like that!" said Susan, almost crying.

"Yes – yes – so it would. It is only that which makes me feel ye an innocent woman. But – to lead me into this!"

"What, Michael?" she asked, alarmed.

"Why, this difficulty about our living together again, and Elizabeth-Jane. She cannot be told all – she would so despise us both that – I could not bear it!"

"That was why she was brought up in ignorance of you. I could not bear it either."

"Well – we must talk of a plan for keeping her in her present belief, and getting matters straight in spite of it. You have heard I am in a large way of business here – that I am Mayor of the town, and church-warden, and I don't know what all?"

"Yes," she murmured.

"These things, as well as the dread of the girl discovering our disgrace, makes it necessary to act with extreme caution. So that I don't see how you two can return openly to my house as the wife and daughter I once treated badly, and banished from me; and there's the rub o't."[8]

"We'll go away at once. I only came to see—"

"No, no, Susan; you are not to go – you mistake me!" he said with kindly severity. "I have thought of this plan: that you and Elizabeth take a cottage in the town as the widow Mrs. Newson and her daughter; that I meet you, court you, and marry you, Elizabeth-Jane coming to my house as my stepdaughter. The thing is so natural and easy that it is half done in thinking o't. This would leave my shady, headstrong, disgraceful life as a young man absolutely unopened; the secret would be yours and mine only; and I should have the pleasure of seeing my own only child under my roof, as well as my wife."

"I am quite in your hands, Michael," she said meekly. "I came here for the sake of Elizabeth; for myself, if you tell me to leave again to-morrow morning, and never come near you more, I am content to go."

"Now, now; we don't want to hear that," said Henchard gently. "Of course you won't leave again. Think over the plan I have proposed for a few hours; and if you can't hit upon a better one we'll adopt it. I have to be away for a day or two on business, unfortunately; but during that time you can get lodgings – the only ones in the town fit for you are those over the china-shop in High Street – and you can also look for a cottage."

"If the lodgings are in High Street they are dear, I suppose?"

"Never mind – you *must* start genteel, if our plan is to be carried out. Look to me for money. Have you enough till I come back?"

"Quite," said she.

"And are you comfortable at the inn?"

"Oh, yes."

"And the girl is quite safe from learning the shame of her case and ours? – that's what makes me most anxious of all."

"You would be surprised to find how unlikely she is to dream of the truth. How could she ever suppose such a thing!"

"True!"

"I like the idea of repeating our marriage," said Mrs. Henchard, after a pause. "It seems the only right course, after all this. Now I think I must go back to Elizabeth-Jane, and tell her that our kinsman, Mr. Henchard, kindly wishes us to stay in the town."

"Very well – arrange that yourself. I'll go some way with you."

"No, no. Don't run any risk!" said his wife anxiously. "I can find my way back – it is not late. Please let me go alone."

"Right," said Henchard. "But just one word. Do you forgive me, Susan?"

She murmured something; but seemed to find it difficult to frame her answer.

"Never mind – all in good time," said he. "Judge me by my future works – good-bye."

He retreated, and stood at the upper side of the Amphitheatre while his wife passed out through the lower way, and descended under the trees to the town. Then Henchard himself went homeward, going so fast, that by the time he reached his door he was almost upon the heels of the unconscious woman from whom he had just parted. He watched her up the street, and turned into his house.

CHAPTER XII

On entering his own door, after watching his wife out of sight, the Mayor walked on through the tunnel-shaped passage into the garden, and thence by the side door towards the stores and granaries. A light shone from the office-window, and, there being no blind to screen the interior, Henchard could see Donald Farfrae still seated where he had left him, initiating himself into the managerial work of the house by overhauling the books. Henchard entered, merely observing, "Don't let me interrupt you, if ye will stay so late."

He stood behind Farfrae's chair, watching his dexterity in clearing up the numerical fogs which had been allowed to grow so thick in Henchard's books as almost to baffle even the Scotchman's perspicacity. The corn-factor's mien was half admiring, and yet it was not without a dash of pity for the tastes of any one who could care to give his mind to such finikin details. Henchard himself was mentally and physically unfit for grubbing subtleties from soiled paper; he had in a modern sense received the education of Achilles,[1] and found penmanship a tantalizing art.

"You shall do no more to-night," he said at length, spreading his great hand over the paper. "There's time enough to-morrow. Come indoors with me and have some supper. Now you shall! I am determined on't." He shut the account-books with friendly force.

Donald had wished to get to his lodgings; but he already saw that his friend and employer was a man who knew no moderation in his requests and impulses, and he yielded gracefully. He liked Henchard's warmth, even if it inconvenienced him; the great difference in their characters adding to the liking.

They locked up the office, and the young man followed his companion through the private little door which, admitting directly into Henchard's garden, permitted a passage from the utilitarian to the beautiful at one step. The garden was silent, dewy, and full of perfume. It extended a long way back from the house, first as lawn and flowerbeds, then as fruit-garden, where the long-tied espaliers, as old as the old house itself, had grown so stout and cramped and gnarled that they had pulled their stakes out of the ground, and stood distorted and writhing in vegetable agony, like leafy Laocoons.² The flowers which smelt so sweetly were not discernible; and they passed through them into the house.

The hospitalities of the morning were repeated, and when they were over Henchard said, "Pull your chair round to the fireplace, my dear fellow, and let's make a blaze – there's nothing I hate like a black grate, even in September." He applied a light to the laid-in fuel, and a cheerful radiance spread around.

"It is odd," said Henchard, "that two men should meet as we have done on a purely business ground, and that at the end of the first day I should wish to speak to 'ee on a family matter. But, d—³ it all, I am a lonely man, Farfrae: I have nobody else to speak to; and why shouldn't I tell it to you?"

"I'll be glad to hear it, if I can be of any service," said Donald, allowing his eyes to travel over the intricate wood-carvings of the chimney-piece, representing garlanded lyres, shields, and quivers, on either side of a draped ox-skull, and flanked by heads of Apollo and Diana in low relief.

"I've not been always what I am now," continued Henchard, his firm deep voice being ever so little shaken. He was plainly under that strange influence which sometimes prompts men to confide to the new-found friend what they will not tell to the old. "I began life as a working hay-trusser, and when I was eighteen I married on the strength o' my calling. Would you think me a married man?"

"I heard in the town that you were a widower."

"Ah, yes – you would naturally have heard that. Well, I lost my wife eighteen years ago[4] – by my own fault. . . . . This is how it came about. One summer evening I was travelling for employment, and she was walking at my side carrying the baby, our only child. We came to a booth in a country fair. I was a drinking man at that time."

Henchard paused a moment, threw himself back so that his elbow rested on the table, his forehead being shaded by his hand, which, however, did not hide the marks of introspective inflexibility on his features as he narrated in fullest detail the incidents of the transaction with the sailor. The tinge of indifference which had at first been visible in the Scotchman now disappeared.

Henchard went on to describe his attempts to find his wife; the oath he swore; the solitary life he led during the years which followed. "I have kept my oath for eighteen years," he went on; "I have risen to what you see me now."

"And it's not a small counterbalance to the immoral years that ye've done so much since!"[5]

"Well – no wife could I hear of in all that time; and being by nature something of a woman-hater, I have found it no hardship to keep at a distance[6] from the sex. No wife could I hear of, I say, till this very day. And now – she has come back."

"Come back, has she!"

"This morning – this very morning. And what's to be done?"

"Can't ye take her and live with her, and so make amends?"

"That's what I've planned and proposed. But Farfrae," said Henchard gloomily, "by doing right with Susan I wrong another innocent woman."

"Ye don't say that?"

"In the nature of things, Farfrae, it is almost impossible that a man of my sort should have the good fortune to tide through twenty years o' life without making more blunders than one. It has been my custom for many years to run across to Jersey in the way of business, particularly in the potato and root season. I do a large trade wi' them in that line. Well, one autumn when stopping there I fell quite ill, and in my illness I sank into one of those gloomy fits I sometimes suffer from, on account o' the loneliness of my domestic life, when the world seems to have the blackness of hell, and, like Job,[7] I could curse the day that gave me birth."

"Ah, now, I never feel like it," said Farfrae.

"Then pray to God that you never may, young man. While in this state I was taken pity on by a woman – a young lady I should call her, for she was of good family, well bred, and well educated – the daughter of some harum-scarum military officer[8] who had got into difficulties, and had his pay sequestrated. He was dead now, and her mother, too, and she was as lonely as I. This young creature was staying at the boarding-house where I happened to have my lodging; and when I was pulled down she took upon herself to nurse me. From that she got to have a foolish liking for me. Heaven knows why, for I didn't encourage any such thing.[9] But, being together in the same house, and her feelings warm,[10] there arose a terrible scandal, which did me no harm, but was of course ruin to her. Though Farfrae, between you and me, as man and man, I solemnly declare that I did her no wrong. Devotion to women-folk has neither been my vice nor my virtue. But I am bound to admit that she was terribly careless of appearances,[11] and that I was perhaps more, because o' my dreary state; and it was through this that the scandal arose. At last I was well, and came away. When I was gone she suffered much on my account, and didn't forget to tell me so in letters one after another; till, latterly, I felt I owed her something, and thought that, as I had not heard of Susan for so long, I would make this other one the only return I could make, and ask her if she would run the risk of Susan being alive (very slight as I believed) and marry me, such as I was. She jumped for joy, and we should no doubt soon have been married – but, behold, Susan appears!"

Donald showed his deep concern at a complication so far beyond the degree of his simple experiences.

"Now see what injury a man may cause around him. Even after that wrong-doing at the fair when I was young, if I had never been so selfish as to let this giddy girl devote herself to me over at Jersey, to the injury of her name, all might now be well. Yet, as it stands, I must bitterly disappoint one of these women; and it is the second. My first duty is to Susan – there's no doubt about that."

"They are both in a very melancholy position, and that's true!" murmured Donald.

"They are! For myself I don't care – 'twill all end one way. But these two." Henchard paused in reverie. "I feel I should like to treat the second, no less than the first, as kindly as a man can in such a case."

"Ah, well, it cannet be helped!" said the other, with philosophic woefulness. "You must write to the young lady, and in your letter you must put it plain and honest that it turns out she cannet be your wife, the first having come back; that ye cannet see her more; and that – ye wish her weel."

"That won't do. 'Od seize it, I must do a little more than that. I must – though she did always brag about her rich uncle or rich aunt, and her expectations from 'em – I must send a useful sum of money to her, I suppose – just as a little recompense, poor girl. . . . Now, will you help me in this, and draw up an explanation to her of all I've told ye, breaking it as gently as you can? I'm so bad at letters."

"And I will."[12]

"Now, I haven't told you quite all yet. My wife Susan has my daughter with her – the baby that was in her arms at the fair; and this girl knows nothing of me beyond that I am some sort of relation by marriage. She has grown up in the belief that the sailor to whom I made over her mother, and who is now dead, was her father, and her mother's husband. What her mother has always felt, she and I together feel now – that we can't proclaim our disgrace to the girl by letting her know the truth. Now what would you do – I want your advice?"

"I think I'd run the risk, and tell her the truth. She'll forgive ye both."

"Never!" said Henchard. "I am not going to let her know the truth. Her mother and I are going to marry again; and it will not only enable us to retain[13] our child's respect, but it will be more proper. Susan looks upon herself as the sailor's widow, and won't think of living with me as formerly without another religious ceremony – and she's right."

Farfrae thereupon said no more. The letter to the young Jersey woman was carefully framed by him, and the interview ended, Henchard saying, as the Scotchman left: "I feel it a great relief, Farfrae, to tell some friend of this! You see now that the Mayor of Casterbridge is not so thriving in his mind as it seems he might be from the state of his pocket."

"I do. And I am sorry for it!" said Farfrae.

When he was gone, Henchard copied the letter, and, enclosing a cheque, took it to the post-office, from which he walked back thoughtfully.

"Can it be that it will go off so easily!" he said. "Poor thing – God knows! Now then, to make amends to Susan!"

CHAPTER XIII

The cottage which Michael Henchard hired for his wife Susan, under her name of Newson – in pursuance of their plan – was in the upper or western part of the town, near the wall, and the avenue which overshadowed it. The evening sun seemed to shine more yellowly there than anywhere else this autumn – stretching its rays, as the hours grew later, under the lowest sycamore boughs, and steeping the ground-floor of the dwelling, with its green shutters, in a substratum of radiance which the foliage screened from the upper parts. Beneath these sycamores on the town walls could be seen from the sitting-room the tumuli and earth forts of the distant uplands; making it altogether a pleasant spot, with the usual touch of melancholy that a western prospect[1] lends.

As soon as the mother and daughter were comfortably installed, with a white-aproned servant and all complete, Henchard paid them a visit, and remained to tea. During the entertainment Elizabeth was carefully hoodwinked by the very general tone of the conversation that prevailed – a proceeding which seemed to afford some humour to Henchard, though his wife was not particularly happy in it. The visit was repeated again and again with business-like determination by the Mayor, who seemed to have schooled himself into a course of strict mechanical rightness towards this woman of prior claim, at any expense to the later one, and to his own sentiments.

One afternoon the daughter was not indoors when Henchard came, and he said drily, "This is a very good opportunity for me to ask you to name the happy day, Susan."

The poor woman smiled faintly; she did not enjoy pleasantries on a situation into which she had entered solely for the sake of her girl's reputation. She liked them so little, indeed, that there was room for wonder why she had countenanced deception at all, and had not bravely let the girl know her history. But the flesh is weak;[2] and the true explanation came in due course.

"Oh Michael," she said, "I am afraid all this is taking up your time and giving trouble – when I did not expect any such thing!" And she looked at him and at his dress as a man of affluence, and at the furniture he had provided for the room – ornate and lavish to her eyes.

"Not at all," said Henchard, in rough benignity. "This is only a cottage – it costs me next to nothing. And as to taking up my time" – here his red and black visage kindled with satisfaction – "I've a splendid fellow to superintend my business now – a man whose like I've never been able to lay hands on before. I shall soon be able to leave everything to him, and have more time to call my own than I've had for these last twenty years."

Henchard's visits here grew so frequent and so regular that it soon became whispered, and then openly discussed in Casterbridge, that the masterful, coercive Mayor of the town was captured and enervated by the genteel widow, Mrs. Newson. His well-known haughty indifference to the society of womankind, his silent avoidance of converse with the sex, contributed a piquancy to what would otherwise have been an unromantic matter enough. That such a poor fragile woman should be his choice was inexplicable, except on the ground that the engagement was a family affair in which sentimental passion had no place; for it was known that they were related in some way. Mrs. Henchard was so pale that the boys called her "The Ghost." Sometimes Henchard overheard this epithet when they passed together along the Walks – as the avenues on the walls were named – at which his face would darken with an expression of destructiveness towards the speakers ominous to see; but he said nothing.

He pressed on the preparations for his union, or rather re-union, with this pale creature in a dogged unflinching spirit which did credit to his conscientiousness. Nobody would have conceived from his outward demeanour that there was no amatory fire or pulse of romance acting as stimulant to the bustle going on in his gaunt, great house; nothing but three large resolves: one to make amends to his neglected Susan, another to provide a comfortable home for Elizabeth-Jane under his paternal eye; and a third to castigate himself with the thorns which these restitutory acts brought in their train; among them the lowering of his dignity in public opinion by marrying so comparatively humble a woman.

Susan Henchard entered a carriage for the first time in her life when she stepped into the plain brougham which drew up at the door on the wedding-day to take her and Elizabeth-Jane to church. It was a windless morning of warm November rain, which floated down like meal, and lay in a powdery form on the nap of hats and coats. Few people had gathered round the church door, though they were well packed within. The Scotchman, who assisted as groomsman, was of course the only one present, beyond the chief actors, who knew the true situation of the contracting parties. He, however, was too inexperienced, too thoughtful, too judicial, too strongly conscious of the serious side of the business, to enter into the scene in its dramatic aspect. That required the special genius of Christopher Coney, Solomon Longways, Buzzford, and their fellows. But they knew nothing of the secret; though as the time for coming out of church drew on they gathered on the pavement adjoining, and expounded the subject according to their lights.

"'Tis five-and-forty years since I had my settlement in this here town," said Coney; "but daze me if ever I see a man wait so long before to take so little! There's a chance even for thee after this, Nance Mockridge." The remark was addressed to a woman who stood behind his shoulder – the same who had exhibited Henchard's bad bread in public when Elizabeth and her mother entered Casterbridge.

"Be cust if I'd marry any such as he, or thee either," replied that lady. "As for thee, Christopher, we know what ye be, and the less said the better. And as for he – well, there – (lowering her voice) 'tis said 'a was a poor parish 'prentice – I wouldn't say it for all the world – but 'a was a poor parish 'prentice, that began life wi' no more belonging to 'en than a carrion crow."

"And now he's worth ever so much a minute," murmured Longways. "When a man is said to be worth so and so a minute he's a man to be considered!"

Turning, he saw a circular disc reticulated with creases, and recognized the smiling countenance of the fat woman who had asked for another song at the King of Prussia. "Well, Mother Cuxsom," he said, "how's this? Here's Mrs. Newson, a mere skellinton, has got another husband to keep her, while a woman of your tonnage have not."

"I have not. Nor another to beat me. . . . Ah, yes, Cuxsom's gone, and so shall leather breeches!"

"Yes; with the blessing of God leather breeches shall go."

" 'Tisn't worth my old while to think of another husband," continued Mrs. Cuxsom. "And yet I'll lay my life I'm as respectable born as she."

"True; your mother was a very good woman – I can mind her. She were rewarded by the Agricultural Society for having the greatest number of healthy children without parish assistance, and other virtuous marvels."

" 'Twas that that kept us so low upon ground – that great family."

"Ay. Where the pigs be many the wash runs thin."

"And dostn't mind how mother would sing, Christopher?" continued Mrs. Cuxsom, kindling at the retrospection: "and how we went with her to the party at Mellstock, do ye mind; – at old Dame Ledlow's, farmer Penny's sister,[3] do ye mind? – she we used to call Toadskin, because her face were so yaller and freckled, do ye mind?"

"I do, hee-hee, I do!" said Christopher Coney.

"And well do I – for I was getting up husband-high at that time – one-half girl, and t'other half woman, as one may say. And canst mind" – she prodded Solomon's shoulder with her finger-tip, while her eyes twinkled between the crevices of their lids – "canst mind the sherry-wine, and the silver snuffers, and how Joan Dummett was took bad when we were coming home, and Jack Griggs was forced to carry her through the mud; and how 'a let her fall in Dairyman Sweetapple's cow-barton, and we had to clane her gown wi' grass – never such a mess as 'a were in?"

"Ay – that I do – hee-hee – such doggery as there was in them ancient days to be sure! Ah, the miles I used to walk then; and now I can hardly step over a furrow!"

Their reminiscences were cut short by the appearance of the re-united pair – Henchard looking round upon the idlers with that ambiguous gaze of his, which at one moment seemed to mean satisfaction, and at another fiery disdain.

"Well – there's a difference between 'em, though he do call himself a teetotaller," said Nance Mockridge. "She'll wish her cake dough afore she's done of him. There's a bluebeardy look about 'en; and 'twill out in time."

"Stuff – he's well enough. Some folk want their luck buttered. If I had a choice as wide as the ocean sea I wouldn't wish for a better man. A poor twanking woman like her – 'tis a godsend for her, and hardly a pair of jumps to her name."

The plain little brougham drove off in the mist, and the idlers dispersed. "Well, we hardly know how to look at things in these times!" said Solomon. "There was a man dropped down dead yesterday, not so very many miles from here; and what wi' that, and this moist weather, 'tis scarce worth one's while to begin any work of consequence to-day. I'm in such a low key with drinking nothing but small table ninepenny[4] this last week or two that I shall call and warm up at the Prooshia as I pass along."

"I don't know but that I may as well go with 'ee, Solomon," said Christopher; "I'm as clammy as a cockle-snail."

CHAPTER XIV

A Martinmas summer[1] of Mrs. Henchard's life set in with her entry into her husband's large house and respectable social orbit; and it was as bright as such summers well can be. Lest she should pine for deeper affection than he could give, he made a point of showing some semblance of it in external action. Among other things he had the iron railings, that had smiled sadly in dull green for the last eighty years, painted a bright chocolate, and the heavy-barred, small-paned, Georgian sash windows enlivened with three coats of white. He was as kind to her as a man, mayor, and churchwarden could possibly be. The house was large, the rooms lofty, and the landings wide; and the two unassuming women scarcely made a perceptible addition to its contents.

To Elizabeth-Jane the time was a most triumphant one. The freedom she experienced, the indulgence with which she was treated, went beyond her expectations. The reposeful, easy, affluent life to which her mother's marriage had introduced her was, in truth, the beginning of a great change in Elizabeth. She found she could have nice personal possessions and ornaments for the asking, and, as the mediæval saying puts it, "Take, have, and keep, are pleasant words." With peace of mind came development, and with development beauty. Knowledge – the result of great natural insight – she did not lack; learning, accomplishments – those, alas, she had not;[2] but as the winter and spring passed by her thin face and figure filled out in rounder and softer curves; the lines and contractions upon her young brow went away; the muddiness of skin which she had looked upon as her lot by nature departed with a change to abundance of good things, and a bloom came upon her cheek. Perhaps, too, her grey, thoughtful eyes revealed an arch gaiety sometimes; but this was infrequent; the sort of wisdom which looked from their pupils did not readily keep company with these lighter moods. Like all people who have known rough times, lightheartedness seemed to her too irrational and inconsequent to be indulged in except as a reckless dram now and then; for she had been too early habituated to anxious reasoning to drop the habit suddenly. She felt none of those ups and downs of spirit which beset so many people without cause; never – to paraphrase a recent poet – never a gloom in Elizabeth-Jane's soul but she well knew how it came there;[3] and her present cheerfulness was fairly proportionate to her solid guarantees for the same.

It might have been supposed that, given a girl rapidly becoming good-looking, comfortably circumstanced, and for the first time in her life commanding ready money, she would go and make a fool of herself by dress. But no. The reasonableness of almost everything that Elizabeth did was nowhere more conspicuous than in this question of clothes. To keep in the rear of opportunity in matters of indulgence is as valuable a habit as to keep abreast of opportunity in matters of enterprise. This unsophisticated[4] girl did it by an innate perceptiveness that was almost genius. Thus she refrained from bursting out like a water-flower that spring, and clothing herself in puffings and knick-knacks as most of the Casterbridge girls would have done in her circumstances. Her triumph was tempered by circumspection; she had still that field-mouse fear of the coulter of destiny despite fair promise, which is common among the thoughtful who have suffered early from poverty and oppression.

"I won't be too gay on any account," she would say to herself. "It would be tempting Providence to hurl mother and me down, and afflict us again as He used to do."[5]

We now see her in a black silk bonnet, velvet mantle or silk spencer, dark dress, and carrying a sunshade. In this latter article she drew the line at fringe, and had it plain edged, with a little ivory ring for keeping it closed. It was odd about the necessity for that sunshade. She discovered that with the clarification of her complexion and the birth of pink cheeks her skin had grown more sensitive to the sun's rays. She protected those cheeks forthwith, deeming spotlessness part of womanliness.

Henchard had become very fond of her, and she went out with him more frequently than with her mother now. Her appearance one day was so attractive that he looked at her critically.

"I happened to have the ribbon by me, so I made it up," she faltered, thinking him perhaps dissatisfied with some rather bright trimming she had donned for the first time.

"Ay – of course – to be sure," he replied in his leonine way. "Do as you like – or rather as your mother advises ye. 'Od send – I've nothing to say to 't!"

Indoors she appeared with her hair divided by a parting that arched like a white rainbow from ear to ear. All in front of this line was covered with a thick encampment of curls; all behind was dressed smoothly, and drawn to a knob.

The three members of the family were sitting at breakfast one day, and Henchard was looking silently, as he often did, at this head of hair, which in colour was brown – rather light than dark. "I thought Elizabeth-Jane's hair – didn't you tell me that Elizabeth-Jane's hair promised to be black when she was a baby?" he said to his wife.

She looked startled, jerked his foot warningly, and murmured, "Did I?"

As soon as Elizabeth was gone to her own room Henchard resumed. "Begad, I nearly forgot myself just now! What I meant was that the girl's hair certainly looked as if it would be darker, when she was a baby."

"It did; but they alter so," replied Susan.

"Their hair gets darker, I know – but I wasn't aware it lightened ever?"

"Oh yes." And the same uneasy expression came out on her face, to which the future held the key.[6] It passed as Henchard went on:

"Well, so much the better. Now, Susan, I want to have her called Miss Henchard – not Miss Newson. Lots o' people do it already in carelessness – it is her legal name – so it may as well be made her usual name – I don't like t'other name at all for my own flesh and blood. I'll advertise it in the Casterbridge paper – that's the way they do it. She won't object."

"No. Oh no. But—"

"Well, then, I shall do it," said he, peremptorily. "Surely, if she's willing, you must wish it as much as I?"

"Oh yes – if she agrees let us do it by all means," she replied.

Then Mrs. Henchard acted somewhat inconsistently; it might have been called falsely, but that her manner was emotional and full of the earnestness of one who wishes to do right at great hazard. She went to

Elizabeth-Jane, whom she found sewing in her own sitting-room upstairs, and told her what had been proposed about her surname. "Can you agree – is it not a slight upon Newson – now he's dead and gone?"

Elizabeth reflected. "I'll think of it, mother," she asked.[7]

When, later in the day, she saw Henchard, she adverted to the matter at once, in a way which showed that the line of feeling started by her mother had been persevered in. "Do you wish this change so very much, sir?" she asked.

"Wish it? Why, my blessed fathers, what an ado you women make about a trifle! I proposed it – that's all. Now, 'Lizabeth-Jane, just please yourself. Curse me if I care what you do. Now, you understand, don't 'ee go agreeing to it to please me."

Here the subject dropped, and nothing more was said, and nothing was done, and Elizabeth still passed as Miss Newson, and not by her legal name.

Meanwhile the great corn and hay traffic conducted by Henchard throve under the management of Donald Farfrae as it had never thriven before. It had formerly moved in jolts; now it went on oiled castors. The old crude *vivâ voce* system of Henchard, in which everything depended upon his memory, and bargains were made by the tongue alone, was swept away. Letters and ledgers took the place of "I'll do't," and "You shall hae't;" and, as in all such cases of advance, the rugged picturesqueness of the old method disappeared with its inconveniences.

The position of Elizabeth-Jane's room – rather high in the house, so that it commanded a view of the hay-stores and granaries across the garden – afforded her opportunity for accurate observation of what went on there. She saw that Donald and Mr. Henchard were insepar-ables. When walking together Henchard would lay his arm familiarly on his manager's shoulder, as if Farfrae were a younger brother, bearing so heavily that his slight figure bent under the weight. Occasionally she would hear a perfect cannonade of laughter from Henchard, arising from something Donald had said, the latter looking quite innocent and not laughing at all. In Henchard's somewhat lonely life he evidently found the young man as desirable for comradeship as he was useful for consultations. Donald's brightness of intellect maintained in the corn-factor the admiration it had won at the first hour of their meeting.

The poor opinion, and but ill-concealed, that he entertained of the slim Farfrae's physical girth, strength, and dash, was more than counter-balanced by the immense respect he had for his brains.

Her quiet eye discerned that Henchard's tigerish affection for the younger man, his constant liking to have Farfrae near him, now and then resulted in a tendency to domineer, which, however, was checked in a moment when Donald exhibited marks of real offence. One day, looking down on their hats from on high, she heard the latter remark, as they stood in the doorway between garden and yard, that their habit of walking and driving about together rather neutralized Farfrae's value as a second pair of eyes, which should be used in places where the principal was not. "Od d—n it," cried Henchard, "what's all the world! I like a fellow to talk to. Now come along and hae some supper, and don't take too much thought about things, or ye'll drive me crazy."

When she walked with her mother, on the other hand, she often beheld the Scotchman looking at them with a curious interest. The fact that he had met her at the King of Prussia was insufficient to account for it, since the assistance she had ill-advisedly tendered there had passed unobserved by him, who, on the occasions on which she had entered his room, had never raised his eyes. Besides, it was at her mother more particularly than at herself that he looked, as it sometimes seemed, to Elizabeth-Jane's half-unconscious, simple-minded, perhaps pardonable, disappointment. Thus she could not account for this interest by her own attractiveness, and she decided that it might be apparent only – a way of turning his eyes that Mr. Farfrae had. She did not divine the ample explanation of his manner, without personal vanity, that was afforded by the fact of Donald being the depositary of Henchard's confidence in respect of his past treatment of the pale, chastened mother who walked by her side. Her conjectures on that past never went further than faint ones based on things casually heard and seen – mere guesses that Henchard and her mother might have been lovers in their younger days, who had quarrelled and parted.

Casterbridge, as has been hinted, was a place deposited in the block upon a corn-field. There was no suburb in the modern sense, or transitional intermixture of town and down. It stood, with regard to the wide fertile land adjoining, clean-cut and distinct, like a chess-board on a green table-cloth. The farmer's boy could sit under his barley-mow and pitch a stone into the office-window of the town-clerk; reapers at work among the sheaves nodded to acquaintances standing on the pavement-corner; the red-robed judge, when he condemned a sheep-stealer, pronounced sentence to the tune of Baa, that floated in at the window from the remainder of the flock browsing hard by; and at executions the waiting crowd stood in a meadow immediately before the drop, out of which the cows had been temporarily driven to give the spectators room.

The corn grown on the upland side of the borough was garnered by farmers who lived in an eastern purlieu called Dummerford.[8] Here wheat-ricks overhung the old Roman street, and thrust their eaves against the church tower; green-thatched barns, with doorways as high as the gates of Solomon's Temple, opened directly upon the main thoroughfare. Barns indeed were so numerous as to alternate with every half-dozen houses along the way. Here lived burgesses who daily walked the fallow; shepherds in an intramural squeeze. A street of farmers' homesteads – a street ruled by a mayor and corporation, yet echoing with the thump of the flail, the flutter of the winnowing-fan, and the purr of the milk into the pails – a street which had nothing urban in it whatever – this was the Dummerford end of Casterbridge.

Henchard, as was natural, dealt largely with this nursery or bed of small farmers close at hand – and his waggons were often down that way. One day, when arrangements were in progress for getting home corn from one of the aforesaid farms, Elizabeth-Jane received a note by hand, asking her to oblige the writer by coming at once to a granary on Dummerford Hill. As this was the granary whose contents Henchard was removing, she thought the request had something to do with his business, and proceeded thither as soon as she had put on her bonnet. The granary was just within the farmyard, and stood on stone staddles, high enough for persons to walk under. The gates were open, but nobody was within. However, she entered and waited. Presently she saw a figure approaching the gate – that of Donald Farfrae. He looked up at the church clock, and came in. By some unaccountable shyness, some wish not to meet him there alone, she quickly ascended the step-ladder leading to the granary door, and entered it before he had seen her. Farfrae advanced, imagining himself in solitude; and a few drops of rain beginning to fall, he moved and stood under the shelter where she had just been standing. Here he leant against one of the staddles, and gave himself up to patience. He too was plainly expecting some one; could it be herself; if so, why? In a few minutes he looked at his watch, and then pulled out a note, a duplicate of the one she had herself received.

The situation began to be very awkward, and the longer she waited the more awkward it became. To emerge from a door just above his head and descend the ladder, and show she had been in hiding there, would look so very foolish, that she still waited on. A winnowing machine stood close beside her, and to relieve her suspense she gently moved the handle; whereupon a cloud of wheat husks flew out into her face, and covered her clothes and bonnet, and stuck into the fur of her victorine. He must have heard the slight movement, for he looked up, and then ascended the steps.

"Ah – it's Miss Newson," he said, as soon as he could see into the granary. "I didn't know you were there. I have kept the appointment, and am at your service."

"O Mr. Farfrae," she faltered; "so have I. But I didn't know it was you who wished to see me, otherwise I—"

"I wished to see you? Oh, no – at least, that is, I am afraid there may be a mistake."

"Didn't you ask me to come here? Didn't you write this?" Elizabeth held out her note.

"No. Indeed, at no hand would I have thought of it! And for you – didn't you ask me? This is not your writing?" And he held up his.

"By no means."

"And is it even so! Then it's somebody wanting to see us both. Perhaps we would do well to wait a little longer."

Acting on this consideration they lingered, Elizabeth-Jane's face being arranged to an expression of preternatural composure, and the young Scot, at every footstep in the street without, looking from under the granary to see if the passer were about to enter and declare himself their summoner. They watched individual drops of rain creeping down the thatch of the opposite rick – straw after straw – till they reached

PLATE VI

' *"Then it's somebody wanting to see us both."* '

the bottom; but nobody came, and the granary roof began to drip.

"The person is not likely to be coming," said Farfrae. "It's a trick perhaps, and if so, it's a great pity to waste our time like this, and so much to be done."

"'Tis a great liberty," said Elizabeth.

"It's true, Miss Newson. We'll hear news of this some day, depend on't, and who it was that did it. I wouldn't stand for it hindering myself; but you, Miss Newson——"

"I don't mind – much," she replied.

"Nor do I."

They lapsed again into silence. "You are anxious to get back to Scotland, I suppose, Mr. Farfrae?" she inquired.

"Oh, no, Miss Newson. Why would I be?"

"I only supposed you might be from the song you sang at the King of Prussia – about Scotland and home, I mean – which you seemed to feel so deep down in your heart; so that we all felt for you."

"Ay – and I did sing there – I did——. But Miss Newson" – and Donald's voice musically undulated between two semitones, as it always did when he became earnest – "it's well you feel a song, for a few minutes, and your eyes they get quite tearful; but you finish it, and for all you felt you don't mind it or think of it again for a long while. Oh, no, I don't want to go back! Yet I'll sing the song to you wi' pleasure whenever you like. I could sing it now, and not mind at all?"

"Thank you, indeed. But I fear I must go – rain or no."

"Ay! Then, Miss Newson, ye were best to say nothing about this hoax, and take no heed of it. And if the person should say anything to you, be civil to him or her, as if you did not mind it – so you'll take the clever person's laugh away." In speaking his eyes became fixed upon her dress, still sown with wheat husks. When she was stepping out he added:[9] "There's husks and dust on you. Perhaps you don't know it?" in tones of extreme delicacy.

"Yes," she said. "I turned the handle, and they flew out suddenly."

"But it's very bad to let rain come upon clothes when there's chaff on them. It washes in and spoils them. Let me help you – blowing is the best."

As Elizabeth neither assented nor dissented, Donald Farfrae inflated his mouth and began blowing her back hair, and her side hair, and her neck, and the crown of her bonnet, and the fur of her victorine, Elizabeth saying, "Oh, thank you," at every puff, and picking out the chaff and dust in front with her own hands. At last she was fairly clean, though Farfrae, having got over his first concern at the situation, seemed in no manner of hurry to be gone.

"Ah – now I'll go and get ye an umbrella," he said.

"Oh, no. I don't mind the rain at all."

She stepped out and was gone. Farfrae walked slowly after, looking thoughtfully at her diminishing figure, and whistling in undertones, "As I came down through Cannobie."[10]

CHAPTER XV

At first Miss Newson's budding beauty was not regarded with much interest by anybody in Casterbridge. Donald Farfrae's gaze, it is true, was now attracted by the Mayor's so-called stepdaughter, but he was only one. The truth is that she was but a poor illustrative instance of the prophet Baruch's sly definition: "The virgin that loveth to go gay."[1] This particular virgin was just a shade too far the other way; and she paid the penalty. Sober and discreet, she was yet so hearty, that her homespun simplicity afforded none of those piquant problems which are afforded by the simplicity that is carefully constructed by art.[2] When she walked abroad she seemed to be occupied with an inner chamber of ideas, and to have slight need for visible objects. In short, it was obvious to real philosophers that Casterbridge young-manhood of the deep-seeing sort ought to have had a solicitous regard for her. So they took no notice of her at all.

If the news got abroad that she was unwell, Henchard's door was not haunted by young fellows with cigars, making some excuse for inquiring indirectly about her. But, to set against this, at inn gatherings of the rollicking sort, where discussions of the female world were apt to take a turn irreverent to the sex, the criticism was stopped when it came to Elizabeth with, "I say, now, we'll leave *her* alone."

Perhaps the young men were penetrating enough to see that she was too honest to be a woman of correct education.[3] This view of her was helped by the curious resolves that she had formed on checking gay fancies in the matter of clothes, because it was inconsistent with her past life to blossom gaudily the moment she had become possessed of money. But nothing is more insidious than the evolution of wishes from mere fancies, and of wants from mere wishes. Henchard gave Elizabeth-Jane a box of delicately tinted gloves one spring day. She wanted to wear them to show her appreciation of his kindness, but she had no bonnet that would harmonize. As an artistic indulgence she thought she would have such a bonnet. When she had a bonnet that would go with the gloves she had no dress that would go with the bonnet. It was now absolutely necessary to finish; she ordered the requisite article, and found that she had no sunshade to go with the dress. In for a penny in for a pound; she bought the sunshade, and the whole structure was at last complete.

Everybody was attracted, and some said that her bygone simplicity was the art that conceals art, the "delicate imposition" of Rochefoucauld;[4] she had produced an effect, a contrast, and it had been done on purpose. As a matter of fact this was not true, but it had its result; for as soon as young Casterbridge thought her artful it thought her worth notice. "It is the first time in my life that I have been so much admired," she said to herself; "though perhaps it is by those whose admiration is not worth having."

But Donald Farfrae admired her, too; and altogether the time was an exciting one; sex had never before asserted itself in her so strongly, for in former days she had perhaps been too impersonally human to be distinctively feminine. After an unprecedented success one day she came indoors, went upstairs, and leant upon her bed face downwards, quite forgetting the possible creasing and damage. "Good Heaven," she whispered, "can it be? Here am I setting up as the town beauty!"

When she had thought it over, her usual fear of exaggerating appearances engendered a deep sadness. "There is something wrong in all

this," she mused. "If they only knew what an unfinished[5] girl I am –
that I can't talk Italian, or use globes, or show any of the accomplishments
they learn at boarding-schools, how they would despise me! Better sell
all this finery and buy myself grammar-books, and dictionaries, and a
history of all the philosophies!"[6]

She looked from the window, and saw Henchard and Farfrae in the
hay-yard talking, with that impetuous cordiality on the mayor's part,
and genial modesty on the younger man's, that was now so generally
observable in their intercourse. Friendship between man and man; what
a rugged strength there was in it, as evinced by these two. And yet the
seed that was to lift the foundation of this friendship was at that moment
taking root in a chink of its structure.

It was about six o'clock; the men were dropping off homeward
one by one. The last to leave was a round-shouldered, blinking
young man of nineteen or twenty, whose mouth fell ajar on the slightest
provocation, seemingly because there was no chin to support it. Henchard called aloud to him as he went out of the gate. "Here – Abel
Whittle!"[7]

Whittle turned, and ran back a few steps. "Yes, sir," he said, in
breathless deprecation, as if he knew what was coming next.

"Once more – be in time to-morrow morning. You see what's to be
done, and you hear what I say, and you know I'm not going to be trifled
with any longer."

"Yes, sir." Then Abel Whittle left, and Henchard and Farfrae; and
Elizabeth saw no more of them.

Now there was good reason for this command on Henchard's part.
Poor Abel, as he was called, had an inveterate habit of oversleeping
himself and coming late to his work. His anxious will was to be among
the earliest; but if his comrades omitted to pull the string that he always
tied round his great toe and left hanging out of the window for that
purpose, his will was as wind. He did not arrive in time.

As he was often second hand at the hay-weighing, or at the crane
which lifted the sacks, or was one of those who had to accompany the
waggons into the country to fetch away stacks that had been purchased,
this affliction of Abel's was productive of much inconvenience. For two
mornings in the present week he had kept the others waiting nearly an

hour; hence Henchard's threat. It now remained to be seen what would happen to-morrow.

Six o'clock struck, and there was no Whittle. At half-past six Henchard entered the yard; the waggon was horsed that Abel was to accompany; and the other man had been waiting twenty minutes. Then Henchard swore, and Whittle coming up breathless at that instant, the corn-factor turned on him, and declared with an oath that this was the last time; that if he were behind once more, by G — he would come and drag him out o' bed.

"There is sommit wrong in my make, your worshipful!" said Abel, "especially in the inside, whereas my poor dumb brain gets as dead as a clot afore I've said my few scrags of prayers. Yes – it came on as a stripling, just afore I'd got man's wages, whereas I never enjoy my bed at all, for no sooner do I lie down than I be asleep, and afore I be awake I be up. I've fretted my gizzard green about it, maister, but what can I do? Now last night, afore I went to bed, I only had a scantling o' cheese and—"

"I don't want to hear it!" roared Henchard. "To-morrow the waggons must start at four, and if you're not here, stand clear. I'll mortify thy flesh for thee!"

"But let me clear up my points, your worshipful—"

Henchard turned away.

"He asked me and he questioned me, and then a' wouldn't hear my points!" said Abel, to the yard in general. "Now, I shall twitch like a moment-hand all night to-night for fear o' him!"

The journey to be taken by the waggons next day was a long one, into White Hart Vale,[8] and at four o'clock lanterns were moving about the yard. But Abel was missing. Before either of the other men could run to Abel's and warn him, Henchard appeared in the garden doorway. "Where's Abel Whittle? Not come after all I've said? Now, I'll carry out my word, by my blessed fathers – nothing else will do him any good! I'm going up that way."

Henchard went off, entered Abel's house, a little cottage in Back Street,[9] the door of which was never locked, because the inmates had nothing to lose. Reaching Whittle's bedside, the corn-factor shouted a bass note so vigorously that Abel started up instantly, and beholding

Henchard standing over him, was galvanized into spasmodic movements which had not much relation to getting on his clothes.

"Out of bed, sir, and off to the granary, or you leave my employ to-day! 'Tis to teach ye a lesson. March on; never mind your breeches!"

The unhappy Whittle threw on his sleeve waistcoat, and managed to get into his boots at the bottom of the stairs, while Henchard thrust his hat over his head. Whittle then trotted on down Back Street, Henchard walking sternly behind.

Just at this time Farfrae, who had been to Henchard's house to look for him, came out of the back gate, and saw something white fluttering in the morning gloom, which he soon perceived to be the part of Abel's shirt that showed below his waistcoat.

"For mercy's sake, what object's this?" said Farfrae, following Abel into the yard, Henchard being some way in the rear by this time.

"Ye see, Mr. Farfrae," gibbered Abel with a resigned smile,[10] "he said he'd mortify my flesh if so be I didn't get up sooner, and now he's a doing on't! Ye see it can't be helped, Mr. Farfrae; things do happen queer sometimes. Yes – I'll go to White Hart Vale half naked as I be, since he do command; but I shall kill myself afterwards; I can't outlive the disgrace; for the women-folk will be looking out of their winders at my mortification all the way along, and laughing me to scorn.[11] You know how I feel such things, Maister Farfrae, and how forlorn thoughts get hold upon me. Yes – I shall do myself harm – I feel it coming on!"

"Get back home, and slip on your breeches, and come to wark like a man! If ye go not, you'll hae your death standing there."

"I'm afeard I mustn't! Mr. Henchard said—"

"I don't care what Mr. Henchard said, nor anybody else! 'Tis simple foolishness to do this. Go and dress yourself instantly, Whittle."

"Hullo, hullo!" said Henchard, coming up behind. "Who's sending him back?"

All the men looked towards Farfrae.

"I am," said Donald. "I say this joke has been carried far enough."

"And I say it hasn't. Get up in the waggon, Whittle."

"Not if I am manager," said Farfrae. "He either goes home, or I march out of this yard for good."

Henchard looked at him with a face stern and red. But he paused for a moment, and their eyes met. Donald went up to him, for he saw in Henchard's look that he began to regret this.

"Come," said Donald quietly, "you know better than all this, sir. It is tyrannical and unworthy of you."

"'Tis not tyrannical!" murmured Henchard, like a sullen boy. "It is to make him remember!" He presently added, in a tone of one bitterly hurt: "Why did you speak to me before them like that, Farfrae? You might have stopped till we were alone. Ah – I know why! I've told ye the secret o' my life – fool that I was to do't – and you take advantage of me!"

"I had forgot it," said Farfrae simply.

Henchard looked on the ground, said nothing more, and turned away. During the day Farfrae learnt from the men that Henchard had kept Abel's old mother in coals and snuff all the previous winter, which made him less antagonistic to the corn-factor. But Henchard continued moody and silent, and when one of the men inquired of him if some oats should be hoisted to an upper floor or not, he said shortly, "Ask Mr. Farfrae. He's master here!"

Morally he was; there could be no doubt of it. Henchard, who had hitherto been the most admired man in his circle, was the most admired no longer. One day the daughters of a deceased farmer in Dummerford wanted an opinion on the value of their haystack, and sent a messenger to ask Mr. Farfrae to oblige them with one. The messenger, who was a child, met in the yard not Farfrae, but Henchard.

"Very well," he said. "I'll come."

"But please will Mr. Farfrae come?" said the child.

"I am going that way. . . . . Why Mr. Farfrae?" said Henchard, with the fixed look of thought. "Why do people always want Mr. Farfrae?"

"I suppose because they like him so – that's what they say."

"Oh – I see – that's what they say – hey? They like him because he's cleverer than Mr. Henchard, and because he knows more; and, in short, Mr. Henchard can't hold a candle to him – hey?"

"Yes – that's just it, sir – some of it."

"Oh, there's more. Of course there's more. What besides? Come, here's sixpence for a fairing."

"'And he's better tempered, and Henchard's a fool to him,' they say.

And when some of the women were a walking home they said, 'He's a diment – he's a chap o' wax[12] – he's the best – he's the horse for my money,' says they. And they said, 'He's the most understanding man o' them two by long chalks.[13] I wish he was the master instead of Henchard,'" they said.

"They'll talk any nonsense," Henchard replied, with covered gloom. "Well, you can go now. And *I* am coming to value the hay, d'ye hear? – I." The boy departed, and Henchard murmured, "Wish he were master here, do they?"

He went towards Dummerford. On his way he overtook Farfrae. They walked on together, Henchard looking mostly on the ground.

"And are ye not right to-day?" Donald inquired.

"Yes, I am very well," said Henchard.

"But ye are down – surely ye are down? Why, there's nothing to be angry about. 'Tis splendid stuff that we've got from White Hart Vale. By-the-by, the people in Dummerford want their hay valued."

"Yes. I am going there."

"I'll go with ye."

As Henchard did not reply, Donald practised a piece of music *sotto voce*, till, getting near the bereaved people's door he stopped himself with –

"Ah, as their father is dead, I won't go on with such as that. How could I forget?"

"Do you care so very much about hurting folks' feelings?" observed Henchard with a half sneer. "You do, I know – especially mine."

"I am sorry if I have hurt yours, sir," replied Donald, standing still, with a second expression of the same sentiment in the regretfulness of his face. "Why should you say it – think it?"

The cloud lifted from Henchard's brow, and as Donald finished the corn-merchant turned to him, regarding his breast rather than his face.

"I have been hearing things that vexed me," he said. "'Twas that made me short in my manner – made me overlook what you really are. Now, I don't want to go in here about this hay – Farfrae, you can do it better than I. They sent for ye, too. I have to attend a meeting of the Town Council at eleven, and 'tis drawing on for't."

They parted thus in renewed friendship, Donald forbearing to ask

Henchard for meanings that were not very plain to him. On Henchard's part there was now again repose; and yet, whenever he thought of Farfrae, it was with a dim dread; and he often regretted that he had told the young man his whole heart, and confided to him the secrets of his life.

CHAPTER XVI

On this account Henchard's manner towards Farfrae insensibly became more reserved. He was courteous – too courteous – and Farfrae was quite surprised at the good breeding which now for the first time showed itself among the qualities of a man he had hitherto thought undisciplined, if warm and sincere. The corn-factor seldom or never again put his arm upon the young man's shoulder so as to nearly weigh him down with the pressure of mechanized friendship. He left off coming to Donald's lodgings and shouting into the passage, "Hoy, Farfrae, boy, come and have some dinner with us! Don't sit here in solitary confinement!" But in the daily routine of their business there was little change.

Thus their lives rolled on till a day of public rejoicing was suggested to the country at large in celebration of a national event that had recently taken place.

For some time Casterbridge, by nature slow, made no response. Then one day Donald Farfrae broached the subject to Henchard by asking if he would have any objection to lend some rick-cloths to himself and a few others, who contemplated getting up an entertainment of some sort on the day named, and required a shelter for the same, to which they might charge admission at the rate of so much a head.

"Have as many cloths as you like," Henchard replied.

When his manager had gone about the business Henchard was fired with emulation. It certainly had been very remiss of him, as Mayor, he thought, to call no meeting ere this, to discuss what should be done on this holiday. But Farfrae had been so cursed quick in his movements as to give old-fashioned people in authority no chance of the initiative. However, it was not too late; and on second thoughts he determined to take upon his own shoulders the responsibility of organizing some amusements, if the other Councilmen would leave the matter in his hands. To this they quite readily agreed, the majority being fine old crusted characters who had a decided taste for living without worry.

So Henchard set about his preparations for a really brilliant thing – such as should be worthy of the venerable town. As for Farfrae's little affair, Henchard nearly forgot it; except once now and then when, on it coming into his mind, he said to himself, "Charge admission at so much a head – just like him![1] – who is going to pay anything a head!" The diversions which the Mayor intended to provide were to be entirely free.

He had grown so dependent upon Donald that he could scarcely resist calling him in to consult. But by sheer self-coercion he refrained. No, he thought, Farfrae would be suggesting such improvements in his d—d luminous way, that in spite of himself he, Henchard, would sink to the position of second fiddle, and only scrape harmonics to his manager's talents.

Everybody applauded the Mayor's proposed entertainment, especially when it became known that he meant to pay for it all himself.

Close to the town was an elevated green spot surrounded by an ancient square earthwork – earthworks square, and not square, were as common as blackberries hereabout – a spot whereon the Casterbridge people usually held any kind of merry-making, meeting, or sheep-fair that required more space than the streets would afford. On one side it sloped to a river,[2] and from any point a view was obtained of the country round for many miles. This pleasant upland was to be the scene of Henchard's exploit.

He advertised about the town, in long posters of a pink colour, that games of all sorts would take place here; and set to work a little battalion of men under his own eye. They erected greasy-poles for climbing, with smoked hams and local cheeses at the top. They placed hurdles in rows for jumping over; across the river they laid a slippery pole, with a live pig of the neighbourhood tied at the other end, to become the property of the man who could walk over and get it. There were also provided wheelbarrows for racing, donkeys for the same, a stage for boxing, wrestling, and drawing blood generally; sacks for jumping in. Moreover, not forgetting his principles, Henchard provided a mammoth tea, of which everybody who lived in the borough was invited to partake without payment. The tables were laid parallel with the inner slope of the rampart, and awnings were stretched overhead.

Passing to and fro the Mayor beheld the unattractive exterior of Farfrae's erection,[3] rick-cloths of different sizes and colours being hung up to the arching trees without any regard to appearance. He was easy in his mind now, for his own preparations far transcended these.

The morning came. The sky, which had been remarkably clear down to within a day or two, was overcast, and the weather threatening, the wind having an unmistakable hint of water in it. Henchard wished he had not been quite so sure about the continuance of a fair season. But it was too late to modify or postpone, and the proceedings went on. At twelve o'clock the rain began to fall, small and steady, commencing and increasing so insensibly that it was difficult to state exactly when dry weather ended or wet established itself. The slight moisture resolved itself into a monotonous smiting of earth by heaven in torrents to which no end could be prognosticated.

A number of people had heroically gathered in the field, but by three o'clock Henchard discerned that his project was doomed to end in failure. The hams at the top of the poles dripped watered smoke in the form of a brown liquor, the pig shivered in the wind, the grain of the deal tables showed through the sticking tablecloths, for the awning allowed the rain to drift under at its will, and to enclose the sides at this hour seemed a useless undertaking. The landscape over the river disappeared; the wind played on the tent-cords in Æolian improvisations;[4] and at length rose to such a pitch that the whole erection slanted to the ground, those who had taken shelter within it having to crawl out on their hands and knees.

But towards six the storm abated, and a drier breeze shook the moisture from the grass bents. It seemed possible to carry out the programme after all. The awning was set up again; the band was called out from its shelter, and ordered to begin, and where the tables had stood a space was cleared for dancing.

"But where are the folk?" said Henchard, after the lapse of half-an-hour, during which time only two men and a woman had stood up to dance. "The shops are all shut. Why don't they come?"

"They are at Farfrae's affair in the Chestnut Walk," answered a councilman who stood in the field with the Mayor.

"A few I suppose. But where are the body o' 'em?"

"All out of doors are there."

"Then the more fools they!"

Henchard walked away moodily. One or two young fellows gallantly came to climb the poles, to save the hams from being wasted; but as there were no spectators, and the whole scene presented the most melancholy appearance, Henchard gave orders that the proceedings were to be suspended, and the entertainment closed, the food to be distributed among the poor people of the town. In a short time nothing was left in the field but a few hurdles, the tents, and the poles.

Henchard returned to his house, had tea with his wife and daughter, and then walked out. It was now dusk. He soon saw that the tendency of all promenaders was towards a particular spot in the Walks, and eventually proceeded thither himself. The notes of a stringed band came from the enclosure that Farfrae had erected – the pavilion, as he called it – and when he reached it he perceived that a gigantic tent had been ingeniously constructed without poles or ropes. The densest point of the avenue of chestnuts had been selected, where the boughs made a closely interlaced vault overhead; to these boughs the canvas had been hung, and a barrel roof was the result. The end towards the wind was enclosed, the other end was open. Henchard went round and saw the interior.

In form it was like a nave of a cathedral with one gable removed, but the scene within was anything but devotional. A reel or fling of some sort was in progress; and the usually sedate Farfrae was in the midst of the other dancers in the costume of a wild Highlander, flinging himself about and spinning to the tune. For a moment Henchard could not help laughing. Then he perceived the immense admiration for the Scotchman that revealed itself in the women's faces; and when this exhibition was over, and a new dance proposed, and Donald had disappeared for a time to return in his natural garments, he had an unlimited choice of partners, every girl being in a coming-on disposition towards one who so thoroughly understood the poetry of motion as he.

All the town crowded to the Walk, such a delightful idea of a ball-room never having occurred to the inhabitants before. Among the rest of the on-lookers were Elizabeth and her mother – the former thoughtful yet much interested, her eyes beaming with a longing lingering light, as if Nature had been advised by Correggio[5] in their creation. The dancing progressed with unabated spirit, and Henchard walked and waited till his wife should be disposed to go home. He did not care to keep in the light, and when he went into the dark it was worse, for there he heard remarks of a kind which were becoming too frequent:

"Mr. Henchard's rejoicings couldn't say good morning to this," said one. "A man must be a headstrong stunpoll to think folk would go up to that bleak place to-day."

The other answered that people said it was not only in such things as those that the Mayor was wanting. Where would his business be if it were not for this young fellow? 'Twas verily Fortune sent him to Henchard. His accounts had been like a bramble-wood when Mr. Farfrae came. He had used to reckon his sacks by chalk strokes all in a row like garden-palings, measure his ricks by stretching with his arms, weigh his trusses by a lift, judge his hay by a "chaw," and settle the price with a curse. But now this accomplished young man did it all by smooth ciphering, and machines, and mensuration. Then the wheat – that sometimes had used to taste so strongly of mice when made into bread that people could fairly tell the breed – Farfrae had a plan for purifying, so that nobody would dream the smallest four-legged beast had walked over it once.[6] "Oh yes, everybody is full of him, and the care Mr. Henchard has to keep him, to be sure!" concluded this gentleman.

"But he won't do it for long, good-now," said the other.

"No!" said Henchard to himself behind the tree. "Or if he do, he'll be honeycombed clean out of all the character and standing that he's built up in these eighteen years!"

He went back to the dancing pavilion. Farfrae was footing a quaint little dance with Elizabeth-Jane – an old country thing, the only one

PLATE VII
'Farfrae was footing a quaint little dance with Elizabeth-Jane.'

she knew, and though he considerately toned down his movements to suit her demurer gait, the pattern of the shining little nails in the soles of his boots became familiar to the eyes of every bystander. The tune had enticed her into it; being a tune of a busy, vaulting, leaping sort – some low notes on the silver string of each fiddle, then a skipping on the small, like running up and down ladders – "Miss McLeod of Ayr"[7] was its name, so Mr. Farfrae had said, and that it was very popular in his own country.

It was soon over, and the girl looked at Henchard for approval; but he did not give it. He seemed not to see her. "Look here, Farfrae," he said, like one whose mind was elsewhere; "I'll go to Port-Bredy[8] Great Market to-morrow myself. You can stay and put things right in your clothes-box and recover strength to your knees after your vagaries." He planted on Donald an antagonistic glare that had begun as a smile.

Some other townsmen came up, and Donald drew aside. "What's this, Henchard," said Alderman Tubber, applying his thumb to the corn-factor like a cheese-taster. "An opposition randy to yours, eh? Jack's as good as his master, eh? Eclipsed ye quite, hasn't he?"

"You see, Mr. Henchard," said the lawyer, another good-natured friend, "where you made the mistake was in going so far afield. You should have taken a leaf out of his book, and have had your sports in a sheltered place like this. But you didn't think of it, you see; and he did, and that's where he's beat you."

"He'll be top-sawyer soon of you two, and carry all afore him," added jocular Mr. Tubber.

"No," said Henchard gloomily. "He won't be that, because he's shortly going to leave me." He looked towards Donald, who had again come near. "Mr. Farfrae's time as my manager is drawing to a close – isn't it, Farfrae?"

The young man, who could now read the lines and folds of Henchard's strongly-traced face as if they were clear verbal inscriptions, quietly assented; and when people deplored the fact, and asked why it was, he simply replied that Mr. Henchard no longer required his help.

Henchard went home, apparently satisfied. But in the morning, when his jealous temper had passed away, his heart sank within him at what he had said and done. He was the more disturbed when he found that this time Farfrae was determined to take him at his word.

CHAPTER XVII

Elizabeth-Jane had perceived from Henchard's manner that in assenting to dance she had made a mistake of some kind. In her simplicity she did not know what it was, till a hint from a nodding acquaintance enlightened her. As the Mayor's stepdaughter, she learnt, she had not been quite in her place in treading a measure amid such a mixed throng as filled the dancing pavilion.

Thereupon her ears, cheeks, and chin glowed like live coals at the dawning of the idea that her manners and tastes were not good enough for her position, and would bring her into disgrace.

This made her very miserable, and she looked about for her mother; but Mrs. Henchard, who had less idea of conventionality than Elizabeth herself, had gone away, leaving her daughter to return at her own pleasure. The latter moved on into the dark dense old avenues, or rather vaults of living woodwork, which ran along the town boundary, and stood reflecting.

A man followed in a few minutes, and her face being towards the shine from the tent, he recognized her. It was Farfrae – just come from the dialogue with Henchard which had signified his dismissal.

"And it's you, Miss Newson? – and I've been looking for ye everywhere!" he said, overcoming a sadness imparted by the estrangement with the corn-merchant. "May I walk on with you as far as your street-corner?"

She thought there might be something wrong in this; but did not utter any objection. So together they went on, first down the Old Walk,[1] and then into the Bowling Walk, till Farfrae said, "It's like that I'm going to leave you soon."

She faltered "Why?"

"Oh – as a mere matter of business – nothing more. But we'll not concern ourselves about it – it is for the best. I hoped to have another dance with you."

She said she could not dance – in any proper way.

"Oh, but you do. It's the feeling for it rather than the learning of steps that makes pleasant dancers. . . . I fear I offended your father by getting up this! And now, perhaps, I'll have to go to another part o' the worrld altogether!"

This seemed such a melancholy prospect that Elizabeth-Jane breathed a sigh – letting it off in fragments that he might not hear her. But darkness makes people truthful, and the Scotchman went on impulsively – perhaps he had heard her after all:

"I wish I was richer, Miss Newson; and your step-father had not been offended; I would ask you something in a short time – yes, I would ask you to-night. But that's not for me!"

What he would have asked her he did not say; and instead of encouraging him she remained incompetently silent. Thus afraid one of another, they continued their promenade along the walls till they got near the bottom of the Bowling Walk: twenty steps further and the trees would end, and the street-corner and lamps appear. In consciousness of this they stopped.

"I never found out who it was that sent us to Durnmerford granary on a fool's errand that day," said Donald, in his undulating tones. "Did ye ever know yourself, Miss Newson?"

"Never," said she.

"I wonder why they did it?"

"For fun, perhaps."

"Perhaps it was not for fun. It might have been that they thought they would like us to stay waiting there, talking to one another. Ah, well! I hope you Casterbridge people won't forget me if I go."

"That I'm sure we won't!" she said, earnestly. "I – wish you wouldn't go at all."

They had got into the lamplight. "Now, I'll think over that," said Donald Farfrae. "And I'll not come up to your door; but part from ye here; lest it make your father more angry still."

They parted, Farfrae returning into the dark Bowling Walk, and Elizabeth-Jane going up the street. Without any consciousness of what she was doing she started running with all her might till she reached her father's door. "Oh, dear me – what am I at?" she thought, as she pulled up breathless.

Indoors she fell to conjecturing the meaning of Farfrae's enigmatic words about not daring to ask her what he fain would. Elizabeth, that silent observing woman, had long noted how he was rising in favour among the townspeople; and, knowing Henchard's nature now, she had feared that Farfrae's days as manager were numbered; so that the announcement gave her little surprise. Would Mr. Farfrae stay in Casterbridge despite his words and her father's dismissal? His occult breathings to her might be solvable by his course in that respect.

The next day was windy – so windy that walking in the garden she picked up a portion of the draft of a letter on business in Donald Farfrae's writing, which had flown over the wall from the office. The useless scrap she took indoors, and began to copy the caligraphy, which she much admired. The letter began "Dear sir," and presently writing on a loose slip "Elizabeth-Jane," she laid the latter over "Sir," making the phrase "Dear Elizabeth-Jane." When she saw the effect a quick red ran up her face and warmed her through, though nobody was there to see what she had done. She quickly tore up the slip, and threw it away. After this she grew cool, and laughed at herself, walked about the room, and laughed again; not joyfully, but distressfully rather.

It was quickly known in Casterbridge that Farfrae and Henchard had decided to dispense with each other. Elizabeth-Jane's anxiety to know if Farfrae was going away from the town reached a pitch that disturbed her, for she could no longer conceal from herself the cause. At length the news reached her that he was not going to leave the place. A man following the same trade as Henchard, but on a very small scale, had sold his business to Farfrae, who was forthwith about to start as corn and hay-merchant on his own account.

Her heart fluttered when she heard of this step of Donald's, proving that he meant to remain; and yet, would a man who cared one little bit for her have endangered his suit by setting up a business in opposition to Mr. Henchard's? Would he not have tried at any sacrifice to please the corn-factor on her account? Surely yes; and it must have been a passing impulse only which had led him to address her so softly.

To solve the problem whether her appearance on the evening of the dance were such as to inspire a fleeting love at first sight, she dressed herself up exactly as she had dressed then – the muslin, the spencer, the sandals, the parasol – and looked in the mirror. The picture glassed back was, in her opinion, precisely of such a kind as to inspire that fleeting regard, and no more – "just enough to make him silly, and not enough to keep him so," she said luminously; and Elizabeth thought, in a much lower key, that by this time he had discovered how plain and homely was the informing spirit of that pretty outside.

Hence, when she felt her heart going out to him she would say to herself with a mock pleasantry that carried an ache with it, "No, no, Elizabeth-Jane – such dreams are not for you!" She tried to prevent herself from seeing him, and thinking of him; succeeding fairly well in the former attempt, in the latter not so completely.

Henchard, who had been hurt at finding that Farfrae did not mean to put up with his temper any longer, was incensed beyond measure when he learnt what the young man had done as an alternative. It was in the town hall, after a council meeting, that he first became aware of Farfrae's *coup* for establishing himself independently in the town; and his voice might have been heard as far as the town-pump expressing his feelings to his fellow councilmen. Those tones showed that, though under a long reign of self-control he had become Mayor and church-warden and what not, there was still the same unruly volcanic stuff beneath the rind of Michael Henchard as when he had sold his wife at Weydon Fair.

"Well, he's a friend of mine, and I'm a friend of his – or if we are not, what are we? 'Od send, if I've not been his friend, who has, I should like to know? Didn't he come here without a sound shoe to his voot? Didn't I keep him here – help him to a living? Didn't I help him to money, or whatever he wanted? I stuck out for no terms – I said 'Name your own price.' I'd have shared my last crust with that young fellow at one time, I liked him so well. And now he's defied me! But d — him, I'll have a tussle with him now – at fair buying and selling, mind – at fair buying and selling! And if I can't overbid such a stripling as he then I'm not worth a varden. We'll show that we know our business as well as one here and there."

His friends of the Corporation did not specially respond. Henchard was less popular now than he had been when, nearly two years before, they had voted him to the chief magistracy on account of his amazing energy. While they had collectively profited by this quality of the corn-factor's, they had been made to wince individually on more than one occasion. So he went out of the hall and down the street alone.

Reaching home he seemed to recollect something with a sour satisfaction. He called Elizabeth-Jane. Seeing how he looked when she entered she appeared alarmed.

"Nothing to find fault with," he said, observing her concern. "Only I want to caution you, my dear. That man, Farfrae – it is about him. I've seen him talking to you two or three times – he danced with 'ee at the rejoicings, and came home with 'ee. Now, now, no blame to you. But just hearken: Have you made him any foolish promise? Gone the least bit beyond sniff and snaff at all?"

"No. I have promised him nothing."

"Good. All's well that ends well. I particularly wish you not to see him again."

"Very well, sir."

"You promise?"

She hesitated for a moment, and then said,

"Yes, if you much wish it."

"I do. He's an enemy to our house."

When she had gone he sat down, and wrote in a heavy hand to Farfrae thus: –

"Sir,

"I make request that henceforth you and my step-daughter be as strangers to each other. She on her part has promised to welcome no more addresses from you; and I trust, therefore, you will not attempt to force them upon her.

"M. Henchard."

One would almost have supposed Henchard to have had policy to see that no better *modus vivendi* could be arrived at with Farfrae than by encouraging him to become his son-in-law. But such a scheme for buying over a rival had nothing to recommend it to the Mayor's headstrong faculties. With all domestic *finesse* of that kind he was hopelessly at variance. Loving a man or hating him, his diplomacy was as wrongheaded as a buffalo's; and his wife had not ventured to suggest the course which she, for many reasons, would have welcomed gladly.

Meanwhile, Donald Farfrae had opened the gates of commerce on his own account at a spot on Dummerford Hill – as far as possible from Henchard's stores, and with every intention of keeping clear of his former friend and employer's customers. There was, it seemed to the younger man, room for both of them and to spare. The town was small, but the corn and hay-trade was proportionately large, and with his native sagacity he saw honest[2] opportunity for a share of it. So determined was he to do nothing which should seem like trade-antagonism to the Mayor that he refused his first customer – a large farmer of good repute – because Henchard and this man had dealt together within the preceding three months.

"He was once my friend," said Farfrae, "and it's not for me to take business from him. I am sorry to disappoint you, but I cannot hurt the trade of a man who's been so kind to me."

In spite of this praiseworthy course the Scotchman's trade increased. Whether it were that his northern energy was an overmastering force among the easy-going Wessex worthies, or whether it was sheer luck, the fact remained that whatever he touched he prospered in. Like Jacob in Padan-Aram, he would no sooner humbly limit himself to the ringstraked-and-spotted exceptions of trade, than the ringstraked-and-spotted would multiply and prevail.[3]

But most probably luck had little to do with it. Character is Fate, said Novalis,[4] and Farfrae's character was just the reverse of Henchard's, who might not inaptly be described as Faust has been described[5] – as a vehement, gloomy being, who had quitted the ways of vulgar men without light to guide him on a better way.

Farfrae duly received the request to discontinue attentions to

Elizabeth-Jane. His acts of that kind had been so slight that the request was almost superfluous. Yet he had felt a considerable interest in her, and after some cogitation he decided that it would be as well to enact no Romeo part just then – for the young girl's own sake no less than his own. Thus the incipient attachment was stifled down.

A time came when, avoid collision with his former friend as he might, Farfrae was compelled, in sheer self-defence, to close with Henchard in mortal commercial combat. He could no longer parry the fierce attacks of the latter by simple avoidance. As soon as their war of prices began everybody was interested, and some few guessed the end. It was, in some degree, Northern insight matched against Southron doggedness – the dirk against the cudgel[6] – and Henchard's weapon was one which, if it did not deal ruin at the first or second stroke, left him afterwards well-nigh at his antagonist's mercy.

Almost every Saturday they encountered each other amid the crowd of farmers which thronged about the market-place in the weekly course of their business. Donald was always ready, and even anxious, to say a few friendly words; but the Mayor invariably gazed stormfully past him, like one who had endured and lost on his account, and could in no sense forgive the wrong; nor did Farfrae's snubbed manner of perplexity at all appease him. The large farmers, corn-merchants, millers, auctioneers, and others had each an official stall in the corn-market room, with their names painted thereon; and when to the familiar series of "Henchard," "Everdene," "Darton," and so on,[7] was added one inscribed "Farfrae," in staring new letters, Henchard was stung into bitterness; like Bellerophon,[8] he wandered away from the crowd, cankered in soul.

From that day Donald Farfrae's name was seldom mentioned in Henchard's house. If at breakfast or dinner Elizabeth-Jane's mother inadvertently alluded to her favourite's movements, the girl would implore her by a look to be silent; and her husband would say, "What – are you, too, my enemy?"

CHAPTER XVIII

There came a shock which had been foreseen for some time by Elizabeth, as the box-passenger foresees the approaching jerk from some channel across the highway.

Her mother was ill – too unwell to leave her room. Henchard, who treated her kindly, except in moments of irritation, sent at once for the richest, busiest doctor, whom he supposed to be the best. Bedtime came, and they burnt a light all night. In a day or two she rallied.

Elizabeth, who had been staying up, did not appear at breakfast on the second morning, and Henchard sat down alone. He was startled to see a letter for him from Jersey in a writing he knew too well, and had expected least to behold again. He took it up in his hands and looked at it as at a picture, a vision, a vista of past enactments; and then he read it as an unimportant finale to conjecture.

The writer said that she at length perceived how impossible it would be for any further communications to proceed between them now that his re-marriage had taken place. That such re-union had been the only straightforward course open to him she was bound to admit. "On calm reflection, therefore," she went on, "I quite forgive you for landing me in such a dilemma, remembering that you concealed nothing before our ill-advised acquaintance; and that you really did set before me in your grim way the fact of there being a certain risk in loving you, slight as it seemed to be after eighteen years[1] of silence on your wife's part. I thus look upon the whole as a misfortune of mine, and not a fault of yours.

"So that, Michael, I must ask you to overlook those letters with which I pestered you day after day in the heat of my feelings. They were written whilst I thought your conduct to me cruel; but now I know more particulars of the position you were in I see how inconsiderate my reproaches were.

"Now you will, I am sure, perceive that the one condition which will make any future happiness possible for me, is that the past connection between our lives be kept secret outside this isle. Speak of it I know you will not; and I can trust you not to write of it. One safeguard more remains to be mentioned – that no writings of mine, or trifling articles belonging to me, should be left in your possession through neglect or forgetfulness. To this end may I request you to return to me any such you may have, particularly the letters written in the first abandonment of feeling.

"For the handsome sum you forwarded to me as a plaster to the wound, I heartily thank you.

"I am now on my way to Bristol, to see my only relative.[2] She is rich, and I hope will do something for me. I shall return through Casterbridge and Budmouth, where I shall take the steamboat. Can you meet me with the letters and other trifles? I shall be in the coach which changes horses at the Stag[3] Hotel at half-past five Wednesday evening; I shall be wearing a Paisley shawl with a red centre, and thus may easily be found. I should prefer this plan of receiving them to having them sent.[4]

"I remain still, yours ever,
"LUCETTA."

Henchard breathed heavily. "Poor thing – better you had not known me![5] Upon my heart and soul, if ever I should be left in a position to carry out that marriage with thee, I *ought* to do it – I ought to do it, indeed!"

The contingency that he had in his mind was, of course, the death of Mrs. Henchard.

As requested, he sealed up Lucetta's letters, and put the parcel aside till the day she had appointed; this plan of returning them by hand being apparently a little *ruse* of the young lady's for exchanging a word or two with him on past times. He would have preferred not to see her; but deeming that there could be no great harm in acquiescing thus far, he went at dusk and stood opposite the coach-office.

The evening was chilly, and the coach was late. Henchard crossed over to it while the horses were being changed; but there was no Lucetta inside or out. Concluding that something had happened to modify her arrangements he gave the matter up and went home, not without a sense of relief.[6]

Meanwhile Mrs. Henchard was weakening visibly. She could not go out of doors any more. One day, after much thinking which seemed to distress her, she said she wanted to write something. A desk was put upon her bed with pen and paper, and at her request she was left alone. She remained writing for a short time, folded her paper carefully, called Elizabeth-Jane to bring a taper and wax, and then, still refusing assistance, sealed up the sheet, directed it, and locked it in her desk. She had directed it in these words:–

"*Mr. Michael Henchard. Not to be opened till Elizabeth-Jane's wedding-day.*"

The latter sat up with her mother to the utmost of her strength night after night. To learn to take the universe seriously there is no quicker way than to watch – to be a "waker," as the country-people call it. Between the hours at which the last toss-pot went by and the first sparrow shook himself, the silence in Casterbridge – barring the rare sound of the watchman – was broken in Elizabeth's ear only by the time-piece in the bedroom ticking frantically against the clock on the stairs; ticking harder and harder till it seemed to clang like a gong; and all this while the subtle-souled girl asking herself why she was born, why sitting in a room, and blinking at the candle; why things around her had taken the shape they wore in preference to every other possible shape. Why they stared at her so helplessly, as if waiting for the touch of some wand that should release them from terrestrial constraint; what that chaos called consciousness, which spun in her at this moment like a top, tended to, and began in. Her eyes fell together; she was awake, yet she was asleep.

A word from her mother roused her. Without preface, and as the continuation of a scene already progressing in her mind, Mrs. Henchard said: "You remember the note sent to you and Mr. Farfrae – asking you to meet some one in Dummerford Barton – and that you thought it was a trick to make fools of you?"

"Yes."

"It was not to make fools of you – it was done to bring you together. 'Twas I did it."

"Why?" said Elizabeth, with a start.

"I – wanted you to marry Mr. Farfrae."

"Oh, mother!" Elizabeth-Jane bent down her head so much that she looked quite into her own lap. But as her mother did not go on, she said, "What reason?"

"Well, I had a reason. 'Twill out one day. I wish it could have been in my time! But there – nothing is as you wish it. Henchard hates him."

"Perhaps they'll be friends again," murmured the girl.

"I don't know – I don't know." After this her mother was silent, and dozed; and she spoke on the subject no more.

Some little time later on, Farfrae was passing Henchard's house on a Sunday morning, when he observed that the blinds were all down. He rang the bell so softly that it only sounded a single full note and a small one; and then he was informed that Mrs. Henchard was dead – just dead – that very hour.

At the town-pump there were gathered when he passed a few old inhabitants, who came there for water whenever they had, as at present, spare time to fetch it, because it was purer from that original fount than from their own wells. Mrs. Cuxsom, who had been standing there for an indefinite time with her pitcher, was describing the incidents of Mrs. Henchard's death, as she had learnt them from the nurse.

"And she was as white as marble-stone," said Mrs. Cuxsom. "And likewise such a thoughtful woman, too – ah, poor soul – so thoughtful that a' minded every little thing that wanted tending. 'Yes,' says she, 'when I'm gone, and my last breath's blowed, look in the top drawer o' the chest in the back room by the window, and you'll find all my coffin clothes; a piece of flannel – that's to put under me, and the little piece is to put under my head; and my new stockings for my feet – they are folded alongside, and all my other things. And there's four ounce pennies, the heaviest I could find, a-tied up in bits of linen, for weights – two for my right eye and two for my left,' she said. 'And when you've used 'em, and my eyes don't open no more, bury the pennies, good souls, and don't ye go spending 'em, for I shouldn't like it. And open the windows as soon as I am carried out, and make it as cheerful as you can for my Elizabeth-Jane.'"

"Ah, poor heart!"

"Well, and Martha did it, and buried the ounce pennies in the garden.

But if ye'll believe words, that man, Christopher Coney, went and dug 'em up, and spent 'em at the King o' Prussia. 'Faith,' he said, 'why should death deprive life of fourpence?[7] Death's not of such good report that we should respect 'en to that extent,' says he."

"'Twas a cannibal deed!" deprecated her listeners.

"Gad, then, I won't quite hae it," said Solomon Longways. "I say it to-day, and 'tis a Sunday morning, and I wouldn't speak wrongfully for a silver sixpence at such a time. I don't see harm in it.[8] To respect the dead is sound doxology; and I wouldn't sell skellintons – leastwise respectable skellintons – to be varnished for 'natomies, except I were out o' work. But money is scarce, and throats get dry. Why *should* death deprive life of fourpence? I say there was no treason in it."

"Well, poor soul; she's helpless to hinder that or anything now," answered Mother Cuxsom. "And all her shining keys will be took from her, and her cupboards opened; and things a' didn't wish seen, anybody will see; and her little wishes and ways will all be as nothing!"

CHAPTER XIX

Henchard and Elizabeth sat conversing by the fire. It was three weeks after Mrs. Henchard's funeral; the candles were not lighted, and a flexuous acrobatic flame, poised on a coal, called from the shady walls the smiles of all shapes that could respond – the old pier-glass, with gilt columns and huge entablature, the picture-frames, sundry knobs and handles, and the brass rosette at the bottom of each riband bell-pull on either side of the chimney-piece.

"Elizabeth, do you think much of old times?" said Henchard.

"Yes, sir; often," said she.

"Who do you put in your pictures of 'em?"

"Mother and father – nobody else hardly."

Henchard always looked like one bent on resisting pain when

Elizabeth-Jane spoke of Richard Newson as "father." "Ah! I am out of all that, am I not?" he said. . . . . "Was Newson a kind father?"

"Yes, sir; very."

Henchard's face settled into an expression of stolid loneliness which gradually modulated into something softer. "Suppose I had been your real father?" he said. "Would you have cared for me as much as you cared for Richard Newson?"

"I can't think it," she said quickly. "I can think of no other as my father except my father."

Henchard's wife was dissevered from him by death; his friend and helper Farfrae by estrangement; Elizabeth-Jane by ignorance. It seemed to him that only one of them could possibly be recalled, and that was the girl. His mind began vibrating between the wish to reveal himself to her, and the policy of leaving well alone, till he could no longer sit still. He walked up and down, and then he came and stood behind her chair, looking down upon the top of her head. He could no longer restrain his impulse. "What did your mother tell you about me – my history?" he asked.

"That you were related by marriage."

"She should have told more – before you knew me. Then my task would not have been such a hard one. . . . . Elizabeth, it is I who am your father, and not Richard Newson. Shame alone prevented your wretched parents from owning this to you while both of 'em were alive."

The back of Elizabeth's head remained still, and her shoulders did not denote even the movements of breathing. Henchard went on: "I'd rather have your scorn, your fear, anything, than your ignorance; 'tis that I hate. Your mother and I were man and wife when we were young. What you saw was our second marriage. Your mother was too honest. We had thought each other dead – and – Newson became her husband."

This was the nearest approach Henchard could make to the full truth. As far as he personally was concerned he would have screened nothing; but he showed a respect for the young girl's sex and years worthy of a better man.

When he had gone on to give details which a whole series of slight

PLATE VIII

*'"Don't cry – don't cry," said Henchard, with vehement pathos,
"I can't bear it, I won't bear it."'*

and unregarded incidents in her past life strangely corroborated; when, in short, she believed his story to be true, she became greatly agitated, and, turning round to the table, flung her face upon it weeping.

"Don't cry – don't cry," said Henchard, with vehement pathos, "I can't bear it, I won't bear it. I am your father; why should you cry? Am I so dreadful, so hateful to 'ee? Don't take against me, Elizabeth-Jane!" he cried, grasping her wet hand. "Don't take against me – though I was a drinking man once, and used your mother roughly – I'll be kinder to you than *he* was! I'll do anything, if you will only look upon me as your father!"

She tried to stand up and confront him trustfully; but she could not; she was troubled at his presence, like the brethren at the avowal of Joseph.[1]

"I don't want you to come to me all of a sudden," said Henchard, in jerks, and moving like a great tree in a wind. "No, Elizabeth, I don't. I'll go away and not see you till to-morrow, or when you like; and then I'll show 'ee papers to prove my words. There, I am gone and won't disturb you any more. . . . . .'Twas I that chose your name, my daughter; your mother wanted it Susan. There, don't forget 'twas I gave you your name." He went out at the door and shut her softly in, and she heard him go away into the garden. But he had not done. Before she had moved, or in any way recovered from the effect of his disclosure, he reappeared.

"One word more, Elizabeth," he said. "You'll take my surname now – hey? Your mother was against it; but it will be much more pleasant to me. 'Tis legally yours, you know. But nobody need know that. You shall take it as if by choice. I'll talk to my lawyer – I don't know the law of it exactly; but will you do this – let me put a few lines into the newspaper that such is to be your name?"

"If it is my name I must have it, mustn't I?" she asked.

"Well, well; usage is everything in these matters."

"I wonder why mother didn't wish it?"

"Oh, some whim of the poor soul's. Now get a bit of paper and draw up a paragraph as I shall tell you. But let's have a light."

"I can see by the firelight," she answered. "Yes – I'd rather."

"Very well."

She got a piece of paper, and bending over the fender, wrote at his dictation words which he had evidently got by heart from some advertisement or other – words to the effect that she, the writer, hitherto known as Elizabeth-Jane Newson, was going to call herself Elizabeth-Jane Henchard forthwith. It was done, and fastened up, and directed to the office of the *Casterbridge Chronicle*.

"Now," said Henchard, with the blaze of satisfaction that he always emitted when he had carried his point – though tenderness softened it this time – "I'll go upstairs and hunt for some documents that will prove it all to you. But I won't trouble you with them till to-morrow. Good night, my Elizabeth-Jane."

He was gone before the bewildered girl could realize what it all meant, or adjust her filial sense to the new centre of gravity. She was thankful that he had left her to herself for the evening, and sat down over the fire. Here she remained in silence, and wept – not for her mother now, but for the genial sailor, Richard Newson, to whom she seemed doing a wrong.

Henchard, in the meantime, had gone upstairs. Papers of a domestic nature he kept in a drawer in his bedroom, and this he unlocked. Before turning them over he leant back and indulged in reposeful thought. Elizabeth was his at last, and she was a girl of such good sense and kind heart that she would be sure to like him. He was the kind of man to whom some human object for pouring out his heat upon – were it affective or were it choleric – was almost a necessity. The craving of his heart for the re-establishment of this tenderest human tie had been great during his wife's lifetime, and now he had submitted to its mastery without reluctance and without fear. He bent over the drawer again, and proceeded in his search.

Among the other papers had been placed the contents of his wife's little desk, the keys of which had been handed to him at her request. Here was the letter addressed to him with the restriction, "*Not to be opened till Elizabeth-Jane's wedding-day.*"

Mrs. Henchard, though better educated[2] than her husband, had been no practical hand at anything. In sealing up the sheet, which was folded and tucked in without an envelope, in the old-fashioned way, she had overlaid the junction with a large mass of wax without the requisite under-touch of the same. The seal had cracked, and the letter was open.

Henchard had no reason to suppose the restriction one of serious weight, and his feeling for his late wife had not been of the nature of deep respect. "Some trifling fancy or other of poor Susan's, I suppose," he said; and without curiosity he allowed his eyes to scan the letter:

> "MY DEAR MICHAEL,
>
> "For the good of all three of us, I have kept one thing a secret from you till now. I hope you will understand why; I think you will; though perhaps you may not forgive me. But, dear Michael, I have done it for the best. I shall be in my grave when you read this, and Elizabeth-Jane will have a home. Don't curse me, Mike – think of how I was situated. I can hardly write it, but here it is. Elizabeth-Jane is not your Elizabeth-Jane – the child who was in my arms when you sold me. No; she died three months after that, and this living one is my other husband's. I christened her by the same name we had given to the first, and she filled up the ache I felt at the other's loss. Michael, I am dying, and I might have held my tongue; but I could not. Tell her husband of this or not, as you may judge; and forgive, if you can, a woman you once deeply wronged, as she forgives you.
>
> "SUSAN HENCHARD."

Her husband regarded the paper as if it were a window-pane through which he saw for miles. His lip twitched, and he seemed to compress his frame, as if to bear better. His usual habit was not to consider whether destiny were hard upon him or not – the shape of his ideas in cases of affliction being simply a moody "I am to suffer, I perceive." "So much scourging as this, then, is it for me?" But now through his passionate head there stormed this thought – that the blasting disclosure was what he had deserved.

His wife's extreme reluctance to have the girl's name altered from Newson to Henchard was now accounted for fully. It furnished another illustration of that honesty in dishonesty which had characterized her in other things.

He remained unnerved and purposeless for near a couple of hours; till he suddenly said,[3] "Ah – I wonder if it is true!"

He jumped up in an impulse, kicked off his slippers, and went with a candle to the door of Elizabeth-Jane's room, where he put his ear to the keyhole and listened. She was breathing profoundly. Henchard softly turned the handle, entered, and shading the light, approached the bedside. Gradually bringing the light from behind a screening curtain he held it in such a manner that it fell slantwise on her face without shining on her eyes. He steadfastly regarded her features.

They were fair: his were dark. But this was an unimportant preliminary. In sleep there come to the surface buried genealogical facts, ancestral curves, dead men's traits, which the mobility of daytime animation screens and overwhelms. In the present statuesque repose of the young girl's countenance Richard Newson's was unmistakably reflected. He could not endure the sight of her, and hastened away.

Misery taught him nothing more than defiant endurance of it. His wife was dead, and the first impulse for revenge died with the thought that she was beyond him. He looked out at the night as at a fiend. Henchard, like all his kind, was superstitious, and he could not help thinking that the concatenation of events this evening had produced was the scheme of some sinister intelligence bent on punishing him. Yet they had developed naturally. If he had not revealed his past history to Elizabeth he would not have searched the drawer for papers, and so on. The mockery was, that he should have no sooner taught a girl to claim the shelter of his paternity than he discovered her to have no kinship with him.

This ironical sequence of things angered him like an impish trick from a fellow-creature. Like Prester John's, his table had been spread, and infernal harpies had snatched up the food.[4] He went out of the house, and moved sullenly onward down the pavement till he came to the bridge at the bottom of the High Street. Here he turned in upon a bypath on the river bank, skirting the north-eastern limits of the town.

These precincts embodied the mournful phases of Casterbridge life, as the south avenues embodied its cheerful moods. The whole way along here was sunless, even in summer time; in spring white frosts lingered here when other places were steaming with warmth; while in winter it was the seed-field of all the aches, rheumatisms, and torturing cramps of the year. The Casterbridge doctors must have pined away for want of sufficient nourishment, but for the configuration of the landscape on the north-eastern side.

The river – slow, noiseless, and dark – the Schwarzwasser[5] of Caster-bridge – ran beneath a low cliff, the two together forming a defence which had rendered walls and artificial earthworks on this side unneces-sary. Here were ruins of a Franciscan priory, and a mill attached to the same, the water of which roared down a back-hatch like the voice of desolation. Above the cliff, and behind the river, rose a pile of buildings, and in the front of the pile a square mass cut into the sky. It was like a pedestal lacking its statue. This missing feature, without which the design remained incomplete, was, in truth, the corpse of a man; for the square mass formed the base of the gallows, the extensive buildings at the back being the county gaol. In the meadow where Henchard now walked the mob were wont to gather whenever an execution took place, and there to the tune of the roaring weir they stood and watched the spectacle.

The exaggeration which darkness imparted to the glooms of this region impressed Henchard more than he had expected. The lugubrious harmony of the spot with his domestic situation was too perfect for him, impatient of effects, scenes, and adumbrations. It reduced his heartburning to melancholy, and he exclaimed, "Why the deuce did I come here!" He went on past the cottage in which the old local hang-man had lived and died, in times before that calling was monopolized by a single gentleman;[6] and climbed up by a steep back lane into the town.[7]

For the sufferings of that night, engendered by his bitter disappoint-ment, he might well have been pitied. He was like one who had half-fainted, and could neither recover nor complete the swoon. In words he could blame his wife, but not in his heart; and had he obeyed the wise directions outside her letter this pain would have been spared him for long – possibly for ever, Elizabeth-Jane seeming to show no ambition to quit her safe and secluded maiden courses for the speculative path of matrimony.

The morning came after this night of unrest, and with it the necessity for a plan. He was far too self-willed to recede from a position, especially as it would involve humiliation. His daughter he had asserted her to be, and his daughter she should always think herself, no matter what hypocrisy it involved.

But he was ill-prepared for the first step in this new situation. The moment he came into the breakfast-room Elizabeth advanced with open confidence to him and took him by the arm.

"I have thought and thought all night of it," she said frankly. "And I see that everything must be as you say. And I am going to look upon you as the father that you are, and not to call you Mr. Henchard any more. It is so plain to me now. Indeed, father, it is. For, of course, you would not have done half the things you have done for me, and let me have my own way so entirely, and bought me presents, if I had only been your stepdaughter. He – Mr. Newson – whom my poor mother married by such a strange mistake" (Henchard was glad that he had disguised matters here) "was very kind – oh, so kind!" (she spoke with tears in her eyes) "but that is not the same thing as being one's real father after all. Now, father, breakfast is ready," said she cheerfully.

Henchard bent and kissed her cheek. The moment and the act he had contemplated for weeks with a thrill of pleasure; yet it was no less than a miserable insipidity to him now that it had come. His reinstation of her mother had been chiefly for the girl's sake, and the fruition of the whole scheme was such dust and ashes as this.

CHAPTER XX

Of all the enigmas which ever confronted a girl[1] there can have been seldom one like that which followed Henchard's announcement of himself to Elizabeth as her father. He had done it in an ardour and an agitation which had half carried the point of affection with her; yet, behold, from the next morning onwards his manner was constrained as she had never seen it before.

The coldness soon broke out into open chiding. One grievous failing of Elizabeth's was her occasional pretty and picturesque use of dialect words – those terrible marks of the beast[2] to the truly genteel.

It was dinner-time – they never met except at meals – and she happened to say when he was rising from table, wishing to show him something, "If you'll bide where you be a minute, father, I'll get it."

" 'Bide where you be,' " he echoed sharply. "Good G—, are you only fit to carry wash to a pig-trough, that ye use such words as those?"

She reddened with shame and sadness.

"I meant 'Stay where you are,' father," she said, in a low, humble voice. "I ought to have been more careful."

He made no reply, and went out of the room.

The sharp reprimand was not lost upon her, and in time it came to pass that for "fay" she said "succeed;" that she no longer spoke of "dumbledores" but of "humble bees;" no longer said of young men and women that they "walked together," but that they were "engaged;" that she grew to talk of "greggles" as "wild hyacinths;" that when she had not slept she did not quaintly tell the servants next morning that she had been "hag-rid," but that she had "suffered from indigestion."

These improvements, however, are somewhat in advance of the story. Henchard, being uncultivated himself, was the bitterest critic the fair girl could possibly have had of her own lapses – really slight now, for she read omnivorously. A gratuitous ordeal was in store for her in the matter of her handwriting. She was passing the dining-room door one evening, and had occasion to go in for something. It was not till she had opened the door that she knew the Mayor was there in the company of a man with whom he transacted business.

"Here, Elizabeth-Jane," he said, looking round at her, "just write down what I tell you – a few words of an agreement for me and this gentleman to sign. I am a poor tool with a pen."

"Be jowned, and so be I," said the gentleman.

She brought forward blotting-book, paper, and ink, and sat down.

"Now then – 'An agreement entered into this sixteenth day of October' – write that first."

She started the pen in an elephantine march across the sheet. It was a splendid round, bold hand of her own conception, a style that would have stamped a woman as Minerva's[3] own in more recent days. But other ideas reigned then: Henchard's creed was that proper young girls wrote ladies'-hand – nay, he believed that bristling characters were as innate and inseparable a part of refined womanhood as sex itself. Hence when, instead of scribbling, like the Princess Ida,[4] –

> "In such a hand as when a field of corn
> Bows all its ears before the roaring East,"

Elizabeth-Jane produced a line of chain-shot and sand-bags, he reddened in angry shame for her, and, peremptorily saying, "Never mind – I'll finish it," dismissed her there and then.

Her considerate and willing disposition became a pitfall to her now. Whenever she took upon herself any domestic duty that the servants could have done – which she often did – he set it down to her faults of breeding.[5] She was, it must be admitted, sometimes provokingly and unnecessarily willing to saddle herself with manual labours. She would go to the kitchen instead of ringing, "Not to make Phœbe come up twice;" she went down on her knees, shovel in hand, when the cat overturned the coal-scuttle; moreover, she would persistently thank the parlourmaid for everything, till one day, as soon as the girl was gone from the room, Henchard broke out with, "Good G—, why dostn't leave off thanking that girl as if she were a goddess-born! Don't I pay her a dozen pound a year to do things for 'ee?" Elizabeth shrank so visibly at the exclamation that he became sorry a few minutes after, and said that he did not mean to be so rough.[6]

These domestic exhibitions were the small protruding needle-rocks which suggested rather than revealed what was underneath. But his passion had less terror for her than his coldness. The increasing frequency of the latter mood told her the sad news that he disliked her with a growing dislike. The more interesting that her appearance and manners became under the softening influences which she could now command, and in her wisdom did command, the more she seemed to estrange him. Sometimes she caught him looking at her with a louring invidiousness that she could hardly bear. Not knowing his secret, it was a cruel mockery that she should for the first time excite his animosity when she had taken his surname.

But the most terrible ordeal was to come. Elizabeth had latterly been accustomed of an afternoon to take out a cup of cider or ale and bread-and-cheese to Nance Mockridge,[7] who worked in the yard, wimbling hay-bonds. Nance accepted this offering thankfully at first; afterwards as a matter of course. On a day when Henchard was on the premises he saw his stepdaughter enter the hay-barn on this errand; and, as there was no clear spot on which to deposit the provisions, she at once set to work arranging two trusses of hay as a table, Mockridge meanwhile standing with her hands on her hips, easefully looking at the preparations on her behalf.

"Elizabeth, come here!" said Henchard; and she obeyed.

"Why do you lower yourself so confoundedly?" he said with suppressed passion. "Haven't I told you o't fifty times? Hey? Making yourself a drudge for a common work-woman of such a character as hers! Why, ye'll disgrace me to the dust!"

Now these words were uttered loud enough to reach Nance inside the barn door, who fired up immediately at the slur upon her personal character. Coming to the door, she cried, regardless of consequences, "Come to that, Mr. Michael Henchard; I can let 'ee know she've waited on worse!"

"Then she must have had more charity than sense," said Henchard.

"Oh, no, she hadn't. 'Twere not for charity but for hire; and at a public-house in this town."

"It is not true," cried Henchard indignantly.

"Just ask her," said Nance, folding her naked arms in such a manner that she could comfortably scratch her elbows.

Henchard glanced at Elizabeth-Jane, whose complexion, now pink and white from confinement, lost nearly all of the former colour. "What does this mean?" he said to her. "Anything or nothing?"

"It is true," said Elizabeth-Jane. "But it was only—"

"Did you do it, or didn't you? Where was it?"

"At the King of Prussia; one evening for a little while, when we were staying there."

Nance glanced triumphantly at Henchard, and sailed into the barn; for, assuming that she was to be discharged on the instant, she had resolved to make the most of her victory. Henchard, however, said nothing about discharging her. Unduly sensitive on such points by

PLATE IX

'"Did you do it, or didn't you? Where was it?"'

reason of his own past, he had the look of one completely ground down to the last indignity. Elizabeth followed him to the house like a culprit; but when she got inside she could not see him. Nor did she see him again that day.

Convinced of the scathing damage to his local repute and position that must have been caused by such a fact, though it had never before reached his own ears, Henchard showed a positive distaste for the presence of this girl not his own, whenever he encountered her. He mostly dined with the farmers at the market-room of one of the two chief hotels, leaving her in utter solitude. Could he have seen how she made use of those silent hours he might have found reason to reverse his judgment on her quality. She read and took notes incessantly, mastering facts with painful laboriousness, but never flinching from her self-imposed task. She began the study of Latin, incited by the Roman characteristics of the town she lived in. "If I am not well-informed it shall be by no fault of my own," she would say to herself through the tears that would occasionally glide down her peachy cheeks when she was fairly baffled by the portentous obscurity of many of these educational works.

Thus she lived on, a dumb, deep-feeling, great-eyed creature, con-strued by not a single contiguous being; quenching with patient fortitude her incipient interest in Farfrae, because it seemed to be one-sided, unmaidenly, and unwise. True, that for reasons best known to herself, she had, since Farfrae's dismissal, shifted her quarters from the back room affording a view of the yard (which she had occupied with such zest) to a front chamber overlooking the street; but as for the young man, whenever he passed the house he seldom or never turned his head.

Winter had almost come, and unsettled weather made her still more dependent upon indoor resources. But there were certain early winter days in Casterbridge – days of firmamental exhaustion which followed angry south-westerly tempests – when, if the sun shone, the air was like velvet. She seized on these days for her periodical visits to the spot where her mother lay buried – the still-used burial-ground of the old Roman-British city, whose curious feature was this its continuity as a place of sepulture. Mrs. Henchard's dust mingled with the dust of women who lay ornamented with glass hairpins and amber necklaces, and men who held in their mouths coins of Hadrian, Posthumus, and the Constantines.[8]

Half-past ten in the morning was about her hour for seeking this spot – a time when the promenades were deserted as the pillared avenues of Karnac. Business had long since passed down them into its daily cells, and Leisure had not arrived there. So Elizabeth-Jane walked and read, or looked over the edge of the book to think, and thus reached the churchyard.[9]

There, approaching her mother's grave, she saw a solitary dark figure in the middle of the gravel-walk. This figure, too, was reading; but not from a book: the words which engrossed it being the inscription on Mrs. Henchard's tombstone. The personage was in mourning like herself, was about her age and size, and might have been her wraith or double, but for the fact that it was a lady much more beautifully dressed than she. Indeed, comparatively indifferent as Elizabeth-Jane was to dress, unless for some temporary whim or purpose, her eyes were arrested by the artistic perfection of the lady's appearance. Her gait, too, had a flexuousness about it, which seemed to avoid angularity of movement less from choice than from predisposition. It was a revelation to Elizabeth that human beings could reach this stage of external development – she had never suspected it. She felt all the freshness and grace to be stolen from herself on the instant by the neighbourhood of such a stranger. And this was in face of the fact that Elizabeth could now have been writ handsome, while the young lady was simply pretty.[10]

Had she been envious she might have hated the woman; but she did not do that – she allowed herself the pleasure of feeling fascinated. She wondered where the lady had come from. The stumpy and practical walk of honest homeliness which mostly prevailed there, the two styles of dress thereabout, the simple and the mistaken, equally avouched that this figure was no Casterbridge woman's, even if a book in her hand resembling a guide-book had not also suggested it.

The stranger presently moved from the tombstone of Mrs. Henchard, and vanished behind the corner of the wall. Elizabeth went to the tomb herself; beside it were two footprints distinct in the soil, signifying that the lady had stood there a long time. She returned homeward, musing on what she had seen, as she might have mused on a rainbow or the Northern Lights, a rare butterfly or a cameo.

Interesting as things had been out of doors, at home it turned out to be one of her bad days. Henchard, whose two years' mayoralty was ending, had been made aware that he was not to be chosen to fill a vacancy in the list of aldermen; and that Farfrae was likely to become one of the Council. This caused the unfortunate discovery that she had played the waiting-maid in the town of which he was Mayor to rankle in his mind yet more poisonously. He had learnt by personal inquiry at the time that it was to Donald Farfrae – that treacherous upstart – that she had thus humiliated herself. And though Mrs. Stannidge seemed to attach no great importance to the incident – the cheerful souls at the King of Prussia having exhausted its aspects long ago – such was Henchard's haughty spirit that the simple thrifty deed was regarded as little less than a social catastrophe by him.

Ever since the evening of his wife's arrival with her daughter there had been something in the air which had changed his luck. That dinner at the Golden Crown with his friends had been Henchard's Austerlitz:[11] he had had his successes since, but his course had not been upward. He was not to be numbered among the aldermen – that Peerage of burghers – as he had expected to be, and the consciousness of this soured him to-day.

"Well, where have you been?" he said to her, with off-hand laconism.

"I've been strolling in the Walks and churchyard, father, till I feel quite leery." She clapped her hand to her mouth, but too late.

This was just enough to incense Henchard after the other crosses of the day. "I *won't* have you talk like that!" he thundered. " 'Leery,' indeed. One would think you worked upon a farm. One day I learn that you lend a hand in public-houses. Then I hear you talk like a clodhopper. I'm burned, if it goes on, this house can't hold us two."

The only way of getting a single pleasant thought to go to sleep upon after this was by recalling the lady she had seen that day, and hoping she might see her again.

Meanwhile Henchard was sitting up, thinking over his jealous folly in forbidding Farfrae to pay his addresses to this girl who did not belong to him, when if he had allowed them to go on he might not have been encumbered with her. At last he said to himself with satisfaction as he jumped up and went to the writing table: "Ah! – he'll think it means peace, and a marriage portion – not that I don't want my house to be troubled with her, and no portion at all." He wrote as follows: –

"SIR, – On consideration I don't wish to interfere with your courtship of Elizabeth-Jane, if you care for her. I therefore withdraw my objection; excepting in this – that the business be not carried on in my house.

"Yours,

"Mr. Farfrae.   "M. HENCHARD."

The morrow, being fairly fine, found Elizabeth-Jane again in the churchyard; but while looking for the lady she was startled by the apparition of Farfrae, who passed outside the gate. He glanced up for a moment from a pocket-book in which he appeared to be making figures as he went; whether or not he saw her he took no notice, and disappeared.

Unduly depressed by a sense of her own superfluity she thought he probably scorned her; and quite broken in spirit sat down on a bench. She fell into painful thought on her position, which ended with her saying quite loud, "Oh, I wish I was dead with dear mother!"[12]

Behind the bench was a little promenade under the wall where people sometimes walked instead of on the gravel. The bench seemed to be touched by something; she looked round, and a face was bending over her, veiled, but still distinct, the face of the young woman she had seen yesterday.

Elizabeth-Jane looked confounded for a moment, knowing she had been overheard, though there was pleasure in her confusion. "Yes, I heard you," said the lady, in a vivacious voice, answering her look. "What can have happened?"

"I don't – I can't tell you," said Elizabeth, putting her hand to her face to hide a quick flush that had come.

There was no movement or word for a few seconds; then the girl felt that the young lady was sitting down beside her.

"I guess how it is with you," said the latter. "That was your mother."

She waved her hand towards the tombstone. Elizabeth looked up at her as if inquiring of herself whether there should be confidence. The lady's manner was so desirous, so anxious, that the girl decided there should be confidence. "It was my mother," she said, "my only friend."

"But your father, Mr. Henchard. He is living?"

"Yes, he is living," said Elizabeth-Jane.

"Is he not kind to you?"

"I've no wish to complain of him."

"There has been a disagreement?"

"A little."

"Perhaps you were to blame," suggested the stranger.

"I was – in many ways," sighed the meek Elizabeth. "I swept up the coals when the servant ought to have done it; and I said I was leery; and he was angry with me."

The lady seemed to warm towards her for that reply. "Do you know the impression your words give me?" she said ingenuously. "That he is a hot-tempered man – a little proud – perhaps ambitious; but not a bad man." Her anxiety not to condemn Henchard, while siding with Elizabeth, was curious.

"Oh no; certainly not *bad*," agreed the honest girl. "And he has not even been unkind to me till lately – since mother died. But it has been very much to bear while it has lasted. All is owing to my defects, I dare say; and my defects are owing to my history."

"What is your history?"

Elizabeth-Jane looked wistfully at her questioner; found that her questioner was looking at her; turned her eyes down; and then seemed compelled to look back again. "My history is not gay nor attractive," she said. "And yet I can tell it, if you really want to know."

The lady assured her that she did want to know; whereupon Elizabeth-Jane told the tale of her life as she understood it, which was in general the true one, except that the sale at the fair had no part therein.

Contrary to the girl's expectation her new friend was not shocked. This cheered her; and it was not till she thought of returning to that home in which she had been treated so roughly of late that her spirits fell.

"I don't know how to return," she murmured. "I think of going away. But what can I do? Where can I go?"

"Perhaps it will be better soon," said her friend gently. "So I would not go far. Now what do you think of this: I shall soon want somebody to live in my house, partly as housekeeper, partly as companion; would you mind coming to me? But perhaps——"

"Oh, yes," cried Elizabeth with tears in her eyes. "I would, indeed – I would do anything to be independent; for then perhaps my father might get to love me. But, ah!"

"What?"

"I am no accomplished person. And a companion to *you*, dear madam,[13] must be that."

"Oh, not necessarily."

"Not? But I can't help using rural words sometimes, when I don't mean to."

"Never mind. I shall like to know them."

"And – oh, I know I sha'n't do!" – she cried with a distressful laugh. "I accidentally learned to write round-hand instead of ladies'-hand. And, of course, you want some one who can write that?"

"Well, no."

"What, not necessary to write ladies'-hand?" cried the joyous Elizabeth.

"Not at all."

"But where do you live, madam?"

"In Casterbridge, or rather I shall be living here after twelve o'clock to-day."

Elizabeth expressed her astonishment.

"I have been staying at Budmouth for a few days while my house was getting ready. The house I am going into is that one they call High Street Hall – the old stone one overlooking the Market.[14] Two or three rooms are fit for occupation, though not all: I sleep there to-night for the first time. Now will you think over my proposal, and meet me here the first fine day next week, and say if you are still in the same mind?"

Elizabeth, her eyes shining at this prospect of a change from an unbearable position, joyfully assented; and the two parted at the gate of the churchyard.

CHAPTER XXI

As a maxim glibly repeated from childhood remains practically un-marked till some mature experience enforces it, so did this High Street Hall now for the first time really show itself to Elizabeth-Jane, though her ears had heard its name on a hundred occasions.

Her mind dwelt upon nothing else but the lady, and the house, and her own chance of living there, all the rest of the day. In the afternoon she had occasion to pay a few bills in the town and do a little shopping, when she learnt that what was a new discovery to herself had become a common topic about the streets. High Street Hall was undergoing repair; a lady was coming there to live shortly; all the shop-people knew it, and had already discounted the chance of her being a customer.

Elizabeth-Jane could, however, add a capping touch to information so new to her in the bulk. The lady, she said, had arrived that day.

When the lamps were lighted, and it was yet not so dark as to render chimneys, attics, and roofs invisible, Elizabeth, almost with a lover's feeling, thought she would like to look at the outside of High Street Hall. She went up the street in that direction.

The Hall, with its grey *façade* and parapet, was the only residence of its sort so near the centre of the town. It had, in the first place, the characteristics of a country mansion – birds'-nests in its chimneys, damp nooks where fungi grew, and irregularities of surface direct from Nature's trowel. At night the forms of passengers were patterned by the lamps in black shadows upon the pale walls.

This evening motes of straw lay around, and other signs of the premises having been in that lawless condition which accompanies the entry of a new tenant. The house was entirely of stone, and formed an example of dignity without great size. It was not altogether aristocratic, still less consequential, yet the old-fashioned stranger instinctively said, "Blood built it, and Wealth enjoys it," however vague his opinions of those accessories might be.

Yet as regards the enjoying it, the stranger would have been wrong, for until this very evening, when the new lady had arrived, the house had been empty for a year or two, while before that interval its occupancy had been irregular. The reason of its unpopularity was soon made manifest. Its rooms overlooked the market-place; and such a prospect from such a house was not considered desirable or seemly by its would-be occupiers.

Elizabeth's eyes sought the upper rooms, and saw lights there. The lady had obviously arrived. The impression that this woman of comparatively practised manner had made upon the studious[1] girl's mind was so deep that she enjoyed standing under an opposite archway merely to think that the charming lady was inside the confronting walls, and to wonder what she was doing. Her admiration for the architecture of that front was entirely on account of the inmate it screened. Though for that matter the architecture deserved admiration, or at least study, on its own account. It was Palladian, and, like all architecture[2] erected since the Gothic age, was a compilation rather than a design. But its reasonableness made it impressive. It was not rich, but rich enough. A timely consciousness of the ultimate vanity of human architecture, no less than of other human things, had prevented artistic superfluity.

Men had till quite recently been going in and out with parcels and packing-cases, rendering the door and hall within like a public thoroughfare. Elizabeth trotted through the open door in the dusk, but becoming alarmed at her own temerity, she went quickly out again by another which stood open in the lofty wall of the back court. To her surprise she found herself in one of the little-used blind alleys of the town. Looking round at the door which had given her egress, by the light of the solitary lamp fixed in the alley, she saw that it was arched and old – older even than the house itself. The door was studded, and the keystone of the arch was a mask. Originally the mask had exhibited a comic leer, as could still be discerned; but generations of Casterbridge boys had thrown stones at the mask, aiming at its open mouth; and the blows thereof had chipped off the lips and jaws as if they had been eaten away by disease. The appearance was so ghastly by the weakly lamp glimmer that she could not bear to look at it – the first unpleasant feature of her visit.

The position of the queer old door and the odd presence of the leering mask suggested one thing above all others as appertaining to the mansion's past history – intrigue. By the alley it had been possible to come unseen from all sorts of quarters in the town – the old play-house, the old bull-stake, the old cock-pit, the pool wherein nameless infants had been used to disappear. High Street Hall could boast of its conveniences undoubtedly.

She turned to come away in the nearest direction homeward, which was up the alley,[3] but hearing footsteps approaching in that quarter, and having no great wish to be found in such a place at such a time, she quickly retreated. There being no other way out, she stood behind a brick pier till the intruder should have gone his ways.

Had she watched she would have been surprised. She would have seen that the pedestrian on coming up made straight for the arched doorway: that as he paused with his hand upon the latch the lamplight fell upon the face of Henchard.

But Elizabeth-Jane clung so closely to her nook that she discerned nothing of this. Henchard passed in, as ignorant of her presence as she was ignorant of his identity, and disappeared in the darkness. Elizabeth came out a second time into the alley, and made the best of her way home.

Henchard's chiding, by begetting in her a nervous fear of doing anything definable as unlady-like, had operated thus curiously in keeping them unknown to each other at a critical moment. Much might have resulted from recognition – at the least a query on either side in one and the self-same form: What could he or she possibly be doing there?

Henchard, whatever his business at the lady's house, reached his own home only a few minutes later than Elizabeth-Jane. Her plan was to broach the question of leaving his roof this evening; the events of the day had urged her to the course. But its execution depended upon his mood, and she anxiously awaited his manner towards her. She found that it had changed. He showed no further tendency to be angry; he showed something worse. Absolute indifference had taken the place of irritability; and his coldness was such that it encouraged her to departure, even more than hot temper could have done.

"Father, have you any objection to my going away?" she asked.

"Going away? No – none whatever. Where are you going?"

She thought it undesirable and unnecessary to say anything at present about her destination to one who took so little interest in her. He would know that soon enough. "I have heard of an opportunity of getting more cultivated and finished, and being less idle," she answered, with hesitation. "A chance of a place in a household where I can earn my living, and have advantages of study, and seeing refined life."

"Then make the best of it, in Heaven's name – if you can't get cultivated where you are."

"You don't object?"

"Object – I? Ho – no! Not at all." After a pause he said, "But you won't have enough money for this lively scheme without help, you know? If you like I should be willing to make you an allowance, so that you be not bound to live upon the starvation wages refined folk are likely to pay 'ee."

She thanked him for this offer.

"It had better be done properly," he added, after a pause. "A small annuity is what I should like you to have – so as to be independent of me – and so that I may be independent of you. Would that please ye?"

"Certainly."

"Then I'll see about it this very day." He seemed relieved to get her off his hands by this arrangement, and as far as they were concerned the matter was settled. She now simply waited to see the lady again.

The day and the hour came; but a drizzling rain fell. Elizabeth-Jane, having now changed her orbit from one of gay independence to laborious self-help, thought the weather good enough for such declined glory as hers, if her friend would only face it – a matter of doubt. She went to the boot-room where her pattens had hung ever since her apotheosis; took them down, had their mildewed leathers blacked, and put them on as she had done in old times. Thus mounted, and with cloak and umbrella, she went off to the place of appointment – intending, if the lady were not there, to call at the house.

One side of the churchyard – the side towards the weather – was sheltered by an ancient thatched mud wall, whose eaves overhung as much as one or two feet. At the back of the wall was a corn-yard with its granary and barns – the place wherein she had met Farfrae many months earlier. Under the projection of the thatch she saw a figure. The young lady had come.

Her presence so exceptionally substantiated the girl's utmost hopes that she almost feared her good fortune. Fancies find room in the strongest minds. Here, in a churchyard old as civilization, in the worst of weathers, was a strange woman of curious fascinations never seen elsewhere: there might be some devilry about her presence. However, Elizabeth went on to the church tower, on whose summit the rope of a flag-staff rattled in the wind; and thus she came to the wall.

The lady had such a cheerful aspect in the drizzle that Elizabeth forgot her fancy. "Well?" said the lady, a little of the whiteness of her teeth appearing with the word through the black fleece that protected her face, "have you decided?"

"Yes, quite," said the other, eagerly.

"Your father is willing?"

"Yes."

"Then come along."

"When, ma'am?"

"Now – as soon as you like. I had a good mind to send to you to come to my house, thinking you might not venture up here in the wind. But, as I like getting out of doors, I thought I would come and see first."

"It was my own thought."

"That shows we shall agree. Then can you come to-day? My house is so hollow and dismal that I want some living thing there."

"I think I might be able to," said the girl, reflecting.

Voices were borne over to them at that instant on the wind and raindrops from the other side of the wall. There came such words as "sacks," "quarters," "threshing," "tailing," "next Saturday's market," each sentence being disorganized by the gusts like a face in a curved mirror. Both the women listened. "Who are those?" said the lady.

"One is my father. He rents that yard and barn."

The lady seemed to forget the immediate business in listening to the technicalities of the corn trade. At last she said suddenly, "Did you tell him where you were going to?"

"No."

"Oh – how was that?"

"I thought it safer to get away first – as he is so uncertain in his temper."

"Perhaps you are right. . . . . Besides, I have never told you my name. It is Miss Templeman. . . . . Are they gone – on the other side?"

"No. They have only gone up into the granary."

"Well, it is getting damp here. I shall expect you to-day – this evening, say, at six."

"Which way shall I come, ma'am?"

"The front way – through the door. There is no other."[4]

Elizabeth-Jane had been thinking of the door in the alley.

"Perhaps, as you have not mentioned your destination, you may as well keep silent upon it till you are clear off. Who knows but that he may alter his mind?"

Elizabeth-Jane shook her head. "On consideration I don't fear it," she said, sadly. "He has grown quite cold to me."

"Very well. Six o'clock then."

When they had emerged upon the open road and parted they found enough to do in holding their bowed umbrellas to the wind. Nevertheless, the lady looked in at the corn yard gates as she passed them, and paused on one foot for a moment. But nothing was visible there save the ricks, and the hump-backed barn, cushioned with moss, and the granary, rising against the church tower behind, where the smacking of the rope against the flag-staff still went on.

Now Henchard had not the slightest suspicion that Elizabeth-Jane's movement was to be so prompt. Hence when, just before six, he reached home and saw a fly at the door from the Golden Crown, and his stepdaughter, with all her little bags and boxes, getting into it, he was taken by surprise.

"But you said I might go, father?" she explained, through the carriage window.

"Said! – yes. But I thought you meant next month, or next year. 'Od, seize it – you take time by the forelock. This, then, is how you be going to treat me for all my trouble about ye?"

"Oh, father, how can you speak like that? It is unjust of you!" she said with spirit.

"Well, well, have your own way," he replied. He entered the house, and, seeing that all her things had not yet been brought down, went up to her room to look on. He had never been there since she had occupied it. Evidences of her care, of her endeavours for improvement, were visible all around, in the form of books, sketches, maps, and little arrangements for tasteful effects. Henchard had known nothing of these efforts. He gazed at them, turned suddenly about, and came down to the door.

"Look here," he said, in an altered voice – he never called her by name now – "Don't 'ee go away from me. It may be I've spoke roughly to you – but I've been grieved beyond everything by you – there's something that caused it."

"By me?" she said, with deep concern. "What have I done?"

"I can't tell you now. But if you'll stop, and go on living as my daughter, I'll tell you all in time."

But the proposal had come ten minutes too late. She was in the fly – was already, in imagination, at the house of the lady whose manner had such charms for her. "Father," she said, as considerately as she could, "I think it best for us that I go on now. I need not stay long; I shall not be far away; and if you want me badly I can soon come back again."

He nodded ever so slightly, as a receipt of her decision, and no more. "You are not going far, you say. What will be your address, in case I wish to write to you? Or am I not to know?"

"O yes – certainly. It is only in the town – High Street Hall."

"Where?" said Henchard, his face stilling.

She repeated the words. He neither moved nor spoke, and waving her hand to him in utmost friendliness, she signified to the flyman to drive up the street.

CHAPTER XXII

We go back for a moment to the preceding night, to account for Henchard's attitude.

At the hour when Elizabeth-Jane was contemplating her stealthy reconnoitring excursion to the abode of the lady of her fancy, he had been not a little amazed at receiving a letter by hand in Lucetta's well-known characters. The self-repression, the resignation of her previous communication had vanished from her mood; she wrote with some of the natural lightness which had marked her in their early acquaintance.

> "High Street Hall.

"MY DEAR MR. HENCHARD,

"Don't be surprised. It is for your good and mine, as I hope, that I have come to live at Casterbridge – for how long I cannot tell. That depends upon another; and he is a man, and a merchant, and a Mayor, and one who has the first right to my affections.

"Seriously, *mon ami*, I am not so light-hearted as I may seem to be from this. I have come here in consequence of hearing of the death of your wife – whom you used to think of as dead so many years before! Poor woman, she seems to have been a sufferer, though uncomplaining, and though weak in intellect not an imbecile.[1] I am glad you acted fairly by her. As soon as I knew she was no more, it was brought home to me very forcibly by my conscience that I ought to endeavour to disperse the shade which my *étourderie* flung over my name, by asking you to carry out your promise to me.[2] I hope you are of the same mind, and that you will take steps to this end. As, however, I did not know how you were situated, or what had happened since our separation, I decided to come and establish myself here before communicating with you.

"You probably feel as I do about this. I shall be able to see you in a day or two. Till then, farewell.

"Yours,
"Lucetta.

"P.S. – I was unable to keep my appointment to meet you for a moment or two in passing through Casterbridge the other day. My plans were altered by a family event, which it will surprise you to hear of."

Henchard had already heard that High Street Hall was being prepared for a tenant. He said with a puzzled air to the first person he encountered, "Who is coming to live at the Hall?"

"A lady of the name of Templeman, I believe, sir," said his informant.

Henchard thought it over. "Lucetta is governess or housekeeper there,[3] I suppose," he said to himself. "Yes, I must put her in her proper position, undoubtedly."

It was by no means with the oppression that would once have accompanied the thought that he regarded the moral necessity now; it was, indeed, with interest, if not warmth. His bitter disappointment at finding Elizabeth-Jane to be none of his, and himself a childless man, had left an emotional void in Henchard that he unconsciously craved to fill. In this frame of mind, though without strong feeling, he had strolled up the blind alley and into High Street Hall by the postern at which Elizabeth had so nearly encountered him. He had gone on thence into the court, and inquired of a man whom he saw unpacking china from a crate, if Miss Le Sueur was living there. Miss Le Sueur had been the name under which he had known Lucetta – or "Lucette" as she had called herself at that time.

The man replied in the negative; that Miss Templeman only had come. Henchard went away, concluding that Lucetta had not as yet settled in.

He was in this interested stage of the inquiry when he witnessed Elizabeth-Jane's departure the next day. On hearing her announce the address there suddenly took possession of him the strange thought that Lucetta and Miss Templeman were one and the same person, for he could recall that in her season of intimacy with him the name of the rich relative whom he had deemed somewhat a mythical personage had been given as Templeman. Though not a fortune-hunter, the possibility that Lucetta had been sublimed into a lady of means by some munificent testament on the part of this relative lent a charm to her image which it might not otherwise have acquired. He was getting on towards the dead level of middle age, when material things increasingly possess the mind.

But Henchard was not left long in suspense. Lucetta was rather addicted to scribbling, as had been shown by the torrent of letters after the *fiasco* in their marriage arrangements, and hardly had Elizabeth gone away when another note came to the Mayor's house from High Street Hall.

"I am in residence," she said, "and comfortable, though getting here has been a wearisome undertaking. You probably know what I am going to tell you, or do you not? My good Aunt Templeman, the banker's widow, whose very existence you used to doubt, leave alone her affluence, has lately died, and bequeathed some of her property to me. I will not enter into details except to say that I have taken her name – as a means of escape from mine, and its wrongs.

"I am now my own mistress, and have chosen to settle among the *gentilhommerie* of Casterbridge[4] – to be tenant of High Street Hall, that at least you may be put to no trouble if you wish to see me. My first intention was to keep you in ignorance of the changes in my life till you should meet me by accident; but I have thought better of this.

"You probably are aware of my arrangement with your daughter, and have doubtless laughed at the – what shall I call it? – practical joke (in all affection) of my getting her to live with me. But my first meeting with her was purely an accident. Do you see, Michael, partly why I have done it? – why, to give you an excuse for coming here as if to visit *her*, and thus to form my acquaintance naturally. She is a dear, good girl, and she thinks you have treated her with undue severity. You may have done so in your haste, but not deliberately, I am sure. As the result has been to bring her to me, I am not disposed to upbraid you. – In haste, yours always,

"LUCETTA."

The excitement which these announcements produced in Henchard's gloomy soul was to him most pleasurable. He sat over his dining-table long and dreamily, and by an almost mechanical transfer the sentiments which had run to waste since his estrangement from Elizabeth-Jane and Donald Farfrae gathered around Lucetta before they had grown dry. She was plainly in a very coming-on disposition for marriage. But what else could a poor woman be who had given her time and attention[5] to him so thoughtlessly, at that former time, as to lose her credit by it? Probably conscience no less than affection had brought her here. On the whole he did not blame her.

"The artful little woman!" he said, smiling (with reference to Lucetta's adroit and pleasant manœuvre with Elizabeth-Jane).

To feel that he would like to see Lucetta was with Henchard to start for her house. He put on his hat and went. It was between eight and nine o'clock when he reached her door. The answer brought him was that Miss Templeman was engaged for that evening; but that she would be happy to see him the next day.

"That's rather like giving herself airs!" he thought.[6] But, after all, she plainly had not expected him, and he took the refusal quietly. Nevertheless, he resolved not to go next day. "These cursed women – there's not an inch of straight grain in 'em!" he said.

Let us follow the track of Mr. Henchard's thought as if it were a clue line, and view the interior of High Street Hall on this particular evening.

On Elizabeth-Jane's arrival she had been phlegmatically asked by an elderly woman to go upstairs and take off her things. She had replied with great earnestness that she would not think of giving that trouble, and on the instant divested herself of her bonnet and cloak in the passage. She was then conducted to the first door on the landing, and left to find her way further alone.

The room disclosed was prettily furnished as a boudoir or small drawing-room, and on a sofa with two cylindrical pillows reclined a dark-haired, large-eyed, pretty woman, of unmistakably French extraction on one side or the other. She was probably somewhat older[7] than Elizabeth, and had a sparkling light in her eye. In front of the sofa was a small table, with a pack of cards scattered upon it faces upward.

The attitude had been so full of abandonment that she bounded up like a spring on hearing the door open.

Perceiving that it was Elizabeth she lapsed into ease, and came across to her with a reckless skip that innate grace only prevented from being boisterous.

"Why, you are late," she said, taking hold of Elizabeth-Jane's hands.

"There were so many little things to put up."

"And you seem dead-alive and tired. Let me try to enliven you by some wonderful tricks I have learnt, to kill time. Sit there and don't move." She gathered up the pack of cards, pulled the table in front of her, and began to deal them rapidly, telling Elizabeth to choose some.

"Well, have you chosen?" she asked, flinging down the last card.

"No," stammered Elizabeth, arousing herself from a reverie. "I quite forgot, I was thinking of – you, and me – and how strange it is that I am here."

Miss Templeman looked at Elizabeth-Jane with interest, and laid down the cards. "Ah! you are another sort than that," she said. "I'll lie here while you sit by me; and we'll talk."

Elizabeth drew up silently to the head of the sofa, but with obvious pleasure. It could be seen that in years she was rather younger than her entertainer, while in manner and general vision she seemed more of the sage. Miss Templeman deposited herself on the sofa in her former flexuous position, and throwing her arm above her brow – somewhat in the pose of a well-known conception of Titian's[8] – talked up at Elizabeth-Jane invertedly across her forehead and arm.

"I must tell you something," she said. "I wonder if you have suspected it. I have only been mistress of a large house and fortune a little while."

"Oh! only a little while?" murmured Elizabeth-Jane, her countenance slightly falling.

"As a girl I lived about in garrison-towns and elsewhere with my father, till I was quite flighty and unsettled. He was an officer in the army. I should not have mentioned this had I not thought it best you should know the truth."

"Yes, yes." She looked thoughtfully round the room – at the little square piano with brass inlayings, at the window-curtains, at the lamp, at the fair and dark kings and queens on the card-table, and finally at the inverted face of Lucetta Templeman, whose large lustrous eyes had such an odd effect upside down.

Elizabeth's mind ran on acquirements to an almost morbid degree. "You speak French and Italian fluently, no doubt," she said. "I have not been able to get beyond a wretched bit of Latin yet."[9]

"Well, for that matter, in my native isle speaking French does not go for much. It is rather the other way."

"Where is your native isle?"

It was with rather more reluctance that Miss Templeman said, "Jersey. There they speak French on one side of the street and English on the other, and a mixed tongue in the middle of the road. But it is a long time since I was there. Bath is where my people really belong to, though my ancestors in Jersey were as good as anybody in England. They were the Le Sueurs,[10] an old family who have done great things in their time. I went back and lived there after my father's death. But I don't value such past matters, and am quite an English person in my feelings and tastes."

Lucetta's tongue had for a moment outrun her discretion. She had arrived at Casterbridge as a Bath lady, and there were obvious reasons why Jersey should drop out of her life. But Elizabeth had tempted her to make free, and a deliberately-formed resolve had been broken.

It could not, however, have been broken in safer company. Lucetta's words went no further, and after this day she was so much upon her guard that there appeared no chance of her identification with the young Jersey woman who had been Henchard's attached comrade at a critical time. Not the least amusing of her safeguards was her resolute avoidance of a French word, if one by accident came to her tongue more readily than its English equivalent. She shirked it with the suddenness of the weak Apostle at the accusation, "Thy speech bewrayeth thee!"[11]

Expectancy sat visibly upon Lucetta the next morning. She dressed herself for Mr. Henchard, and restlessly awaited his call before mid-day;

as he did not come she waited on through the afternoon. But she did not tell Elizabeth that the person expected was her stepfather.

They sat in adjoining windows of the same room in Lucetta's great stone mansion, netting, and looking out upon the market, which formed an animated scene. Elizabeth could see the crown of her stepfather's hat among the rest beneath, and was not aware that Lucetta watched the same object with yet intenser interest. He moved about amid the throng, at this point lively as an ant-hill; elsewhere more reposeful, and broken up by stalls of fruit and vegetables. The farmers as a rule preferred the open *carrefour* for their transactions, despite its inconvenient jostlings and the danger from crossing vehicles, to the gloomy sheltered market-room provided for them. Here they surged on this one day of the week, forming a little world of leggings, switches, and sample-bags; men of extensive stomachs, sloping like mountain sides; men whose heads in walking swayed as the trees in November gales; who in conversing varied their attitudes much, lowering themselves by spreading their knees, and thrusting their hands into the pockets of remote inner jackets. Their faces radiated tropical warmth; for though when at home their countenances varied with the seasons, their market-faces all the year round were glowing little fires.

All over-clothes here were worn as if they were an inconvenience, a hampering necessity. Some men were well-dressed; but the majority were careless in that respect, appearing in suits which were historical records of their wearer's deeds, sun-scorchings, and daily struggles for many years past. Yet they carried ruffled cheque-books in their pockets which regulated at the bank hard by a balance of never less than four figures. In fact, what these gibbous human shapes specially represented was ready money – money insistently ready – not ready next year like a nobleman's – often not merely ready at the bank like a professional man's, but ready in their large plump hands.

It happened that to-day there rose in the midst of them all two or three tall apple-trees standing as if they grew on the spot; till it was perceived that they were held by men from the cider-districts who came here to sell them, bringing the clay of their county on their boots. Elizabeth-Jane, who had often observed them, said, "I wonder if the same trees come every week?"

"What trees?" said Lucetta, absorbed in watching for Henchard.

Elizabeth replied vaguely, for an incident checked her. Behind one of the trees stood Farfrae, briskly discussing a sample-bag with a farmer. Henchard had come up, accidentally encountering the young man, whose face seemed to inquire, "Do we speak together?"

She saw her stepfather throw a shine into his eye, which answered "No!" Elizabeth-Jane sighed.

"Are you particularly interested in anybody out there?" said Lucetta.

"Oh no," said her companion, a quick red shooting over her face.

Luckily Farfrae's figure was immediately covered by the apple-tree.

Lucetta looked hard at her. "Quite sure?" she said.

"Oh yes," said Elizabeth-Jane.

Again Lucetta looked out. "They are all farmers, I suppose?" she said.

"No. There's Mr. Bulge; he's a wine merchant: there's Benjamin Brownlet – a horse-dealer; and Kitson, the pig-breeder; and Yopper, the auctioneer; besides maltsters, and millers – and so on." Farfrae stood out quite distinctly now; but she did not mention him.

The Saturday afternoon slipped on thus desultorily. The market changed from the sample-showing hour to the idle hour before starting homewards, when tales were told. Henchard had not called on Lucetta, though he had stood so near. He must have been too busy, she thought. He would come on Sunday or Monday.

The days came, but not the visitor, though Lucetta repeated her dressing with scrupulous care. She was disheartened. It may at once be declared that Lucetta no longer bore towards Henchard all that warm allegiance which had characterized her in their first acquaintance; the then unfortunate issue of things had chilled pure love considerably. But there remained a conscientious wish to bring about her union with him, now that there was nothing to hinder it – to right her position – which in itself was a happiness to sigh for. With strong social reasons on her side why their marriage should take place,[12] there had ceased to be any worldly reason on his why it should be postponed, since she had succeeded to comparative fortune.

Tuesday was the great Candlemas fair.[13] At breakfast she said to Elizabeth-Jane quite coolly: "I imagine your father may call to see you to-day? I suppose he stands close by in the market-place, with the rest of the corndealers?"

She shook her head. "He won't come."

"Why?"

"He has taken against me," she said in a husky voice.

"You have quarrelled more deeply than I know of."

Elizabeth, wishing to shield the man she believed to be her father from any charge of unnatural dislike, said "Yes."

"Then where you are is, of all places, the one he will avoid?"

Elizabeth nodded sadly.

Lucetta looked blank, twitched up her lovely eyebrows and lip, and burst into hysterical sobs. Here was a *contretemps* – her ingenious scheme completely stultified!

"Oh, my dear Miss Templeman – what's the matter?" cried her companion.

"I like your company much," said Lucetta, as soon as she could speak.

"Yes, yes – and so do I yours!" Elizabeth chimed in soothingly.

"But – but—" She could not finish the sentence, which was, naturally, that if Henchard had such a rooted dislike for the girl as now seemed to be the case, Elizabeth-Jane would have to be got rid of – a disagreeable necessity.

A provisional resource suggested itself. "Miss Henchard – will you go on an errand for me as soon as breakfast is over? – Ah, that's very good of you. Will you go and order—" Here she enumerated several commissions at sundry shops, which would occupy Elizabeth's time for the next hour or two, at least.

"And have you ever seen the Museum?"

Elizabeth-Jane had not.

"Then you should do so at once. You can finish the morning by going there. It is an old house in a back street – I forget where – but you'll find out – and there are crowds of interesting things – skeletons, teeth, old pots and pans, ancient boots and shoes, birds' eggs – all charmingly instructive. You'll be sure to stay till you get quite hungry."

Elizabeth hastily put on her things and departed. "I wonder why she wants to get rid of me to-day!" she said sorrowfully, as she went. That her absence, rather than her services or instruction, was in request, had been readily apparent to Elizabeth-Jane, simple as she seemed, and difficult as it was to attribute a motive for the desire.

She had not been gone ten minutes when one of Lucetta's servants was sent to Henchard's with a note. The contents were briefly: –

"DEAR MICHAEL, –

"You will be standing close to my house to-day for two or three hours in the course of your business, so do please call and see me. I am sadly disappointed that you have not come before, for can I help anxiety about my own equivocal relation to you? – especially now my aunt's fortune has brought me more prominently before society. Your daughter's presence here may be the cause of your neglect; and I have therefore sent her away for the morning. Say you come on business – I shall be quite alone.

"LUCETTA."

When the messenger returned, her mistress gave directions that if a gentleman called he was to be admitted at once, and sat down to await results.

Sentimentally she did not much care to see him – his delays had wearied her; but it was necessary; and with a sigh she arranged herself picturesquely in the chair; first this way, then that; next so that the light fell over her head. Next she flung herself on the couch in the cyma-recta curve which so became her, and, with her arm over her head, looked towards the door. This, she decided, was the best position after all; and thus she remained till a man's step was heard on the stairs. Whereupon Lucetta, forgetting her curve (for Nature was too strong for Art as yet), jumped up, and ran and hid herself behind one of the window-curtains in a freak of timidity. In spite of the waning of passion the situation was an agitating one – she had not seen Henchard since his (supposed) temporary parting from her in Jersey.[14]

She could hear the servant showing the visitor into the room, shutting the door upon him, and leaving as if to go and look for her mistress. Lucetta flung back the curtain with a nervous greeting. The man before her was not Henchard.[15]

PLATE X

'The man before her was not Henchard.'

CHAPTER XXIII

A conjecture that her visitor might be some other person had, indeed, flashed through Lucetta's mind when she was on the point of bursting out; but it was just too late to recede.

He was years younger than the Mayor of Casterbridge; fair, fresh, and slenderly handsome. He wore genteel cloth leggings with white buttons, polished boots with infinite lace holes, light cord breeches, and black velveteen coat and waistcoat; and he had a silver-topped switch[1] in his hand. Lucetta blushed, and said with a curious mixture of pout and laugh on her face – "Oh, I've made a mistake!"

The visitor, on the contrary, did not laugh half a wrinkle. "But I'm very sorry!" he said, in deprecating tones. "I came and I inquired for Miss Henchard, and they showed me up here, and at no hand would I have caught ye so unmannerly if I had known!"

"I was the unmannerly one," said she.

"But is it that I have come to the wrong house, madam?" said Mr. Farfrae, blinking a little in his bewilderment, and nervously tapping his legging with his switch.

"Oh no, sir – sit down. You must come and sit down now you are here," replied Lucetta, kindly, to relieve his embarrassment. "Miss Henchard will be here directly."

Now this was not strictly true; but that something about the young man – that Hyperborean crispness, constringency, and charm, as of a well-braced musical instrument, which had awakened the interest of Henchard, and of Elizabeth-Jane, and of the King of Prussia's jovial crew, at sight, made his unexpected presence here attractive to Lucetta. He hesitated, looked at the chair, thought there was no danger in it (though there was), and sat down.

Farfrae's presence here was simply the result of Henchard's permission to him to see Elizabeth, if he were minded to woo her. At first he had taken no notice of Henchard's brusque letter; but an exceptionally fortunate business transaction put him on good terms with everybody, and revealed to him that he could undeniably marry if he chose. Then who so pleasing, thrifty, and satisfactory in every way as Elizabeth-Jane? Apart from her personal recommendations, a reconciliation with his former friend Henchard would, in the natural course of things, flow from such a union. He therefore forgave the Mayor his curtness; and this morning on his way to the fair he had called at her house, where he learnt that she was staying at Miss Templeman's. A little stimulated at not finding her ready and waiting – so fanciful are men – he hastened on to High Street Hall, to encounter no Elizabeth, but its mistress herself.

"The fair to-day seems a large one," she said, when, by a natural deviation, their eyes sought the busy scene without. "Your numerous fairs and markets keep me interested. How many things I think of while I watch from here!"

He seemed in doubt how to answer, and the babble without reached them as they sat – voices as of wavelets on a lopping sea, one ever and anon rising above the rest. "Do you look out often?" he asked.

"Yes – very often."

"Do you look for any one you know?"

Why should she have answered as she did? "I look as at a picture merely. But," she went on, turning pleasantly to him, "I may do so now – I may look for you. You are always there, are you not? Ah – I don't mean it seriously! But it is amusing to look for somebody one knows in a crowd, even if one does not want him. It takes off the terrible oppressiveness of being surrounded by a throng, and having no point of junction with it through a single individual."

"Ah! Maybe you'll be very lonely, ma'am?"

"Nobody knows how lonely."

"But you are rich, they say?"

"If so I don't know how to enjoy my riches. I came to Casterbridge thinking I should like to live here. But I wonder if I shall."

"Where did ye come from, ma'am?"

"The neighbourhood of Bath."

"And I from near Edinboro'," he murmured. "It's better to stay at home, and that's true; but a man must live where his money is made. It is a great pity, but it's even so! Yet I've done very well this year. Oh, yes," he went on with ingenuous enthusiasm. "You see that man with the drab kerseymere coat? I bought largely of him in the autumn when wheat was down, and then afterwards when it rose a little I sold off all I had. It brought only a small profit to me; while the farmers kept theirs, expecting higher figures, yes, though the rats were gnawing the ricks hollow. Just when I sold the markets went lower, and I bought up the corn of those who had been holding back, at less price than my first purchases. And then," cried Farfrae, impetuously, his face alight, "I sold it a few weeks after when it happened to go up again! And so, by contenting myself with small profits frequently repeated I soon made five hundred pounds – yes!" – (bringing down his hand upon the table, and quite forgetting where he was) – "while the others by keeping theirs in hand made nothing at all!"

Lucetta regarded him with a critical interest. He was quite a new type of person to her. At last his eye fell upon the lady's, and their glances met.

"Ah, now, I'm wearying you!" he exclaimed.

She said, "No, indeed," colouring a shade.

"What then?"

"Quite otherwise. You are most interesting."

It was now Farfrae who showed the modest pink.

"I mean all you Scotchmen," she added in hasty correction. "So free from Southern extremes. We common people are all one way or the other – warm or cold, passionate or frigid. You have both temperatures going on in you at the same time."

"But how do you mean that? Ye were best to explain clearly, ma'am."

"You are animated – then you are thinking of getting on. You are sad the next moment – then you are thinking of Scotland and friends."

"Yes. I think of home sometimes!" he said, simply.

"So do I – as far as I can. But it was an old house where I was born, and they pulled it down for improvements, so I seem hardly to have any home to think of now."

Lucetta did not add, as she might have done, that the house was in St. Helier, and not in Bath.

"But the mountains and the mists and the rocks, they are there! And don't they seem like home?"

She shook her head.

"They do to me – they do to me," he murmured. And his mind could be seen flying away northwards. Whether its origin were national or personal, it was quite true what Lucetta had said, that the curious double strands in Farfrae's thread of life – the commercial and the romantic – were very distinct at times. Like the colours in a variegated cord those contrasts could be seen intertwisted, yet not mingling.

"You are wishing you were back again," said she.

"Ah, no, ma'am," said Farfrae, suddenly recalling himself.

The fair without the windows was now raging thick and loud. It was the chief hiring fair of the year, and differed quite from the market of a few days earlier. In substance it was a whitey-brown crowd flecked with white – this being the body of labourers waiting for places. The wing-bonnets² of women like waggon-tilts, their cotton gowns and checked shawls, mixed with the carters' smockfrocks; for they, too, entered into the hiring. Among the rest, at the corner of the pavement, stood an old shepherd, who attracted the eyes of Lucetta and Farfrae by his stillness. He was evidently a chastened man. The battle of life had been a sharp one with him, for, to begin with, he was a man of small frame. He was now so bowed by hard work and years that, approaching from behind, a person could hardly see his head. He had planted the stem of his crook in the gutter and was resting upon the bow, which was polished to silver brightness by the long friction of his hands. He had quite forgotten where he was, and what he had come for, his eyes being bent on the ground. A little way off negotiations were proceeding which had reference to him; but he did not hear them, and there seemed to be passing through his mind pleasant visions of the hiring successes of his prime, when his skill laid open to him any farm for the asking.

The negotiations were between a farmer from a distant county and the old man's son. In these there was a difficulty. The farmer would not take the crust without the crumb of the bargain, in other words, the old man without the younger; and the son had a sweetheart on his present farm, who stood by, waiting the issue with pale lips.

"I'm sorry to leave ye, Nelly," said the young man with emotion.

"But, you see, I can't starve father, and he's out o' work at Lady-day.[3] 'Tis only seventy mile."

The girl's lips quivered. "Seventy mile!" she murmured. "Ah! 'tis enough! I shall never see 'ee again!" It was, indeed, a hopeless length of traction for Dan Cupid's magnet; for young men were young men at Casterbridge as elsewhere.

"Oh! no, no – I never shall," she insisted, when he pressed her hand; and she turned her face to Lucetta's wall to hide her weeping. The farmer said he would give the young man half-an-hour for his answer, and went away, leaving the group sorrowing.

Lucetta's eyes, full of tears, met Farfrae's. His, too, to her surprise, were moist at the scene.

"It is very hard," she said with strong feeling. "Lovers ought not to be parted like that! Oh, if I had my wish I'd let people live and love at their pleasure!"

"Maybe I can manage that they'll not be parted," said Farfrae. "I want a young carter; and perhaps I'll take the old man too – yes; he'll not be very expensive, and doubtless he will answer me parrpose somehow."

"Oh, you are so good!" she cried delighted. "Go and tell them, and let me know if you have succeeded."

Farfrae went out, and she saw him speak to the group. The eyes of all brightened; the bargain was soon struck. Farfrae returned to her immediately it was concluded.

"It is kind-hearted of you, indeed," said Lucetta. "For my part, I have resolved that all my servants shall have lovers if they want them. Do you make the same resolve?"

Farfrae looked more serious, waving his head a half-turn. "I must be a little stricter than that," he said.

"Why?"

"You are a – a thriving lady; and I am a struggling hay-and-corn merchant."

"I am a very unambitious lady."

"Ah well, I cannot explain. I don't know how to talk to ladies, ambitious or no; and that's true," said Donald with grave regret. "I try to be civil to a' folk – no more!"

"I see you are as you say," replied she, sensibly getting the upper hand in these exchanges of sentiment. Under this revelation of insight Farfrae again looked out of the window into the thick of the fair.

Two farmers met and shook hands, and being quite near the window their remarks could be heard as others' had been.

"Have you seen young Mr. Farfrae this morning?" asked one. "He promised to meet me here at the stroke of twelve; but I've gone athwart and about the fair half-a-dozen times, and never a sign of him: though he's mostly a man to his word."

"I quite forgot the engagement," murmured Farfrae.

"Now you must go," said she; "must you not?"

"Yes," he replied. But he still remained.

"You had better go," she urged. "You will lose a customer."

"Now, Miss Templeman, you will make me angry," exclaimed Farfrae.

"Then suppose you don't go; but stay a little longer?"

He looked anxiously at the farmer who was seeking him, and who just then ominously walked across to where Henchard was standing, and he looked into the room and at her. "I like staying; but I fear I must go!" he said. "Business ought not to be neglected, ought it?"

"Not for a single minute."

"It's true. I'll come another time – if I may, ma'am?"

"Certainly," she said. "What has happened to us to-day is very curious."

"Something to think over when we are alone, it's like to be."

"Oh, I don't know that. It is commonplace after all."

"No, miss; I'll not say that. Oh, no!"

"Well, whatever it has been, it is now over; and the market calls you to be gone."

"Yes, yes. Market – business! I wish there were no business in the warrld."

Lucetta almost laughed – she would quite have laughed – but that there was a little emotion going in her at the time. "How you change!" she said. "You should not change like this."

"I have never wished such things before," said the Scotchman, with a simple, shamed, apologetic look for his weakness. "It is only since coming here, and seeing you."

"If that's the case you had better not look at me any longer. Dear me, I feel I have quite demoralized you!"

"But look or look not, I will see you in my thoughts. Well, I'll go – thank you for the pleasure of this visit."

"Thank you for staying."[4]

"Maybe I'll get into my market-mind when I've been out a few minutes," he murmured. "But I don't know – I don't know!"

As he went she said eagerly, "You may hear them speak of me in Casterbridge as time goes on. If they tell you I'm a coquette, which some may, because of the incidents of my life, don't believe it, for I am not."

"I swear I will not!" he said, fervidly.

Thus the two. She had enkindled the young man's enthusiasm till he was quite brimming with sentiment, while he, from merely affording her a new form of idleness, had gone on to wake her serious solicitude. Why was this? They could not have told.

Lucetta as a young girl would hardly have looked at a tradesman. But her ups-and-downs, capped by her indiscretions in relation to Henchard, had made her uncritical as to station. In her poverty she had met with repulse from the society to which she had belonged, and she had no great zest for renewing an attempt upon it now. Her heart longed for some ark into which it could fly and be at rest. Rough or smooth she did not care, so long as it was warm.[5]

Farfrae was shown out, it having entirely escaped him that he had called to see Elizabeth. Lucetta at the window watched him threading the maze of farmers and farmers' men. She could see by his gait that he was conscious of her eyes, and her heart went out to him for his modesty – pleaded with her sense of his unfitness that he might be allowed to come again. He entered the market-house, and she could see him no more.

Three minutes later, when she had left the window, a knock, not of multitude but of strength, sounded through the house, and the waiting-maid tripped up.

"Mr. Henchard," she said.

Lucetta had reclined herself, and was looking dreamily through her fingers. She did not answer at once, and the maid repeated the information with the addition, "And he's afraid he hasn't much time to spare, he says."

"Oh! Then tell him that as I have a headache I won't detain him to-day."

The message was taken down, and she heard the door close.

Lucetta had come to Casterbridge to quicken Henchard's feelings with regard to her. She had quickened them, and now she was indifferent to the achievement.

Her morning view of Elizabeth-Jane as a disturbing element changed, and she no longer felt strongly the necessity of getting rid of the girl for her stepfather's sake. When the young woman came in, sweetly unconscious of the turn in the tide, Lucetta went up to her, and said quite sincerely:

"I'm so glad you've come. You'll live with me a long time, won't you?"

Elizabeth as a watch-dog to keep her father off – what a new idea. Yet it was not unpleasing. Henchard had neglected her all these days, after compromising her indescribably in the past.[6] The least he could have done when he found himself free, and herself affluent, would have been to respond heartily and promptly to her invitation.

Her emotions rose, fell, undulated, filled her with wild surmise at their suddenness; and so passed Lucetta's experience, of that day.

END OF VOL. I.

VOLUME II

CHAPTER XXIV

Poor Elizabeth-Jane, little thinking what her malignant star had done to blast the budding attentions she had won from Donald Farfrae, was glad to hear Lucetta's words about remaining.

For in addition to Lucetta's house being a home, that raking view of the market-place which it afforded had as much attraction for her as for Lucetta. The *carrefour* was like the regulation Open Place in spectacular dramas, where the incidents that occur always happen to bear on the lives of the adjoining residents. Farmers, merchants, dairymen, quacks, hawkers, appeared there from week to week, and disappeared as the afternoon wasted away. It was the node of all orbits.[1]

From Saturday to Saturday was as from day to day with the two young women now. In an emotional sense they did not live at all during the intervals. Wherever they might go wandering on other days, on market-day they were sure to be at home. Both stole sly glances out of the window at Farfrae's shoulders and poll. His face they seldom saw, for, either through shyness, or not to disturb his mercantile mood, he avoided looking towards their quarters.

Thus things went on, till a certain market-morning brought a new sensation. Elizabeth and Lucetta were sitting at breakfast when a parcel containing two dresses arrived for the latter from London. She called Elizabeth from her breakfast, and entering her friend's bedroom Elizabeth saw the gowns spread out on the bed, one of a deep cherry colour, the other lighter – a glove lying at the end of each sleeve, a bonnet at the top of each neck, and parasols across the gloves, Lucetta standing beside the suggested human figure in an attitude of contemplation.

"I wouldn't think so hard about it," said Elizabeth, marking the intensity with which Lucetta was alternating the question whether this or that would suit best.

"But settling upon new clothes is so trying," said Lucetta. "You are that person" (pointing to one of the arrangements), "or you are *that* totally different person" (pointing to the other) "for the whole of the coming spring: and one of the two, you don't know which, may turn out to be very objectionable."

It was finally decided by Miss Templeman that she would be the cherry-coloured person at all hazards. The dress was pronounced to be a fit, and Lucetta walked with it into the front room, Elizabeth following her.

The morning was exceptionally bright for the time of year. The sun fell so flat on the market-house and church and pavement opposite Lucetta's residence that they poured their brightness into her rooms. Suddenly, after a rumbling of wheels, there were added to this steady light a fantastic series of circling irradiations upon the ceiling, and the companions turned to the window. Immediately opposite a vehicle of strange description had come to a standstill, as if it had been placed there for exhibition.

It was the new-fashioned agricultural implement called a horse-drill, till then unknown, in its modern shape, in this part of the country, where the venerable seed-lip was still used for sowing as in the days of the Heptarchy. Its arrival created about as much sensation in the corn-market as a flying machine would create at Charing Cross. The farmers crowded round it, women drew near it, children crept under and into it. The machine was painted in bright hues of green, yellow, and red, and it resembled as a whole a compound of hornet, grasshopper, and shrimp, magnified enormously. Or it might have been likened to an upright musical instrument with the front gone. That was how it struck Lucetta. "Why, it is a sort of agricultural piano," she said.

"It has something to do with corn," said Elizabeth.

"I wonder who thought of introducing it here?"

Donald Farfrae was in the minds of both as the innovator, for though not a farmer he was closely leagued with farming operations. And as if in response to their thought he came up at that moment, looked at the machine, walked round it, and handled it as if he knew something about its make. The two watchers had inwardly started at his coming, and Elizabeth left the window, went to the back of the room, and stood as if absorbed in the panelling of the wall. She hardly knew that she had done this till Lucetta, animated by the conjunction of her new attire with the sight of Farfrae, spoke out: "Let us go and look at the instrument, whatever it is."

Elizabeth-Jane's bonnet and shawl were pitchforked on in a moment, and they went out. Among all the agriculturists gathering round, the only appropriate possessor of the new machine seemed to be Lucetta, because she alone rivalled it in colour.

They examined it curiously; observing the rows of trumpet-shaped tubes one within the other, the little scoops, like revolving salt-spoons, which tossed the seed into the upper ends of the tubes that conducted it to the ground; till somebody said "Good morning, Elizabeth-Jane." She looked up, and there was her stepfather.

His greeting had been somewhat dry and thunderous, and Elizabeth-Jane, embarrassed out of her equanimity, stammered at random, "This is the lady I live with, father – Miss Templeman."

Henchard put his hand to his hat, which he brought down with a great wave till it met his body at the knee. Miss Templeman bowed. "I am happy to become acquainted with you, Mr. Henchard," she said. "This is a curious machine."

"Yes," Henchard replied; and he proceeded to explain it, and still more forcibly to ridicule it.

"Who brought it here?" said Lucetta.

"Oh, don't ask me, ma'am!" said Henchard. "The thing – why 'tis impossible it should act. 'Twas brought here by one of our machinists on the recommendation of a jumped-up jackanapes of a fellow who thinks——" His eye caught Elizabeth-Jane's imploring face, and he stopped, probably thinking that the suit might be progressing.

He turned to go away. Then something seemed to occur which his stepdaughter fancied must really be a hallucination of hers. A murmur apparently came from Henchard's lips in which she detected the words, "You refused to see me!" reproachfully addressed to Lucetta. She could not believe that they had been uttered by her stepfather; unless, indeed, they might have been spoken to one of the yellow-gaitered farmers near them. Yet Lucetta seemed silent; and then all thought of the incident was dissipated by the humming of a song, which sounded as though from the interior of the machine. Henchard had by this time vanished into the market-house, and both the women glanced towards the corn-drill. They could see behind it the bent back of a man who was pushing his head into the internal works to master their simple secrets. The hummed song went on:

> "Tw—s on a s—m—r aftern—n
> A wee bef—re the s—n w—nt d—n,
> When Kitty wi' a braw n—w g—wn
> C—me ow're the h—lls to Gowrie."

Elizabeth-Jane had apprehended the singer in a moment, and looked guilty of she did not know what. Lucetta next recognized him, and more mistress of herself, said archly, "The 'Lass of Gowrie'[2] from the inside of a seed-drill – what a phenomenon!"

Satisfied at last with his investigation, the young man stood upright, and met their eyes across the summit.

"We are looking at the wonderful new drill," Miss Templeman said. "But practically it is a stupid thing – is it not?" she added, on the strength of Henchard's information.

"Stupid? Oh, no!" said Farfrae, gravely. "It will revolutionize sowing hereabout. No more sowers flinging about their seed broadcast, so that some falls by the wayside, and some among thorns, and all that.[3] Each grain will go straight to its intended place, and nowhere else at all!"

"Then the romance of the sower is gone for ever," observed Elizabeth-Jane, who felt herself at one with Farfrae in Bible-reading at least. "'He that observeth the wind shall not sow,' so the Preacher said;[4] but his words will not be to the point any more. How things change."

"Yes, yes—It must be so!" Donald admitted, his gaze fixing itself on a small point far away. "But the machines are already very common in the East and North of England," he added, apologetically.

Lucetta seemed to be rather outside this train of sentiment, her acquaintance with the Scriptures being somewhat limited. "Is the machine yours?" she asked of Farfrae.

"Oh, no, madam," said he, becoming embarrassed and deferential at the sound of her voice, though with Elizabeth-Jane he was quite at his ease. "No, no – I merely recommended that it should be got."

In the silence which followed Farfrae appeared only conscious of her; to have passed from perception of Elizabeth into a brighter sphere of existence than she appertained to. Lucetta, discerning that he was much mixed that day – partly in his mercantile mood and partly in his romantic one – said gaily to him,

"Well, don't forsake the machine for us," and went indoors with her companion.

The latter felt that she had been in the way, though why was unaccountable to her. Lucetta explained the matter somewhat by saying, when they were again in the sitting-room:

"I had occasion to speak to Mr. Farfrae the other day, and so I knew him this morning."

Lucetta was very kind towards Elizabeth that day. Together they saw the market thicken, and in course of time thin away with the slow decline of the sun towards the upper end of the town, its rays taking the street endways and enfilading the long thoroughfare from top to bottom. The gigs and vans disappeared one by one till there was not a vehicle in the street. The time of the riding world was over; the pedestrian world held sway. Field labourers and their wives and children trooped in from the villages for their weekly shopping, and instead of a rattle of wheels and a tramp of horses ruling the sound as earlier, there was nothing but the shuffle of many feet. All the implements were gone; all the farmers; all the moneyed class. The character of the town's trading had changed from bulk to multiplicity, and pence were handled now as pounds had been handled earlier in the day.

Lucetta and Elizabeth looked out upon this, for though it was night, and the street lamps were lighted, they had kept their shutters unclosed. In the faint blink of the fire they spoke more freely.

"Your father was distant with you," said Lucetta.

"Yes." And having forgotten the momentary mystery of Henchard's seeming speech to Lucetta, she continued, "It is because he does not think I am respectable. I have tried to be so more than you can imagine, but in vain! My mother's separation from my father was unfortunate for me. You don't know what it is to have shadows like that upon your life."

Lucetta seemed to wince. "I do not – of that kind precisely," she said; "but you may feel a – sense of disgrace – shame – in other ways."

"Have you ever had any such feeling?" said the younger innocently.

"Oh, no," said Lucetta quickly. "I was thinking of – what happens sometimes when women get themselves in strange positions in the eyes of the world from no fault of their own."

"It must make them very unhappy afterwards."

"It makes them anxious; for might not other women despise them?"

"Not altogether despise them. Yet not quite like or respect them."

Lucetta winced again. Her past was by no means secure from investigation, even in Casterbridge. For one thing, Henchard had never returned to her the cloud of letters she had written and sent him in her first excitement.[5] Possibly they were destroyed; but she could have wished that they had never been written.

The rencounter with Farfrae and his bearing towards Lucetta had made the reflective Elizabeth more observant of her brilliant and amiable companion. A few days afterwards, when her eyes met Lucetta's as the latter was going out, she somehow knew that Miss Templeman was nourishing a hope of seeing the attractive Scotchman. The fact was printed large all over Lucetta's cheeks and eyes to any one who read her as Elizabeth-Jane was beginning to do. Lucetta passed on and closed the street-door.

A seer's spirit took command of Elizabeth, impelling her to sit down by the fire, and divine events so surely from *data* already her own that they could be held as witnessed. She followed Lucetta thus mentally – saw her encounter Donald somewhere as if by chance – saw him wear his special look when meeting women, with an added intensity because this one was Lucetta. She depicted his impassioned manner; beheld the indecision of both between their lothness to separate, and their desire not to be observed; depicted their shaking of hands; how they probably parted with frigidity in their general contour and movement, only in the smaller features showing the spark of passion, thus invisible to all but themselves. This discerning silent witch had not done thinking of these things when Lucetta came noiselessly behind her, and made her start.

It was all true as she had pictured – she could have sworn it. Lucetta had a heightened luminousness in her eye over and above the advanced colour of her cheeks.

"You've seen Mr. Farfrae," said Elizabeth, demurely.

"Yes," said Lucetta. "How did you know?"

She knelt down on the hearth and took her friend's hands excitedly in her own. But after all she did not say when or how she had seen him or what he had said.

That night she became restless; in the morning she was feverish; and at breakfast time she told her companion that she had something on her mind – something which concerned a person in whom she was interested much. Elizabeth was earnest to listen and sympathize.

"This person – a lady – once admired a man much – very much," she said, tentatively.

"Ah," said Elizabeth-Jane.

"He did not think so deeply of her as she did of him. But in an impulsive moment, purely out of gratitude,[6] he proposed to make her his wife. She agreed. But there was an unexpected hitch in the proceedings; though she had been so far compromised with him that she felt she could never belong to another man, as a pure matter of conscience, even if she should wish to. After that they were much apart, heard nothing of each other for a long time, and she felt her life quite closed up for her."

"Ah – poor girl!"

"She suffered much on account of him; though I should add that he could not altogether be blamed for what had happened. At last the obstacle which separated them was providentially removed; and he came to marry her."

"How delightful!"

"But in the interval she – my poor friend – had seen a man she liked better than him. Now comes the point: Could she in honour dismiss the first?"

"A man she liked better – that's bad!"

"Yes," said Lucetta, looking pained at a boy who was swinging the town pump-handle. "It is bad! Though you must remember that she was forced into an equivocal position with the first man by an accident – that he was not so well educated or refined as the second, and that she had discovered some qualities in the first that rendered him less desirable as a husband than she had at first thought him to be."

PLATE XI
'She knelt down on the hearth, and took her friend's hand excitedly in her own.'

"I cannot answer," said Elizabeth-Jane, thoughtfully. "It is so difficult. It wants a Pope to settle that."

"You prefer not to, perhaps?" Lucetta showed in her appealing tone how much she leant on Elizabeth's judgment.

"Yes, Miss Templeman," admitted Elizabeth. "I would rather not say."

Nevertheless, Lucetta seemed relieved by the simple fact of having opened out the situation a little, and was slowly convalescent of her headache. "Bring me a looking-glass. How do I appear to people?" she said languidly.

"Well – a little worn," answered Elizabeth, eyeing her as a critic eyes a doubtful painting; fetching the glass, she enabled Lucetta to survey herself in it, which Lucetta anxiously did.

"I wonder if I wear well, as times go!" she observed after a while.

"Yes – fairly."

"Where am I worst?"

"Under your eyes – I notice a little brownness there."

"Yes. That is my worst place, I know.[7] How many years more do you think I shall last before I get hopelessly plain?"

There was something curious in the way in which Elizabeth, though the younger, had come to play the part of experienced sage in these discussions. "It may be five years," she said judicially. "Or, with a quiet life, as many as ten. With no love you might calculate on ten."

Lucetta seemed to reflect on this as on an unalterable, impartial verdict. She told Elizabeth-Jane no more of the past attachment she had roughly adumbrated as the experiences of a third person; and Elizabeth, who in spite of her philosophy was very tender-hearted, wept that night in bed at the thought that her pretty, rich Lucetta did not treat her to the full confidence of names and dates in her confessions. For by the "she" of Lucetta's story Elizabeth had not been beguiled.

CHAPTER XXV

The next phase of the supercession of Henchard in Lucetta's heart was an experiment in calling on her, performed by Farfrae with some apparent trepidation. Conventionally speaking, he conversed with both Miss Templeman and her companion; but in fact it was rather that Elizabeth sat invisible in the room. Donald appeared not to see her at all, and answered her wise, homely little remarks with curtly[1] indifferent monosyllables, his looks and faculties hanging on the woman who could boast of a more Protean variety in her phrases, moods, opinions, and also principles, than could Elizabeth. Lucetta had persisted in dragging her into the circle; but she had remained like an awkward third point which that circle would not touch.

Susan Henchard's daughter bore up against the frosty ache of this treatment, as she had borne up under worse things, and contrived as soon as possible to get out of the inharmonious room without being missed. The Scotchman seemed hardly the same Farfrae who had danced with her, and walked with her, in a delicate poise between love and friendship – that period in the history of a love when alone it can be said to be unalloyed with pain.

She stoically looked from her bedroom window, and contemplated her fate as if it were written on the top of the church-tower hard by. "Yes," she said at last, bringing down her palm upon the sill with a pat: "*He* is the second man of that story she told me!"

All this time Henchard's smouldering sentiments towards Lucetta had been fanned into higher and higher inflammation by the circumstances of the case. He was discovering that the young woman, for whom he once felt a pitying warmth, which had been almost chilled out of him by reflection, was, when now qualified with a slight inaccessibility and a more matured beauty, the very being to make him satisfied with life. Day after day proved to him, by her silence, that it was no use to think of bringing her round by holding aloof; so he gave in, and called upon her again, Elizabeth-Jane being absent.

He crossed the room to her with a heavy tread of some awkwardness, his strong, warm gaze upon her – like the sun beside the moon in comparison with Farfrae's modest look – and with something of a hail-fellow bearing, as, indeed, was not unnatural. But she seemed so transubstantiated by her change of position, and held out her hand to him in such cool friendship, that he became deferential, and sat down with a perceptible loss of power. He understood but little of fashion in dress, yet enough to feel himself inadequate in appearance beside her whom he had hitherto been dreaming of as almost his property. She said something very polite about his being good enough to call. This caused him to recover balance. He looked her oddly in the face, losing his awe.

"Why, of course I have called, Lucetta," he said. "What does that nonsense mean? You know I couldn't have helped myself if I had wished – that is, if I had any kindness at all. I've called to say that I am ready, as soon as custom will permit, to give you my name, in return for your devotion, and what you lost by it, in thinking too little of yourself and too much of me; to say that you can fix the day or month, with my full consent, whenever in your opinion it would be seemly; you know more of these things than I."

"It is full early yet," she said evasively.

"Yes, yes; I suppose it is. But you know, Lucetta, I felt directly my poor ill-used Susan died, and when I could not bear the idea of marrying again, that after what had happened between us it was my duty not to let any unnecessary delay occur before putting things to rights. Still, I wouldn't call in a hurry, because – well, you can guess how this money you've come into made me feel." His voice slowly fell; he was conscious that in this room his accents and manner wore a roughness not observable in the street. He looked about the room, at the novel hangings and ingenious furniture with which she had surrounded herself.

"Upon my life I didn't know such furniture as this could be bought in Casterbridge," he said.

"Nor can it be," said she. "Nor will it till fifty years more of civilization have passed over the town. It took a waggon and four horses to get it here."

"H'm.² The fact is, your setting up like this makes my bearings towards you rather awkward."

"Why?"

An answer was not really needed, and he did not furnish one. "Well," he went on; "there's nobody in the world I would have wished to see enter into this wealth before you, Lucetta; and nobody, I am sure, who will become it more." He turned to her with congratulatory admiration so fervid that she shrank somewhat, notwithstanding that she knew him so well.

"I am greatly obliged to you for all that," said she, rather with an air of speaking ritual. The stint of reciprocal feeling was perceived, and Henchard showed chagrin at once – nobody was more quick to show that than he.

"You may be obliged or not for 't. Though the things I say may not have the polish of what you've lately learnt to expect for the first time in your life, they are real, my lady Lucetta."

"That's rather a rude way of speaking to me," pouted Lucetta, with stormy eyes.

"Not at all!" replied Henchard hotly. "But there, there, I don't want to quarrel with ye. I come with an honest proposal for silencing your Jersey enemies, and you ought to be thankful."

"How can you speak so!" she answered, firing quickly. "Knowing that my only crime was the indulging in a foolish girl's passion for you with too little regard for appearances, and that I was what I call innocent all the time they called me guilty, you ought not to be so cutting! I suffered enough at that worrying time, when you wrote to tell me of your wife's return, and my consequent dismissal, and if I am a little independent now, surely the privilege is due to me?"

"Yes, it is," he said. "But it is not by what is, in this life, but by what appears, that you are judged; and I therefore think you ought to accept me – for your own good name's sake. What is known in your native Jersey may get known here."

"How you keep on about Jersey. I am English."[3]

"Yes, yes. Well, what do you say to my proposal?"

For the first time in their acquaintance Lucetta had the move; and yet she was backward. "For the present let things be," she said with some embarrassment. "Treat me as an acquaintance; and I'll treat you as one. Time will—" she stopped; and he said nothing to fill the gap for a while, there being no pressure of half-acquaintance to drive them into speech if they were not minded for it.

"That's the way the wind blows, is it?" he said at last grimly, nodding an affirmative to his own thoughts.

A yellow flood of reflected sunlight filled the room for a few instants. It was produced by the passing of a load of newly-trussed hay from the country in a waggon marked with Farfrae's name. Beside it rode Farfrae himself on horseback. Lucetta's face became – as a woman's face becomes when the man she loves rises upon her gaze like an apparition.

A turn of the eye by Henchard, a glance from the window, and the secret of her inaccessibility would have been revealed. But Henchard in estimating her tone was looking down so plumb-straight that he did not note the warm consciousness upon Lucetta's face.

"I shouldn't have thought it – I shouldn't have thought it of woman!" he said emphatically by-and-by, rising and shaking himself into activity; while Lucetta was so anxious to divert him from any suspicion of the truth, that she asked him to be in no hurry. Bringing him some apples, she insisted upon paring one for him.

He would not take it. "No, no; such is not for me," he said drily, and moved to the door. At going out he turned his eye upon her.

"You come to live in Casterbridge entirely on my account," he said. "Yet now you are here you won't have anything to say to my offer!"

He had hardly gone down the staircase when she dropped upon the sofa, and jumped up again in a fit of desperation. "I will love him!" she cried passionately; "as for *him* – he's hot-tempered and stern, and it would be madness to bind myself to him, knowing that. I won't be a slave to the past – I'll love where I choose!"

Yet having decided to break away from Henchard, one might have supposed her capable of aiming higher than Farfrae. But Lucetta reasoned nothing: she feared hard words from the people with whom she had been earlier associated; she had no relatives left; and with native lightness of heart took kindly to what fate offered.[4]

Elizabeth-Jane, surveying the position of Lucetta between her two lovers from the crystalline sphere of a straightforward mind, did not fail to perceive that her father, as she called him, and Donald Farfrae became more desperately enamoured of her friend every day. On Farfrae's side it was the unforced passion of youth. On Henchard's the artificially stimulated coveting of maturer age.

The pain she experienced from the almost absolute obliviousness to her existence that was shown by the pair of them became at times half-dissipated by her sense of its humorousness. When Lucetta had pricked her finger they were as deeply concerned as if she were dying; when she herself had been seriously sick or in danger they uttered a conventional word of sympathy at the news, and forgot all about it immediately. But, as regarded Henchard, this perception of hers also caused her some filial grief; she could not help asking what she had done to be neglected so, after the professions of solicitude he had made. As regarded Farfrae, she thought, after honest reflection, that it was quite natural. What was she beside Lucetta? – as one of the "meaner beauties of the night"[5] when the moon had risen in the skies.

She had learnt the lesson of renunciation, and was as familiar with the wreck of each day's wishes as with the diurnal setting of the sun. If her earthly career had taught her few book philosophies it had at least well practised her in this. Yet her experience had consisted less in a series of pure disappointments than in a series of substitutions. Continually it had happened that what she had desired had not been granted her, and that what had been granted her she had not desired. So she viewed with an approach to equanimity the now cancelled days when Donald had been her undeclared lover, and wondered what unwished-for thing Heaven might send her in place of him.

CHAPTER XXVI

It chanced that on a fine spring morning Henchard and Farfrae met in the chesnut-walk which ran along the south wall of the town. Each had just come out from his early breakfast, and there was not another soul near. Henchard was reading a letter from Lucetta, sent in answer to a note from him, in which she made some excuse for not immediately granting him a second interview that he had desired.

Donald had no wish to enter into conversation with his former friend on their present constrained terms; neither would he pass him in scowling silence. He nodded, and Henchard did the same. They had receded from each other several paces when a voice cried "Farfrae!" It was Henchard's, who stood regarding him.

"Do you remember," said Henchard, as if it were the presence of the thought and not of the man which made him speak, "do you remember my story of that second woman – who suffered for her thoughtless devotion to[1] me?"

"I do," said Farfrae.

"Do you remember my telling 'ee how it all began, and how it ended?"

"Yes."

"Well, I have offered to marry her now that I can; but she won't marry me. Now what would you think of her – I put it to you?"

"Well, ye owe her nothing more now,"[2] said Farfrae heartily.

"It is true," said Henchard, and went on.

That he had looked up from a letter to ask his questions completely shut out from Farfrae's mind all vision of Lucetta as the culprit. Indeed, her present position was so different from that of the young woman of Henchard's story as of itself to be sufficient to blind him absolutely to her identity. As for Henchard, he was reassured by Farfrae's words and manner against a suspicion which had crossed his mind. They were not those of a conscious rival.

Yet that there was rivalry by some one he was firmly persuaded. He could feel it in the air around Lucetta, see it in the turn of her pen. There was an antagonistic force in exercise, so that when he had tried to hang near her he seemed standing in a refluent current. That it was not innate caprice he was more and more certain. Her windows gleamed as if they did not want him; her curtains seemed to hang slily, as if they screened an ousting presence. To discover whose presence that was – whether really Farfrae's after all, or another's – he exerted himself to the utmost to see her again; and at length succeeded.

At the interview, when she offered him tea, he made it a point to launch a cautious inquiry if she knew Mr. Farfrae.

Oh, yes, she knew him, she declared: she could not help knowing almost everybody in Casterbridge, living in such a gazebo over the centre and arena of the town.

"Pleasant young fellow," said Henchard.

"Yes," said Lucetta.

"We both know him," said kind Elizabeth-Jane, to relieve her companion's divined embarrassment.

There was a knock at the door; literally, three full knocks and a little one at the end.

"That kind of knock means half-and-half – somebody between gentle and simple," said the corn-merchant to himself. "I shouldn't wonder therefore if it is he." In a few seconds surely enough Donald walked in.

Lucetta was full of little fidgets and flutters, which increased Henchard's suspicions without affording any special proof of their correctness. He was well-nigh ferocious at the sense of the queer situation in which he stood towards this woman. One who had reproached him for deserting her when calumniated, who had urged claims upon his consideration on that account, who had lived waiting for him, who at the first decent moment had come to ask him to rectify, by making her his, the false position into which she had placed herself for his sake: such she had been. And now he sat at her tea-table eager to gain her attention, and, in his amatory rage, feeling the other man present to be a villain, just as any young fool of a lover might feel.

They sat stiffly side by side at the darkening table, like some Tuscan painting of the two disciples supping at Emmaus.[3] Lucetta, forming the third and chief figure, was opposite them; Elizabeth-Jane, being out of the game, and out of the group, could observe from afar all things:[4] that there were long spaces of taciturnity, when all exterior circumstance was subdued to the touch of spoons and china, the click of a heel on the pavement under the window, the passing of a wheelbarrow or cart, the whistling of the carter, the gush of water into householders' buckets at the town-pump opposite; the exchange of greetings among their neighbours, and the rattle of the yokes by which they carried off their evening supply.

"More bread-and-butter?" said Lucetta to Henchard and Farfrae equally, holding out between them a plateful of long slices. Henchard took a slice by one end and Donald by the other; each feeling certain he was the man meant; neither let go, and the slice came in two.

"Oh – I am so sorry!" cried Lucetta, with a nervous titter. Farfrae tried to laugh; but he was too much in love to see the incident in any but a tragic light.

"How ridiculous of all three of them!" said Elizabeth to herself.

Henchard left the house with a ton of conjecture, though without a grain of proof, that the counter attraction was Farfrae; and therefore he would not make up his mind. Yet to Elizabeth-Jane it was plain as the town-pump that Donald and Lucetta were incipient lovers. More than once, in spite of her care, Lucetta had been unable to restrain her glance from flitting across into Farfrae's eyes like a bird to its nest. But Henchard was constructed upon too large a scale to discern such minutiæ as these by an evening light, which to him were as the notes of a grasshopper that lie above the compass of the human ear.

But he was disturbed. And the sense of occult rivalry in suitorship was so much superadded to the palpable rivalry of their business lives. To the coarse materiality of that rivalry it added an inflaming soul.

The thus vitalized antagonism took the form of action by Henchard sending for Jopp, the manager originally displaced by Farfrae's arrival. Henchard had frequently met this man about the streets, observed that his clothing spoke of neediness, heard that he lived in Mixen Lane[5] – a back slum of the town, the *pis aller* of Casterbridge domiciliation – itself almost a proof that a man had reached a stage when he would not stick at trifles.

Jopp came after dark, by the gates of the store-yard, and felt his way through the hay and straw to the office where Henchard sat in solitude awaiting him.

"I am again out of a foreman," said the corn-factor. "Are you in a place?"

"Not so much as a beggar's, sir."

"How much do you ask?"

Jopp named his price, which was very moderate.

"When can you come?"

"At this hour and moment, sir," said Jopp, who, standing hands-pocketed at the street corner till the sun had faded the shoulders of his coat to scarecrow green, had regularly watched Henchard in the market-place, measured him, and learnt him, by virtue of the power which the still man has in his stillness of knowing the busy one better than he knows himself. Jopp, too, had had a convenient experience; he was the only one in Casterbridge besides Henchard and the close-lipped Elizabeth who knew that Lucetta came truly from Jersey, and but proximately from Bath. "I know Jersey, too, sir," he said. "Was living there when you used to do business that way. Oh yes – have often seen ye there."

"Indeed! Very good. Then the thing is settled. The testimonials you showed me when you first tried for't are sufficient."

That characters deteriorate in time of need possibly did not occur to Henchard. Jopp said, "Thank you," and stood more firmly, in the consciousness that at last he officially belonged to that spot.

"Now," said Henchard, digging his strong eyes into Jopp's face, "one thing is necessary to me, as the biggest corn and hay dealer in these parts. The Scotchman who's taking the town trade so bold into his hands must be cut out. D'ye hear? We two can't live side by side – that's clear and certain."

"I've seen it all," said Jopp.

"By fair competition I mean, of course," Henchard continued. "But as hard, keen, and unflinching as fair – rather more so. By such a desperate bid against him for the farmers' custom as will grind him into the ground – starve him out. I've capital, mind ye, and I can do it."

"I'm all that way of thinking," said the new foreman. Jopp's dislike of Farfrae as the man who had once usurped his place, while it made him a willing tool, made him, at the same time, commercially as unsafe a colleague as Henchard could have chosen.

"I sometimes think," he added, "that he must have some glass that he sees next year in. He has such a knack of making everything bring him fortune."

"He's deep beyond all honest men's discerning; but we must make him shallower. We'll under-sell him, and over-buy him, and so snuff him out."

They then entered into specific details of the process by which this would be accomplished, and parted at a late hour.

Elizabeth-Jane heard by accident that Jopp had been engaged by her stepfather. She was so fully convinced that he was not the right man for the place that, at the risk of making Henchard angry, she expressed her apprehension to him when they met. But it was done to no purpose. Henchard shut up her argument with a sharp rebuff.

The season's weather seemed to favour their scheme. The time was in the years immediately before foreign competition had revolutionized the trade in grain, when still, as from the earliest ages, the wheat quotations from month to month depended entirely upon the home harvest. A bad harvest, or the prospect of one, would double the price of corn in a few weeks; and the promise of a good yield would lower it as rapidly. Prices were like the roads of the period, steep in gradient, reflecting in their phases the local conditions, without engineering, levellings, or averages.

The farmer's income was ruled by the wheat-crop within his own horizon, and the wheat-crop by the weather. Thus, in person, he became a sort of flesh-barometer, with feelers always directed to the sky and wind around him. The local atmosphere was everything to him; the atmospheres of other countries a matter of indifference. The people, too, who were not farmers, the rural multitude, saw in the god of the weather a more important personage than they do now. Indeed, the feeling of the peasantry in this matter was so intense as to be almost unrealizable in these equable days. Their impulse was well-nigh to prostrate themselves in lamentation before untimely rains and tempests, which came as the Alastor of those households whose crime it was to be poor.

After midsummer they watched the weather-cocks as men waiting in ante-chambers watch the lackey. Sun elated them; quiet rain sobered them; weeks of watery tempest stupefied them. That aspect of the sky which they now regard as disagreeable they then beheld as furious.

It was June, and the weather was very unfavourable. Casterbridge, being, as it were, the bell-board on which all the adjacent hamlets and villages sounded their notes, was decidedly dull. Instead of new articles in the shop-windows, those that had been rejected in the foregoing summer were brought out again; superseded reap-hooks, badly-shaped rakes, shop-worn leggings, and time-stiffened water-tights reappeared, furbished up as near to new as possible.

Henchard, backed by Jopp, read a disastrous garnering, and resolved to base his strategy against Farfrae upon that reading. But before acting he wished – what so many have wished – that he could know for certain what was at present only strong probability. He was superstitious – as such headstrong natures often are – and he nourished in his mind an idea bearing on the matter; an idea he shrank from disclosing even to Jopp.

In a lonely hamlet a few miles from the town – so lonely, that what are called lonely villages were teeming by comparison – there lived a man of curious repute as a forecaster or weather-prophet. The way to his house was crooked and miry – even difficult in the present unpropitious season. One evening when it was raining so heavily that ivy and laurel resounded like distant musketry, and an out-door man could be excused for shrouding himself to his ears and eyes, such a shrouded figure on foot might have been perceived travelling in the direction of the hazel-copse which dripped over the prophet's cot. The turnpike-road became a lane, the lane a cart-track; the cart-track a bridle-path, the bridle-path a foot-way, the foot-way overgrown. The solitary walker slipped here and there, and stumbled over the natural springes formed by the brambles, till at length he reached the house, which, with its garden, was surrounded with a high, dense hedge. The cottage, comparatively a large one, had been built of mud by the occupier's own hands, and thatched also by himself. Here he had always lived, and here it was presumed he would die.

He existed on unseen supplies; for it was an anomalous thing that while there was hardly a soul in the neighbourhood but affected to laugh at this man's assertions, uttering the formula, "There's nothing in 'em," with full assurance on the surface of their faces, very few of them were unbelievers in their secret hearts. Whenever they consulted him they did it "for a fancy." When they paid him they said, "Just a trifle for Christmas," or "Candlemas," as the case might be.

He would have preferred more honesty in his clients, and less sham ridicule; but fundamental belief consoled him for superficial irony. As stated, he was enabled to live; people supported him with their backs turned. He was sometimes astonished that men could profess so little and believe so much at his house when at church they professed so much and believed so little.

Behind his back he was called "Wide-oh," on account of his reputation; to his face "Mr." Fall.

The hedge of his garden formed an arch over the entrance, and a door was inserted as in a wall. Outside the door the tall traveller stopped, bandaged his face with a handkerchief as if he were suffering from toothache, and went up the path. The window shutters were not closed, and he could see the prophet within, preparing his supper.

In answer to the knock Fall came to the door, candle in hand. The visitor stepped back a little from the light, and said, "Can I speak to ye?" in significant tones. The other's invitation to come in was responded to by the country form, "This will do, thank ye," after which the householder has no alternative but to come out. He placed the candle on the corner of the dresser, took his hat from a nail, and joined the stranger in the porch, shutting the door behind him.

"I've long heard that you can – do things of a sort?" began the other, repressing his individuality as much as he could.

"Maybe so, Mr. Henchard," said the weather-caster.

"Ah – why do you call me that?" asked the visitor with a start.

"Because it's your name. Feeling you'd come, I've waited for ye; and thinking you might be leery from your walk I laid two supper plates – look ye here." He threw open the door and disclosed the supper-table, at which appeared a second chair, knife and fork, plate and mug, as he had declared.

Henchard felt like Saul at his reception by Samuel;[6] he remained in silence for a few moments, then throwing off the disguise of frigidity which he had hitherto preserved, he said, "Then I have not come in vain. . . . . Now, for instance, can ye charm away warts?"

"Without trouble."

"Cure the evil?"[7]

"That I've done – with consideration – if they will wear the toad-bag by night as well as by day."

"Forecast the weather?"

PLATE XII

'In answer to the knock Fall came to the door, candle in hand.'

"With labour and time."

"Then take this," said Henchard. "'Tis a crown-piece. Now, what is the harvest fortnight to be? When can I know?"

"I've worked it out already, and you can know at once." (The fact was that five farmers had already been there on the same errand from different parts of the country.) "By the sun, moon, and stars, by the clouds, the winds, the trees, and grass, the candle-flame and swallows, the smell of the herbs; likewise by the cats' eyes, the ravens, the leeches, the spiders, and the dung-mixen, the last fortnight in August will be – rain and tempest."

"You are not certain, of course?"

"As one can be in a world where all's unsure. 'Twill be more like living in Revelations[8] this autumn than in England. Shall I sketch it out for ye in a scheme?"

"Oh no, no," said Henchard. "I don't altogether believe in forecasts, come to second thoughts on such. But I——"

"You don't – you don't – 'tis understood," said Wide-oh, without a sound of scorn. "You have given me a crown because you've one too many. But won't you join me at supper, now 'tis waiting and all?"

Henchard would gladly have joined; for the savour of the stew had floated from the cottage into the porch with such appetising distinctness, that the meat, the onions, the pepper, and the herbs could be severally recognized by his nose. But as sitting down to hob-and-nob there would have seemed to mark him too implicitly as the weather-caster's apostle, he declined, and went his way.

The next Saturday Henchard bought grain to such an enormous extent that there was quite a talk about his purchases among his neighbours, the lawyer, the wine merchant, and the doctor; also on the next, and on all available days. When his granaries were full to choking, all the weather-cocks of Casterbridge creaked and set their faces in another direction, as if tired of the south-west. The weather changed; the sunlight which had been like tin for weeks assumed the hues of topaz. The temperament of the welkin passed from the phlegmatic to the sanguine; an excellent harvest was almost a certainty; and as a consequence prices rushed down.

All these transformations, lovely to the outsider, to the wrong-headed corn-dealer were terrible. He was reminded of what he had well known before, that a man might gamble upon the square green areas of fields as readily as upon those of a card-room.

Henchard had backed bad weather, and apparently lost. He had mistaken the turn of the flood for the turn of the ebb. His dealings had been so extensive that settlement could not long be postponed, and to settle, he was obliged to sell off corn that he had bought only a few weeks before at figures higher by many shillings a quarter. Much of the corn he had never seen; it had not even been moved from the ricks in which it lay stacked miles away. Thus he lost heavily.

In the blaze of an early August day he met Farfrae in the market-place. Farfrae knew of his dealings (though he did not guess their intended bearing on himself) and commiserated him; for since their exchange of words in the South Walk they had been on stiffly-speaking terms. Henchard, for the moment, appeared to resent the sympathy; but he suddenly took a careless turn.

"Ho, no, no! – nothing serious, man!" he cried with fierce gaiety. "These things always happen, don't they? I know it has been said that figures have touched me tight lately; but is that anything rare? The case is not so bad as folk make out perhaps. And dammy, a man must be a fool to mind the common hazards of trade!"

But he had to enter the Casterbridge Bank that day for reasons which had never before sent him there – and to sit a long time in the partners' room with a constrained bearing. It was rumoured soon after that much real property, as well as vast stores of produce, in the town and neighbourhood, which had stood in Henchard's name, was actually the property of his bankers.

Coming down the steps of the Bank he encountered Jopp. The gloomy transactions just completed within had added fever to the original sting of Farfrae's sympathy that morning, which Henchard fancied might be satire disguised, so that Jopp met with anything but a bland reception. The latter was in the act of taking off his hat to wipe his forehead, and saying, "A fine hot day," to an acquaintance.

"You can wipe and wipe, and say 'A fine hot day,' can ye!" cried Henchard in a savage undertone, imprisoning Jopp between himself and the bank-wall. "If it hadn't been for your fool's advice it might have been a fine day enough. Why did ye let me go on, hey? – when a word of doubt from you or anybody would have made me think twice, that you can never be sure of weather till 'tis past."

"My advice, sir, was to do what you thought best."

"A useful fellow: and the sooner you help somebody else in that way the better!" Henchard continued his address to Jopp in similar terms till it ended in Jopp's dismissal there and then, Henchard turning upon his heel and leaving him.

"You shall be sorry for this, sir; sorry as a man can be!" said Jopp, standing pale, and looking after the corn-merchant as he disappeared in the crowd of market-men hard by.

CHAPTER XXVII

It was the eve of harvest. Prices being low Farfrae was buying. As was usual, after reckoning too surely on famine weather, the local farmers had flown to the other extreme, and (in Farfrae's opinion) were selling off too recklessly – calculating with just a trifle too much certainty upon an abundant yield. So he went on buying old corn at its comparatively ridiculous price: for the produce of the previous year, though not large, had been of excellent quality.

When Henchard had squared his affairs in a disastrous way, and got rid of his burdensome purchases at a monstrous loss, the harvest began. There were three days of excellent weather, and then – "What if that cust conjuror should be right after all!" said Henchard.

The fact was that no sooner had the sickles begun to play than the atmosphere suddenly felt as if cress would grow in it without other nourishment. It rubbed people's cheeks like damp flannel when they walked abroad. There was a gusty, high, warm wind; isolated raindrops starred the window-panes at remote distances; the sunlight would flap out like a quickly-opened fan, throw the pattern of the window upon the floor of the room in a milky, colourless shine, and withdraw as suddenly as it had appeared.

From that day and hour it was clear that there was not to be so successful an ingathering after all. If Henchard had only waited long enough he might at least have avoided loss, though he had not made a profit. But the momentum of his character knew no patience. At this third turn of the scales he remained silent. The movements of his mind seemed to tend to the thought that some power was working against him.

"I wonder," he asked himself with eerie misgiving; "I wonder if it can be that somebody has been roasting a waxen image of me,[1] or stirring an unholy brew to confound me! I don't believe in such power; and yet – what if they should ha' been doing it!" Even he could not admit that the perpetrator, if any, might be Farfrae. These isolated hours of superstition came to Henchard in time of moody depression, when all his practical largeness of view had oozed out of him.

Meanwhile Donald Farfrae prospered. He had purchased in so depressed a market that the present moderate stiffness of prices was sufficient to pile for him a large heap of gold where a little one had been.

"Why, he'll soon be Mayor!" said Henchard. It was indeed hard that the speaker should, of all others, have to follow the triumphal chariot of this man to the Capitol.[2]

The rivalry of the masters was taken up by the men.

September night-shades had fallen upon Casterbridge; the clocks had struck half-past eight, and the moon had risen. The streets of the town were curiously silent for such a comparatively early hour. A sound of jangling horse-bells and heavy wheels passed up the street. These were followed by angry voices outside Lucetta's house, which led her and Elizabeth-Jane to run to the windows, and pull up the blinds.

The opposite Market House and Town Hall abutted against its next neighbour the Church except in the lower storey, where an arched thoroughfare gave admittance to a large square called Bull Stake.[3] A stone post rose in the midst, to which the oxen had formerly been tied for baiting with dogs to make them tender before they were killed in the adjoining shambles. In a corner stood the stocks.

The thoroughfare leading to this spot was now blocked by two four-horse waggons and horses, laden[4] with hay-trusses, the leaders having already passed each other, and become entangled head to tail. The passage of the vehicles might have been practicable if empty; but built up with hay to the bedroom windows as they were it was impossible.

"You must have done it a' purpose!" said Farfrae's waggoner. "You can hear my horses' bells half-a-mile such a night as this."

"If ye'd been minding your business instead of zwailing along in such a gawk-hammer way, you would have seed me," retorted the wroth representative of Henchard.

However, according to the strict rule of the road it appeared that Henchard's man was most in the wrong; he therefore attempted to back into the High Street. In doing this the near hind-wheel rose against the churchyard wall, and the whole mountainous load went over, two of the four wheels rising in the air, and the legs of the thill-horse.

Instead of considering how to gather up the load the two men closed in a fight with their fists. Before the first round was quite over Henchard came upon the spot, somebody having run for him.

Henchard sent the two men staggering in contrary directions by collaring one with each hand, turned to the horse that was down, and extricated him after some trouble. He then inquired into the circumstances; and seeing the state of his waggon and its load, began hotly rating Farfrae's man.

Lucetta and Elizabeth-Jane had by this time run down to the door and opened it,[5] whence they watched the bright heap of new hay lying in the moon's rays, and passed and re-passed by the forms of Henchard and the waggoners. The women had witnessed what nobody else had seen – the origin of the mishap; and Lucetta spoke.

"I saw it all, Mr. Henchard," she cried; "and your man was most in the wrong!"

Henchard paused in his harangue and turned. "Oh, I didn't notice you, Miss Templeman," said he. "My man in the wrong? Ah, to be sure; to be sure! But I beg your pardon notwithstanding. The other's is the empty waggon, and he must have been most to blame for coming on."

"No; I saw it, too," said Elizabeth-Jane. "And I can assure you he couldn't help it."

"You can't trust *their* senses!" murmured Henchard's man.

"Why not?" asked Henchard sharply.

"Why, you see, sir, all the women side with Farfrae – being a young dand, and of the sort that he is – one that creeps into the maiden heart like the giddying worm into the sheep's brain[6] – making crooked seem straight to their eyes."

"But do you know what that lady is you talk about in such a fashion? Do you know that I pay my attentions to her, and have for some time? Just be careful!"

"Not I. I know nothing, sir, outside eight shillings a week."

"And that Mr. Farfrae is well aware of that? He's sharp in trade, but he wouldn't do anything so underhand as what you hint at."

Whether because Lucetta heard this low dialogue, or not, her white figure disappeared from her doorway inward, and the door was shut before Henchard could reach it to converse with her further. This disappointed him, for he had been sufficiently disturbed by what the man had said to wish to speak to her more closely. While pausing the old constable came up.

"Just see that nobody drives against that hay and waggon to-night, Stubberd," said the corn-merchant. "It must bide till the morning, for all hands are in the fields still. And if any coach or road-waggon wants to come along, tell 'em they must go round by the back street, and be hanged to 'em. . . . . Any case to-morrow up in Hall?"

"Yes, sir. One in number, sir."

"Oh, what's that?"

"A old flagrant female, sir, swearing and staggering[7] in a horrible profane manner against the church wall, sir, as if 'twere no more than a pot-house. That's all, sir."

"Oh. The Mayor's out o' town, isn't he?"

"He is, sir."

"Very well, then I'll be there. Don't forget to keep an eye on that hay. Good night t'ye."

During those moments Henchard had determined to follow up Lucetta, notwithstanding her elusiveness, and he knocked for admission.

The answer he received was an expression of Miss Templeman's sorrow at being unable to see him again that evening, because she had an engagement to go out.

Henchard walked away from the door to the opposite side of the street, and stood by his hay in a lonely reverie, the constable having strolled elsewhere, and the horses being removed. Though the moon was not bright as yet there were no lamps lighted, and he entered the shadow of one of the projecting jambs which formed the thoroughfare to Bull Stake; here he watched Lucetta's door.

Candle-lights were flitting in and out of her bedroom, and it was obvious that she was dressing for the appointment, whatever the nature of that might be at such an hour. The lights disappeared, the clocks struck nine, and almost at the moment Farfrae came round the opposite corner and knocked. That she had been waiting just inside for him was certain, for she instantly opened the door herself. They went together by the way of All Saints' Lane southward,[8] avoiding the front street; guessing at last where they were going, he determined to follow.

The harvest had been so delayed by the capricious weather, that whenever a fine day occurred all sinews were strained to save what could be saved of the damaged crops. On account of the rapid shortening of the days the harvesters worked by moonlight. Hence to-night the wheat-fields abutting on the two sides of the square formed by Caster-bridge town were animated by the gathering hands. Their shouts and laughter had reached Henchard at the Market House, while he stood there waiting, and he had little doubt from the turn which Farfrae and Lucetta had taken that they were bound for the spot.

Nearly the whole town had gone into the fields. The Casterbridge populace still retained the primitive habit of helping one another in time of need; and thus, though the corn belonged to the farming section of the little community – that inhabiting the Dummerford quarter – the remainder was no less interested in the labour of getting it home.

Reaching the end of the lane Henchard crossed the shaded avenue on the walls, slid down the green rampart, and stood amongst the stubble. The "stitches" or shocks rose like tents about the yellow expanse, those in the distance becoming lost in the moonlit hazes.

He had entered at a point removed from the scene of immediate operations; but two others had entered at that place, and he could see them winding among the shocks. They were paying no regard to the direction of their walk, whose vague serpentining soon began to bear down towards Henchard. A meeting promised to be awkward, and he therefore stepped into the hollow of the nearest shock, and sat down.

"You have my leave," Lucetta was saying, gaily. "Speak what you like."

"Well, then," replied Farfrae, with the unmistakable inflection of the lover pure, which Henchard had never heard in full resonance on his lips before; "you are sure to be much sought after for your position, wealth, talents, and beauty. But will ye resist the temptation to be one of those ladies with lots of admirers – ay – and be content to have only a homely one?"

"And he the speaker?" said she laughing. "Very well, sir, what next?"

"Ah! I'm afraid that what I feel will make me forget my manners!"

"Then I hope you'll never have any, if you lack them only for that cause." After some broken words, which Henchard lost, she added, "Are you sure you won't be jealous?"

Farfrae seemed to assure her that he would not, by taking her hand.

"You are convinced, Donald, that I love nobody else," she presently said. "But I should wish to have my own way in some things."

"In everything! What special thing did you mean?"

"If I wished not to live always in Casterbridge, for instance; on finding that I should not be happy here?"

Henchard did not hear the reply; he might have done so and much more, but he did not care to play the eavesdropper. They went on towards the scene of activity, where the sheaves were being handed, a dozen a minute, upon the carts and waggons which carried them away.

Lucetta insisted on parting from Farfrae when they drew near the workpeople. He had some business with them, and, though he entreated her to wait a few minutes, she was inexorable, and tripped off homeward alone.

Henchard thereupon left the field, and followed her. His state of mind was such that on reaching Lucetta's door he did not knock, but opened it, and walked straight up to her sitting-room, expecting to find her there. But the room was empty, and he perceived that in his haste he had somehow passed her on the way hither. He had not to wait many minutes, however, for he soon heard her dress rustling in the hall, followed by a soft closing of the door. In a moment she appeared.

The light was so low that she did not notice Henchard at first. As soon as she saw him she uttered a little cry, almost of terror.

"How can you frighten me so!" she exclaimed, with a flushed face. "It is past ten o'clock, and you have no right to surprise me here at such a time."

"I don't know that I've not the right. At any rate, I have the excuse. Is it so necessary that I should stop to think of manners and customs?"

"It is too late for propriety, and might injure me."

"I called an hour ago, and you would not see me, and I thought you were in when I called now. It is you, Lucetta, who are doing wrong. It is not proper in ye to throw me over like this. I have a little matter to remind you of, which you seem to forget."

She sank into a chair, and turned pale.

"I don't want to hear it – I don't want to hear it!" she said through her hands, as he, standing close to the edge of her dress, began to allude to the Jersey days.

"But you ought to hear it," said he.

"It came to nothing; and through you. Then why not leave me the freedom that I gained with such sorrow! Had I found that you proposed to marry me⁹ for pure love I might have felt bound now. But I soon learnt that you had planned it out of mere charity – almost as an unpleasant duty – because I had nursed you, and compromised myself somewhat, and you thought you must repay me. After that I did not care for you so deeply as before."

"Why did you come here to find me, then?"

"I thought I ought to marry you for conscience sake, since you were free, even though I – did not like you so well."

"And why then don't you think so now?"

She was silent. It was only too obvious that conscience had ruled well enough till new love had intervened, and usurped that rule. In feeling this she herself forgot for the moment her partially-justifying argument – that having discovered Henchard's infirmities of temper, she had some excuse for not risking her happiness in his hands after once escaping them. The only thing she could say was, "I was a poor girl then; and now my circumstances have altered, so I am hardly the same person."

"That's true. And it makes the case awkward for me. But I don't want to touch your money. I am quite willing that every penny of your property shall remain to your personal use. Besides, that argument has nothing in it. The man you are thinking of is no better than I."

"If you were as good as he you would leave me!" she cried passionately.

This unluckily aroused Henchard. "You cannot in honour refuse me," he said. "And unless you give me your promise this very night to be my wife, before a witness, I'll reveal our intimacy – in common fairness to other men!"

A look of resignation settled upon her. Henchard saw its bitterness; and had Lucetta's heart been given to any other man in the world than Farfrae he would probably have had pity upon her at that moment. But the supplanter was the upstart (as Henchard called him) who had mounted into prominence upon his shoulders, and he could bring himself to show no mercy.

Without another word she rang the bell, and directed that Elizabeth-Jane should be fetched from her room. The latter appeared, surprised in the midst of her lucubrations. As soon as she saw Henchard she went across to him dutifully.

"Elizabeth-Jane," he said, taking her hand, "I want you to hear this." And turning to Lucetta: "Will you, or will you not, marry me?"

"If you – wish it, I must agree!"

"You say yes?"

"I do."

No sooner had she given the promise than she fell back in a fainting state.[10]

"What dreadful thing drives her to say this, father, when it is such a pain to her?" asked Elizabeth, kneeling down by Lucetta. "Don't compel her to do anything against her will. I have lived with her, and know that she cannot bear much."

"Don't be a no'thern simpleton!" said Henchard drily. "This promise will leave him free for you, if you want him, won't it."

At this Lucetta seemed to wake from her swoon with a start.

"Him? Who are you talking about?" she said wildly.

"Nobody, as far as I am concerned," said Elizabeth firmly.

"Oh – well. Then it is my mistake," said Henchard. "But the business is between me and Miss Templeman. She agrees to be my wife."

"But don't dwell on it just now," entreated Elizabeth, holding Lucetta's hand.

"I don't wish to, if she promises," said Henchard.

"I have, I have," groaned Lucetta, her limbs hanging like flails, from very misery and faintness. "Michael, please don't argue it any more!"

"I will not," he said. And taking up his hat he went away.

Elizabeth-Jane continued to kneel by Lucetta. "What is this?" she said. "You called my father 'Michael' as if you knew him well? And how is it he has got this power over you, that you promise to marry him against your will? Ah – you have many, many secrets from me!"

"Perhaps you have some from me," Lucetta murmured, with closed eyes, little thinking, however, so unsuspicious was she, that the secret of Elizabeth's heart concerned the young man who had caused this damage to her own.

"I would not – do anything against you at all!" stammered Elizabeth, keeping in all signs of emotion till she was ready to burst. "I cannot understand how my father can command you so; I don't sympathize with him in it at all. I'll go to him and ask him to release you."

"No, no," said Lucetta. "Let it all be."

CHAPTER XXVIII

The next morning Henchard went to the Town Hall opposite Lucetta's house, to attend Petty Sessions, being still a magistrate for the year by virtue of his late position as Mayor. In passing he looked up at her windows, but nothing of her was to be seen.

Henchard, as a Justice of the Peace, may at first seem to be an even greater incongruity than Shallow and Silence[1] themselves. But his rough and ready perceptions, his sledge-hammer directness, had often served him better than nice legal knowledge in despatching such simple business as fell to his hands in this Court. To-day, Dr. Chalkfield, the Mayor for the year, being absent, the corn-merchant took the big chair, his eyes still abstractedly stretching out of the window to the ashlar front of High Street Hall.

There was one case only, and the offender stood before him. She was an old woman of mottled countenance, attired in a shawl of that nameless tertiary hue which comes, but cannot be made – a hue neither tawny, russet, hazel, nor ash; a sticky black bonnet that seemed to have been worn in the country of the Psalmist where the clouds drop fatness;[2] and an apron that had been white in times so comparatively recent as still to contrast visibly with the rest of her clothes. The steeped[3] aspect of the woman as a whole showed her to be no native of the country-side, or even of a country-town.

She looked cursorily at Henchard and the second magistrate, and Henchard looked at her, with a momentary pause, as if she had reminded him indistinctly of somebody or something which passed from his mind as quickly as it had come. "Well, and what has she been doing?" he said, looking down at the charge-sheet.

"She is charged, sir, with the offence of disorderly female and vagabond," whispered Stubberd.

"Where did she do that?" said the other magistrate.

"By the church, sir, of all the wrong places in the world for shouts and rolling.[4] I caught her in the act, your worship."

"Stand back then," said Henchard, "and let's hear what you've got to say."

Stubberd was sworn, the magistrate's clerk dipped his pen, Henchard being no notetaker himself, and the constable began:

"Hearing an illegal noise I went down the street at twenty-five minutes past eleven P.M. on the night of the fifth instinct, Hannah Dominy. When I had—"

"Don't go on so fast, Stubberd," said the clerk.

The constable waited, with his eyes on the clerk's pen, till the latter stopped scratching, and said "yes." Stubberd continued: "When I had proceeded to the spot, I saw defendant at another spot, namely, the gutter." He paused, watching the point of the clerk's pen again.

"Gutter, yes, Stubberd."

"Spot measuring twelve feet nine inches or thereabouts, from where I—" Still careful not to outrun the clerk's penmanship, Stubberd pulled up again; for having got his evidence by heart, it was immaterial to him whereabouts he broke off.

"I object to that," spoke up the old woman, "'spot measuring twelve feet nine or thereabouts from where I,' is not good evidence."

The magistrates consulted, and the second one said that the Bench was of opinion that twelve feet nine inches from a man on his oath was admissible evidence. Stubberd, with a suppressed gaze of victorious rectitude at the old woman, continued: "Was standing myself. She was wambling about quite dangerous to the thoroughfare, and when I approached to draw near, she insulted me."[5]

"'Insulted me'. . . . Yes, what did she say?"

"She said, 'Put away that dee lantern,' says she."

"Yes."

"Says she, 'Dost hear, old turmit-head? Put away that dee lantern. I have floored fellows a dee sight finer-looking than thee,[6] dee me if I haint,' she says."

"I object to that conversation!" interposed the old woman. "I was not capable enough to hear what I said, and what's said out of my hearing is not evidence."

There was another stoppage for consultation, a book was referred to, and finally Stubberd was allowed to go on again. The truth was that the old woman had appeared in court so many more times than the magistrates themselves, that they were obliged to keep a sharp look out upon their procedure. However, when Stubberd had rambled on a little further, Henchard broke out impatiently, "Come – we don't want to hear any more of them cust d's! Say the word out like a man, and don't be so modest, Stubberd; or else leave it alone!" Turning to the woman, "Now then, have you any questions to ask him, or anything to say?"

"Yes," she replied with a twinkle in her eye; and the clerk dipped his pen.

"Twenty years ago[7] I was a selling of furmity in a tent at Weydon Fair—"

"'Twenty years ago' – well, that's beginning at the beginning – suppose you go back to the Creation?" said the clerk, not without satire.

But Henchard stared, and quite forgot what was evidence and what was not.

"A man and a woman with a little child came into my tent," the woman continued. "They sat down and had a basin apiece. Ah, Lord's my life! I was of a more respectable station in life then than I am now, being a land smuggler[8] in a large way of business; and I used to season my furmity with rum for them who asked for't. I did it for the man; and then he had more and more; till at last he quarrelled with his wife, and offered to sell her to the highest bidder. A sailor came in and bid five guineas, and paid the money, and led her away. And the man who sold his wife in that fashion is the man sitting there in the great big chair." The speaker concluded by nodding her head at Henchard, and folding her arms.

Everybody looked at Henchard. His face seemed strange, and in tint as if it had been powdered over with ashes. "We don't want to hear your life and adventures," said the second magistrate sharply, filling the pause which followed. "You've been asked if you've anything to say bearing on the case."

"That bears on the case. It proves that he's no better than I, and has no right to sit there in judgment upon me."

"'Tis a concocted story," said the clerk. "So hold your tongue."

"No – 'tis true." The words came from Henchard. "'Tis as true as the light," he said slowly. "And upon my soul it does prove that I'm no better than she! And to keep out of any temptation to treat her hard for her revenge I'll leave her to you."

The sensation in the Court was indescribably great. Henchard left the chair, and came out, passing through a group of people on the steps and outside that was much larger than usual; for it seemed that the old furmity dealer had mysteriously hinted to the denizens of the lane in which she had been lodging since her arrival, that she knew a queer thing or two about their great local man Mr. Henchard, if she chose to tell it. This had brought them hither.

"Why are there so many idlers round the Town Hall to-day?" said Lucetta to her servant when the case was over. She had risen late, and had just looked out of the window.

"Oh, please ma'am, 'tis this larry about Mr. Henchard. A woman has proved that before he became a gentleman he sold his wife for five guineas in a booth at a fair."

In all the accounts which Henchard had given her of the separation from his wife Susan for so many years, of his belief in her death, and so on, he had never clearly explained the actual and immediate cause of that separation. The story she now heard for the first time.

A gradual misery overspread Lucetta's face as she dwelt upon the promise wrung from her the night before. At bottom, then, Henchard was this. How terrible a contingency for a woman who should commit herself to his care.

During the day she went out to the Ring, and to other places, not coming in till nearly dusk.[9] As soon as she saw Elizabeth-Jane after her return indoors she told her that she had resolved to go away from home to the seaside for a few days – to Port-Breedy, Casterbridge was so gloomy.

Elizabeth seeing that she looked wan and disturbed, encouraged her in the idea, thinking a change would afford her relief. She could not help suspecting that the gloom which seemed to have come over Casterbridge in Lucetta's eyes might be partially owing to the fact that Farfrae was away from home.

Elizabeth saw her friend depart for Port-Breedy, and took charge of High Street Hall till her return. After two or three days of solitude and incessant rain Henchard called at the house. He seemed disappointed to hear of Lucetta's absence, and though he nodded with outward indifference, he went away handling his beard with a nettled mien.

The next day he called again. "Is she come now?" he asked.

"Yes. She returned this morning," replied his stepdaughter. "But she is not indoors. She has gone for a walk along the turnpike-road to Port-Breedy. She will be home by dusk."

After a few words which only served to reveal his restless impatience he left the house again.

CHAPTER XXIX

At this hour Lucetta was bounding along the road to Port-Breedy just as Elizabeth had announced. That she had chosen for her afternoon walk the road along which she had returned to Casterbridge three hours earlier in a carriage was curious – if anything should be called curious in concatenations of phenomena wherein each is known to have its accounting cause. It was the day of the chief market – Saturday – and Farfrae for once had been missed from his corn-stand in the dealers' room. Nevertheless it was known that he would be home that night – "for Sunday," as Casterbridge expressed it.

Lucetta, in continuing her walk, had at length reached the end of the ranked trees which bordered the highway in this and other directions out of the town. This end marked a mile; and here she stopped.

The spot was a vale between two gentle acclivities, and the road, still adhering to its Roman foundation, stretched onward straight as a surveyor's line till lost to sight on the most distant ridge. There was neither hedge nor tree in the prospect now, the road clinging to the stubbly expanse of corn-land like a stripe to an undulating garment. Near her was a barn – the single building of any kind within her horizon.

She strained her eyes up the lessening road, but nothing appeared thereon – not so much as a speck. She sighed one word – "Donald!" and turned her face to the town for retreat.

Here the case was different. A single figure was approaching her – Elizabeth-Jane's.

Lucetta, in spite of her loneliness, seemed a little vexed. Elizabeth came on, her face, as soon as she recognized her friend, shaping itself into affectionate lines, while yet beyond speaking distance. "I suddenly thought I would come and meet you," she said smiling.

Lucetta's reply was taken from her lips by an unexpected diversion. A by-road on her right hand descended from the fields into the highway at the point where she stood, and down the track a bull was rambling uncertainly towards her and Elizabeth, who, facing the other way, did not observe him.

In the latter quarter of each year cattle were at once the mainstay and the terror of families about Casterbridge and its neighbourhood, where breeding was carried on with Abrahamic success.[1] The head of stock driven into and out of the town at this season to be sold by the local auctioneer was very large; and all these horned beasts, in travelling to and fro, sent women and children to shelter as nothing else could do. In the main the animals would have walked along quietly enough; but the Casterbridge tradition was that to drive stock it was indispensable that hideous cries, coupled with Yahoo antics and gestures, should be used, large sticks flourished, stray dogs called in, and in general everything done that was likely to infuriate the viciously-disposed and terrify the mild. Nothing was commoner than for a householder, on going out of his parlour, to find his hall or passage full of little children, nursemaids, aged women, or a ladies'-school, who apologized for their presence by saying, "A bull passing down street from the sale."

Lucetta and Elizabeth regarded the animal in doubt, he meanwhile drawing vaguely towards them. It was a large specimen of the breed, in colour rich dun, though disfigured at present by splotches of mud about his seamy sides. His horns were thick and tipped with brass; his two nostrils like the Thames Tunnel[2] as seen in the perspective toys of yore. Between them, through the gristle of his nose, was a stout copper ring, welded on, and irremovable as Gurth's collar of brass.[3] To the ring was attached an ash staff about a yard long, which the bull with the motions of his head flung about like a flail.

It was not till they observed this dangling stick that the young women were really alarmed; for it revealed to them that the bull was an old one, too savage to be driven, which had in some way escaped, the staff being the means by which the drover controlled him and kept his horns at arms length.

They looked round for some shelter or hiding-place, and thought of the barn hard by. As long as they had kept their eyes on the bull he had shown some deference in his manner of approach; but no sooner did they turn their backs to seek the barn than he tossed his head, and decided to thoroughly terrify them. This caused the two helpless girls to run wildly, whereupon the bull advanced in a deliberate charge.

The barn stood behind a green slimy pond, and it was closed with the exception of one of the usual pair of doors facing them, which had been propped open by a hurdle-stake, and for this opening they made. The interior had been cleared by a recent bout of threshing, except at one end, where there was a stack of dry clover. Elizabeth-Jane took in the situation. "We must climb up there," she said.

But before they had even approached it they heard the bull scampering through the pond without, and in a second he dashed into the barn, knocking down the hurdle-stake, in passing; the heavy door slammed behind him; and all three were imprisoned in the barn together. The mistaken creature saw them, and stalked towards the end of the barn into which they had fled. The girls doubled, so adroitly, that their pursuer was against the wall when the fugitives were already half way to the other end. By the time that his length would allow him to turn and follow them thither they had crossed over; thus the pursuit went on, the hot air from his nostrils blowing over them like a sirocco, and not a moment being attainable by Elizabeth or Lucetta in which to open the door. What might have happened had their situation continued cannot be said; but in a few moments a rattling of the door distracted their adversary's attention, and a man appeared.[4] He ran forward towards the leading-staff, seized it, and wrenched the animal's head as if he would snap it off. The wrench was in reality so violent that the thick neck seemed to have lost its stiffness and to become half-paralyzed, whilst the nose dropped blood. The premeditated human contrivance of the nose-ring was too cunning for impulsive brute force, and the creature flinched.

The man was seen in the partial gloom to be large-framed, and unhesitating. He led the bull to the door, and the light revealed Henchard. He made the bull fast without, and re-entered to the succour of Lucetta; for he had not perceived Elizabeth, who had climbed on to the clover-heap. Lucetta was hysterical, and Henchard took her in his arms and carried her to the door.

"You – have saved me!" she cried, as soon as she could speak.

"I have returned your kindness," he responded tenderly. "You once saved me."

"How – comes it to be you – you?" she asked, not heeding his reply.

"I came out here to look for you. I have been wanting to tell you something these two or three days; but you have been away, and I could not. Perhaps you cannot talk now?"

"Oh – no. Where is Elizabeth?"

"Here am I!" cried the missing one cheerfully; and without waiting for the ladder to be placed she slid down the face of the clover-stack to the floor.[5]

Henchard supporting Lucetta on one side, and Elizabeth-Jane on the other, they went slowly along the rising road. They had reached the top and were descending again when Lucetta, now much recovered, recollected that she had left her muff in the barn.

"I'll run back," said Elizabeth-Jane. "I don't mind it at all, as I am not tired as you are." She thereupon hastened down again to the barn, the others pursuing their way.

Elizabeth soon found the muff, such an article being by no means small at that time. Coming out she paused to look for a moment at the bull, now rather to be pitied with his bleeding nose, having perhaps rather intended a practical joke than a murder. Henchard had secured him by jamming the staff into the hinge of the barn-door, and wedging it there with a stake. At length she turned to hasten onward after her contemplation, when she saw a green-and-black gig approaching from the contrary direction, the vehicle being driven by Farfrae.

His presence here seemed to explain Lucetta's walk that way. Donald saw her, drew up, and was hastily made acquainted with what had occurred. At Elizabeth-Jane mentioning how greatly Lucetta had been jeopardized he exhibited an agitation different in kind no less than in intensity from any she had seen in him before. He became so absorbed in the circumstances that he scarcely had sufficient knowledge of what he was doing to think of helping her up beside him.

"She has gone on with Mr. Henchard, you say?" he inquired at last.

"Yes. He is taking her home. They are almost there by this time."

"And you are sure she can get home?"

Elizabeth-Jane was quite sure.

"Your stepfather saved her?"

"Entirely."

PLATE XIII

'"She has gone on with Mr. Henchard, you say?"'

Farfrae checked his horse's pace; she guessed why. He was thinking that it would be best not to intrude on the other two just now. Henchard had saved Lucetta, and to provoke a possible exhibition of her deeper affection for himself was as ungenerous as it was unwise.

The immediate subject of their talk being exhausted, she felt more embarrassed at sitting thus beside her past lover; but soon the two figures of the others were visible at the entrance to the town. The face of the woman was frequently turned back, but Farfrae did not whip on the horse. When these reached the town walls Henchard and his companion had disappeared down the street; Farfrae set down Elizabeth-Jane, on her expressing a particular wish to alight there, and drove round to the stables at the back of his lodgings.

On this account he entered the house through his garden, and going up to his apartments found them in a particularly disturbed state, his boxes being hauled out upon the landing, and his bookcase standing in three pieces. These phenomena, however, seemed to cause him not the least surprise. "When will everything be sent up?" he said to the mistress of the house, who was superintending.

"I am afraid not before eight, sir," said she. "You see we wasn't aware till this morning that you were going to move, or we could have been forwarder."

"A – well, never mind, never mind!" said Farfrae, cheerily. "Eight o'clock will do well enough if it be not later. Now, don't ye be standing here talking, or it will be twelve I doubt." Thus speaking he went out by the front door and up the street.

During this interval Henchard and Lucetta had had experiences of a different kind. After Elizabeth's departure for the muff, the corn-merchant opened himself frankly, holding her hand within his arm, though she would fain have withdrawn it. "Dear Lucetta, I have been very, very anxious to see you these two or three days," he said; "ever since I saw you last. I have thought over the way I got your promise that night. You said to me, 'If I were a man I should not insist.' That cut me deep. I felt that there was some truth in it. I don't want to make you wretched; and to marry me just now would do that as nothing else could – it is but too plain. Therefore I agree to an indefinite engagement – to put off all thought of marriage for a year or two."

"But – but – can I do nothing of a different kind?" said Lucetta. "I am full of gratitude to you – you have saved my life. And your care of me is like coals of fire on my head.[6] I am rich. Surely I can do something in return for your goodness – something practical?"

Henchard remained in thought. He had evidently not expected this. "There is one thing you might do, Lucetta," he said. "But not exactly of that kind."

"Then of what kind is it?" she asked, with renewed misgiving.

"I must tell you a secret to ask it—. You may have heard that I have been unlucky this year. I did what I have never done before – speculated rashly; and I lost. That's just put me in a strait."

"And you would wish me to advance some money?"

"No, no!" said Henchard, almost in anger. "I'm not the man to sponge on a woman, even though she may be so nearly my own as you. No, Lucetta; what you can do is this; and it would save me. My great creditor is Grower,[7] and it is at his hands I shall suffer if at anybody's; while a fortnight's forbearance on his part would be enough to allow me to pull through. This may be got out of him in one way – that you would let it be known to him that you are my intended – that we are to be quietly married in the next fortnight—. Now stop, you haven't heard all! Let him have this story, without of course any prejudice to the fact that the actual engagement between us is to be a long one. Nobody else need know: you could go with me to Mr. Grower, and just let me speak to ye before him as if we were on such terms. We'll ask him to keep it secret. He will willingly wait then. At the fortnight's end I shall be able to face him; and I can coolly tell him all is postponed between us for a year or two. Not a soul in the town need know how you've helped me. Since you wish to be of use, there's your way."

It being now what the people call the "pinking in" of the day, that is, the quarter-hour just before dusk, he did not at first observe the result of his words upon her.

"If it were anything else," she began, and the dryness of her lips was represented in her voice.

"But it is such a little thing!" he said, with a deep reproach. "Less than you have offered – just the beginning of what you have so lately promised! I could have told him as much myself, but he would not have believed me."

"It is not because I won't – it is because I absolutely can't," she said, with rising distress.

"You are provoking!" he burst out. "It is enough to make me force you to carry out at once what you have promised."

"I cannot!" she insisted, desperately.

"Why? When I have only within these few minutes released you from your promise to do the thing off-hand."

"Because—he was a witness!"

"Witness! Of what?"

"If I must tell you—Don't, don't upbraid me!"

"Well? Let's hear what you mean?"

"Witness of my marriage – Mr. Grower was."

"Marriage?"

"Yes. With Mr. Farfrae. O Michael, I am already his wife. We were married this week at Port-Breedy. There were reasons against our doing it here. Mr. Grower was a witness because he happened to be at Port-Breedy at the time."

Henchard stood as if idiotised. She was so alarmed at his silence that she murmured something about lending him sufficient money to tide over the perilous fortnight.

"Married him?" said Henchard at length. "My good – what, married him whilst – bound to marry me?"

"It was like this," she explained, with tears in her eyes and quavers in her voice; "don't – don't be cruel! I loved him so much, and I thought you might tell him of the past – and that grieved me. And then, when I had promised you, I learnt of the rumour that you had – sold your first wife at a fair, like a horse or cow. How could I keep my promise after hearing that? I could not risk myself in your hands; it would have been letting myself down to take your name after such a scandal. But I knew I should lose Donald if I did not secure him at once – for you would carry out your threat of telling him of our former acquaintance, as long as there was a chance of keeping me for yourself by doing so. But you will not do so now, will you, Michael; for it is too late to separate us?"

The notes of St. Jude's[8] bells in full peal had been wafted to them while she spoke; and now the genial thumping of the town band, renowned for its unstinted use of the drumstick, throbbed down the street.

"Then this racket they are making is on account of it, I suppose?" said he.

"Yes – I think he has told them, or else Mr. Grower has. . . . May I leave you now? My – he was detained at Port-Breedy to-day, and sent me on a few hours before him."

"Then it is *his wife's* life I have saved this afternoon."

"Yes – and he will be for ever grateful to you."

"I am much obliged to him. . . . . Oh, you false woman!" burst from Henchard. "You promised me!"

"Yes, yes. But it was under compulsion, and I did not know all your past—"

"And now I've a mind to punish you as you deserve! One word to this bran-new husband of how you courted me, and your precious happiness is blown to atoms."

"Michael – pity me, and be generous."

"You don't deserve pity. You did; but you don't now."

"I'll help you to pay off your debt."

"A pensioner of Farfrae's wife – not I! Don't stay with me longer – I shall say something worse. Go home."

She disappeared under the trees of the south walk as the band came round the corner, awaking the echoes of every stock and stone in celebration of her happiness. Lucetta took no heed, but ran up the back street and reached her own home unperceived.

CHAPTER XXX

Farfrae's words to his landlady had referred to the removal of his boxes and other effects from his late lodgings to Lucetta's house. The work was not heavy, but it had been much hindered on account of the frequent pauses necessitated by exclamations of surprise at the event, of which she had been briefly informed by letter a few hours earlier.

At the last moment of leaving Port-Breedy Farfrae, like John Gilpin,[1] had been detained by important customers, whom, even in the exceptional circumstances, he was not the man to neglect. Moreover, there was a convenience in Lucetta arriving first at her house. Nobody there as yet knew what had happened; and she was best in a position to break the news to the inmates, and give directions for her husband's accommodation. He had, therefore, sent on his two-days' bride in a hired brougham, whilst he went across the country to a certain group of wheat and barley ricks a few miles off, telling her the hour at which he might be expected the same evening. This accounted for her trotting out to meet him after their separation of four hours.

By a strenuous effort, after leaving Henchard, she calmed herself in readiness to receive Donald at High Street Hall when he came on from his lodging. One supreme fact empowered her to this, the sense that, come what would, she had secured him. Half-an-hour after her arrival he walked in, and she met him with a relieved gladness, which a month's perilous absence could not have intensified.

"There is one thing I have not done; and yet it is important," she said earnestly, when she had finished talking about the adventure with the bull. "That is, broken the news of our marriage to my dear Elizabeth-Jane."

"Ah, and you have not," he said thoughtfully. "I gave her a lift from the barn homewards; but I did not tell her either; for I thought she might have heard of it in the town, and was keeping back her congratulations from shyness, and all that."

"She can hardly have heard of it. But I'll find out; I'll go to her now. And, Donald, you don't mind her living on with me just the same as before? She is so quiet and unassuming."

"Oh no, indeed I don't," Farfrae answered with, perhaps, a faint awkwardness. "But I wonder if she would care to?"

"Oh yes," said Lucetta eagerly. "I am sure she would like to. Besides, poor thing, she has no other home."

Farfrae looked at her, and saw that she did not suspect the secret of her more reserved friend. He liked her all the better for the blindness. "Arrange as you like with her, by all means," he said. "It is I who have come to your house, not you to mine."

"I'll run and speak to her," said Lucetta.

When she got upstairs to Elizabeth-Jane's room, the latter had taken off her out-door things, and was resting over a book. Lucetta found in a moment that she had not as yet learnt the news.

"I did not come down to you, Miss Templeman," she said simply. "I was coming to ask if you had quite recovered from your fright, but I found you had a visitor. What are the bells ringing for, I wonder? and the band, too, is playing. Somebody must be married; or else they are practising for Christmas."

Lucetta uttered a vague "Yes," and seating herself by the other young woman, looked musingly at her. "What a lonely creature you are," she presently said; "never knowing what's going on, or what people are talking about everywhere with keen interest. You should get out, and gossip about as other women do, and then you wouldn't be obliged to ask me a question of that kind. Well, now I have something to tell you."

Elizabeth-Jane said she was so glad, and made herself receptive.

"I must go rather a long way back," said Lucetta; the difficulty of explaining herself satisfactorily to the pondering one beside her growing more apparent at each syllable. "You remember that trying case of conscience I told you of some time ago – about the first lover, and the second lover." She let out in jerky phrases a leading word or two of the story she had told.

"Oh yes – I remember; the story of *your friend*," said Elizabeth drily, regarding the irises of Lucetta's eyes as though to catch their exact shade. "The two lovers – the old and the new: how she wanted to marry the second, but felt she ought to marry the first; so that the good she would have done she did not, and the evil that she would not, that she did – exactly like the Apostle Paul."[2]

"Oh, no; she didn't do evil!" said Lucetta hastily.

"But you said that she – or as I may say *you*" – answered Elizabeth, dropping the mask, "were in honour and truth bound to marry the first."

Lucetta's blush at being seen through came and went again before she replied anxiously, "You will never breathe this, will you, Elizabeth-Jane?"

"Certainly not, if you say not."

"Then I will tell you that the case is more complicated – worse, in fact – than it seemed in my story. I and the first man were thrown together in a strange way, and felt that we ought to be united, as the world had misrepresented us.[3] He was a widower, as he supposed. He had not heard of his first wife for many years. But the wife returned, and we parted. She is now dead; and the husband comes paying me addresses again, saying, 'Now we'll complete our purpose.' But, Elizabeth-Jane, all this amounts to a new courtship of me by him; I was absolved from all vows by the return of the other woman."

"Have you not lately renewed your promise?" said the younger with quiet surmise. She had divined Man Number One.

"That was wrung from me by a threat."

"Yes, it was. But I think when any one gets coupled up with a man in the past so unfortunately as you have done, she ought to become his wife, if she can, even if she were innocent."

Lucetta's countenance lost its sparkle. "He turned out to be a man I should be afraid to marry," she pleaded. "Really afraid. And it was not till after my renewed promise that I knew it."

"Then there is only one course left to honesty. You must remain a single woman.'

"But think again. Do consider—"

"I am certain," interrupted her companion, hardily. "I have guessed very well who the man is. My father; and I say it is him or nobody for you."

Any suspicion of lack of respectability[4] was to Elizabeth-Jane like a red rag to a bull. Her craving for correctness of environment was, indeed, almost vicious. Owing to her early troubles with regard to her mother, a semblance of irregularity had terrors for her which those whose names are safeguarded from suspicion know nothing of. "You ought to marry Mr. Henchard or nobody – certainly not another man," she went on with a quivering lip, in whose movement two passions shared.

"I don't admit that," said Lucetta, passionately.

"Admit it or not, it is true."

Lucetta covered her eyes with her right hand, as if she could plead no more, holding out her left to Elizabeth-Jane.

"Why you *have* married him!" cried the latter, jumping up with pleasure after a glance at Lucetta's fingers. "When did you do it? Why did you not tell me, instead of teasing me like this? How very honourable of you! He did treat my mother badly once, it seems, in a moment of intoxication. And it is true that he is stern sometimes. But you will rule him entirely, I am sure, with your beauty and wealth and accomplishments. You are the woman he will adore, and we shall all three be happy together now."

"Oh, my Elizabeth-Jane!" cried Lucetta, distressfully. "'Tis somebody else that I have married! I was so desperate – so afraid of being forced to anything else – so afraid of revelations that would quench his love for me, that I resolved to do it off-hand, come what might, and purchase a week of happiness at any cost."

"You – have – married Mr. Farfrae!" cried Elizabeth-Jane, in Nathan tones.[5]

Lucetta bowed. She had recovered herself.

"The bells are ringing on that account," she said. "My husband is downstairs. He will live here till a more suitable house is ready for us; and I have told him that I want you to stay with me just as before."

"Let me think of it alone," the girl quickly replied, corking up the turmoil of her feeling with grand control.

"You shall. I am sure we shall be happy together."

Lucetta departed to join Donald below, a vague uneasiness floating over her joy at seeing him quite at home there. Not on account of her friend Elizabeth did she feel it: for of the bearings of Elizabeth-Jane's emotions she had not the least suspicion; but on Henchard's alone.

Now the instant decision of Susan Henchard's daughter was to dwell in that house no more. Apart from her estimate of the propriety of Lucetta's conduct, Farfrae had been so nearly her avowed lover that she felt she could not live there.

It was still early in the evening when she hastily put on her things and went out. In a few minutes, knowing the ground, she had found a suitable lodging, and arranged to enter it that night. Returning and entering noiselessly she took off her pretty dress and arrayed herself in a plain one, packing up the other to keep as her best; for she would have to be very economical now. She wrote a note to leave for Lucetta, who was closely shut up in the drawing-room with Farfrae; and then Elizabeth-Jane called a man with a wheelbarrow; and seeing her boxes put into it she trotted off down the street to her rooms. They were in the street in which Henchard lived, and almost opposite his door.

Here she sat down and considered the means of subsistence. The little annual sum settled on her by her stepfather would keep body and soul together. A wonderful skill in netting of all sorts – acquired in childhood by making seines in Newson's home – might serve her in good stead; and her studies, which were pursued unremittingly, might serve her in still better.

By this time the marriage that had taken place was known throughout Casterbridge; had been discussed noisily on kerbstones, confidentially behind counters, and jovially at the King of Prussia. Whether Farfrae would sell his business and set up for a gentleman on his wife's money, or whether he would show independence enough to stick to his trade in spite of his brilliant alliance, was a great point of interest.

CHAPTER XXXI

The retort of the furmity-woman before the magistrates had spread; and in four-and-twenty hours there was not a person in Casterbridge who remained unacquainted with the story of Henchard's mad freak at Weydon Priors Fair, long years before. The amends he had made in after life were lost sight of in the dramatic glare of the original act. Had the incident been well known of old and always, it might by this time have grown to be lightly regarded as the rather tall wild oat, but the single one, of a young man with whom the steady and mature (if somewhat headstrong) burgher of to-day had scarcely a point in common. But the act having lain as dead and buried ever since, the interspace of years was unperceived; and the black spot of his youth wore the aspect of a recent crime.

Small as the Court incident had been in itself, it formed the edge or turn in the incline of Henchard's fortunes. On that day – almost at that minute – he passed the ridge of prosperity and honour, and began to descend rapidly on the other side. It was strange how soon he sank in esteem. Socially he had received a startling fillip downwards; and, having already lost commercial buoyancy from rash transactions, the velocity of his descent in both aspects became accelerated every hour.

He now gazed more at the pavements, and less at the house-fronts, when he walked about; more at the feet and leggings of men, and less into the pupils of their eyes with the blazing regard which formerly had made them blink.

New events combined to undo him. It had been a bad year for others besides himself, and the heavy failure of a debtor whom he had trusted implicitly[1] completed the overthrow of his tottering credit. And now, in his desperation, he failed to preserve that strict correspondence between bulk and sample, which is the soul of commerce in grain. For this, one of his men was mainly to blame; that worthy, in his great unwisdom, having picked over the sample of an enormous quantity of second-rate corn which Henchard had in hand, and removed the pinched, blasted, and smutted grains[2] in great numbers. The produce, if honestly offered, would have created no scandal; but the blunder of misrepresentation, coming at such a moment, dragged Henchard's name into the ditch.

The details of his failure were of the ordinary kind. One day Elizabeth-Jane was passing the Golden Crown, when she saw people bustling in and out more than usual when there was no market. A bystander informed her, with some surprise at her ignorance, that it was a meeting of the Commissioners under Mr. Henchard's bankruptcy. She felt quite tearful, and when she heard that he was present in the hotel she wished to go in and see him, but was advised not to intrude that day.

The room in which debtor and creditors had assembled was a front one, and Henchard, looking out of the window, had caught sight of

Elizabeth-Jane through the wire blind. His examination had closed, and the creditors were leaving. The appearance of Elizabeth threw him into a reverie; till, turning his face from the window, and towering above all the rest, he called their attention for a moment more. His countenance had somewhat changed from its flush of prosperity; the black hair and whiskers were the same as ever, but a film of ash was over the rest.

"Gentlemen," he said, "over and above the assets that we've been talking about, and that appear on the balance-sheet, there be these. It all belongs to ye, as much as everything else I've got, and I don't wish to keep it from you, not I." Saying this, he took his gold watch from his pocket, and laid it on the table; then his purse – the yellow canvas money-bag, such as was carried by all farmers and dealers – untying it, and shaking the money out upon the table beside the watch. The latter he drew back quickly for an instant, to remove the hair-guard made and given him by Lucetta. "There, now you have all,"[3] he said. "And I wish for your sakes 'twas more."

The creditors, farmers almost to a man, looked at the watch, and at the money, and into the street; when Farmer James Everdene[4] spoke.

"No, no, Henchard," he said warmly. "We don't want that. 'Tis honourable in ye; but keep it. What do you say, neighbours – do ye agree?"

"Ay, sure: we don't wish it at all," said Grower, another creditor.

"Let him keep it, of course," murmured another in the background – a silent, reserved young man, named Boldwood;[5] and the rest responded unanimously.

"Well," said the senior Commissioner, addressing Henchard, "though the case is a desperate one, I am bound to admit that I have never met a debtor who behaved more fairly. I've proved the balance-sheet to be as honestly made out as it could possibly be; we have had no trouble; there have been no evasions and no concealments. The rashness of dealing which led to this unhappy situation is obvious enough; but as far as I can see every attempt has been made to avoid wronging anybody."

Henchard was more affected by this than he cared to let them perceive, and he turned aside to the window again. A general murmur of agreement followed the Commissioner's words; and the meeting dispersed. When they were gone Henchard regarded the watch they had returned to him. "'Tisn't mine by rights," he said to himself. "Why the devil didn't they take it? – I don't want what don't belong to me." Moved by a recollection he took the watch to the maker's just opposite, sold it there and then for what the tradesman offered, and went with the proceeds to one among the smaller of his creditors, a cottager of Dummerford, in straitened circumstances, to whom he handed the money.

When everything was ticketed that Henchard had owned, and the auctions were in progress, there was quite a sympathetic reaction in the town, which till then for some time past had done nothing but condemn him. Now that Henchard's whole career was pictured distinctly to his neighbours, and they could see how admirably he had used his one talent of energy to creat a position of affluence out of absolutely nothing – which was really all he could show when he came to the town as a journeyman hay-trusser, with his wimble and knife in his basket – they wondered, and regretted his fall.

Try as she might, Elizabeth could never meet with him. She believed in him still, though nobody else did; and she wanted to be allowed to forgive him for his roughness to her, and to help him in his trouble.

She wrote to him; he did not reply. She then went to his house – the great house she had lived in so happily for a time – with its front of dun brick, vitrified here and there, and its heavy sash-bars – but Henchard was to be found there no more. The ex-Mayor had left the home of his prosperity, and gone into Jopp's cottage by the Priory Mill – the sad purlieu to which he had wandered on the night of his discovery that she was not his daughter. Thither she went.

Elizabeth thought it odd that he had fixed on this spot to retire to, but assumed that necessity had no choice. Trees which seemed old enough to have been planted by the friars still stood around, and the back hatch of the original mill yet formed a cascade which had raised its terrific roar for centuries. The cottage itself was built of old stones from the long-dismantled Priory, scraps of tracery, moulded window-jambs, and arch-labels, being mixed in with the rubble of the walls.

In this cottage he occupied a couple of rooms, Jopp, whom Henchard had employed, abused, cajoled, and dismissed by turns, being the householder. But even here her stepfather could not be seen.

"Not by his daughter?" pleaded Elizabeth.

"By nobody – at present: that's his order," she was informed.

Afterwards she was passing by the corn-stores and hay-barns which had been the headquarters of his business. She knew that he ruled there no longer; but it was with amazement that she regarded the familiar gateway. A smear of decisive lead-coloured paint had been laid on to obliterate Henchard's name, though its letters dimly loomed through like ships in a fog. Over these, in fresh white, spread the name of Farfrae.

Abel Whittle was edging his skeleton in at the wicket, and she said, "Mr. Farfrae is master here?"

"Yaas, Miss Henchet," he said, "Mr. Farfrae have bought the concern and all of we work-folk with it; and 'tis better for us than 'twas – though I shouldn't say that to you as a daughter-law. We work harder, but we bain't made afeard now. It was fear made my few poor hairs so thin. No busting out, no slamming of doors, no meddling with yer eternal soul and all that; and though 'tis a shilling a week less I'm the richer man; for what's all the world if yer mind is always in a larry, Miss Henchet?"

The intelligence was in a general sense true; and Henchard's stores, which had remained in a paralyzed condition during the settlement of his bankruptcy, were stirred into activity again when the new tenant had possession. Thenceforward the full sacks, looped with the shining chain, went scurrying up and down under the cat-head, hairy arms were thrust out from the different doorways, and the grain was hauled in; trusses of hay were tossed anew in and out of the barns, and the wimbles creaked; while the scales and steelyards began to be busy where guess-work had formerly been the rule.

CHAPTER XXXII

Two bridges[1] stood near the lower part of Casterbridge town.

The first, of weather-stained brick, was immediately at the end of High Street, where a diverging branch of that thoroughfare ran round to the low-lying Dummerford lanes; so that the precincts of the bridge formed the merging point of respectability and indigence. The second bridge, of stone, was further out on the highway – in fact, fairly in the meadows, though still within the town boundary.

These bridges had speaking countenances. Every projection in each was worn down to obtuseness, partly by weather, more by friction from generations of loungers, whose toes and heels had from year to year made restless movements against these parapets as they had stood there meditating on the aspect of affairs. In the case of the more friable bricks and stones even the flat faces were worn into hollows by the same mixed mechanism. The masonry of the top was clamped with iron at each joint; since it had been no uncommon thing for desperate men to wrench the coping off and throw it down the river, in reckless defiance of the magistrates.

For to this pair of bridges gravitated all the failures of the town; those who had failed in business, in love, in sobriety, in crime. Why the unhappy hereabout usually chose the bridges for their meditations in preference to a railing, a gate, or a stile, was not so clear.

There was a marked difference of quality between the personages who haunted the near bridge of brick, and the personages who haunted the far one of stone. Those of lowest character preferred the former, adjoining the town; they did not mind the glare of the public eye. They had been of comparatively no account during their successes; and, though they might feel dispirited, they had no particular sense of shame in their ruin. Their hands were mostly kept in their pockets; they wore a leather strap round their waists, and boots that required a great deal of lacing, but seemed never to get any. Instead of sighing at their adversities they spat, and instead of saying the iron had entered into their souls they said they were down on their luck. Jopp in his times of distress had often stood here; so had Mother Cuxsom, Christopher Coney, and poor Abel Whittle.[2]

The *misérables* who stood on the remoter bridge were of a politer stamp. They included bankrupts, hypochondriacs, persons who were what is called "out of a situation" from fault or lucklessness, the inefficient of the professional class – shabby-genteel men, who did not know how to get rid of the weary time between breakfast and dinner, and the yet more weary time between dinner and dark. The eyes of this group were mostly directed over the parapet upon the running water below. A man seen there looking thus fixedly into the river was pretty sure to be one whom the world did not treat kindly for some reason or other. While those in straits on the townward bridge did not mind who saw them so, and kept their backs to the parapet to survey the passers-by, those in straits on this never faced the road, never turned their heads at coming footsteps, but, sensitive to their condition, watched the current whenever a stranger approached, as if some strange fish interested them, though every finned thing had been poached out of the river years before.

There and thus they would muse; if their grief were the grief of oppression they would wish themselves kings; if their grief were poverty, wish themselves millionaires; if sin, they would wish they were saints or angels; if despised love, that they were some much-courted Adonis of county fame. Some had been known to stand and think so long with this fixed gaze downward, that eventually they had allowed their poor carcases to follow that gaze; and they were discovered the next morning in the pool beneath out of reach of their troubles.[3]

To this bridge came Henchard as the other unfortunates had come before him, his way thither being by the riverside path on the chilly edge of the town. Here he was standing one windy afternoon when Dummerford church clock struck five. While the gusts were bringing the notes to his ears across the damp intervening flat a man passed behind him, and greeted Henchard by name. Henchard turned slightly, and saw that the comer was Jopp, his old foreman, now employed elsewhere, to whom, though he hated him, he had gone for lodgings because Jopp was the one man in Casterbridge whose observation and

PLATE XIV

'Henchard turned slightly, and saw that the comer was Jopp, his old foreman.'

opinion the fallen corn-merchant despised to the point of indifference.

Henchard returned him a scarcely perceptible nod, and Jopp stopped.

"He and she are gone into their new house to-day," said Jopp.

"Oh," said Henchard, absently. "Which house is that?"

"Your old one."

"Gone into my house?" And, starting up, Henchard added, "*My* house of all others in the town!"

"Well, as somebody was sure to live there, and you couldn't, it can do ye no harm that he's the man."

It was quite true: he felt that it was doing him no harm. Farfrae, who had already taken the yards and stores, had acquired possession of the house for the obvious convenience of its contiguity. And yet this act of his taking up residence within those roomy chambers while he, their former tenant, lived in a cottage, galled him indescribably.

Jopp continued: "And you heard of that fellow who bought all the best furniture at your sale? He was bidding for no other than Farfrae all the while. It has never been moved out of the house, as he'd already got the lease."

"My furniture too! Surely he'll buy my body and soul likewise."[4]

"There's no saying he won't, if you be willing to sell." And having planted these wounds in the heart of his once imperious master, Jopp went on his way; while Henchard stared and stared into the racing river till the bridge seemed moving backward with him.

The low land grew blacker, and the sky a deeper grey. When the landscape looked like a picture blotted in with ink, another traveller approached the great stone bridge. He was driving a gig, his direction being also townwards. On the round of the middle of the arch the gig stopped. "Mr. Henchard?" came from it in the voice of Farfrae. Henchard turned his face.

Finding that he had guessed rightly, Farfrae told the man who accompanied him to drive home; while he alighted, and went up to his former friend.

"I have heard that you think of emigrating, Mr. Henchard," he said. "Is it true? I have a real reason for asking."

Henchard withheld his answer for several instants, and then said, "Yes; it is true. I am going where you were going to a few years ago, when I prevented you and got you to bide here. 'Tis turn and turn about, isn't it? Do ye mind how we stood like this on the bridge[5] when I persuaded ye to stay? You then stood without a chattel to your name, and I was the master of the house in Corn Street. But now I stand without a stick or a rag, and the master of that house is you."

"Yes, yes; it is so. Such is the course of things," said Farfrae.

"Ha, ha, true!" cried Henchard, throwing himself into a mood of jocularity. "Up and down! I'm used to it. What's the odds after all!"

"Now listen to me, if it's no taking up your time," said Farfrae, "just as I listened to you. Don't go. Stay at home."

"But I can do nothing else, man," said Henchard scornfully. "The little money I have will just keep body and soul together for a few weeks, and no more. I have not felt inclined to go back to journey-work yet: but I can't stay doing nothing, and my best chance is elsewhere."

"No; but what I propose is this – if ye will listen. Come and live in your old house. We can spare some rooms very well – I am sure my wife would not mind it at all – until there's an opening for ye."

Henchard started. Probably the picture drawn by the unsuspecting Donald of himself under the same roof with Lucetta was too striking to be received with equanimity. "No, no," he said gruffly; "we should quarrel."

"You should hae a part to yourself," said Farfrae; "and nobody would interrupt you. It will be healthier than down there by the river where you live now."

Still Henchard refused. "You don't know what you ask," he said. "However, I can do no less than thank ye."

They walked into the town together side by side, as they had done when Henchard persuaded the young Scotchman to remain. "Will you come in and have some supper?" said Farfrae, when they reached the middle of the town where their paths diverged right and left.

"No, no."

"By-the-by, I had nearly forgot. I bought a good deal of your furniture."

"So I have heard."

"Well, it was no that I wanted it so very much for myself; but I wish ye to pick out all that you care to have – such things as may be endeared to ye by associations, or particularly suited to your use. And take them to your own house – it will not be depriving me; we can do with less very well, and I will have plenty of opportunities of getting more."

"What – give it to me for nothing?" said Henchard. "But you paid the creditors for it."

"Ah, yes; but maybe it's worth more to you than it is to me."

Henchard was a little moved. "I – sometimes think I've wronged ye!" he said, in tones which showed the disquietude that the night shades hid in his face. He shook Farfrae abruptly by the hand, and hastened away as if unwilling to betray himself further. Farfrae saw him turn through the thoroughfare into Bull Stake and vanish down towards the Priory Mill.

Meanwhile Elizabeth-Jane, in an upper room no larger than the Prophet's chamber,[6] and with the silk attire of her palmy days packed away in a box, was netting with great industry between the hours which she devoted to studying such books as she could get hold of.

Her lodgings being nearly opposite her stepfather's former residence, now Farfrae's, she could see Donald and Lucetta speeding in and out of their door with all the bounding enthusiasm of their situation. She avoided looking that way as much as possible, but it was hardly in human nature to keep the eyes averted when the door slammed.

While living on thus quietly she heard the news that Henchard had caught cold and was confined to his room – possibly a result of standing about the meads in damp weather. She went off to his house at once. This time she was determined not to be denied admittance, and made her way upstairs. He was sitting up in the bed with a great-coat round him, and at first resented her intrusion. "Go away – go away," he said. "I don't like to see ye!"

"But, father—"

"I don't like to see ye," he repeated.

However, the ice was broken, and she remained. She made the room more comfortable, gave directions to the people below, and by the time she went away had reconciled her stepfather to her visiting him.

The effect, either of her ministrations or of her mere presence, was a rapid recovery. He soon was well enough to go out; and now things seemed to wear a new colour in his eyes. He no longer thought of emigration, and thought more of Elizabeth. The having nothing to do made him more dreary than any other circumstance; and one day, with better views of Farfrae than he had held for some time, and a sense that honest work was not a thing to be ashamed of, he stoically went down to Farfrae's yard and asked to be taken on as a journeyman hay-trusser. He was engaged at once.

This hiring of Henchard was done through a foreman, Farfrae feeling that it was undesirable to come personally in contact with the ex-cornfactor more than was absolutely necessary. While anxious to help him he was well aware by this time of his uncertain temper, and thought reserved relations best. For the same reason, his orders to Henchard to proceed to this and that country farm trussing in the usual way were always given through a third person.

For a time these arrangements worked well, it being the custom to truss in the respective stack-yards, before bringing it away, the hay bought at the different farms about the neighbourhood; so that Henchard was often absent at such places the whole week long. When this was all done, and Henchard had become in a measure broken in, he came to work daily on the home premises like the rest. And thus the once flourishing merchant and Mayor and what not stood as a day-labourer in the barns and granaries he formerly had owned.

"I have worked as a journeyman before now, ha'n't I?" he would say in his defiant way; "and why shouldn't I do it again?" But he looked a far different journeyman from the one he had been in his earlier days. Then he had worn clean, suitable clothes, light and cheerful in hue; leggings yellow as marigolds, corduroys immaculate as new flax, and a neckerchief like a flower-garden. Now he wore the remains of an old blue cloth suit of his gentlemanly times, a rusty silk hat, and a once black satin stock, soiled and shabby. Clad thus, he went to and fro, still comparatively an active man – for he was not much over forty – and saw with the other men in the yard Donald Farfrae going in and out the green door that led to the garden, and the big house, and Lucetta.

At the beginning of the winter it was rumoured about Casterbridge that Mr. Farfrae, already in the Town Council, was to be proposed for Mayor in a year or two.

"Yes; she was wise, she was wise in her generation!"[7] said Henchard to himself when he heard of this one day on his way to Farfrae's hay-barn. He thought it over as he wimbled his bonds, and the piece of news acted as a reviviscent breath to that old view of his – of Donald Farfrae as his triumphant rival who rode rough-shod over him.

"A fellow of his age going to be Mayor, indeed!" he murmured with a corner-drawn smile on his mouth. "But 'tis her money that floats en upward. Ha-ha – how cust odd it is! Here be I, his former master, working for him as man, and he the man standing as master, with my house and my furniture and my intended wife[8] all his own."

He repeated these things a hundred times a day. During the whole period of his acquaintance with Lucetta he had never wished to claim her as his own so desperately as he now regretted her loss. It was no mercenary hankering after her fortune that moved him; though that fortune had been the means of making her so much the more desired by giving her the air of independence and sauciness which attracts men of his composition. It had given her servants, house, and fine clothing – a setting that invested Lucetta with a startling novelty in the eyes of him who had known her in her narrow days.

He accordingly lapsed into moodiness, and at every allusion to the possibility of Farfrae's near election to the municipal chair his former hatred of the Scotchman returned. Concurrently with this he underwent a moral change. It resulted in his significantly saying every now and then, in tones of recklessness, "Only a fortnight more!" – "Only a dozen days!" and so forth, lessening his figures day by day.

"Why d'ye say only a dozen days?" asked Solomon Longways as he worked beside Henchard in the granary weighing oats.

"Because in twelve days I shall be released from my oath."

"What oath?"

"The oath to drink no spirituous liquid. In twelve days it will be twenty years since I swore it, and then I mean to enjoy myself, please God."

Elizabeth-Jane sat at her window one Sunday, and while there she heard in the street below a conversation which introduced Henchard's name. She was wondering what was the matter, when a third person who was passing by asked the question in her mind.

"Michael Henchard have busted out drinking after taking nothing for twenty years."

Elizabeth-Jane jumped up, put on her things, and went out.

CHAPTER XXXIII

At this date there prevailed in Casterbridge a convivial custom – scarcely recognized as such, yet none the less established. On the afternoon of every Sunday a large contingent of the Casterbridge journeymen – steady church-goers and sedate characters – having attended service, filed from the church doors across the way to the King of Prussia Inn. The rear was usually brought up by the choir,[1] with their bass-viols, fiddles, and flutes under their arms.

The great point, the point of honour, on these sacred occasions was for each man to strictly limit himself to half-a-pint of liquor. This scrupulosity was so well understood by the landlord, that the whole company was served in cups of that measure. They were all exactly alike – straight-sided, with leafless lime-trees done in eel-brown on the sides – one towards the drinker's lips, the other confronting his comrade. To wonder how many of these cups the landlord possessed altogether was a favourite exercise of children in the marvellous. Forty at least might have been seen at these times in the large room, forming a ring round the margin of the great sixteen-legged oak table, like the monolithic circle at Stonehenge[2] in its pristine days. Outside and above the forty cups came a circle of forty smoke-jets from forty clay pipes; outside the pipes the countenances of the forty church-goers, supported at the back by a circle of forty chairs.

The conversation was not the conversation of week days, but a thing altogether finer in point and higher in tone. They invariably discussed the sermon, dissecting it, weighing it, as above or below the average – the general tendency being to regard it as a scientific feat or performance which had no relation to their own lives, except as between critics and the thing criticized. The bass-viol player and the clerk usually spoke with more authority than the rest on account of their official connection with the preacher.

Now the King of Prussia was the inn chosen by Henchard as the place for closing his long term of dramless years. He had so timed his entry as to be well established in the large room by the time the forty church-goers entered to their customary cups. The flush upon his face proclaimed at once that the vow of twenty years had lapsed, and the era of recklessness begun anew. He was seated on a small table, drawn up to the side of the massive oak board reserved for the churchmen, a few of whom nodded to him as they took their places, and said, "How be ye, Mr. Henchard? Quite a stranger here."

Henchard did not take the trouble to reply for a few moments, and his eyes rested on his stretched-out legs and boots. "Yes," he said at length; "that's true. I've been down in spirit for weeks; some of ye know the cause. I am better now; but not quite serene. I want you fellows of the choir to strike up a tune; and what with that and this brew of Stannidge's I am in hopes of getting altogether out of my minor key."

"With all my heart," said the first fiddle. "We've let back our strings, that's true; but we can soon pull 'em up again. Sound A, neighbours, and give the man a stave."

"I don't care a curse what the words be," said Henchard. "Hymns, ballets, or rantipole rubbish; the Rogue's March[3] or the cherubim's warble – 'tis all the same to me if 'tis good harmony, and well put out."

"Well – heh, heh – it may be we can do that, and not a man among us that have sat in the gallery less than twenty year," said the leader of the band. "As 'tis Sunday, neighbours, suppose we raise the fourth Psa'am,[4] to Samuel Wakely's tune, as improved by me?"

"Hang Samuel Wakely's tune as improved by thee!" said Henchard. "Chuck across one of your psalters – old Wiltshire[5] is the only tune worth singing – the psalm-tune that would make my blood ebb and flow like the sea when I was a steady chap. I'll find some words to fit en." He took one of the psalters, and began turning over the leaves.

Chancing to look out of the window at that moment, he saw a flock of people passing by, and perceived them to be the congregation of the upper church, now just dismissed, their sermon having been a longer one than that the lower parish was favoured with. Among the rest of the leading inhabitants walked Mr. Councillor Farfrae, with Lucetta upon his arm, the observed and imitated of all the smaller tradesmen's womankind. Henchard's mouth changed a little, and he continued to turn over the leaves.

"Now then," he said, "Psalm the Hundred-and-Ninth, to the tune of Wiltshire: verses ten to fifteen. I gie ye the words:

> "His seed shall orphans be, his wife
>   A widow plunged in grief;
> His vagrant children beg their bread
>   Where none can give relief.
>
> "His ill-got riches shall be made
>   To usurers a prey;
> The fruit of all his toil shall be
>   By strangers borne away.
>
> "None shall be found that to his wants
>   Their mercy will extend,
> Or to his helpless orphan seed
>   The least assistance lend.
>
> "A swift destruction soon shall seize
>   On his unhappy race;
> And the next age his hated name
>   Shall utterly deface."

"I know the Psa'am – I know the Psa'am!" said the leader hastily; "but I would as lief not sing it. 'Twasn't made for singing. We chose it once when the gipsies stole the pa'son's mare, thinking to please him, but he were quite upset. Whatever Servant David wer thinking about when he made a Psalm that nobody can sing without disgracing himself, I can't fathom! Now then, the Fourth Psalm to Samuel Wakely's tune, as improved by me."

"'Od seize your sauce – I tell ye to sing the Hundred-and-Ninth, to

Wiltshire, and sing it you shall!" roared Henchard. "Not a single one of all the droning crew of ye goes out of this room till that Psalm is sung!" He slipped off the table, seized the poker, and going to the door placed his back against it. "Now then, go ahead, if you don't wish to have your cust pates broken!"

"Don't 'ee, don't 'ee take on so! – As 'tis the Sabbath-day, and 'tis Servant David's words and not ours, perhaps we don't mind for once, hey?" said one of the terrified choir, looking round upon the rest. So the instruments were tuned and the comminatory verses sung.

"Thank ye, thank ye," said Henchard in a softened voice, his eyes growing downcast, and his manner that of a man much moved by the strains. "Don't you blame David," he went on in low tones, shaking his head without raising his eyes. "He knew what he was about when he wrote that. If I could afford it, be hanged if I wouldn't keep a church choir at my own expense to play and sing to me at these low, dark times of my life. But the bitter thing is that when I was rich I didn't need what I could have, and now I be poor I can't have what I need!"

While they paused, Lucetta and Farfrae passed again, this time homeward, it being their custom to take, like others, a short walk out on the highway and back, between church and tea-time. "There's the man we've been singing about," said Henchard.

The players and singers turned their heads, and saw his meaning.

"Heaven forbid!" said the bass-player.

"'Tis the man," repeated Henchard doggedly.

"Then if I'd known," said the performer on the clarionet solemnly, "that 'twas meant for a living man, nothing should have drawn out of my wynd-pipe the breath for that Psalm, so help me!"

"Nor from mine," said the first singer. "But, thought I, as it was made so long ago, and so far away, perhaps there isn't much in it, so I'll oblige a neighbour; for there's nothing to be said against the tune."

"Ah, my boys, you've sung it," cried Henchard triumphantly. "As for him, it was partly by his songs that he got over me, and heaved me out. . . . . I could double him up like that – and yet I don't." He laid the poker across his knee, bent it as if it were a twig, flung it down, and came away from the door.

It was at this time that Elizabeth-Jane, having heard where her

THE MAYOR OF CASTERBRIDGE

stepfather was, entered the room with a pale and agonized countenance. The choir and the rest of the company moved off, in accordance with their half-pint regulation. Elizabeth-Jane went up to Henchard, and entreated him to accompany her home.

By this hour the volcanic fires of his nature had burnt down, and having drunk no great quantity as yet, he was inclined to acquiesce. She took his arm, and together they went on. Henchard walked blankly, like a blind man, repeating to himself the last words of the singers:

> "And the next age his hated name
> Shall utterly deface."

At length he said to her, "I am a man to my word. I have kept my oath for twenty years; and now I can drink with a good conscience. . . . . If I don't do for him – well, I am a fearful practical joker when I choose. He has taken away everything from me, and by heavens, if I meet him I won't answer for my deeds!"

These half-uttered words alarmed Elizabeth – all the more by reason of the still determination of Henchard's mien.

"What will you do?" she asked cautiously, while trembling with disquietude, and guessing Henchard's allusion only too well.

Henchard did not answer, and they went on till they had reached his cottage. "May I come in?" she said.

"No, no; not to-day," said Henchard; and she went away; feeling that to caution Farfrae was almost her duty, as it was certainly her strong desire.

As on the Sunday, so on the weekdays, Farfrae and Lucetta might have been seen flitting about the town like two butterflies – or rather like a bee and a butterfly in league for life. She seemed to take no pleasure in going anywhere except in her husband's company; and hence when business would not permit him to waste an afternoon she remained indoors, waiting for the time to pass till his return, her face being visible to Elizabeth-Jane from her window aloft. The latter, however, did not say to herself that Farfrae should be thankful for such devotion, but, full of her reading, she cited Rosalind's exclamation: "Mistress, know yourself; down on your knees and thank heaven fasting for a good man's love."[6]

232

She kept her eye upon Henchard also. One day he answered her inquiry for his health by saying that he could not endure Abel Whittle's[7] pitying eyes upon him while they worked together in the yard. "He is such a fool," said Henchard, "that he can never get out of his mind the time when I was master there."

"I'll come and wimble for you instead of him, if you will allow me," said she. Her motive on going to the yard was to get an opportunity of observing the general position of affairs on Farfrae's premises now that her stepfather was a workman there. Henchard's threats had alarmed her so much, that she wished to see his behaviour when the two were face to face.

For two or three days after her arrival Donald did not make any appearance. Then one afternoon the green door opened, and through came, first Farfrae, and at his heels Lucetta. Donald brought his wife forward without hesitation, it being obvious that he had no suspicion whatever of any antecedents in common between her and the now journeyman hay-trusser.

Henchard did not turn his eyes towards either of the pair, keeping them fixed on the bond he twisted as if that alone absorbed him. A feeling of delicacy, which even prompted Farfrae to avoid anything that might seem like triumphing over a fallen rival, led him to keep away from the hay-barn where Henchard and his daughter were working, and to go on to the corn department. Meanwhile Lucetta, never having been informed that Henchard had entered her husband's service, rambled straight on to the barn, where she came suddenly upon Henchard, and gave vent to a little "Oh!" which the happy and busy Donald was too far off to hear.

Henchard, with withering humility of demeanour, touched the brim of his hat to her as Whittle and the rest had done, to which she breathed a dead-alive "Good afternoon."

"I beg your pardon, ma'am?" said Henchard, as if he had not heard.

"I said good afternoon," she faltered.

"O yes, good afternoon, ma'am," he replied, touching his hat again. "I am glad to see you, ma'am." Lucetta looked embarrassed, and Henchard continued: "For we humble workmen here feel it a great honour that a lady should look in and take an interest in us."

PLATE XV

'Henchard, with withering humility of demeanour, touched the brim of his hat to her.'

She glanced at him entreatingly; the sarcasm was too bitter, too unendurable.

"Can you tell me the time, ma'am?" he asked.

"Yes," she said hastily; "half-past four."

"Thank ye. An hour and a half longer before we are released from work. Ah, ma'am, we of the lower classes know nothing of the gay leisure that such as you enjoy."

As soon as she could do so Lucetta left him, nodded and smiled to Elizabeth-Jane, and joined her husband at the other end of the enclosure, where she could be seen leading him away by the outer gates, so as to avoid passing Henchard again. That she had been taken by surprise was obvious.

The result of this casual rencounter was, that the next morning a note was put into Henchard's hand by the postman.

"Will you," said Lucetta, with as much bitterness as she could put into a small communication, "will you kindly undertake not to speak to me in the biting undertones you used to-day, if I walk through the yard at any time? I bear you no ill-will, and I am only too glad that you should have employment of my dear husband; but in common fairness treat me as his wife, and do not try to make me wretched by covert words. I have committed no crime, and done you no injury."

"Poor fool!" said Henchard with fond savagery, holding out the note. "To know no better than commit herself in writing like this! Why, if I were to show that to her dear husband – pooh!" He threw the letter into the fire.

Lucetta took care not to come again among the hay and corn. She would rather have died than run the risk of encountering Henchard at such close quarters a second time. The gulf between them was growing wider every day. Farfrae was always considerate to his fallen acquaintance; but it was impossible that he should not, by degrees, cease to regard the ex-corn merchant as more than one of his other workmen. Henchard saw this, and concealed his feelings under a cover of stolidity, fortifying his heart by drinking more freely at the King of Prussia every evening.

Often did Elizabeth-Jane, in her endeavours to prevent his taking other liquor, carry tea to him in a little basket at five o'clock. Arriving one day on this errand, she found her stepfather was measuring up clover-seed and rape-seed in the corn-stores on the top floor, and she ascended to him. Each floor had a door opening into the air under a cat-head, from which a chain dangled for hoisting the sacks.

When Elizabeth's head rose through the trap she perceived that the upper door was open, and that her stepfather and Farfrae stood just within it in conversation, Farfrae being nearest the dizzy edge, and Henchard a little way behind. Not to interrupt them she remained on the steps without raising her head any higher. While waiting thus she saw – or fancied she saw, for she had a terror of feeling certain – her stepfather slowly raise his hand to a level behind Farfrae's shoulders, a curious expression taking possession of his face. The young man was quite unconscious of the action, which was so indirect that, if Farfrae had observed it, he might almost have regarded it as an idle outstretching of the arm. But it would have been possible, by a comparatively light touch, to push Farfrae off his balance, and send him head over heels into the air.

Elizabeth felt quite sick at heart on thinking of what this *might* have meant. As soon as they turned she mechanically took the tea to him, left it, and went away. Reflecting, she endeavoured to assure herself that the movement was an idle eccentricity, and no more. Yet, on the other hand, his subordinate position in an establishment where he once had been master might be acting on him like an irritant poison; and she finally resolved to caution Donald.

CHAPTER XXXIV

Next morning, accordingly, she rose at five o'clock, and went into the street. It was not yet light; a dense fog prevailed, and the town was as silent as it was dark, except that from the rectangular avenues which framed in the borough there came a chorus of tiny rappings, caused by the fall of water drops condensed on the boughs; now it was wafted from the West Walk, now from the South Walk; and then from both quarters simultaneously. She moved on to the bottom of Corn Street, and, knowing his time well, waited only a few minutes before she heard the familiar bang of his door, and then his quick walk towards her. She met him at the point where the last tree of the engirdling avenue flanked the last house in the street.

He could hardly discern her till, glancing inquiringly, he said, "What – Miss Henchard – and are ye up so early?"

She asked him to pardon her for waylaying him at such an unseemly time. "But I am anxious to mention something," she said. "And I wished not to alarm Mrs. Farfrae by calling."

"Yes?" said he, with the cheeriness of a superior. "And what may it be? It's very kind of ye, I'm sure."

She now felt the difficulty of conveying to his mind the exact aspect of possibilities in her own. But she somehow began, and introduced Henchard's name. "I sometimes fear," she said with an effort, "that he may be betrayed into some attempt to – insult you, sir."

"But we are the best of friends."

"Or to play some practical joke upon you, sir. Remember that he has been hardly used."

"But we are quite friendly."

"Or to do something – that would injure you – hurt you – wound you." Every word cost her twice its length of pain. And she could see that Farfrae was still incredulous. Henchard, a poor man in his employ, was not, to Farfrae's view, the Henchard who had ruled him. Yet he was not only the same man, but that man with the sinister qualities formerly latent quickened into life by his buffetings.

Farfrae, happy, and thinking no evil, persisted in making light of her fears. Thus they parted, and she went homeward, journeymen now being in the street, waggoners going to the harness-makers for articles left to be repaired, farm-horses going to the shoeing-smiths, and the sons of labour being generally on the move. Elizabeth entered her lodging unhappily, thinking she had done no good, and only made herself appear foolish by her weak note of warning.

But Donald Farfrae was one of those men upon whom an incident is never absolutely lost. He revised impressions from a subsequent point of view, and the impulsive judgment of the moment was not always his permanent one. The vision of Elizabeth's earnest face in the rimy dawn came back to him several times during the day. Knowing the solidity of her character, he did not treat her hints altogether as idle sounds.

But he did not desist from a kindly scheme on Henchard's account that engaged him just then; and when he met Lawyer Joyce, the town-clerk, later in the day, he spoke of it as if nothing had occurred to damp it.

"About that little seedsman's shop," he said; "the shop overlooking the churchyard, which is to let. It is not for myself I want it; but for our unlucky fellow-townsman, Henchard. It would be a new beginning for him, if a small one; and I have told the Council that I would head a private subscription among them to set him up in it – that I would be fifty pounds, if they would make up the other fifty among them."

"Yes, yes; so I've heard; and there's nothing to say against it for that matter," the town-clerk replied, in his plain, frank way. "But, Farfrae, others see what you don't. Henchard hates ye – ay, hates ye; and 'tis right that you should know it. To my knowledge he was at the King of Prussia last night, saying in public that about you which a man ought not to say about another."

"Is it so – and is it so!" said Farfrae, looking down. "Why should he do it?" added the young man, bitterly; "what harm have I done him that he should try to wrong me?"

"God only knows," said Joyce, lifting his eyebrows. "It shows much long-suffering in you to put up with him, and keep him in your employ."

"But I cannet discharge a man who was once a good friend to me. How can I forget that when I came here 'twas he enabled me to make a footing for myself? No, no. As long as I've a day's wark to offer he shall do it if he chooses. 'Tis not I who will deny him such a little as that. But I'll drop the idea of establishing him in a shop till I can think more about it."

It grieved Farfrae much to give up this scheme. But a damp having been thrown over it by these and other voices in the air, he went and countermanded his orders. The then occupier of the shop was in it when Farfrae spoke to him, and feeling it necessary to give some explanation of his withdrawal from the negotiation, Donald mentioned

Henchard's name, and stated that the intentions of the Council had been changed.

The occupier was much disappointed, and straightway informed Henchard, as soon as he saw him, that a scheme of the Council for setting him up in a shop had been knocked on the head by Farfrae. And thus out of error enmity grew.

When Farfrae got indoors that evening the tea-kettle was singing on the high hob of the semi-egg-shaped grate. Lucetta, light as a sylph, ran forward and seized his hands, whereupon Farfrae duly kissed her.

"Oh!" she cried playfully, turning to the window. "See – the blinds are not drawn down, and the people can look in – what a scandal!"

When the candles were lighted, the curtains drawn, and the twain sat at tea, she noticed that he looked serious. Without directly inquiring why, she let her eyes linger solicitously on his face.

"Who has called?" he absently asked. "Any folk for me?"

"No," said Lucetta. "What's the matter, Donald?"

"Well – nothing worth talking of," he responded sadly.

"Then, never mind it. You will get through it. Scotchmen are always lucky."

"No – not always!" he said, shaking his head gloomily as he contemplated a crumb on the table. "I know many who have not been so! There was Sandy Macfarlane, who started to America to try his fortune, and he was drowned; and Archibald Leith, he was murdered! And poor Willie Dunbleeze and Maitland Macfreeze – they fell into bad courses, and went the way of all such!"

"Why – you old goosey – I was only speaking in a general sense, of course. You are always so literal. Now when we have finished tea, sing me that funny song about high-heeled shoon and siller tags, and the one-and-forty wooers."[1]

"No, no. I couldna sing to-night! It's Henchard – he hates me; so that I may not be his friend if I would. I would understand why there should be a wee bit envy; but I cannot see a reason for the whole intensity of what he feels. Now can you, Lucetta? It is more like old-fashioned rivalry in love than just a bit of rivalry in trade."

Lucetta had grown somewhat wan. "No," she replied.

"I give him employment – I cannot refuse it. But neither can I blind myself to the fact that with a man of passions such as his, there is no safeguard for conduct!"

"What have you heard – oh Donald, dearest?" said Lucetta in alarm. The words on her lips were "anything about me?" – but she did not utter them. She could not, however, suppress her agitation, and her eyes filled with tears.

"No, no – it is not so serious as ye fancy," declared Farfrae soothingly; though he did not know its seriousness so well as she.

"I wish you would do what we have talked of," mournfully remarked Lucetta. "Give up business, and go away from here. We have plenty of money, and why should we stay?"

Farfrae seemed seriously disposed to discuss this move, and they talked thereon till a visitor was announced. Their neighbour Alderman Vatt came in.

"You've heard, I suppose, of poor Dr. Chalkfield's death? Yes – died this afternoon at five," said Mr. Vatt. Chalkfield was the Councilman who had succeeded to the Mayoralty in the preceding November.

Farfrae was sorry at the intelligence, and Mr. Vatt continued: "Well, we know he's been going some days, and as his family is well provided for we must take it all as it is. Now I have called to ask ye this – quite privately. If I should nominate ye to succeed him, and there should be no particular opposition, will ye accept the chair?"

"But there are folk whose turn is before mine; and I'm over young, and may be thought pushing?" said Farfrae after a pause.

"Not at all. I don't speak for myself only, several have named it. You won't refuse?"

"We thought of going away," interposed Lucetta, looking at Farfrae anxiously.

"It was only a fancy," Farfrae murmured. "I wouldna refuse if it is the wish of a respectable majority in the Council."

"Very well, then, look upon yourself as elected. We have had old men long enough."

When he was gone Farfrae said musingly, "See now how it's ourselves that are ruled by the powers above us! We plan this, but we do that. If they want to make me Mayor I will stay, and Henchard must rave as he will."

From this evening onward Lucetta was very uneasy. If she had not been imprudence incarnate, she would not have acted as she did when she met Henchard by accident a day or two later. It was in the bustle of the market, when no one could readily notice their discourse.

"Michael," said she, "I must again ask you what I asked you months ago – to return me any letters or papers of mine that you may have – unless you have destroyed them. You must see how desirable it is that the time at Jersey should be blotted out, for the good of all parties."

"Why, bless the woman – I packed up every scrap of your handwriting to give you in the coach – but you never appeared."

She explained how the death of her aunt had prevented her taking the journey on that day. "And what became of the parcel then?" she asked.

He could not say – he would consider. When she was gone he recollected that he had left a heap of useless papers in his former dining-room safe – built up in the wall of his old house – now occupied by Farfrae. The letters might have been amongst them.

A grotesque grin shaped itself on Henchard's face. Had that safe been opened?[2]

On the very evening which followed this there was a great ringing of bells in Casterbridge, and the combined brass, wood, catgut, and leather bands played round the town with more prodigality of percussion-notes than ever. Farfrae was Mayor – the two-hundredth odd of a series forming an elective dynasty dating back to the days of Charles I. – and the fair Lucetta was the courted of the town. . . . . But, ah! that worm i' the bud[3] – Henchard; what he could tell!

He, in the meantime, festering with indignation at some erroneous intelligence of Farfrae's opposition to the scheme for installing him in the little seed-shop, was greeted with the news of the municipal election (which, by reason of Farfrae's comparative youth and his Scottish nativity – a thing unprecedented in the case – had an interest far beyond the ordinary). The bell-ringing and the band-playing, loud as Tamerlane's trumpet,[4] goaded the down-fallen Henchard indescribably; the ousting now seemed to him to be complete.

The next morning he went to the corn-yard as usual, and about eleven o'clock Donald entered through the green door, with no trace of the worshipful about him. The yet more emphatic change of places between him and Henchard which this election had established renewed a slight embarrassment in the manner of the modest younger man; but Henchard showed the front of one who had overlooked all this; and Farfrae met his amenities half-way at once.

"I was going to ask you," said Henchard, "about a packet that I may possibly have left in my old safe in the dining-room." He added particulars.

"If so, there it is now," said Farfrae. "I have never opened the safe at all as yet; for I keep my few securities at the bank, to sleep easy o' nights?"[5]

"It was not of much consequence – to me," said Henchard. "But I'll call for it this evening, if you don't mind."

It was quite late when he fulfilled his promise. He had primed himself with grog, as he did very frequently now, and a curl of sardonic humour hung on his lip as he approached the house, as though he were contemplating some terrible form of amusement. Whatever it was, the incident of his entry did not diminish its force, this being his first visit to the house since he had lived there as owner. The ring of the bell spoke to him like the voice of a familiar drudge who had been bribed to forsake him; the movements of the doors were revivals of dead days.

Farfrae invited him into the dining-room, where he at once unlocked the iron safe built into the wall, *his*, Henchard's safe, made by an ingenious locksmith under his direction. Farfrae drew thence the parcel, and other papers, with apologies for not having returned them.

"Never mind," said Henchard drily. "The fact is they are letters mostly. . . . Yes," he went on, sitting down and unfolding Lucetta's passionate bundle, "here they be. That ever I should see 'em again! I hope Mrs. Farfrae is well after her exertions of yesterday?"

"She has felt a bit weary; and has gone to bed early on that account."

Henchard returned to the letters, sorting them over with interest, Farfrae being seated at the other end of the dining-table. "You don't forget, of course," he resumed, "that curious chapter in the history of my past, which I told you of, and that you gave me some assistance in? These letters are, in fact, related to that unhappy business. Though, thank God, it is all over now."

"What became of the poor girl?" asked Farfrae.

"Luckily she married, and married well," said Henchard. "So that these reproaches she poured out on me do not now cause me any twinges, as they might otherwise have done. . . . Just listen to what an angry woman will say!"

Farfrae, willing to humour Henchard, though quite uninterested, and bursting with yawns, gave well-mannered attention.

"For me," the letter went on,[6] "there is practically no future. A creature too unconventionally devoted to you – who feels it impossible that she can be wife of any other man; and who is yet no more to you than the first woman you meet in the street – such am I. I quite acquit you of any intention to wrong me, yet you are the door through which wrong has come to me. That in the event of your present wife's death you will place me in her position is a consolation so far as it goes – but how far does it go? Thus I sit here, forsaken by my few acquaintance, and forsaken by you."

"That's how she went on to me," said Henchard; "acres of words like that, when what had happened was no fault of mine."

"Yes," said Farfrae absently, "such is the way of women." But the fact was that he knew very little of the sex; yet detecting a sort of resemblance in style between the effusions of the woman he worshipped and those of the supposed stranger, he concluded that Aphrodite ever spoke thus, whose-soever the personality she assumed.

Henchard unfolded another letter, and read it through likewise, stopping at the subscription as before. "Her name I don't give," he said blandly. "As I didn't marry her, and another man did, I can scarcely do that in fairness to her."

"Tr-rue, tr-rue," said Farfrae. "But why didn't you marry her when your wife Susan died?" Farfrae asked this, and the other questions, in the comfortably indifferent tone of one whom the matter very remotely concerned.

"Ay – well you may ask that," said Henchard, the new-moon-shaped grin adumbrating itself again upon his mouth. "In spite of all her protestations, when I came forward to do so, as in generosity bound, she was not the woman for me."

"She had already married another – I presume?"

Henchard seemed to think it would be sailing too near the wind to descend further into particulars, and he answered "Yes."

"The young lady must have had a heart that bore transplanting very readily."

"She had, she had," said Henchard emphatically.

He opened a third and fourth letter, and read. This time he approached the conclusion as if the signature were indeed coming with the rest. But again he stopped short. The truth was that, as may be divined, he had quite intended to effect a grand catastrophe at the end of this drama by reading out the name; he had come to the house with no other thought. But sitting here in cold blood he could not do it. Such a wrecking of hearts appalled even him. His quality was such that he could have annihilated them both in the heat of action; but to accomplish the deed by oral poison was beyond the nerve of his enmity.

CHAPTER XXXV

As Donald stated, Lucetta had retired early to her room because of fatigue. She had, however, not gone to rest, but sat in the bedside chair reading, and thinking over the events of the day. At the ringing of the door-bell by Henchard she wondered who it should be that would call at that comparatively late hour. The dining-room was almost under her bedroom; she could hear that somebody was admitted there, and presently the indistinct murmur of a person reading became audible.

The usual time for Donald's arrival upstairs came and passed, yet still the reading and conversation went on. This was very singular. She could think of nothing but that some extraordinary crime had been committed, and that the visitor, whoever he might be, was reading an account of it from a special edition of the *Casterbridge Chronicle*. At last she left the room, and descended the stairs. The dining-room door was ajar, and in the silence of the resting household the voice and the words were recognizable before she reached the lower flight. She stood transfixed. Her own words greeted her, in Henchard's voice, like spirits from the grave.

Lucetta leant upon the bannister with her cheek against the smooth hand-rail, as if she would make a friend of it in her misery. Rigid in this position, more and more words fell successively upon her ear. But what amazed her most was the tone of her husband. He spoke merely in the accents of a man who made a present of his time.

"One word," he was saying, as the crackling of paper denoted that Henchard was unfolding yet another sheet. "Is it quite fair to this young woman's memory to read at such length to a stranger what was intended for your eye alone?"

"Well, yes," said Henchard. "By not giving her name I make it an example of all womankind, and not a scandal to one."

"If I were you I would destroy them," said Farfrae, giving more thought to the letters than he had hitherto done. "As another man's wife it would injure the woman if it were known."

"No, I shall not destroy them," murmured Henchard, putting the letters away. Then he arose, and Lucetta heard no more.

She went back to her bedroom in a semi-paralyzed state. For very fear she could not undress, but sat on the edge of the bed, waiting. Would Henchard let out the secret in his parting words? Her suspense was terrible. Had she confessed all to Donald in their early acquaintance he might possibly have got over it, and married her just the same – unlikely as it had once seemed; but for her or any one else to tell him now would be fatal.

The door slammed: she could hear her husband bolting it. After looking round in his customary way he came leisurely up the stairs. The spark in her eyes well-nigh went out when he appeared round the bedroom door. Her gaze hung doubtful for a moment, then to her joyous amazement she saw that he looked at her with the rallying smile of one who had just been relieved of a scene that was irksome. She could hold out no longer, and sobbed hysterically.

When he had restored her Farfrae naturally enough spoke of Henchard. "Of all men he was the least desirable as a visitor," he said; "but it is my belief that he's just a bit crazed. He has been reading to me a long lot of letters relating to his past life; and I could do no less than indulge him by listening."

This was sufficient. Henchard, then, had not told. Henchard's last words to Farfrae, in short, as he stood on the door-step, had been these: "Well – I'm much obliged to ye for listening. I may tell more about her some day."[1]

Finding this, she was much perplexed as to Henchard's motives in opening the matter at all; for in such cases we attribute to an enemy a power of consistent action which we never find in ourselves or in our friends; and forget that abortive efforts from want of heart are as possible to revenge as to generosity.

Next morning Lucetta remained in bed, meditating how to parry this incipient attack. The bold stroke of telling Donald the truth, dimly conceived, was yet too bold; for she dreaded lest, in doing so, he, like the rest of the world, should believe appearances and not her story.[2]

She decided to employ persuasion – not with Donald, but with the enemy himself. It seemed the only practicable weapon left her as a woman. Having laid her plan she rose, and wrote to him who kept her on these tenterhooks:

"I overheard your interview with my husband last night, and saw the drift of your revenge. The very thought of it crushes me. Have pity on a distressed woman. If you could see me you would relent. You do not know how anxiety has told upon me lately. I will be at the Ring at the time you leave work – just before the sun goes down. Please come that way. I cannot rest till I have seen you face to face, and heard from your mouth that you will carry this horse-play no further."

To herself she said, on closing up this appeal: "If ever tears and pleadings have served the weak to fight the strong, let them do so now!"

With this view she made a toilette which differed from all she had ever attempted before. To heighten her natural attractions had hitherto been the unvarying endeavour of her adult life, and one in which she was no novice. But now she neglected this, and even proceeded to impair the natural presentation. She had not slept all the previous night,[3] and this had produced upon her naturally pretty though slightly worn features the aspect of a countenance ageing prematurely from extreme sorrow. She selected – as much from want of spirit as design – her poorest, plainest, and longest discarded attire.

To avoid the contingency of being recognized she veiled herself, and slipped out of the house quickly. The sun was resting on the hill like a drop of blood on an eyelid by the time she had got up the road opposite the amphitheatre, which she speedily entered. The interior was shadowy, and emphatic of the absence of every living thing.

She was not disappointed in the fearful hope with which she awaited him. Henchard came over the top, descended, and Lucetta waited breathlessly. But having reached the arena she saw a change in his bearing: he stood still, at a little distance from her; she could not think why.

Nor could any one else have known. The truth was that in appointing this spot, and this hour, for the rendezvous, Lucetta had unwittingly backed up her entreaty by the strongest argument she could have used outside words, with this man of moods, glooms and superstitions. Her figure in the midst of the huge enclosure, the unusual plainness of her dress, her attitude of hope and appeal, so strongly revived in his soul the memory of another ill-used woman who had stood there and thus in bygone days, and had now passed away into her rest, that he was unmanned, and his heart smote him for having attempted reprisals on one of a sex so weak. When he approached her, and before she had spoken a word, her point was half gained.[4]

His manner as he had come down had been one of cynical carelessness; but he now put away his grim half-smile, and said, in a kindly subdued tone, "Good night t'ye. Of course I'm glad to come if you want me."

"Oh, thank you," she said apprehensively.

"I am sorry to see you looking so ill," he stammered, with unconcealed compunction.

She shook her head. "How can you be sorry," she asked, "when you deliberately cause it?"

"What?" said Henchard, uneasily. "Is it anything I have done that has pulled you down like that?"

"It is all your doing," said she. "I have no other grief. My happiness would be secure enough but for your threats. Oh, Michael, don't wreck me like this! You might think that you have done enough! When I came here I was a young woman; now I am rapidly becoming an old one.

Neither my husband nor any other man will regard me with interest long."

Henchard was disarmed. His old feeling of supercilious pity for womankind in general was intensified by this suppliant appearing here as the double of the first. Moreover, that thoughtless want of foresight which had led to all her trouble remained with poor Lucetta still; she had come to meet him here in this compromising way without perceiving the risk. Such a woman was very small deer to hunt; he felt ashamed, lost all zest and desire to humiliate Lucetta[5] there and then, and no longer envied Farfrae his bargain. He had married money, but nothing more. Henchard was anxious to wash his hands of the game.

"Well, what do you want me to do?" he said gently. "I am sure I shall be very willing. My reading of those letters was only a sort of practical joke, and I revealed nothing."

"To give me back the letters and any papers you may have that breathe of matrimony or worse."

"So be it. Every scrap shall be yours. . . . . But, between you and me, Lucetta, he is sure to find out something of the matter, sooner or later."

"Ah!" she said with eager tremulousness; "but not till I have proved myself a faithful and deserving wife to him, and then he may forgive me everything."

Henchard silently looked at her: he almost envied Farfrae such love as that, even now. "H'm – I hope so," he said. "But you shall have the letters without fail. And your secret shall be kept. I swear it."

"How good you are! – how shall I get them?"

He reflected, and said he would send them the next morning. "Now don't doubt me," he added. "I can keep my word."[6]

PLATE XVI

'"Well, Lucetta, I've a bit of news for ye," he said gaily.'

[Scene deleted from serial for book editions.
See Chapter XXXV, n. 6.]

CHAPTER XXXVI

Returning from her appointment Lucetta saw a man waiting by the lamp nearest to her own door. When she stopped to go in he came and spoke to her. It was Jopp.

He begged her pardon for addressing her. But he had heard that Mr. Farfrae had been applied to by a neighbouring corn-merchant to recommend a working partner; if so, he wished to offer himself. He could give good security, and had stated as much to Mr. Farfrae in a letter; but he would feel much obliged if Lucetta would say a word in his favour to her husband.

"It is a thing I know nothing about," said Lucetta coldly.

"But you can testify to my trustworthiness better than anybody, ma'am," said Jopp. "I was in Jersey several years, and knew you there by sight."

"Indeed," she replied. "But I knew nothing of you."

"I think, ma'am, that a word or two from you would secure for me what I covet very much," he persisted.

She steadily refused to have anything to do with the affair, and, cutting him short, because of her anxiety to get indoors before her husband should miss her, left him on the pavement.

He watched her till she had vanished, and then went home. When he got there he sat down in the fireless chimney-corner looking at the iron dogs, and the wood laid across them for heating the morning kettle. A movement upstairs disturbed him, and Henchard came down from his bedroom, where he seemed to have been rummaging boxes.

"I wish," said Henchard, "you would do me a service, Jopp, now, to-night, I mean, if you can. Leave this at Mrs. Farfrae's for her. I should take it myself, of course, but I don't wish to be seen there."

He handed a package in brown paper, sealed. Henchard had been as good as his word. Immediately on coming indoors he had searched over his few belongings; and every scrap of Lucetta's writing that he possessed was here. Jopp indifferently expressed his willingness.

"Well, how have ye got on to-day?" his lodger asked. "Any prospect of an opening?"

"I am afraid not," said Jopp, who had not told the other of his application to Farfrae.

"There never will be in Casterbridge," declared Henchard decisively. "You must roam further afield." He said good-night to Jopp, and returned to his own part of the house.

Jopp sat on till his eyes were attracted by the shadow of the candle-snuff on the wall, and looking at the original he found that it had formed itself into a head like a red-hot cauliflower. Henchard's packet next met his gaze. He knew there had been something of the nature of wooing between Henchard and the now Mrs. Farfrae; and his vague ideas on the subject narrowed themselves down to these: Henchard had a parcel belonging to Mrs. Farfrae, and he had reasons for not returning that parcel to her in person. What could be inside it? So he went on and on till, animated by resentment at Lucetta's haughtiness, as he thought it, and curiosity to learn if there were any weak sides to this transaction with Henchard, he examined the package. The pen and all its relations being awkward tools in Henchard's hands, he had affixed the seals without an impression, it never occurring to him that the efficacy of such a fastening depended on this. Jopp was far less of a tyro; he lifted one of the seals with his penknife, peeped in at the end thus opened, saw that the bundle consisted of letters; and, having satisfied himself thus far, sealed up the end again by simply softening the wax with the candle, and went off with the parcel as requested.

His path was by the river-side at the foot of the town. Coming into the light at the bridge which stood at the end of High Street, he beheld lounging thereon Mother Cuxsom and Nance Mockridge.

"We be just going down Mixen Lane way, to look into Saint Peter's Finger[1] afore creeping to bed," said Mrs. Cuxsom. "There's a fiddle and tambourine going on there. Lord, what's all the world – do ye come along too, Jopp – 'twon't hinder ye five minutes."

Jopp had mostly kept himself out of this company, but present circumstances made him somewhat more reckless than usual, and without many words he decided to go to his destination that way.

*

Though the upper part of Dummerford was mainly composed of a curious congeries of barns and farmsteads, there was a less picturesque side to the parish. This was Mixen Lane, now in great part pulled down.

Mixen Lane was the Adullam[2] of all the surrounding villages. It was the hiding-place of those who were in distress, and in debt, and trouble of every kind. Farm-labourers and other peasants, who combined a little poaching with their farming, and a little brawling and bibbing with their poaching, found themselves sooner or later in Mixen Lane. Rural mechanics too idle to mechanise, rural servants too rebellious to serve, drifted or were forced into Mixen Lane.

The lane and its surrounding thicket of thatched cottages stretched out like a spit into the moist and misty lowland. Much that was sad, much that was low, some things that were shameful, could be seen in Mixen Lane. Vice ran freely in and out certain of the doors of the neighbourhood; recklessness dwelt under the roof with the crooked chimney; shame in some bow-windows; theft (in times of privation) in the thatched and mud-walled houses by the sallows. Even slaughter had not been altogether unknown here. In a block of cottages up an alley there might have been erected an altar to disease in years gone by. Such was Mixen Lane in the times when Henchard and Farfrae were Mayors.

Yet this mildewed leaf in the sturdy and flourishing Casterbridge plant lay close to the open country: not a hundred yards from a row of noble elms, and commanding a view across the moor of airy uplands and corn-fields, and mansions of the great. A brook divided the moor from the tenements, and to outward view there was no way across it – no way to the houses but round about by the road. But under every householder's stairs there was kept a mysterious plank nine inches wide; which plank was a secret bridge.

If you, as one of those refugee householders, came in from business after dark – and this was the business time here – you stealthily crossed the moor, approached the border of the aforesaid brook, and whistled opposite the house to which you belonged. A shape thereupon made its appearance on the other side bearing the bridge on end against the sky; it was lowered; you crossed, and a hand helped you to land yourself, together with the pheasants and hares gathered from neighbouring manors. You sold them slily the next morning, and the day after you stood before the magistrates, with the eyes of all your sympathizing neighbours concentrated on your back. You disappeared for a time: then you were again found quietly living in Mixen Lane.

Walking along the lane at dusk the stranger was struck by two or three peculiar features therein. One was an intermittent rumbling from the back premises of the inn half-way up; this meant a skittle alley. Another was the extensive prevalence of whistling in the various domiciles – a piped note of some kind coming from nearly every open door. Another was the frequency of white aprons over dingy gowns among the women around the doorways. A white apron is a suspicious vesture in situations where spotlessness is difficult; moreover, the industry and cleanliness which the white apron expressed were belied by the postures and gaits of the women who wore it – their knuckles being mostly on their hips (an attitude which lent them the aspect of two-handled mugs), and their shoulders against doorposts; while there was a curious alacrity in the turn of each honest woman's head upon her neck, and in the twirl of her honest eyes, at any noise resembling a masculine footfall along the lane.

Yet amid so much that was bad needy respectability also found a home. Under some of the roofs abode pure and virtuous souls whose presence there was due to the iron hand of necessity, and to that alone. Families from decayed villages – families of that once bulky, but now nearly extinct, section of village society called "liviers," or lifeholders–copyholders,[3] and others whose roof-trees had fallen for some reason or other, compelling them to quit the rural spot that had been their home for generations – came here, unless they chose to lie under a hedge by the wayside.

The inn called Saint Peter's Finger was the church of Mixen Lane.

It was centrally situate, as such places should be, and bore about the same social relation to the King of Prussia as the latter bore to the Golden Crown. At first sight the inn was so respectable as to be puzzling. The front door was kept shut, and the step was so clean that evidently but few persons entered over its sanded surface. But at the corner of the public-house was an alley, a mere slit, dividing it from the next building. Half-way up the alley was a narrow door, shiny and paintless from the rub of infinite hands and shoulders. This was the actual entrance to the inn.

A pedestrian would be seen abstractedly passing along Mixen Lane; and then, in a moment, he would vanish, causing the gazer to blink like Ashton at the disappearance of Ravenswood.[4] That abstracted pedestrian had edged into the slit by the adroit fillip of his person sideways; from the slit he edged into the tavern by a similar exercise of skill.

The company at the King of Prussia were persons of quality in comparison with the company which gathered here; though it must be admitted that the lowest fringe of the King's party touched the crest of Peter's at points. Waifs and strays of all sorts loitered about here. The landlady was a virtuous woman, who had been unjustly sent to gaol as an accessory to something or other after the fact. She underwent her year, and had worn a martyr's countenance ever since, except at times of meeting the constable who apprehended her, when she winked her eye.

To this house Jopp and his acquaintances had arrived. The settles on which they sat down were thin and tall, their tops being guyed by pieces of twine to hooks in the ceiling; for when the guests grew boisterous the settles would rock and overturn without some such security. The thunder of bowls echoed from the backyard; swingels hung behind the blower of the chimney; and ex-poachers and ex-gamekeepers, whom squires had persecuted without a cause (in their own view), sat elbowing each other – men who in past times had met in fights under the moon, till lapse of sentences on the one part, and loss of favour and expulsion from service on the other, brought them here together to a common level, where they sat calmly discussing old times.

"Dos't mind how you could jerk a trout ashore with a bramble, and not ruffle the stream, Charl?" a deposed keeper was saying. "'Twas at that I caught 'ee once, if you can mind?"

"That can I. But the worst larry for me was that pheasant business at Horewood.[5] Your wife swore false that time, Joe – oh, by Gad she did – there's no denying it."

"How was that?" asked Jopp.

"Why – Joe closed with me, and we rolled down together, close to his garden hedge. Hearing the noise, out ran his wife with the oven pyle, and it being dark under the trees she couldn't see which was uppermost. 'Where beest thee, Joe, under or top?" she screeched. 'Oh – under by Gad!' says he. She then began to rap down upon my skull, back and ribs with the pyle till we'd roll over again. 'Where beest now, dear Joe, under or top?" she'd scream again. By George, 'twas through her I was took! And then when we got up in hall she sware that the cock pheasant was one of her rearing, when 'twas not your bird at all, Joe; 'twas Squire Brown's bird – that's whose 'twas – one that we'd picked off as we passed his wood, an hour afore. It did hurt my feelings to be so wronged!. . . . Ah well – 'tis over now."

"I might have had ye days afore that," said the keeper. "I was within a few yards of ye dozens of times, with a sight more of birds than that poor one."

"Yes – 'tis not our greatest doings that the world gets wind of," said the furmity-woman, who, lately settled in this purlieu, sat among the rest. Having travelled a great deal in her time, she spoke with cosmopolitan largeness of idea. It was she who presently asked Jopp what was the parcel he kept so snugly under his arm.

"Ah, therein lies a grand secret," said Jopp. "It is the passion of love. To think that a woman should love one man so well, and hate another so unmercifully."

"Who's the object of your meditation, sir?"

"One that stands high, in this town. I'd like to shame her! Upon my life 'twould be as good as a play to read her love-letters, the proud piece of silk and wax-work! For 'tis her love-letters that I've got here."

"Love-letters? then let's hear 'em, good soul," said Mother Cuxsom. "Lord, do ye mind, Richard, what fools we used to be when we were younger? getting a schoolboy to write ours for us; and giving him a penny, do ye mind, not to tell other folks what he'd put inside, do ye mind?"

By this time Jopp had pushed his finger under the seals, and unfastened the letters, tumbling them over and picking up one here and there at random, which he read aloud. These passages soon began to uncover the secret which Lucetta had so earnestly hoped to keep buried, though the epistles, being allusive only, did not make it altogether plain.

"Mrs. Farfrae wrote that!" said Nance Mockridge. "'Tis a humbling thing for us, as respectable women, that one of the same sex could do it. And now she's vowed herself to another man!"

"So much the better for her," said the furmity-woman. "Ah, I saved her from a real bad marriage, and she's never been the one to thank me."

"I say, what a good foundation for a skimmity-ride,"[6] said Nance.

"True," said Mrs. Cuxsom reflecting. "'Tis as good a ground for a skimmity-ride as ever I knowed; and it ought not to be wasted. The last one seen in Casterbridge must have been ten years ago, if a day."[7]

At this moment there was a shrill whistle, and the landlady said to the man who had been called Charl, "'Tis Jim coming in. Would ye go and let down the bridge for me?"

Without replying Charl and his comrade Joe rose, and receiving a lantern from her went out at the back door and down the garden-path, which ended abruptly at the edge of the stream already mentioned. Beyond the stream was the open moor, from which a clammy breeze smote upon their faces as they advanced. Taking up the board that had lain in readiness one of them lowered it across the water, and the instant its further end touched the ground footsteps entered upon it, and there appeared from the shade a stalwart man with straps round his knees, a double-barrelled gun under his arm and some birds slung up behind him. They asked him if he had had much luck.

"Not much," he said indifferently. "All safe inside?"

Receiving a reply in the affirmative he went on inwards, the others withdrawing the bridge and beginning to retreat in his rear. Before, however, they had entered the house a cry of "Ahoy," from the moor led them to pause.

The cry was repeated. They pushed the lantern into an out-house, and went back to the brink of the stream.

"Ahoy – is this the way to Casterbridge?" said some one from the other side.

"Not in particular," said Charl. "There's a river afore ye."

"I don't care – here's for through it," said the man in the moor. "I've had travelling enough for to-day."

"Stop a minute, then," said Charl, finding that the man was no enemy. "Joe, bring the plank and lantern: here's somebody that's lost his way. You should have kept along the turnpike road, friend, and not have strook across here."

"I should – as I see now. But I saw a light here, and says I to myself, that's a short cut, depend on't."

The plank was now lowered; and the stranger's form shaped itself from the darkness. He was a middle-aged man, with hair and whiskers prematurely grey, and a broad and genial face. He had crossed on the plank without hesitation, and seemed to see nothing odd in the transit. He thanked them, and walked between them up the garden. "What place is this?" he asked, when they reached the door.

"A public-house."

"Oh. Perhaps it will suit me to put up at. Now then, come in and wet your whistle at my expense for the lift over you have given me."

They followed him into the inn, where the increased light exhibited him as one who would stand higher in an estimate by the eye than in one by the ear. He was dressed with a certain clumsy richness – his coat being furred, and his head covered by a cap of sealskin, which, though the nights were chilly, must have been warm for the daytime, spring being somewhat advanced. In his hand he carried a small mahogany case, strapped, and clamped with brass.

Apparently surprised at the kind of company which confronted him through the kitchen door, he at once abandoned his idea of putting up at the house; but taking the situation lightly, he called for glasses of the best, paid for them as he stood in the passage, and turned to proceed on his way by the front door. This was barred, and while the landlady was unfastening it the conversation about the skimmington was continued in the sitting-room, and reached his ears.

"What do they mean by a 'skimmity-ride?'" he asked.

"Oh, sir," said the landlady, swinging her long ear-rings with deprecating modesty; "'tis a old foolish thing they do in these parts when a man's wife is – well, a bad bargain in any way.[8] But as a respectable householder I don't encourage it."

"Still, are they going to do it shortly? It is a good sight to see, I suppose?"

"Well, sir," she simpered. And then, bursting into naturalness, and glancing from the corner of her eye; "'Tis the funniest thing under the sun! And it costs money."

"Ah! I remember hearing of some such thing. Now I shall be in Casterbridge for two or three weeks to come, and should not mind seeing the performance. Wait a moment." He turned back, entered the sitting-room, and said, "Here, good folks; I should like to see the old custom you are talking of, and I don't mind being something towards it – take that." He threw a sovereign on the table and returned to the landlady at the door, of whom, having inquired the way into the town, he took his leave.

"There were more where that one came from," said Charl, when the sovereign had been taken up and handed to the landlady for safe keeping. "By George! we ought to have got a few more while we had him here."

"No, no," answered the landlady. "This is a respectable house, thank God! and I'll have nothing done but what's honourable."

"Well," said Jopp; "now we'll consider the business begun, and will soon get it in train."

"We will," said Nance. "A good laugh warms my heart more than a cordial, and that's the truth on't."

Jopp gathered up the letters, and it being now somewhat late, he did not attempt to call at Farfrae's with them that night. He reached home, sealed them up as before, and delivered the parcel at its address next morning. Within an hour its contents were reduced to ashes by Lucetta, who, poor soul! was inclined to fall down on her knees in thankfulness that at last no evidence remained[9] of the unlucky episode with Henchard in her past. For, innocent as she had been of deliberately lax intentions therein, that episode, if known, was not the less likely to operate fatally between herself and her husband.

CHAPTER XXXVII

Such was the state of things when the current affairs of Casterbridge were interrupted by an event of such magnitude that its influence reached to the lowest social stratum there, stirring the depths of its society so sensibly as to cut into the midst of the preparations for the skimmington. It was one of those excitements which, when they move a country-town, leave a permanent mark upon its chronicles, as a warm summer permanently marks the ring in the tree-trunk corresponding to its date.

A Royal Personage[1] was about to pass through the borough, on his course further west, to inaugurate an immense engineering work out that way. He had consented to halt half-an-hour or so in the town, and to receive an address from the Corporation of Casterbridge, which, as a representative centre of husbandry, wished thus to express its sense of the great services he had rendered to agricultural science and economics, by his zealous promotion of designs for placing the art of farming on a more scientific footing.

Royalty had not been seen in Casterbridge since the days of the third King George,[2] and then only by candlelight for a few minutes when that monarch, on a night-journey, had stopped to change horses at the Golden Crown. The inhabitants therefore decided to make a thorough *fête carillonnée* of the unwonted occasion. Half-an-hour's pause was not long, it is true; but much might be done in it by a judicious grouping of incidents, above all, if the weather were fine.

The address was prepared on parchment, by an artist,[3] who was handy at ornamental lettering, and was laid on with the best gold-leaf and colours that the sign-painter had in his shop. The Council met on the Tuesday before the appointed day, to arrange the details of procedure. While they were sitting, the door of the Council Chamber standing open, they heard a heavy footstep coming up the stairs. It advanced along the passage, and Henchard entered the room, in clothes of frayed and threadbare shabbiness, the very clothes which he had used to wear in the primal days when he had sat among them.

"I have a feeling," he said, advancing to the table and laying his hand upon the green cloth, "that I should like to join ye in this reception of our illustrious visitor. I suppose I could walk with the rest?"

Embarrassed glances were exchanged by the Council, and Grower nearly ate the end of his quill-pen, so gnawed he it during the silence. Farfrae, the young Mayor, who by virtue of his office sat in the large chair, intuitively caught the sense of the meeting, and as spokesman was obliged to utter it, glad as he would have been that the duty should have fallen to another tongue.

"I hardly see that it would be proper, Mr. Henchard," said he. "The Council are the Council, and as ye are no longer one of the body, there would be an irregularity in the proceeding. If ye were included, why not others?"

"I have a particular reason for wishing to assist at the ceremony."

Farfrae looked round. "I think I have expressed the feeling of the Council," he said.

"Yes, yes," from Dr. Bath, Lawyer Long, Alderman Tubber, and several more.

"Then I am not to be allowed to have anything to do with it officially?"

"I am afraid so; it is out of the question, indeed. But of course you can see the doings full well, such as they are to be, like the rest of the spectators."

Henchard did not reply to that very obvious suggestion, and, turning on his heel, went away.

It had been only a passing fancy of his, but opposition crystallized it into a determination. "I'll welcome his Royalty, or nobody shall!" he went about saying. "I am not going to be sat upon by Farfrae, or any of the rest of the paltry crew. You shall see."

The eventful morning was bright, a full-faced sun confronting early window-gazers eastward, and all perceived (for they were practised in weather-lore) that there was permanence in the glow. Visitors soon began to flock in from county houses, villages, remote copses, and lonely uplands, the latter in oiled boots and tilt bonnets, to see the reception, or if not to see it, at any rate to be near it. There was hardly a work man in the town who did not put a clean shirt on. Solomon Longways, Christopher Coney, Buzzford, and the rest of that fraternity, showed their sense of the occasion by advancing their customary eleven o'clock pint to half-past ten; from which they found a difficulty in getting back to the proper hour for several days.

Henchard had determined to do no work that day. He primed himself in the morning with a glass of rum, and walking down the street met Elizabeth-Jane, whom he had not seen for a week. "It was lucky," he said to her, "my twenty years had expired before this came on, or I should never have had the nerve to carry it out."

"Carry out what?" said she, alarmed.

"This welcome I am going to give our Royal visitor."

She was perplexed. "Shall we go and see it together?" she said.

"See it! I have other fish to fry. You see it. It will be worth seeing!"

She could do nothing to elucidate this, and decked herself out with a heavy heart. As the appointed time drew near she got sight again of her stepfather. She thought he was going to the King of Prussia; but no, he elbowed his way through the gay throng to the shop of Woolfrey, the draper. She waited in the crowd without.

In a few minutes he emerged, wearing, to her surprise, a brilliant rosette, while, more surprising still, in his hand he carried a flag, of somewhat homely construction, formed by tacking one of the small Union Jacks, which abounded in the town to-day, to the end of a deal wand – probably the roller from a piece of calico. Henchard rolled up his flag on the doorstep, put it under his arm, and went down the street.

Suddenly the taller members of the crowd turned their heads, and the shorter stood on tip-toe. It was said that the Royal *cortège* approached. The railway had stretched out an arm towards Casterbridge at this time, but had not reached it by several miles as yet; so that the intervening distance, as well as the remainder of the journey, was to be traversed by road, in the old fashion. People thus waited – the county families in their carriages, the masses on foot – and watched the far-stretching London highway to the ringing of bells and chatter of tongues.

From the background Elizabeth-Jane watched the scene. Some seats had been arranged from which ladies could witness the spectacle, and the front seat was occupied by Lucetta just at present. In the road under her eyes stood Henchard. She appeared so bright and pretty that, as it seemed, he was experiencing the momentary weakness of wishing for her notice. But he was far from attractive to a woman's eye, ruled as that is so largely by the superficies of things. He was not only a journeyman, unable to appear as he formerly had appeared, but he disdained to appear as well as he might. Everybody else, from the Mayor to the washerwoman, shone in new vesture according to means; but Henchard had doggedly retained the fretted and weatherbeaten garments of bygone years.

Hence, alas, this occurred: Lucetta's eyes slid over him to this side and to that without anchoring on a feature – as gaily dressed women's eyes will too often do on such occasions. Her manner signified quite plainly that she meant to know him in public no more.

But she was never tired of watching Donald, as he stood in animated converse with his friends a few yards off, wearing round his young neck the official gold chain with great square links, like that round the Royal unicorn. Every trifling emotion that her husband showed as he talked had its reflex on her face and lips, which moved in little duplicates to his. She was living his part rather than her own, and cared for no one's situation but Farfrae's that day.

At length a man stationed at the furthest turn of the high road, namely, on the second bridge of which mention has been made, gave a signal; and the Corporation in their robes proceeded from the front of the Town Hall to the archway erected at the entrance to the town. The carriages containing the Royal visitor and his suite arrived at the spot in a cloud of dust, a procession was formed, and the whole came on to the Town Hall at a walking pace.

This spot was the centre of interest. There were a few clear yards in front of the Royal carriage; and into this space a man stepped before any one could prevent him. It was Henchard. He had unrolled his private flag, and removing his hat he advanced[4] to the side of the slowing vehicle, waving the Union Jack to and fro with his left hand, while he blandly held out his right to the illustrious personage. All the ladies said with bated breath, "Oh, look there!" and Lucetta was ready to faint. Elizabeth-Jane peeped through the shoulders of those in front, saw what it was, and was terrified; and then her interest in the event as a strange phenomenon got the better of her fear.

Farfrae immediately rose[5] to the occasion. He seized Henchard by the shoulder, dragged him back, and told him roughly to be off. Henchard's eyes met his, and Farfrae observed the fierce light in them, despite his excitement and irritation. For a moment Henchard stood his ground rigidly; then by an unaccountable impulse gave way and retired. Farfrae glanced to the ladies' gallery, and saw that his Calphurnia's cheek was pale.[6]

"Why – it is your husband's old patron!" said Mrs. Blowbody, a lady of the neighbourhood, who sat beside Lucetta.

"Patron!" said Donald's wife with quick indignation.

"Do you say the man is an acquaintance of Mr. Farfrae's?" observed Mrs. Bath, the physician's wife, a new-comer to the town, through her recent marriage with the Doctor.

"He works for my husband," said Lucetta.

"Oh – is that all? They have been saying to me that it was through him your husband first got a footing in Casterbridge. What stories people will tell!"

"They will indeed. It was not so at all. Donald's genius would have enabled him to get a footing anywhere, without anybody's help! He would have been just the same if there had been no Henchard in the world."

It was partly Lucetta's ignorance of the circumstances of Donald's arrival which led her to speak thus; partly the sensation that everybody seemed bent on snubbing her at this triumphant time. The incident had occupied but a few moments, but it was necessarily witnessed by the Royal personage, who, however, with practised tact, affected not to have noticed anything unusual. He alighted, the Mayor advanced, the address was read, the visitor replied, then said a few words to Farfrae, and shook hands with Lucetta, as the Mayor's wife. The ceremony occupied but a few minutes, and the carriages rattled heavily as Pharaoh's chariots up the straight High Street and out upon the great open road,[7] in continuation of the journey coastward.

In the crowd stood Coney, Buzzford, and Longways. "Some difference between him now and when he sang at the King o' Prussia," said the first. "'Tis wonderful how he could get a lady of her quality to go snacks with him[8] in such quick time."

"True. Yet how folk do worship fine clothes. Now there's a better-looking woman than she that nobody notices at all, because she's akin to that mandy fellow Henchard."

"I could worship ye, Buzz, for saying that," remarked Nance Mock-ridge. "I do like to see the trimming pulled off such Christmas candles. I am quite unequal to the part of villain myself, or I'd gie all my small silver to see that lady toppered. . . . . And perhaps I shall soon," she added significantly.

"That's not a noble passion for a woman to keep up," said Longways.

Nance did not reply, but every one knew what she meant. The ideas diffused by the reading of Lucetta's letters at Saint Peter's Finger had condensed into a scandal, which was spreading like a miasmatic fog through Mixen Lane, and thence up the back streets of Casterbridge.

This mixed assemblage of idlers known to each other presently fell apart into two bands, by a process of natural selection, the frequenters of Saint Peter's Finger going off Mixen Lane-wards, where most of them lived, while Coney, Buzzford, Longways, and that connection remained in the street.

"You know what's brewing down there, I suppose?" said Buzzford mysteriously to the others.

Coney looked at him. "Not the skimmity-ride?"

Buzzford nodded.

"I have my doubts if it will be carried out," said Longways. "If they are getting it up they are keeping it mighty close."

"I heard they were thinking of it a fortnight ago, at all events."

"If I were sure o't I'd lay information," said Longways emphatically. "'Tis too rough a joke, and apt to wake riots in towns. We know that the Scotchman is a right enough man, and that his lady has been a right enough woman since she came here, and if there was anything wrong about her afore, that's their business, not ours."

Coney reflected. Farfrae was still liked in the community; but it must be owned that, as the Mayor and man of money, engrossed with affairs and ambitions, he had lost in the eyes of the poorer inhabitants something of that wondrous charm which he had had for them as a light-hearted penniless young man, who sang ditties as readily as the birds in the trees. Hence the anxiety to keep him from annoyance showed not quite the ardour that would have animated it in former days.

"Suppose we make inquiration into it, Christopher," continued Longways; "and if we find there's really anything in it, drop a letter to them most concerned, and advise 'em to keep out of the way?"

This course was decided on, and the group separated, Buzzford saying to Coney, "Come, my ancient friend; let's move on. There's nothing more to see here."

These well-intentioned ones would have been surprised had they known how ripe the great jocular plot really was. "Yes, to-night," Jopp had said to the Peter's party at the corner of Mixen Lane. "As a wind-up to the Royal visit the hit will be all the more pat by reason of their great elevation to-day."

To him, at least, it was not a joke, but a reprisal.

CHAPTER XXXVIII

The proceedings had been brief – too brief – to Lucetta, whom an intoxicating *Weltlust* had fairly mastered; but they had brought her a great triumph nevertheless. The shake of the Royal hand still lingered in her fingers; and the chit-chat she had overheard, that her husband might possibly receive the honour of knighthood, though idle to a degree, seemed not the wildest vision; stranger things had occurred to men so good and captivating as her Scotchman was.

After the collision with the Mayor, Henchard had withdrawn behind the ladies' stand; and there he stood regarding with a stare of abstraction the spot on the lappel of his coat where Farfrae's hand had seized it. He put his own hand there, as if he could hardly realize such an outrage from one whom it had once been his wont to treat with ardent generosity. While pausing in this half-stupefied state the conversation of Lucetta with the other ladies reached his ears; and he distinctly heard her deny him – deny that he had assisted Donald, that he was anything more than a common journeyman.

He moved on homeward, and met Jopp in the archway to the Bull Stake. "So you've had a snub," said Jopp.

"And what if I have?" answered Henchard, sternly.

"Why I've had one too, so we are both under the same displeasure." He briefly related his attempt to win Lucetta's intercession.

Henchard merely heard his story, without taking it deeply in. His own relation to Farfrae and Lucetta overshadowed all kindred ones. He went on saying brokenly to himself, "She has supplicated to me in her time; and now her tongue won't own me nor her eyes see me! . . . And he – how angry he looked. He drove me back as if I were a bull breaking fence. . . . I took it like a lamb, for I saw it could not be settled there. He can rub brine on a green wound![1] . . . But he shall pay for it, and she shall be sorry. It must come to a tussle – face to face; and then we'll see how a coxcomb can front a man!"

Without further reflection the fallen merchant, bent on some wild purpose, ate a hasty dinner, and went forth to find Farfrae. After being injured by him as a rival, and snubbed by him as a journeyman, the crowning degradation had been reserved for this day – that he should be shaken at the collar by him as a vagabond in the face of the whole town.

The crowds had dispersed. But for the green arches which still stood as they were erected Casterbridge life had resumed its ordinary shape. Henchard went down Corn Street till he came to Farfrae's house, where he knocked, and left a message that he would be glad to see his employer at the granaries as soon as he conveniently could come there. Having done this he proceeded round to the back and entered the yard.

Nobody was present, for, as he had been aware, the labourers and carters were enjoying half-holiday on account of the events of the day – though the carters would have to return for a short time later on, to feed and litter down the horses. He had reached the granary steps and was about to ascend, when he said to himself aloud, "I'm stronger than he."

Henchard returned to a shed, where he selected a short piece of rope from several pieces that where lying about; hitching one end of this to a nail he took the other in his right hand and turned himself bodily round, while keeping his left arm against his side; by this contrivance he pinioned the latter effectively. He now went up the ladders to the top floor of the corn-stores.

It was empty, except of a few sacks, and at the further end was the door often mentioned, opening under the cathead and chain that hoisted the sacks. He fixed the door open, and looked over the sill. There was a depth of thirty or forty feet to the ground; here was the spot on which he had been standing with Farfrae when Elizabeth-Jane had seen him lift his arm, with many misgivings as to what the movement portended.

He retired a few steps into the loft, and waited. From this elevated perch his eye could sweep the roofs roundabout, the upper parts of the luxurious chestnut-trees, now delicate in leaves of a week's age, and the drooping boughs of the limes; Farfrae's garden, and the green door leading therefrom. In course of time – he could not say how long – that green door opened and Farfrae came through. He was dressed as if for a journey. The low light of the nearing evening caught his head and face when he emerged from the shadow of the wall, warming them to a complexion of flame-colour. Henchard watched him with his mouth firmly set, the squareness of his jaw and the verticality of his profile being unduly marked.

Farfrae came on with one hand in his pocket, and humming a tune in a way which told that the words were most in his mind. They were those of the song he had sung when he arrived years before at the King of Prussia, a poor young man, adventuring for life and fortune, and scarcely knowing whitherward: –

> "And here's a hand, my trusty fiere,
>   And gie's a hand o' thine."[2]

Nothing moved Henchard like an old melody. He sank back. "No; I can't do it!" he gasped. "Why does the infernal fool begin that now!"

At length Farfrae was silent, and Henchard looked out of the loft door. "Will ye come up here?" he said.

"Ay, man," said Farfrae. "I couldn't see ye. What's amiss?"

A minute later Henchard heard his feet on the lowest ladder. He heard him land on the first floor, ascend and land on the second, begin the ascent to the third. And then his head rose through the trap behind.

"What are you doing up here at this time?" he asked, coming forward. "Why didn't ye take your holiday like the rest of the men?" He spoke in a tone which had just severity enough in it to show that he remembered the untoward event of the forenoon.[3]

Henchard said nothing; but, going back, he closed the stair hatchway, and stamped upon it so that it went tight into its frame; he next turned to the wondering young man, who by this time observed that one of Henchard's arms was bound to his side.

"Now," said Henchard quietly, "we stand face to face – man and man. Your money and your fine wife no longer lift ye above me as they did but now, and my poverty does not press me down."

"What does it all mean?" asked Farfrae simply.

"Wait a bit, my lad. You should have thought twice before you affronted to extremity a man who had nothing to lose. I've borne your rivalry, which ruined me, and your snubbing, which humbled me; but your hustling, that disgraced me, I won't stand!"

Farfrae warmed a little at this. "Ye'd no business there," he said.

"As much as any one among ye. What, you forward stripling, tell a man of my age he'd no business there?" The anger-vein swelled in his forehead as he spoke.

"You insulted Royalty, Henchard; and 'twas my duty, as the chief magistrate, to stop you."

"Royalty be—,"[4] said Henchard. "I am as loyal as you, come to that."

"I am not here to argue. Wait till you are cool, wait till you are cool; and you will see things as I do."

"You may be the one to cool first," said Henchard, grimly. "Now this is the case. Here be we, in this four-square loft, to finish out that little wrestle you began this morning. There's the door, forty foot above ground. One of us two puts the other out by that door – the master stays inside. If he likes he may go down afterwards and give the alarm that the other has fallen out by accident – or he may tell the truth – that's his business. As the strongest man I've tied one arm to take no advantage of ye. D'ye understand? Then here's at ye!"

There was no time for Farfrae to do aught but one thing, to close with Henchard, for the latter had come on at once. It was a wrestling match, the object of each being to give his antagonist a back fall; and on Henchard's part, unquestionably that it should be through the door.

At the outset Henchard's hold by his only spare hand, the right, was on the left side of Farfrae's collar, which he firmly grappled, the latter holding Henchard by his collar with the contrary hand. With his right he endeavoured to get hold of his antagonist's left arm, which, however, he could not do, so adroitly did Henchard keep it in the rear as he gazed upon the lowered eyes of his fair and slim antagonist.

Henchard planted the first toe forward, Farfrae crossing him with his; and thus far the struggle had very much the appearance of the ordinary wrestling of those parts. Several minutes were passed by them in this attitude, the pair rocking and writhing like trees in a gale, both preserving an absolute silence. By this time their breathing could be heard. Then Farfrae tried to get hold of the other side of Henchard's collar, which was resisted by the larger man exerting all his force in a wrenching movement, and this part of the struggle ended by his forcing Farfrae down on his knees by sheer pressure of one of his muscular arms. Hampered as he was, however, he could not keep him there, and Farfrae finding his feet again the struggle proceeded as before.

By a whirl Henchard brought Donald dangerously near the precipice; seeing his position the Scotchman for the first time locked himself to his adversary, and all the efforts of that infuriated Prince of Darkness – as he might have been called from his appearance just now – were inadequate to lift or loosen Farfrae for a time. By an extraordinary effort he succeeded at last, though not until they had got far back again from the fatal door. In doing so Henchard contrived to turn Farfrae a complete somersault. Had Henchard's other arm been free it would have been all over with Farfrae then. But again he regained his feet, wrenching Henchard's arm considerably, and causing him sharp pain, as could be seen from the twitching of his face. He instantly delivered the younger man an annihilating turn by the left fore-hip, as it used to be expressed, and following up his advantage thrust him towards the door, never loosening his hold till Farfrae's fair head was hanging over the window-sill, and his arm dangling down outside the wall.

PLATE XVII

'"Now," said Henchard between his gasps. "Your life is in my hands."'

"Now," said Henchard between his gasps, "this is the end of what you began this morning. Your life is in my hands."

"Then take it," said Farfrae. "You've wished to long!"

Henchard looked down upon him in silence, and their eyes met. "O, Farfrae – that's not true!" he said, bitterly. "God is my witness that no man ever loved another as I did thee at one time. . . . . And now – though I came here to kill 'ee, I cannot hurt thee! Go and give me in charge – do what you will – I care nothing for what comes of me!"

He withdrew to the back part of the loft,[5] and flung himself into a corner upon some sacks, in the abandonment of remorse. Farfrae regarded him in silence; then went to the hatch and descended through it. Henchard would fain have recalled him; but his tongue failed in its task, and the young man's steps died on his ear.

Henchard took his full measure of shame and self-reproach. The scenes of his first acquaintance with Farfrae rushed back upon him – that time when the curious mixture of romance and thrift in the young man's composition so commanded his heart that Farfrae could play upon him as on an instrument. So thoroughly subdued was he that he remained on the sacks in a crouching attitude, unusual for a man, and for such a man. Its womanliness sat tragically on the figure of so stern a piece of virility. He heard a conversation below, the opening of the coach-house door, and the putting in of a horse, but took no notice.

Here he stayed till the thin shades thickened to opaque obscurity, and the loft-door became an oblong of gray light – the only visible shape around. At length he arose, shook the dust from his clothes wearily, felt his way to the hatch, and gropingly descended the steps till he stood in the yard.

"He thought highly of me once," he murmured. "Now he'll hate me and despise me for ever!"

He became possessed by an overpowering wish to see Farfrae again that night, and by some desperate pleading to attempt the well-nigh impossible task of winning pardon for his late mad attack. But as he walked towards Farfrae's door, he recalled the unheeded doings in the yard while he had lain above in a sort of stupor. Farfrae he remembered had gone to the stable and put the horse into the gig; while doing so, Whittle had brought him a letter; Farfrae had then said that he would not go towards Budmouth as he had intended – that he was unexpectedly summoned to Weatherbury, and meant to call at Mellstock on his way thither, that place lying but three or four miles[6] out of his course.

He must have come prepared for a journey when he first arrived in the yard, unsuspecting enmity; and he must have driven off (though in a changed direction) without saying a word to any one on what had occurred between themselves.

It would therefore be useless to call at Farfrae's house till very late.

There was no help for it but to wait till his return, though waiting was almost torture to his restless and self-accusing soul. He walked about the streets and outskirts of the town, lingering here and there till he reached the stone bridge of which mention has been made, an accustomed halting-place with him now. Here he spent a long time, the purl of waters through the weirs meeting his ear, and the Casterbridge lights glimmering at no great distance off.

While leaning thus upon the parapet, his listless attention was awakened by sounds of an unaccustomed kind from the town quarter. They were a confusion of rhythmical noises, to which the streets added yet more confusion by encumbering them with echoes. His first incurious thought that the clangour arose from the town band, engaged in an attempt to round off a memorable day by a burst of evening harmony, was contradicted by certain peculiarities of reverberation. But inexplicability did not rouse him to more than a cursory heedfulness; his sense of degradation was too strong for the admission of foreign ideas; and he leant against the parapet as before.

CHAPTER XXXIX

When Farfrae descended out of the loft, breathless from his encounter with Henchard, he paused at the bottom to recover himself. He arrived at the yard with the intention of putting the horse into the gig himself (all the men having a holiday), and driving to a village on the Budmouth Road. Despite the fearful struggle he decided still to persevere in his journey, so as to recover himself before going indoors and meeting the eyes of Lucetta. He wished to consider his course in a case so serious.

When he was just on the point of driving off, Whittle arrived with a note, badly addressed, and bearing the word "immediate" upon the outside. On opening it he was surprised to see that it was unsigned. It contained a brief request that he would go to Weatherbury that evening about some business which he was conducting there. Farfrae knew nothing that could make it pressing; but as he was bent upon going out he yielded to the anonymous request, particularly as he had a call to make at Mellstock which could be included in the same tour. Thereupon he told Whittle of his change of direction, in words which Henchard had overheard; and set out on his way. Farfrae had not directed his man to take the message indoors, and Whittle had not been supposed to do so on his own responsibility.

Now the anonymous letter was the well-intentioned but clumsy contrivance of Longways and other of Farfrae's men, to get him out of the way for the evening, in order that the satirical mummery should fall flat, if it were attempted. By giving open information they would have brought down upon their heads the vengeance of those among their comrades who enjoyed these boisterous old games; and therefore the plan of sending a letter recommended itself by its indirectness.

For poor Lucetta they took no protective measure, believing with the majority there was some truth in the scandal, which she would have to bear as she best might.

It was about eight o'clock, and Lucetta was sitting in the drawing-room alone. Night had set in for more than half-an-hour, but she had not had the candles lighted, for when Farfrae was away she preferred waiting for him by the firelight, and, if it were not too cold, keeping one of the window-sashes a little way open that the sound of his wheels might reach her ears early. She was leaning back in her chair, in a more hopeful mood than she had enjoyed since her marriage. The day had been such a success; and the temporary uneasiness which Henchard's show of effrontery had wrought in her disappeared with the quiet disappearance of Henchard himself under her husband's reproof. The floating evidences of her absurd passion for him, and its consequences, had been destroyed, and she really seemed to have no cause for fear.

The reverie in which these and other subjects mingled was disturbed by a hubbub in the distance, that increased moment by moment. It did not greatly surprise her, the afternoon having been given up to recreation by a majority of the populace since the passage of the Royal equipages. But her attention was at once riveted to the matter by the voice of a maid-servant next door, who spoke from an upper window across the street to some other maid even more elevated than she.

"Which way are they going now?" inquired the first with interest.

"I can't be sure for a moment," said the second, "because of the malter's chimney. "Oh, yes – I can see 'em. Well, I declare, I declare!"

"What, what?" from the first, more enthusiastically.

"They are coming up Corn Street after all! They sit back to back!"

"What – two of 'em – are there two figures?"

"Yes. Two images on a donkey, back to back, their elbows tied to one another's. She's facing the head, and he's facing the tail."

"Is it meant for anybody particular?"

"Well – it may be. The man has got on a blue coat and kerseymere leggings; he has black whiskers, and a reddish face. 'Tis a stuffed figure, with a mask."

The din was increasing now – then it lessened a little.

"There – I sha'n't see, after all!" cried the disappointed first maid.

"They have gone into a back street – that's all," said the one who occupied the enviable position in the attic. "There – now I have got 'em all endways nicely."

"What's the woman like? Just say, and I can tell in a moment if 'tis meant for one I've in mind."

"My – why – 'tis dressed just as *she* was dressed when she sat in the front seat at the time the play-actors came to the Town Hall!"

Lucetta started to her feet; and almost at the instant the door of the room was quickly and softly opened. Elizabeth-Jane advanced into the firelight.

"I have come to see you," she said breathlessly. "I did not stop to knock – forgive me. I see you have not shut your shutters, and the window is open."

Without waiting for Lucetta's reply she crossed quickly to the window, and pulled out one of the shutters. Lucetta glided to her side. "Let it be – hush!" she said peremptorily, in a dry voice, while she seized Elizabeth-Jane by the hand, and held up her finger. Their intercourse had been so low and hurried that not a word had been lost of the conversation without; which had thus proceeded: –

"Her neck is uncovered, and her hair in bands, and her back-comb in place; she's got on a puce silk, and white stockings, and coloured shoes."

Again Elizabeth-Jane attempted to close the window; but Lucetta held her by main force.[1]

"'Tis me," she said, with a face pale as death. "A procession – a scandal – an effigy of me, and him!"

The look of Elizabeth betrayed that the latter knew it already.

"Let us shut it out," coaxed Elizabeth-Jane, noting that the rigid wildness of Lucetta's features were growing[2] yet more rigid and wild with the nearing of the noise and laughter. "Let us shut it out!"

"It is of no use!" she shrieked out. "He will see it, won't he? Donald will see it. He is just coming home – and it will break his heart – he will never love me any more – and oh, it will kill me – kill me!"

Elizabeth-Jane was frantic now. "Oh, can't something be done to stop it?" she cried. "Is there nobody to do it – not one?"

She relinquished Lucetta's hands, and ran to the door. Lucetta herself, saying recklessly, "I will see it!" turned to the window, threw up the sash, and went out upon the balcony. Elizabeth immediately followed her, and put her arm round her to pull her in. Lucetta's eyes were straight upon the spectacle of the uncanny revel, now advancing rapidly. The numerous lights around the two effigies threw them up into lurid distinctness: it was impossible to mistake the pair for other than the intended victims.

"Come in, come in," implored Elizabeth; "and let me shut the window!"

"She's me – she's me – even to the parasol – my green parasol!" cried Lucetta with a wild laugh as she stepped in. She stood motionless for one second – then fell heavily to the floor.

Almost at the instant of her fall the rude music of the skimmington

PLATE XVIII
'Lucetta's eyes were straight upon the spectacle of the uncanny revel.'

ceased. The roars of sarcastic laughter went off in ripples, and the tramping died out like the rustle of a spent wind. Elizabeth was only indirectly conscious of this; she had rung the bell, and was bending over Lucetta, who remained convulsed on the carpet in the paroxysms of an epileptic seizure. She rang again and again, in vain; the probability being that the servants had all run out of the house to see more of the Demoniac Sabbath than they could see within.

At last Farfrae's man, who had been agape on the door-step, came up; then the cook. The shutters, hastily pushed to by Elizabeth, were quite closed, a light was obtained, Lucetta carried to her room, and the man sent off for a doctor. While Elizabeth was undressing her she recovered consciousness; but as soon as she remembered what had passed the fit returned.

The doctor arrived with unhoped-for promptitude; he had been standing at his door, like others, wondering what the uproar meant. As soon as he saw the unhappy sufferer he said, in answer to Elizabeth's mute appeal, "This is serious."

"It is a fit," Elizabeth said.

"Yes. But a fit in the present state of her health means mischief. You must send at once for Mr. Farfrae. Where is he?"

"He has driven into the country, sir," said the parlour-maid; "to some place on the Budmouth Road. He's likely to be back soon."

"Never mind; he must be sent for, in case he should not hurry." The doctor returned to the bedside again. The man was despatched, and they soon heard him clattering out of the yard at the back.

Meanwhile Mr. Benjamin Grower, that prominent burgess, of whom mention has been already made, hearing the din of cleavers,[3] kits, crouds, humstrums, serpents, rams'-horns, and other historical kinds of music as he sat indoors in the High Street, had put on his hat and gone out to learn the cause. He came to the corner above Farfrae's, and soon guessed the nature of the proceedings; for being a native of the town he had witnessed such rough jests before. His first move was to search hither and thither for the constables; there were two in the town, shrivelled men whom he ultimately found in hiding up an alley, yet more shrivelled than usual, having some not ungrounded fears that they might be roughly handled if seen.

"What can we two poor lammigers do against such a multitude!" expostulated Stubberd, in answer to Mr. Grower's chiding. "'Tis tempting 'em to commit *felo de se* upon us, and that would be the death of the perpetrator; and we wouldn't be the cause of a fellow-creature's death on no account, not we."

"Get some help, then. Here, I'll come with you. We'll see what a few words of authority can do. Quick now; have ye got your staves?"

"We didn't want the folk to notice us as law officers, being so short-handed, sir; so we pushed our Gover'ment staves[4] up this water-pipe."

"Out with 'em, and come along, for heaven's sake! Ah, here's Mr. Blowbody, that's lucky." Blowbody was one of the magistrates.[5]

"Well, what's the row?" said Blowbody. "Got their names – hey?"

"No. Now," said Grower to one of the constables, "you go with Mr. Blowbody round by the Old Walk, and come up the street; and I'll go with Stubberd straight forward. By this plan we shall have 'em between us. Get their names only: no attack or interruption."

Thus they started. But as Stubberd with Mr. Grower advanced into Corn Street, whence the sounds had proceeded, they were surprised that no procession could be seen. They passed Farfrae's, and looked to the end of the street. The lamp flames waved, the Walk trees soughed, a few loungers stood about with their hands in their pockets. Everything was as usual.

"Have you seen a motley crowd, making a disturbance?" Grower said magisterially to one of these in a fustian jacket, who smoked a short pipe and wore straps round his knees.

"Beg yer pardon, sir?" blandly said the person addressed, who was no other than Charl, of Saint Peter's Finger. Mr. Grower repeated the words.

Charl shook his head to the zero of childlike ignorance. "No; we haven't seen anything; have we, Joe? And you was here afore I."

Joseph was quite as blank as the other in his reply.

"H'm – that's odd," said Mr. Grower. "Ah – here's a respectable man coming that I know by sight. Have you," he inquired, addressing the nearing shape of Jopp, "have you seen any gang of fellows making a devil of a noise – skimmington riding, or something of the sort?"

"Oh, no – nothing, sir," Jopp replied as if receiving the most singular news. "But, I've not been far to-night, so perhaps—"

"Oh, 'twas here – just here," said the magistrate.

"Now I've noticed, come to think o't, that the wind in the Walk trees makes a peculiar poetical-like murmur to-night, sir; more than common; so perhaps 'twas that?" Jopp suggested, as he rearranged his hand in his great-coat pocket (where it ingeniously supported a pair of kitchen tongs and a cow's horn, thrust up under his waistcoat).

"No, no, no – d'ye think I'm a fool? Constable, come this way. They must have gone into the back street."

Neither in back street nor in front street, however, could the disturbers be perceived; and Blowbody and the second constable, who came up at this time, brought similar intelligence. Effigies, donkey, lanterns, band, all had disappeared like the crew of *Comus*.[6]

"Now," said Mr. Grower, "there's only one thing more we can do. Get ye half-a-dozen helpers, and go in a body to Mixen Lane, and into Saint Peter's Finger. I'm much mistaken if you don't find a clue to the perpetrators there."

The rusty-jointed executors of the law mustered assistance as soon as they could, and the whole party marched off to the lane of notoriety. It was no rapid matter to get there at night, not a lamp or glimmer of any sort offering itself to light the way, except an occasional pale radiance through some window-curtain, or through the chink of some door which could not be closed because of the smoky chimney within. At last they entered the inn boldly, by the till then bolted front-door, after a prolonged knocking of loudness commensurate with the importance of their standing.

In the settles of the large room, guyed to the ceiling by cords as usual for stability, an ordinary group sat drinking and smoking with statuesque quiet of demeanour. The landlady looked mildly at the invaders, saying in honest accents, "Good evening, gentlemen; there's plenty of room. I hope there's nothing amiss?"

They looked round the room. "Surely," said Stubberd to one of the men, "I saw you by now in Corn Street – Mr. Grower spoke to 'ee?"

The man, who was Charl, shook his head absently. "I've been here this last hour, hain't I, Nance?" he said to the woman who meditatively sipped her ale near him.

"Faith, that you have. I came in for my quiet supper-time half-pint, and you were here then, as were all the rest."

The other constable was facing the clock-case where he saw reflected in the glass a quick motion by the landlady. Turning sharply, he caught her closing the oven-door.

"Something curious about that oven, ma'am?" he observed advancing, opening it, and drawing out a tambourine.

"Oh," she said, apologetically, "that's what we keep here to use when there's a little quiet dancing. You see damp weather spoils it, so I put it there to keep it dry."

The constable nodded knowingly; but what he knew was nothing. Nohow could anything be elicited from this mute and inoffensive assembly. In a few minutes the investigators went out, and joining those of their auxiliaries who had been left at the door, they pursued their way elsewhither.

CHAPTER XL

Long before this time Henchard, weary of his ruminations on the bridge, had repaired towards the town. When he stood at the bottom of the street a procession burst upon his view, in the act of turning out of an alley just above him. The lanterns, horns, and multitude startled him; he saw the mounted images, and knew what it all meant.

They crossed the way, entered another street, and disappeared. He turned back a few steps and was lost in grave reflection, finally wending his way homeward by the obscure river-side path. Unable to rest there he went to his stepdaughter's lodging, and was told that Elizabeth-Jane had gone to Mrs. Farfrae's. Like one acting in obedience to a charm, and with a nameless apprehension, he followed in the same direction, in the hope of meeting her, the roysterers having vanished. Disappointed in this, he gave the gentlest of pulls to the door-bell, and then learnt particulars of what had occurred, together with the doctor's imperative orders that Farfrae should be brought home, and how they had set out to meet him on the Budmouth Road.

"But he has gone to Mellstock and Weatherbury!" exclaimed Henchard, now unspeakably grieved. "Not Budmouth way at all."

But, alas! for Henchard; he had lost his good name. They would not believe him, taking his words but as the frothy utterances of recklessness. Though Lucetta's life seemed at that moment to depend upon her husband's return (she being in great mental agony lest he should never know the unexaggerated truth of her past relations with Henchard) no messenger was despatched towards Weatherbury. Henchard, in a state of bitter anxiety and contrition, determined to seek Farfrae himself.

To this end he hastened down the town, ran along the eastern road over the moor, up the hill beyond, and thus onward in the moderate darkness of this spring night till he had reached a second and a third hill about three miles distant. In a cutting on the summit of the last he listened.[1] At first nothing, beyond his own heart-throbs, was to be heard but the slow wind making its moan among the masses of spruce and larch which clothed the heights on either hand; but presently there came the sound of light wheels whetting their felloes against the newly stoned patches of road, accompanied by the distant glimmer of lights.

He knew it was Farfrae's gig, from an indescribable personality in its noise, the vehicle having been his own till bought by the Scotchman at the sale of his effects. Henchard thereupon descended the hill on its further side, meeting the gig as its driver slackened speed at the foot of the incline.[2]

It was a point in the highway at which the road to Mellstock branched off from the homeward direction. By diverging to that village, as he had intended to do, Farfrae might probably delay his return by a couple of hours. It soon appeared that his intention was to do so still, the light swerving towards the by-road. Farfrae's off gig-lamp flashed in Henchard's face. At the same time, Farfrae discerned his late antagonist.

"Farfrae – Mr. Farfrae!" cried the breathless Henchard, holding up his hand.

Farfrae allowed the horse to turn several steps into the branch lane before he pulled up. He then drew rein, and said "Yes?" over his shoulder, as one would towards a pronounced enemy.

"Come back to Casterbridge at once!" Henchard said. "There's something wrong at your house – requiring your return. I've run all the way here on purpose to tell ye!"

Farfrae was silent, and at his silence Henchard's soul sank within him. Why had he not before this thought of what was only too obvious? He who, four hours earlier, had enticed Farfrae into a deadly wrestle, stood now in the darkness of late night-time on a lonely road, at a point where it plunged into a cutting through a wood; he invited the man, whom on the first occasion he had let off, to enter that wood, when his purposed way was across an open upland, where there was at least a better opportunity of guarding himself from attack.[3] Henchard could almost feel this view of things in course of passage through Farfrae's mind.

"I have to go to Mellstock," said Farfrae coldly, as he loosened his rein to move on.

"But," implored Henchard, "the matter is more serious than your business at Mellstock. It is – your wife. She is ill. I can tell you particulars as we go along."

The very agitation and hesitancy of Henchard increased Farfrae's suspicion that this was a *ruse* to decoy him into the wood, where might be effectually compassed what, from policy or want of nerve, Henchard had failed to do earlier in the day. He started the horse.

"I know what you think," deprecated Henchard, running after, almost bowed down with despair as he perceived the image of unscrupulous villainy that he had assumed in his former friend's eyes. "But I am not what you think!" he cried hoarsely. "Believe me, Farfrae; I have come entirely on your own and your wife's account. She is in danger. I know no more; and they want you to come. Your man has gone the other way in a mistake. Oh, Farfrae, don't mistrust me – I am a wretched man; but my heart is true to you still!"

Farfrae, however, did distrust him utterly. He had left his wife not long ago in perfect health;[4] and Henchard's treachery was more credible than his story. He had in his time heard bitter ironies from Henchard's lips, and there might be ironies now. He quickened the horse's pace, and had soon risen into the open country lying between there and Mellstock, Henchard's spasmodic run after him lending yet more substance to his thought of evil purposes.

The gig and its driver lessened against the sky in Henchard's eyes; his exertions for Farfrae's good had been in vain. Over this repentant sinner, at least, there was to be no joy in heaven.[5] He cursed himself like a less scrupulous Job,[6] as a vehement man will do when he loses self-respect, the last mental prop under poverty. To this he had come after a time of emotional darkness of which the adjoining woodland shade afforded inadequate illustration. Presently he began to walk back again along the way by which he had come. Farfrae should at all events have no reason for delay upon the road by seeing him there when he took his journey homeward later on.

Arriving at Casterbridge, Henchard went again to Farfrae's house to make inquiries. As soon as the door opened anxious faces confronted his from the staircase, hall, and landing; and they all said in grievous disappointment, "Oh – it is not he!" The man, finding his mistake, had long since returned, and all hopes had been centred upon Henchard.

"But haven't you found him?" said the doctor.

"Yes. . . . . I cannot tell ye!" Henchard replied, as he sank down on a chair within the entrance. "He can't be home for two hours."

"H'm," said the physician, returning upstairs.

"How is she?" asked Henchard of Elizabeth, who formed one of the group.

"In great danger, father. Her anxiety to see her husband makes her fearfully restless. Poor woman – I fear they have killed her!"

Henchard regarded the sympathetic speaker for a few instants as if she struck him in a new light; then, without further remark, went out of the door and onward to his lonely cottage. So much for man's rivalry, he thought. Death was to have the oyster, and Farfrae and himself the shells. But about Elizabeth-Jane; in the midst of his gloom she seemed to him as a pin-point of light. He had liked the look of her face as she answered him from the stairs. There had been affection in it, and above all things what he desired now was affection from anything that was good and pure. She was not his own; yet, for the first time, he had a faint dream that he might get to like her as his own – if she would only continue to love him.

Jopp was just going to bed when Henchard got home. As the latter entered the door Jopp said, "This is rather bad about Mrs. Farfrae's illness."

"Yes," said Henchard shortly, though little dreaming of Jopp's complicity in the night's harlequinade, and raising his eyes just sufficiently to observe that Jopp's face was lined with anxiety.

"Somebody has called for you," continued Jopp, when Henchard was shutting himself into his own apartment. "A kind of traveller, or sea-captain of some sort."

"Oh! – who could he be?"

"He seemed a well-be-doing man – had grey hair and a broadish face; but he gave no name, and no message."

"Nor do I give him any attention." And, saying this, Henchard closed his door.

The divergence to Mellstock delayed Farfrae's return very nearly the two hours of Henchard's estimate. Among the other urgent reasons for his presence had been the need of his authority to send to Budmouth for a second physician; and when at length Farfrae did come back he was in a state bordering on distraction at his misconception of Henchard's motives.

A messenger was despatched to Budmouth, late as it had grown; the night wore on, and the other doctor came in the small hours. Lucetta had been much soothed by Donald's arrival; he seldom or never left her side; and when, immediately after his entry, she had tried to lisp out to him the secret which so oppressed her, he checked her feeble words, lest talking should be dangerous, assuring her there was plenty of time to tell him everything.

Up to this time he knew nothing of the skimmington-ride. The dangerous illness[7] of Mrs. Farfrae was soon rumoured through the town, and an apprehensive guess having been given as to its cause by the protagonists in the exploit, compunction and fear threw a dead silence over all particulars of their orgie; while those immediately around Lucetta would not venture to add to her husband's distress by alluding to the subject.

What, and how much, Farfrae's wife ultimately explained to him of her past entanglement with Henchard, when they were alone in the solitude of that sad night, cannot be told. That she informed him of the bare facts of her peculiar intimacy with[8] the corn-merchant became plain from Farfrae's own statements. But in respect of her subsequent conduct – her motive in coming to Casterbridge to unite herself with Henchard – her assumed justification in abandoning him when she discovered reasons for fearing him (though in truth her inconsequent passion for another man at first sight had most to do with that abandonment) – her method of reconciling to her conscience a marriage with the second when she was in a measure committed to the first: to what extent she spoke of these things remained Farfrae's secret alone.

Besides the watchman who called the hours and weather in Casterbridge that night there walked a figure up and down Corn Street hardly less frequently. It was Henchard's, whose retiring to rest had proved itself a futility as soon as attempted; and he gave it up to go hither and thither, and make inquiries about the patient every now and then. He called as much on Farfrae's account as on Lucetta's, and on Elizabeth-Jane's even more than on either's. Shorn one by one of all other interests, his life seemed centring on the personality of the stepdaughter whose presence but recently he could not endure. To see her on each occasion of his inquiry at Lucetta's was a comfort to him.

The last of his calls was made about four o'clock in the morning, in the steely light of dawn. Lucifer was fading into day over Dummerford Moor, the sparrows were just alighting into the street, and the hens had begun to cackle from the outhouses. When within a few yards of Farfrae's he saw the door gently opened, and a servant raise her hand to the knocker, to untie the piece of cloth which had muffled it. He went across, the sparrows in his way scarcely flying up from the road-litter, so little did they believe in human aggression at so early a time.

"Why do you take off that?" said Henchard.

She turned in some surprise at his presence, and did not answer for an instant or two. Recognizing him, she said, "Because they may knock as loud as they will; she will never hear it any more."

CHAPTER XLI

Henchard went home. The morning having now fully broke he lit his fire, and sat abstractedly beside it. He had not sat there long when a gentle footstep approached the house and entered the passage, a finger tapping lightly at the door. Henchard's face brightened, for he knew the motions to be Elizabeth's. She came into his room, looking pale and sad.

"Have you heard?" she asked. "Mrs. Farfrae? She is – dead! Yes indeed – about an hour ago."

"I know it," said Henchard. "I have but lately come in from there. It is so very good of ye, Elizabeth, to come and tell me. You must be so tired out, too, with sitting up. Now do you bide here with me this morning. You can go and rest in the other room; and I will call you when breakfast is ready."

To please him, and herself – for his recent kindliness was winning a surprised gratitude from the lonely girl – she did as he bade her, and lay down on a sort of couch which Henchard had rigged up out of a settle in the adjoining room. She could hear him moving about in his preparations; but her mind ran most strongly on Lucetta, whose death, in such fulness of life, and amid such cheerful hopes of maternity, was appallingly unexpected. Presently she fell asleep.

Meanwhile her stepfather in the outer room had set the breakfast in readiness; but finding that she dozed he would not call her; he waited on, looking into the fire and keeping the kettle boiling with housewifely care, as if it were an honour to have her in his house. In truth, a great change had come over him with regard to her, and he was developing the dream of a future lit by her filial presence, as though that way alone could happiness lie.

He was disturbed by another knock at the door, and rose to open it, rather deprecating a call from anybody just then. A stoutly-built man stood on the doorstep, with an alien, unfamiliar air about his figure and bearing – an air which might have been called colonial by people of cosmopolitan experience. It was the man who had asked the way at Saint Peter's Finger. Henchard nodded, and looked inquiry.

"Good morning, good morning," said the stranger with profuse heartiness. "Is it Mr. Henchard I am talking to?"

"My name is Henchard."

"Then I caught ye at home – that's right. Morning's the time for business, says I. Can I have a few words with you?"

"By all means," Henchard answered, showing the way in.

"You may remember me?" said his visitor, seating himself.

Henchard observed him indifferently, and shook his head.

"Well – perhaps you may not. My name is Newson."

Henchard's face and eyes seemed to die. The other did not notice it. "I know the name well," Henchard said at last, looking on the floor.

"I make no doubt of that. Well, the fact is, I've been looking for ye this fortnight past. I went through Casterbridge on my way to Weydon Priors,[1] and when I got there, they told me you had some years before been living at Casterbridge. Back came I again, and by long and by late I got here by coach, ten minutes ago. 'He lives down by the mill,' says they. So here I am. Now – that transaction between us some twenty years agone – 'tis that I've called about. 'Twas a curious business. I was younger then than I am now, and perhaps the less said about it, in one sense, the better."

"Curious business? 'Twas worse than curious. I cannot even allow that I'm the man you met then. I was not in my senses, and a man's senses are himself."

"We were young and thoughtless," said Newson. "However, I've come to mend matters rather than open arguments. Poor Susan – her's was a strange experience."

"It was."

"She was a warm-hearted, home-spun woman. She was not what they call shrewd or sharp at all – better she had been."

"She was not."

"As you in all likelihood know, she was simple-minded enough to think that the sale was binding. She was as guiltless o' wrong-doing in that particular as a saint in the clouds."

"I know it, I know it. I found it out directly," said Henchard, still with averted eyes. "There lay the sting o't to me. If she had known the truth she would never have left me.[2] Never! But how should she be expected to know? What advantages had she? None. She could write her own name, and no more."

"Well, it was not in my heart to undeceive her when the deed was done," said the sailor of former days. "I thought, and there was not much vanity in thinking it, that she would be happier with me. She was fairly happy, and I never would have undeceived her till the day of her death. Your child died; she had another, and all went well. But a time came – mark me, a time always does come. A time came – it was some while after she and I and the child returned from America – when somebody she had confided her history to told her my claim to her was a mockery, and made a jest of her belief in my right. After that she was never happy with me. She pined and pined, and socked and sighed. She said she must leave me, and then came the question of our child. Then a man advised me what to do, and I did it, for I thought it was best. I left her at Falmouth, and went off to sea. When I got to the other side of the Atlantic there was a storm, and it was supposed that a lot of us, including myself, had been washed overboard. I got ashore at Newfoundland, and then I asked myself what I should do. 'Since I'm here, here I'll bide,' I thought to myself; "twill be most kindness to her, now she's taken against me, to let her believe me lost; for,' I thought, 'while she supposes us both alive she'll be miserable; but if she thinks me dead she'll go back to him, and the child will have a home.' I've never returned to this country till a month ago, and I found that, as I had supposed, she went to you, and my daughter with her. They told me in Falmouth that Susan was dead. But Elizabeth-Jane – where is she?"

"Dead likewise," said Henchard doggedly. "Surely you learnt that too?"

The sailor started up, and took an enervated pace or two down the room. "Dead!" he said, in a low voice. "Then what's the use of my money to me?"

Henchard, without answering, shook his head, as if that were rather a question for Newson himself than for him.

"Where is she buried?" the traveller inquired.

"Beside her mother," said Henchard, in the same stolid tones.

"When did she die?"

"A year ago, and more,"[3] replied the other without hesitation.

The sailor continued standing. Henchard never looked up from the floor. At last Newson said: "My journey hither has been for nothing. I may as well go as I came! It has served me right. I'll trouble you no longer."

Henchard heard the retreating footsteps of Newson upon the sanded floor, the mechanical lifting of the latch, the slow opening and closing of the door that was natural to a baulked or dejected man; but he did not turn his head. Newson's shadow passed the window. He was gone.

Then Henchard, scarcely believing the evidence of his senses, rose from his seat, amazed at what he had done. It had been the impulse of a moment. The regard he had lately acquired for Elizabeth, the new-sprung hope of his loneliness that she would be to him a daughter of whom he could feel as proud as of the actual daughter she still believed herself to be, had been stimulated by the unexpected coming of Newson to a greedy exclusiveness in relation to her; so that the sudden prospect of her loss had caused him to speak mad lies like a child, in pure mockery of consequences. He had expected questions to close in round him, and unmask his fabrication in five minutes; yet such questioning had not come. But surely they would come; Newson's departure could be but momentary; he would learn all by inquiries in the town; and return to curse him, and carry his last treasure away!

He hastily put on his hat, and went out in the direction that Newson had taken. Newson's back was soon visible up the road.[4] Henchard followed; and saw his visitor stop at the Golden Crown, where the morning coach which had brought him waited half-an-hour for another coach which crossed there. The coach Newson had come by was now about to move again. Newson mounted; his luggage was put in, and in a few minutes the vehicle disappeared with him.

He had not so much as turned his head. It was an act of simple faith in Henchard's words – faith so simple as to be almost sublime. The young sailor who had taken Susan Henchard on the spur of the moment, and on the faith of a glance at her face, more than twenty years before, was still living and acting under the form of the grizzled traveller who had taken Henchard's words on trust so absolute as to shame him as he stood.

Was Elizabeth-Jane to remain his by virtue of this hardy invention of a moment? "Perhaps not for long," said he. Newson might converse with his fellow-travellers, some of whom might be Casterbridge people; and the trick would be discovered.

This probability threw Henchard into a defensive attitude, and instead of considering how best to right the wrong, and acquaint Elizabeth's father with the truth at once, he bethought himself of ways to keep the position he had accidentally won. Towards the young woman herself his affection grew more jealously strong with each new hazard to which his claim to her was exposed.

He watched the distant highway, expecting to see Newson return on foot, enlightened and indignant, to claim his child. But no figure appeared. Possibly he had spoken to nobody on the coach, but buried his grief in his own heart.

His grief! – what was it, after all, to that which he, Henchard, would feel at the loss of her? Newson's affection, cooled by years, could not equal his who had been constantly in her presence. And thus his jealous soul speciously argued to excuse the separation of father and child.

He returned to the house half-expecting that she would have vanished. No; there she was – just coming out from the inner room, the marks of sleep upon her eyelids, and exhibiting a generally refreshed air.

"Oh, father," she said, smiling. "I had no sooner lain down than I napped, though I did not mean to! I wonder I did not dream about poor Mrs. Farfrae, after thinking of her so; but I did not. How strange it is that we do not often dream of latest events, absorbing as they may be."[5]

"I am glad you have been able to sleep," he said, taking her hand with anxious proprietorship – an act which gave her a pleasant surprise.

They sat down to breakfast, and Elizabeth-Jane's thoughts reverted to Lucetta. Their sadness added charm to a countenance whose beauty had ever lain in its meditative soberness.

"Father," she said, as soon as she recalled herself to the outspread meal, "it is so kind of you to get this nice breakfast with your own hands, and I idly asleep the while."

"I do it every day," he replied. "You have left me; everybody has left me; how should I live but by my own hands."

"You are very lonely, are you not?"

"Ay, child – to a degree that you know nothing of. It is my own fault. You are the only one who has been near me for weeks. And you will come no more."

"Why do you say that? Indeed I will, if you would like to see me."

Henchard signified dubiousness. Though he had so lately hoped that Elizabeth-Jane might again live in his house as daughter, he would not ask her to do so now. Newson might return at any moment, and what Elizabeth would think of him for his deception it were best to bear apart from her.

When they had breakfasted his stepdaughter still lingered, till the moment arrived at which Henchard was accustomed to go to his daily work. Then she arose, and with assurances of coming again soon went up the hill in the morning sunlight.

"At this moment her heart is as warm towards me as mine is towards her; she would live with me here in this humble cottage for the asking! Yet before the evening probably he will have come; and then she will despise me."

This reflection, constantly repeated by Henchard to himself, accompanied him everywhere through the day. His mood was no longer that of the rebellious, ironical, reckless misadventurer; but the leaden gloom of one who has lost all that can make life interesting, or even tolerable. There would remain nobody for him to be proud of, nobody to fortify him; for Elizabeth-Jane would soon be but as a stranger, and worse. Susan, Farfrae, Lucetta, Elizabeth – all had gone from him, one after one, either by his fault or by his misfortune.

In place of them he had no interest, hobby, or desire. If he could have summoned music to his aid his existence might even now have been borne; for with Henchard music was of regal power. The merest trumpet or organ tone was enough to move him, and high harmonies transubstantiated him. But fate had ordained that he should be unable to call up this Divine spirit in his need.

The whole land ahead of him was as darkness itself; there was nothing to come, nothing to wait for. Yet in the natural course of life he might possibly have to linger on earth another thirty or forty years – scoffed at, at best pitied.

The thought of it was unendurable.

To the east of Casterbridge lay moors and meadows, through which much water flowed. The wanderer in this direction, who should stand still for a few moments on a quiet night, might hear singular symphonies from these waters, as from a lampless orchestra, all playing in their sundry tones, from near and far parts of the moor. At a hole in a rotten weir they executed a recitative; where a tributary brook fell over a stone breastwork they trilled cheerily; under an arch they performed a metallic cymballing; and at Dummerford Hole they hissed. The spot at which their instrumentation rose loudest was a place called Ten-Hatches, whence during high springs there proceeded a very fugue of sounds.

The river here was deep and strong at all times, and the hatches on this account were raised and lowered by cogs and a winch. A path led from the second bridge over the highway (so often mentioned) to these Hatches, crossing the stream at their head by a narrow plank-bridge. But after nightfall human beings were seldom found going that way, the path leading to no place in particular,[6] and the passage being dangerous.

Henchard, however, leaving the town by the east road, proceeded to the second, or stone bridge, and thence struck into this path of solitude, following its course beside the stream till the dark shapes of the Ten-Hatches cut the sheen thrown upon the river by the weak lustre that still lingered in the west. In a second or two he stood beside the weir-hole where the water was at its deepest. He looked backwards and forwards, and no creature appeared in view. He then took off his coat and hat, and stood on the brink of the stream with his hands clasped in front of him.

While his eyes were bent on the water beneath there slowly became visible a something floating in the circular pool formed by the wash of centuries; the pool he was intending to make his death-bed. At first it was indistinct, by reason of the shadow from the bank; but it emerged thence, and took shape, which was that of a human body, lying stiff and stark upon the surface of the stream.

In the circular current imparted by the central flow the form was brought forward, till it passed under his eyes; and then he perceived with a sense of horror that it was *himself*. Not a man somewhat resembling him, but one in all respects his counterpart, his actual double, was floating as if dead in Ten-Hatches Hole.

The sense of the supernatural was strong in this unhappy man, and he turned away as one might have done in the actual presence of an appalling miracle. He covered his eyes and bowed his head. Without looking again into the stream he took his coat and hat, and went slowly away.

Presently he found himself by the door of his own dwelling. To his surprise Elizabeth-Jane was standing there. She came forward, spoke, called him "father" just as before. Newson, then, had not even yet returned.

"I thought you seemed very sad this morning," she said, "so I have come again to see you. Not that I am anything but sad myself. But everybody and everything seem against you so; and I know you must be suffering."

How this woman divined things! Yet she had not divined their whole extremity.

He said to her, "Are miracles still worked, do ye think, Elizabeth? I am not a read man. I don't know so much as I could wish. I have tried to peruse and learn all my life; but the more I try to know the more ignorant I seem."

"I don't quite think there are any miracles nowadays," she said.

"No interference in the case of desperate intentions, for instance? Well, perhaps not, in a direct way. Perhaps not. But will you come and walk with me, and I will show ye what I mean."

She agreed willingly, and he took her over the highway, and by the lonely path to Ten-Hatches. He walked restlessly, as if some haunting shade, unseen of her, hovered round him and troubled his glance. She would gladly have talked of Lucetta, but feared to disturb him. When they got near the weir he stood still, and asked her to go forward and look into the pool, and tell him what she saw.

She went, and soon returned to him. "Nothing," she said.

"Go again," said Henchard, "and look narrowly."

She proceeded to the river brink a second time. On her return, after some delay, she told him that she saw something floating there; but what it was she could not discern. It seemed to be a bundle of old clothes.

"Are they like mine?" asked Henchard.

"Well – they are. Dear me – I wonder if—Father, let us go away."

"Go and look once more; and then we will get home."

She went back, and he could see her stoop till her head was close to the margin of the pool. She started up, and hastened back to his side.

"Well," said Henchard; "what do you say now?"

"Let us go home."

"But tell me – do – what is it floating there?"

"The effigy," she answered hastily. "They must have thrown it into the river, higher up amongst the willows,⁷ to get rid of it in their alarm at discovery; and it must have floated down here."

"Ah – to be sure – the image o' me! But where is the other? Why that one only?. . . . That performance of theirs killed her, but saved me alive!"

Elizabeth-Jane thought and thought of these words, "saved me alive," as they slowly retraced their way to the town; and at length guessed their meaning. "Father! – I will not leave you alone like this!" she cried. "May I live with you, and tend upon you as I used to do? I do not mind your being poor. I would have agreed to come this morning, but you did not ask me."

"May you come to me?" he cried bitterly. "Elizabeth, don't mock me! If you only would come!"

"I will," said she.

"How will you forgive all my roughness in former days? You cannot!"

"I have forgotten it. Talk of that no more."

Thus she assured him, and arranged their plans for reunion; and at length each went home. Then Henchard shaved for the first time during many days, and put on clean linen, and combed his hair; and was as a man resuscitated thenceforward.

The next morning the fact turned out to be as Elizabeth-Jane had stated: the effigy was discovered by a cowherd, and that of Lucetta a little higher up in the same stream. But as little as possible was said of the matter, and the figures were privately destroyed.

Despite this natural solution of the mystery, Henchard no less regarded it as an intervention that the figure should have been floating there. Elizabeth-Jane heard him say, "Who is such a reprobate as I! And yet it seems that even I am in Somebody's hand!"

CHAPTER XLII

But the emotional conviction that he was in Somebody's hand began to die out of Henchard's breast as time slowly removed into distance the event which had given that feeling birth. The apparition of Newson haunted him. He would surely return.

Yet Newson did not arrive. Lucetta had been borne along the church-yard path; Casterbridge had for the last time turned its regard upon her, before proceeding to its work as if she had never lived. But Elizabeth remained undisturbed in the belief of her relationship to Henchard, and now shared his home. Perhaps, after all, Newson was gone for ever.

In due time the bereaved Farfrae had learnt the at least proximate cause of Lucetta's illness and death; and his first impulse was naturally enough to wreak vengeance in the name of the law upon the perpetrators of the mischief. He resolved to wait till the funeral was over ere he moved in the matter. The time having come he reflected. Disastrous as the result had been, it was obviously in no way foreseen or intended by the thoughtless crew who arranged the motley procession. The tempting prospect of putting to the blush people who stand at the head of affairs – that supreme and piquant enjoyment of those who writhe under the heel of the same – had alone animated them, so far as he could see; for he knew nothing of Jopp's incitements. Other consider-ations were also involved. Lucetta had confessed everything to him before her death, and it was not altogether desirable to make much ado about her history, alike for her sake, for Henchard's, and for his own. To regard the event as an untoward accident seemed, to Farfrae, truest consideration for the dead one's memory, as well as best philosophy.

Henchard and himself mutually forbore to meet. For Elizabeth's sake the former had fettered his pride sufficiently to accept the small seed business which some of the Town Council, headed by Farfrae, had purchased, to afford him a new opening. Had he been only personally concerned, Henchard, without doubt, would have declined assistance even remotely brought about by the man whom he had so fiercely assailed. But the sympathy of the girl seemed necessary to his very existence; and on her account pride itself wore the garments of humility.

Here they settled themselves; and on each day of their lives Henchard anticipated her every wish with a watchfulness in which paternal regard was heightened by a burning, jealous dread of rivalry. Yet that Newson would ever now return to Casterbridge to claim her as a daughter there was little reason to suppose. He was a wanderer and a stranger, almost an alien; he had not seen his daughter for several years; his affection for her could not in the nature of things be keen; other interests would probably soon obscure his recollections of her, and prevent any such renewal of inquiry into the past as would lead to a discovery that she was still a creature of the present. To satisfy his conscience somewhat, Henchard repeated to himself that the lie which had retained for him the coveted treasure had not been deliberately told to that end, but had come from him as the last defiant word of irony which took no thought of consequences. Furthermore he pleaded within himself that no Newson could love her as he loved her, or would tend her to his life's extremity as he was prepared to do cheerfully.

Thus they lived on in the shop overlooking the churchyard, and nothing occurred to mark their days during the remainder of the year. Going out but seldom, and never on a market-day, they saw Donald Farfrae only at rarest intervals, and then mostly as a transitory object in the distance of the street. Yet he was pursuing his ordinary avocations, smiling mechanically to fellow-tradesmen, and arguing with bargainers – as bereaved men do after a while.

"Time, in his own grey style,"[1] taught Farfrae how to estimate his experience of Lucetta – all that it was, and all that it was not. There are men whose hearts insist upon a dogged fidelity to some image or cause, thrown by chance into their keeping, long after their judgment has pronounced it no rarity – even the reverse, indeed; and without them the band of the worthy is incomplete. But Farfrae was not of those. It was inevitable that the insight, briskness, and rapidity of his nature should take him out of the dead blank which his loss threw about him. He could not but perceive that by the death of Lucetta he had exchanged a looming misery for a simple sorrow. After that revelation of her history, which must have come sooner or later in any circumstances, it was hard to believe that life with her would have been productive of further happiness.

But as a memory, notwithstanding such conditions, Lucetta's image still lived on with him, her weaknesses provoking only the gentlest criticism, and her sufferings attenuating wrath at her concealments to a momentary spark now and then.

By the end of a year Henchard's little retail seed and grain shop, not much larger than a cupboard, had developed its trade considerably, and the stepfather and daughter enjoyed much serenity in the pleasant, sunny corner in which it stood. The quiet bearing of one who brimmed with an inner activity characterized Elizabeth-Jane at this period. She took long walks into the country two or three times a week, mostly in the direction of Budmouth. Sometimes it occurred to him that when she sat with him in the evening after these invigorating walks she was civil rather than affectionate; and he was troubled; one more bitter regret being added to those he had already experienced at having, by his severe censorship, frozen up her precious affection when originally offered.

She had her own way in everything now. In going and coming, in buying and selling, her word was law.

"You have got a new muff, Elizabeth," he said to her one day quite humbly.

"Yes; I bought it," she said.

He looked at it again as it lay on an adjoining table. The fur was of a glossy brown, and, though he was no judge of such articles, he thought it seemed an unusually good one for her to possess.

"Rather costly, I suppose, my dear, was it not?" he hazarded.

"It was rather above my figure," she said quietly. "But it is not showy."

"Oh no," said the netted lion, anxious not to pique her in the least.

Some little time after, when the year had advanced into another spring, he paused opposite her empty bedroom in passing it. He thought of the time when she had cleared out of his then large and handsome house in Corn Street, in consequence of his dislike and harshness, and he had looked into her chamber in just the same way. The present room was much humbler, but what struck him about it was the abundance of books lying everywhere. Their number and quality made the meagre furniture that supported them seem absurdly disproportionate. Some, indeed many, must have been recently purchased; and though he encouraged her to buy in reason, he had no notion that she indulged her innate passion so extensively in proportion to the narrowness of their income. For the first time he felt a little hurt by what he thought her extravagance, and resolved to say a word to her about it. But, before he had found the courage to speak, an event happened which set his thoughts flying in quite another direction.

The busy time of the seed trade was over; and the quiet weeks that preceded the hay-season had come – setting their special stamp upon Casterbridge by thronging the market with wood rakes, new waggons in yellow, green, and red, formidable scythes, and pitch-forks of prong sufficient to skewer up a small family. Henchard, contrary to his wont, went out one Saturday afternoon towards the market-place, from a curious feeling that he would like to pass a few minutes on the spot of his former triumphs. Farfrae, to whom he was still a comparative stranger, stood a few steps below the Corn Exchange door – a usual position with him at this hour – and he appeared lost in thought about something he was looking at a little way off.

Henchard's eyes followed Farfrae's, and he saw that the object of his gaze was no sample-showing farmer, but his own stepdaughter, who had just come out of a shop over the way. She, on her part, was quite unconscious of his attention, and in this was less fortunate than those young women whose very plumes, like those of Juno's bird, are set with Argus eyes[2] whenever possible admirers are within ken.

Henchard went away, thinking that perhaps there was nothing significant after all in Farfrae's look at Elizabeth-Jane at that juncture. Yet he could not forget that the Scotchman had once shown a tender interest in her, of a fleeting kind. Thereupon promptly came to the surface that idiosyncrasy of Henchard's which had ruled his courses from the beginning, and had mainly made him what he was. Instead of thinking that a union between his cherished stepdaughter and the energetic thriving Donald was a thing to be desired for her good and his own, he hated the very possibility.

Time had been when such instinctive opposition would have taken shape in action. But he was not now the Henchard of former days. He schooled himself to accept her will, in this as in other matters, as absolute and unquestionable. He dreaded lest an antagonistic word should lose for him such regard as he had regained from her by his devotion, feeling that to retain this under separation was better than to incur her dislike by keeping her near.

But the mere thought of such separation fevered his spirit much, and in the evening he said, with the stillness of suspense, "Have you seen Mr. Farfrae to-day, Elizabeth?"

Elizabeth-Jane started at the question; and it was with some confusion that she replied "No."

"Oh – that's right – that's right. . . . It was only that I saw him in the street when we both were there." He was wondering if her embarrassment justified him in a new suspicion – that the long walks which she had latterly been taking[3] had anything to do with the young man. She did not enlighten him, and lest silence should allow her to shape thoughts unfavourable to their present friendly relations, he diverted the discourse into another channel.

Henchard was, by original make, the last man to act stealthily, for good or for evil. But the *solicitus timor* of his love – the dependence upon Elizabeth's regard into which he had declined (or, in another sense, to which he had advanced) – denaturalized him. He would often weigh and consider for hours together the meaning of such and such a deed or phrase of hers, when a blunt settling question would formerly have been his first instinct. And now, uneasy at the thought of a passion for Farfrae which should entirely usurp her mild filial sympathy with himself, he observed her going and coming more narrowly.

There was nothing secret in Elizabeth-Jane's movements beyond what habitual reserve induced; and it may at once be owned on her account that she was guilty of occasional conversations with Donald when they chanced to meet. Whatever the origin of her walks on the Budmouth Road, her return from those walks was often coincident with Farfrae's emergence from Corn Street for a twenty minutes' blow on that rather windy highway – just to winnow the seeds and chaff out of him before sitting down to tea, as he said. Henchard became aware of this by going to the Ring, and, screened by its enclosure, keeping his eye upon the road till he saw them meet. His face assumed an expression of extreme anguish.

"Of her, too, he means to rob me!" he whispered. "But he has the right. I do not wish to interfere."

The meeting, in truth, was of a very innocent kind, and matters were by no means so far advanced between the young people as Henchard's jealous grief inferred. Could he have heard such conversation as passed he would have been enlightened thus much: –

He. – "You like walking this way, Miss Henchard – is it not so?" (uttered in his undulatory accents, and with an appraising, pondering gaze at her).[4]

She. – "Oh, yes. I have chosen this road latterly. I have a reason for it."[5]

He. – "And that may make a reason for others."

She (reddening). – "I don't know that. My reason, however, is that I wish to get a glimpse of the sea every day."

He. – "Is it a secret why?"

She (reluctantly). – "Yes."

He (with the pathos of one of his native ballads). – "Ah, I doubt there will be any good in secrets! A secret cast a deep shadow over my life. And well you know what it was."

Elizabeth admitted that she did, but she refrained from confessing why the sea attracted her. She could not herself account for it fully, not knowing the secret possibly to be that, in addition to early marine associations, her blood was a sailor's.[6] They proceeded along the road together till they reached the town, and their paths diverged.

Henchard vowed that he would leave them to their own devices, put nothing in the way of their courses, whatever they might mean. If he were doomed to be bereft of her, so it must be. In the situation which their marriage would create he could see no *locus standi* for himself at all. Farfrae would never recognize him more than superciliously; his poverty ensured that, no less than his past conduct. And so Elizabeth would grow to be a stranger to him, and the end of his life would be friendless solitude.

With such a possibility impending he could not help watchfulness. Indeed, within certain lines, he had the right to keep an eye upon her as his charge. The meetings seemed to become matters of course with them on special days of the week.

Once he was standing behind a wall close to the place at which Farfrae encountered her, and he thought he heard the young man address her as "Dearest Elizabeth-Jane."[7]

When they were gone their way Henchard came out from the wall, and mournfully followed them to Casterbridge. The chief looming trouble in this engagement had not decreased. Both Farfrae and Elizabeth-Jane, unlike the rest of the people, must suppose Elizabeth to be his actual daughter, from his own assertion while he himself had the same belief; and though Farfrae must have so far forgiven him as to have no objection to own him as a father-in-law, intimate they could never be. Thus would the girl, who was his only friend, be withdrawn from him by degrees through her husband's influence, and learn to despise him.

Had she lost her heart to any other man in the world than the one he had rivalled, cursed, wrestled with for life in days before his spirit was broken, Henchard would have said, "I am content." But content with the prospect as now depicted was hard to acquire.

There is an outer chamber of the brain in which thoughts unowned, unsolicited, and of noxious kind are sometimes allowed to wander for a moment prior to being sent off whence they came. One of these thoughts sailed into Henchard's ken now.

Suppose he were to communicate to Farfrae the fact that his betrothed was not the child of Michael Henchard at all – legally, nobody's child; how would that correct and leading townsman receive the information? He might possibly forsake Elizabeth-Jane, and then she would be her step-sire's own again.

Henchard shuddered, and exclaimed, "God forbid such a thing! Why should I still be subject to these visitations of the Devil, when I try so hard to keep him away?"

CHAPTER XLIII

What Henchard saw thus early was, naturally enough, seen at a little later date by other people. That Mr. Farfrae "walked with that bankrupt Henchard's stepdaughter, of all women," became a common topic in the town, the simple perambulating term being used hereabout to signify a wooing; and the nineteen superior young ladies of Casterbridge, who had each looked upon herself as the only woman capable of making the merchant Councilman happy, indignantly left off going to the church Farfrae attended, left off conscious mannerisms, left off putting him in their prayers at night amongst their blood relations; in short, reverted to their natural courses.

Perhaps the only inhabitants of the town to whom this looming choice of the Scotchman's gave unmixed satisfaction were the members of the philosophic party, which included Longways, Christopher Coney, Billy Wills, Mr. Buzzford, and the like. The King of Prussia having been, years before, the house in which they had witnessed the young man and woman's first and humble appearance on the Casterbridge stage, they took a kindly interest in their career, not unconnected, perhaps, with visions of festive treatment at their hands hereafter. Mrs. Stannidge, having rolled into the large parlour one evening, and said that it was a wonder such a man as Mr. Farfrae, "a pillow of the town," who might have chosen one of the daughters of the professional men, or private residents, should stoop so low, Coney ventured to disagree with her.

"No, ma'am, no wonder at all. 'Tis she that's a stooping to he – that's my opinion. A widow-man – whose first wife was no credit to him – what is it for a young perusing woman, that's her own mistress and well-liked? But as a neat patching up of things I see much good in it. When a man have put up a tomb of best marble-stone to the other one, as he've done, and weeped his fill, and thought it all over, and said to himself, 'T'other took me in; I knew this one first; she's a sensible piece for a partner, and there's no faithful women in high life now;' –

well, he may do worse than not take her, if she's tender-inclined."

Thus they talked at The King. But we must guard against a too liberal use of the conventional declaration that a great sensation was caused by the prospective event, that all the gossips' tongues were set wagging thereby, and so on, even though such a declaration might lend some *éclat* to the career of our poor only heroine. When all has been said about busy rumourers, a superficial and temporary thing is the concern of anybody with affairs which do not directly touch them. It would be a truer representation to say that Casterbridge (ever excepting the nineteen young ladies) looked up for a moment at the news, and withdrawing its attention, went on labouring and victualling, bringing up its children and burying its dead, without caring a tittle for Farfrae's domestic plans.[1]

Not a hint of the matter was thrown out to her stepfather by Elizabeth herself or by Farfrae either. Reasoning on the cause of their reticence he concluded that, estimating him by his past, the throbbing pair were afraid to broach the subject, and looked upon him as a lion in the path[2] whom they would be heartily glad to get out of the way. Embittered as he was against society, this moody view of himself took deeper and deeper hold of Henchard, till the daily necessity of facing mankind, and of them particularly Elizabeth-Jane, became well-nigh more than he could endure. His health declined; he became morbidly sensitive. He wished he could escape those who did not want him, and hide his head for ever.

But what if he were mistaken in his views, and there were no necessity that his own absolute separation from her should be involved in the incident of her marriage?

He proceeded to draw a picture of the alternative – himself living like a fangless lion about back rooms of a house in which his stepdaughter was mistress; an inoffensive old man, tenderly smiled on by Elizabeth, and good-naturedly tolerated by her husband. It was terrible to his pride to think of descending so low; and yet, for the girl's sake, he might put up with anything; even from Farfrae; even snubbings and masterful tongue-scourgings. The privilege of being in the house she occupied would almost outweigh the personal humiliation.[3]

Whether this were a dim possibility or the reverse, the courtship – which it evidently now was – had an absorbing interest for him.

Elizabeth often took her walks on the Budmouth Road, and Farfrae as often made it convenient to create an accidental meeting with her there. A quarter of a mile from the highway was a pre-historic earthen fort,[4] of huge dimensions and many ramparts, within or upon whose enclosures a human being, as seen from the road, was but an insignificant speck. Hither Henchard often resorted, glass in hand, and scanned the hedgeless *Via* – for it was the original track laid out by the legions of the Empire – to a distance of two or three miles, his object being to read the progress of affairs between Farfrae and his charmer.

One day Henchard was at this spot when a masculine figure came along the road from Budmouth and lingered. Applying his telescope to his eye, Henchard expected that Farfrae's features would be disclosed as usual. But the lenses revealed that to-day the man was not Elizabeth-Jane's lover.

It was one clothed as a merchant-captain; and as he turned in his scrutiny of the road he revealed his face. Henchard lived a lifetime the moment he saw it. The face was Newson's.

Henchard dropped the glass, and for some seconds made no other movement. He stood in dark despair, obscured by "the shade from his own soul upthrown."[5]

Newson waited, and Henchard waited – if that could be called a waiting which was a transfixture. But Elizabeth-Jane did not come. Something or other had caused her to neglect her customary walk that day. Perhaps Farfrae and she had chosen another road for variety's sake. But what did that amount to? She might be here to-morrow, and in any case Newson, if bent on a private meeting and a revelation of the truth to her, would soon make his opportunity.

Then he would tell her not only of his paternity, but of the ruse by which he had been once sent away. Elizabeth's strict nature would cause her for the first time to despise her stepfather, would root out his image as that of an arch deceiver, and Newson would reign in her heart in his stead.

But Newson did not see anything of her that morning. Waiting in vain he at last retraced his steps, and Henchard felt like a condemned man who has a few hours' respite. When he reached his own house he found her there.

"Oh, father," she said innocently, "I have had a letter – a strange one – not signed. Somebody has asked me to meet him, either on the Budmouth Road at noon to-day, or in the evening at Mr. Farfrae's. He says he came to see me some time ago but missed me.[6] I don't understand it; but between you and me I think Donald is at the bottom of the mystery, and that it is a relation of his who wants to pass an opinion on – his choice. But I did not like to go till I had seen you. Shall I go?"

Henchard replied heavily, "Yes; go."

The question of his remaining in Casterbridge was for ever disposed of by this closing in of Newson on the scene. Henchard was not the man to stand the certainty of condemnation on a matter so near his heart. And being an old hand at bearing anguish in silence, and haughty withal, he resolved to make as light as he could of his intention, while immediately taking his measures.

He surprised the young woman, whom he had looked upon as his all in this world, by saying to her, as if he did not care about her more: "I am going to leave Casterbridge, Elizabeth-Jane."

"Leave Casterbridge!" she cried, "and leave – me?"

"Yes, this little shop can be managed by you alone as well as by us both; I don't care about shops and streets and folk – I would rather get into the country by myself, out of sight, and follow my own ways, and leave you to yours."

She looked down, and her tears fell silently. It naturally seemed to her that this resolve of his had come on account of her attachment, and its probable result. She showed her devotion to Farfrae, however, by mastering her emotion and speaking out.

"I am sorry you have decided on this," she said with difficult[7] firmness. "For I thought it probable – possible – that I might marry Mr. Farfrae some little time hence, and I did not know that you disapproved of the step!"

"I approve of anything you desire to do, Izzy," said Henchard huskily. "If I did not approve, it would be no matter. I wish to go away. My presence might make things awkward in the future; and, in short, it is best that I go."

Nothing that her affection could urge would induce him to reconsider his determination; for she could not urge what she did not know – that when she should learn he was not related to her other than as a step-parent she would refrain from despising him, and that when she knew what he had done to keep her in ignorance she would refrain from hating him. It was his conviction that she would not so refrain; and there existed as yet neither word nor event which could argue it away.[8]

"Then," she said at last, "you will not be able to come to my wedding; and that is not as it ought to be."

"I don't want to see it – I don't want to see it!" he exclaimed; adding more softly, "but think of me sometimes in your future life – you'll do that, Izzy? – think of me when you are living as the wife of the richest, the foremost man in the town, and don't let my sins, *when you know them all*, cause ye to quite forget that though I loved 'ee late I loved 'ee well."

"It is because of Donald!" she sobbed.

"I don't forbid you to marry him," said Henchard evasively. "Promise not to quite forget me when——" He meant when Newson should come.[9]

She promised mechanically, in her agitation; and the same evening at dusk Henchard left the town, to whose development he had been one of the chief stimulants for many years.

During the day he had bought a new tool-basket, cleaned up his old hay-knife and wimble, set himself up in fresh leggings, knee-naps and corduroys, and in other ways gone back to the working clothes of his young manhood, discarding for ever the shabby-genteel suit of cloth and rusty silk hat that since his decline had characterized him in the Casterbridge streets as a man who had seen better days.

He went secretly and alone, not a soul of the many who had known him being aware of his departure. Elizabeth-Jane accompanied him as far as the second bridge on the highway – for the hour of her appointment with the unguessed visitor at Farfrae's had not yet arrived – and parted from him with unfeigned wonder and sorrow – keeping him back a minute or two before finally letting him go.[10] She watched his form diminish across the moor, the yellow straw basket at his back moving up and down with each tread, and the creases behind his knees coming and going alternately till she could no longer see them. Though she did not know it, Henchard formed at this moment much the same picture as he had presented when entering Casterbridge for the first time nearly a quarter of a century before; except, to be sure, that the serious addition to his years had considerably lessened the spring of his stride, that his state of hopelessness had weakened him, and imparted to his shoulders, as weighted by the basket, a perceptible bend.

He went on till he came to the first milestone, which stood in the bank, half-way up a steep hill. He rested his basket on the top of the stone, placed his elbows on it, and gave way to a convulsive twitch, which was worse than a sob, because it was so hard and so dry.

"If I had only got her with me – if I only had!" he said. "Hard work would be nothing to me then! But that was not to be. I – Cain – go alone as I deserve – an outcast and a vagabond. But my punishment is *not* greater than I can bear!"[11]

He sternly subdued his anguish, shouldered his basket, and went on.

Elizabeth, in the meantime, had breathed him a sigh, recovered her equanimity, and turned her face to Casterbridge. Before she had reached the first house she was met in her walk by Donald Farfrae. This was evidently not their first meeting that day; they joined hands without ceremony, and Farfrae anxiously asked, "And is he gone – and did you tell him? – I mean of the other matter – not of ours."

"He is gone; and I told him all I knew of your friend. Donald, who is he?"

"Well, well, dearie; you will know soon about that. And Mr. Henchard will hear of it if he does not go far."

"He will go far – he's bent upon getting out of sight and sound!"

She walked beside her lover, and when they reached the Town Pump turned with him into Corn Street, instead of going straight on to her own door. At Farfrae's house they stopped and went in.

Farfrae flung open the door of the ground-floor sitting-room, saying, "There he is waiting for you," and Elizabeth entered. In the arm-chair sat the broad-faced genial man who had called on Henchard on a memorable morning between one and two years before this time, and whom the latter had seen mount the coach and depart within half-an-hour of his arrival. It was Richard Newson.

The meeting with the light-hearted man from whom she had been separated half-a-dozen years, as if by death, need hardly be detailed. It was an affecting one, apart from the question of paternity. Henchard's departure was in a moment explained. When the true facts came to be handled, the difficulty of restoring her to her old belief in Newson was not so great as might have seemed likely, for Henchard's conduct itself was a proof that those facts were true. Moreover, she had grown up under Newson's paternal care; and even had Henchard been her father in nature, this father in early domiciliation might almost have carried the point against him, when the incidents of her parting with Henchard had a little worn off.

Newson's pride in what she had grown up to be was more than he could express. He kissed her again and again.

"I've saved you the trouble to come and meet me – ha-ha!" said Newson. "The fact is that Mr. Farfrae here, he said, 'Come up and stop with me for a day or two, Captain Newson, and I'll bring her round.' 'Faith,' says I, 'so I will;' and here I am."

"Well, Henchard is gone," said Farfrae, shutting the door. "He has done it all voluntarily, and, as I gather from Elizabeth-Jane, he has been very nice with her. I was got rather uneasy; but all is as it should be, and we will have no more difficulties at all."

"Now, that's very much as I thought," said Newson, looking into the face of each by turns. "I said to myself, ay, a hundred times, while I've been living on in my Budmouth lodging, and I said it when I sent her without signature a ten-pound note to buy books and clothes; and I have said it when I have tried to get a peep at her unknown to herself – 'Depend upon it, 'tis best that I should live on quiet like this till something turns up for the better.' I now know you are all right, and what can I wish for more? I should not be happier if I were residing with ye publicly; and Henchard, after all, has more legal claim upon ye."

"*You* sent that ten pounds?" said she, smiling. "Well, I kept it secret, as you requested. But Mr. Henchard wondered about my purchases."[12]

"Well, Captain Newson, I will be glad to se ye here every day now, since it can do no harm," said Farfrae. "And what I've been thinking is, that the wedding may as well be kept under my own roof, the house being large, and you being in lodgings yourself – so that a great deal of trouble and expense would be saved ye – and 'tis a convenience when a couple's married not to hae far to go to get home!"

PLATE XIX

*'"Elizabeth, my child, come and hearken to what we are talking about,
and not bide staring out o' window as if ye didn't hear."'*

"With all my heart," said Captain Newson; "since, as ye say, it can do no harm, now poor Henchard's gone; though I wouldn't have done it otherwise, or put myself in his way at all; for I've already in my lifetime been an intruder into his family quite as far as politeness can be expected to put up with. But what do the young woman say herself about it? Elizabeth, my child, come and hearken to what we be talking about, and not bide staring out o' the window as if ye didn't hear."

"Donald and you must settle it," murmured Elizabeth, still keeping up a scrutinizing gaze at some small object in the street.

"Well, then," continued Newson, turning anew to Farfrae with a face expressing thorough entry into the subject, "that's how we'll have it. And, Mr. Farfrae, as you provide so much, and house room, and all that, I'll do my part in the drinkables, and see to the rum and schiedam – maybe a dozen jars will be sufficient, as many of the folk will be ladies, and perhaps they won't drink hard enough to make a high average in the reckoning? But you know best. I've provided for men and shipmates times enough, but I'm as ignorant as a child how many glasses of grog a woman, that's not a drinking woman, is expected to consume at these ceremonies?"

"Oh, none – we shan't want much of that – oh, no!" said Farfrae, shaking his head with respectable gravity. "Do you leave all to me."

When they had gone a little further in these particulars Newson, leaning back in his chair and smiling reflectively at the ceiling, said, "I've never told ye, or have I, Mr. Farfrae, how Henchard put me off the scent that time?"

He expressed ignorance of what the Captain alluded to.

"Ah, I thought I hadn't. I resolved that I would not, I remember; not to hurt the man's name. But now he's gone I can tell ye. Why, I came to Casterbridge nine or ten months before that day[13] that I found ye out. I had been here twice before then. The first time I passed through the town on my way westward, not knowing Elizabeth lived here. Then hearing at some place – I forget where – that a man of the name of Henchard had been Mayor here, I came back, and called at his house one morning. The joker! – he said Elizabeth-Jane had died years ago."

Elizabeth now gave earnest heed to his story.

"Now, it never crossed my mind that the man was selling me a packet," continued Newson. "And, if you'll believe me, I was that upset, that I went back to the coach that had brought me, and took passage onward without lying in the town half-an-hour. Ha – ha – 'twas a good joke, and well carried out, and I give the man credit for't!"

Elizabeth-Jane was amazed at the intelligence. "A joke? – Oh, no!" she cried. "Then he kept you from me, father, all those months, when you might have been here?"

The father admitted that such was the case.

"He ought not to have done it!" said Farfrae.

Elizabeth sighed. "I said I would never forget him. But, oh! I think I ought to forget him now!"[14]

Newson, like a good many rovers and sojourners among strange men and strange moralities, failed to perceive the enormity of Henchard's crime, notwithstanding that he himself had been the chief sufferer therefrom. Indeed, the attack upon the absent culprit waxing serious, he began to take Henchard's part.

"Well, 'twas not ten words that he said, after all," Newson pleaded. "And how could he know that I should be such a simpleton as to believe him? 'Twas as much my fault as his, poor fellow!"

"No," said Elizabeth-Jane firmly, in her revulsion of feeling. "He knew your disposition – you always were so trusting, father; I've heard my mother say so hundreds of times – and he did it to wrong you. After weaning me from you these five years by saying he was my father, he should not have done this."

Thus they conversed; and there was nobody to set before Elizabeth the palliatives of the absent one's great faults – that he had himself been deceived in her identity, till he had been informed by her mother's letter that his own child had died; that in the second case his lie had been the last desperate throw of a gamester who loved her affection better than his own honour.[15] Even had he been present Henchard might scarce have pleaded these things, so little did he value himself or his good name.

"Well, well – never mind – it is all over and past," said Newson good-naturedly. "Now, about this wedding again."

311

CHAPTER XLIV

Meanwhile, the man of their talk had pursued his solitary way eastward till weariness overtook him, and he looked about for a place of rest. His heart was so exacerbated at parting from the girl that he could not face an inn, or even a household of the most humble kind; and entering a field he lay down under a wheat-rick, feeling no want of food. The very heaviness of his soul caused him to sleep profoundly.

The bright autumn sun shining into his eyes across the stubble awoke him the next morning early. He opened his basket, and ate for his breakfast what he had packed for his supper; and in doing so overhauled the remainder of his kit. Although everything he brought necessitated carriage at his own back, he had secreted among his tools a few of Elizabeth-Jane's cast-off belongings, in the shape of gloves, shoes, a scrap of her handwriting, and the like; and in his pocket he carried a curl of her hair. Having looked at these things he closed them up again, and went onward.

During five consecutive days Henchard's rush basket rode along upon his shoulder between the highway hedges, the new yellow of the rushes catching the eye of an occasional field labourer as he glanced over the quickset, together with the wayfarer's hat and head, and down-turned face, over which the twig shadows moved in endless procession. It now became apparent that the direction of his journey was Weydon Priors, which he reached on the afternoon of the sixth day.

The renowned hill, whereon the annual fair had been held for so many generations, was now bare of human beings, and almost of aught besides. A few sheep grazed thereabout, but these ran off when Henchard halted upon the summit. He deposited his basket upon the turf, and looked about with sad curiosity; till he discovered the road by which his wife and himself had entered on the upland so memorable to both, two or three and twenty years before.[1]

"Yes, we came up that way," he said, after ascertaining his bearings.

"She was carrying the baby, and I was reading a ballet-sheet. Then we crossed about here – she so sad and weary, and I speaking to her hardly at all, because of my cursed pride, and mortification at being poor. Then we saw the tent – that must have stood more this way." He walked to another spot; it was not really where the tent had stood, but it seemed so to him. "Here we went in, and here we sat down. I faced this way. Then I drank, and committed my crime. It must have been just on that very pixy-ring that she was standing when she said her last words to me before going off with him; I can hear their sound now, and the sound of her sobs: 'O, Mike, I've lived with thee all this while, and had nothing but temper. Now I'm no more to 'ee – I'll try my luck elsewhere.'"

He experienced not only the bitterness of a man who finds, in looking back upon an ambitious course, that what he has sacrificed in sentiment was worth as much as what he has gained in substance; but the super-added bitterness of seeing his very recantation nullified. He had been sorry for all this long ago; but his attempts to replace ambition by love had been as fully foiled as his ambition itself. His wronged wife had foiled them by a fraud so grandly simple as to be almost a virtue.

It was an odd sequence that out of all this wronging of social law came that flower of Nature, Elizabeth. Part of his wish to wash his hands of life arose from his perceptions of its contrarious inconsistencies – of Nature's jaunty readiness to support bad social principles.

He intended to go on from this place – visited as an act of penance – into another part of the country altogether. But he could not help thinking of Elizabeth, and the quarter of the horizon in which she lived. Out of this it happened that the centrifugal tendency imparted by weariness of the world was counteracted by the centripetal influence of his love for his step-daughter. As a consequence, instead of following a straight course yet further away from Casterbridge, Henchard gradually, almost unconsciously, deflected from that right line of his first intention; till, by degrees, his path,[2] like that of the Canadian woodsman, became part of a circle, of which Casterbridge formed the centre. In ascending any particular hill, he ascertained the bearings as nearly as he could by means of the sun, moon, or stars, and settled in his mind the exact direction in which Casterbridge and Elizabeth-Jane lay. Sneering at himself for his weakness, he yet every hour – nay, every few minutes –

conjectured her actions for the time being – her sitting down and rising up, her goings and comings, till thought of Newson's and Farfrae's counter-influence would pass like a cold blast over a pool, and efface her image. And then he would say of himself, "O you fool! All this about a daughter who is no daughter of thine!"[3]

And thus Henchard found himself again on the precise standing which he had occupied five-and-twenty years before. Externally there was nothing to hinder his making another start on the upward slope, and by his new lights achieving higher things than his soul in its half-formed state had been able to accomplish. But the ingenious machinery contrived by the gods for reducing human possibilities of amelioration to a minimum – which arranges that wisdom to do shall come *pari passu* with the departure of zest for doing – stood in the way of all that. He had no wish to make an arena a second time of a world that had become a mere painted scene to him.[4]

Very often, as he wandered on, he would survey mankind, and say to himself, "Here and everywhere are folk dying before their time like frosted leaves, though wanted by the world, the country, and their own families, as badly as can be; while I, an outcast and an incumbrance, wanted by nobody, I live on, and can't die if I try."[5]

Had he been able to extend his vision through the night shades as far as Casterbridge that evening, Henchard would have seen that the door of his old house was wide open, that the hall was lighted extravagantly, and that people were going up and down the stairs. It was the wedding-day of Elizabeth and Farfrae. Such an innovation on Casterbridge customs as a flitting of bride and bridegroom from the town immediately after the ceremony had not been thought of, and at that hour Mr. and Mrs. Farfrae were entertaining a houseful of guests at their home in Corn Street.

Donald himself was taking a leading part in the festivity, his voice being distinctly audible in the street, giving expression to a song of his native country. Idlers were standing on the pavement in front, and presently it could be perceived that a dance was proposed, Mr. and Mrs. Farfrae joining in the figure.

Then the people without could discern fractional parts of the dancers

PLATE XX

'"I have done wrong in coming to 'ee . . . I'll never, never
trouble 'ee again, Elizabeth-Jane."'

[See Appendix 1].

whenever their gyrations brought them near the windows, together with about two-fifths of the band in profile, including the restless shadow of a fiddler's elbow and the tip of the bass-viol bow. With the progress of the dance the performers spread out somewhat, and Elizabeth was distinctly visible.

She was in a dress of white silk or satin – the observers were not near enough to say which – snowy white, without a tinge of milk or cream; and the expression of her face was one of nervous pleasure rather than of gaiety. Presently Farfrae came round, his exuberant movement making him conspicuous in a moment. The pair were not dancing together this time, but it was apparent that there was a wordless speech between them; and that whenever the interchanges of the figure made them the partners of a moment their emotions breathed a much subtler essence than at other times.

By degrees the idlers became aware that the measure was also trod by some one who out-Farfraed Farfrae in saltatory intenseness. This was strange, and it was stranger to find that the eclipsing personage was Elizabeth-Jane's partner.

The first time that they saw him he was sweeping grandly round, his head quivering and low down, his legs in the form of an X, and his back towards the door. The next time he came round in the other direction, his white waistcoat preceding his face, and his toes preceding his white waistcoat. That happy form was Captain Newson's.[6]

CHAPTER XLV

It was about a month after the day which closed as in the last chapter. Elizabeth-Jane had grown accustomed to the novelty of her situation, and the only difference between Donald's movements now and formerly was that he hastened indoors rather more quickly after business hours than he had been in the habit of doing for some time.

Newson had stayed in Casterbridge three days after the wedding party (whose gaiety, as might have been surmised, was of his making rather than of the married couple's), and was stared at and honoured as became the returned Crusoe[1] of the hour. But whether or not because Casterbridge was difficult to excite by dramatic returns and disappearances, through having been for centuries an assize town, in which sensational exits from the world, antipodean absences, and such like, were half-yearly occurrences, the inhabitants did not altogether lose their equanimity on his account. On the fourth morning he was discovered disconsolately climbing a hill, in his craving to get a glimpse of the sea from somewhere or other.

The contiguity of salt water proved to be such a necessity of his existence that he preferred Budmouth as a place of residence, notwithstanding the society of his daughter in the other town. Thither he went, and settled in lodgings in a green-shuttered cottage which had a bow-window, jutting out sufficiently to afford glimpses of a vertical strip of blue sea to any one opening the sash, and leaning forward far enough to look through a narrow lane of tall intervening houses.

In exploring her new domain during the first week of residence – gazing with critical satisfaction on this cheerful room and that, penetrating cautiously into dark cellars, sallying with gingerly tread into the garden, now leaf-strewn by the autumn winds, and thus, like a wise field-marshal, estimating the capabilities of the site whereon she was about to open her housekeeping campaign – Mrs. Elizabeth Farfrae had been reminded often of her stepfather, whose house this of hers had formerly been. He was now homeless – possibly penniless. True he had gone away of his own accord.[2] He had not expressed to her any regrets or excuses for what he had done in the past; but it was a part of his nature to extenuate nothing,[3] and live on as one of his own worst accusers.

From that hour her heart softened towards the self-alienated man; till at length she begged Farfrae to help her in finding out, as soon as possible, whither Henchard had banished himself, that she might try to do something to make his life less that of an outcast, and more tolerable to him.

Although Farfrae had never so passionately liked Henchard as Henchard had liked him, he had, on the other hand, never so passionately hated in the same direction as his former friend had done; and he was therefore not the least indisposed to assist Elizabeth-Jane in her laudable plan.

But it was by no means easy to set about discovering Henchard. He had apparently sunk into the earth on leaving Casterbridge. Elizabeth-Jane remembered what he had once attempted; and trembled.

But Henchard had become a changed man since then – as far, that is, as change of emotional base can justify such a radical phrase; and she needed not to fear. In a few days Farfrae's inquiries elicited that Henchard had been seen, less than a month before,[4] by one who knew him, walking steadily along the Melchester highway westward, at twelve o'clock at night – in other words, retracing his steps on the road by which he had gone.

This was enough; and the next morning Farfrae might have been discovered driving his gig out of Casterbridge in that direction, Elizabeth-Jane sitting beside him, wrapped in a thick flat fur – the victorine of the period – her complexion somewhat richer than formerly, and an incipient matronly dignity, which the serene Minerva-eyes of one "whose gestures beamed with mind"[5] made easy, settling on her face. Having herself arrived at a promising haven from at least the grosser troubles of her life, her object was to place Henchard in some similar quietude, before he should sink into that lower stage of existence which was only too possible to him now.

After driving along the highway for a few miles, they made further inquiries, and learnt of a road-mender, who had been working thereabouts for weeks, that he had observed such a man at the time mentioned; he had turned back from the Casterbridge coach-road by a forking highway which crossed Egdon Heath.[6] Into this road they directed the horse's head, and soon were bowling across that ancient country whose surface never had been stirred to a finger's depth, save by the scratchings of rabbits, since brushed by the feet of the earliest tribes. The tumuli these had left behind, dun and shagged with heather, jutted roundly into the sky from the hill above, as though they were the full breasts of Diana Multimammia[7] supinely extended there.

They searched Egdon, but found no Henchard. Farfrae drove

onward, and by the afternoon reached the neighbourhood of some woodland to the east, the first outpost of which,[8] in the form of a blasted clump of firs on the summit of a hill, they soon passed under. That the road they were following had, up to this point, been Henchard's track on foot they were pretty certain; but the ramifications which now began to reveal themselves in the route made further progress in the right direction a matter of pure guess-work, and Donald strongly advised his wife to give up the search in person, and trust to other means for obtaining news of her stepfather. They were now a score of miles at least from home, but, by resting the horse for a couple of hours at a village they had just traversed, it would be possible to get back to Casterbridge that same day; while to go much further afield would reduce them to the necessity of camping out for the night.[9] She pondered the position, and agreed with him.

He accordingly drew rein, but before reversing their direction paused a moment, and looked vaguely around upon the wide country which the elevated position disclosed. While they looked, a solitary human form came from under the clump of trees, and crossed ahead of them. The person was some labourer; his gait was shambling, his regard fixed in front of him as absolutely as if he wore blinkers; and in his hand he carried a few sticks. Having crossed the road he descended into a ravine, where a cottage revealed itself, which he entered.

"If it were not so far away from Casterbridge I should say that must be poor Whittle.[10] 'Tis just like him," observed Elizabeth-Jane.

"And it may be Whittle, for he's never been to the yard these three weeks, going away without saying any word at all; and I owing him for two days' work, without knowing who to pay it to."

The possibility led them to alight, and at least make an inquiry at the cottage. Farfrae hitched the reins to the gate-post, and they approached what was of humble dwellings surely the humblest. The walls, built of kneaded clay originally faced with a trowel, had been worn by years of rain-washings to a lumpy crumbling surface, channelled and sunken from its plane, its grey rents held together here and there by a leafy strap of ivy which could scarcely find substance enough for the purpose.[11] Leaves from the fence had been blown into the corners of the doorway, and lay there undisturbed. The door was ajar; Farfrae knocked; and he who stood before them was Whittle, as they had conjectured.

His face showed marks of deep sadness, his eyes lighting on them with an unfocused gaze; and he still held in his hand the few sticks he had been out to gather. As soon as he recognized them he started.

"What, Abel Whittle; is it that ye are here?" said Farfrae.

"Ay, yes, sir! You see, he was kind-like to mother when she wer here below, though 'a was rough to me."

"Who are you talking of?"

"Oh, sir – Mr. Henchet? Didn't ye know it? He's just gone – about half-an-hour ago, by the sun; for I've got no watch to my name."

"Not – dead?" faltered Elizabeth-Jane.

"Yes, ma'am, he's gone! He was kind-like to mother when she wer here below, sending her the best ship-coal, and hardly any ashes from it at all; and taties, and suchlike that were very needful to her. I couldn't forget him, and traipsed out here to look for him, about the time of your worshipful's wedding to the lady at yer side, and I seed him walking along in the rain,[12] and I thought he looked low and faltering. And I followed en over the road, and he turned and saw me, and said 'You go back!' But I followed, and he turned again, and said, 'Do you hear, sir? Go back!' But I saw that he was low, and I followed on still. Then 'a said, 'Whittle, what do ye follow me for when I've told ye to go back all these times?' And I said, 'Because, sir, I see things be bad with ye, and ye wer kind-like to mother if ye were rough to me, and I would fain be kind-like to you.' Then he walked on, and I followed; and he never complained at me any more. We walked on like that all night; and in the blue o' the morning, when 'twas hardly day, I looked ahead o' me, and I seed that he wambled, and could hardly drag along. By that time we had got past here, but I had seen that this house was empty as I went by, and I got him to come back; and I took down the boards from the windows, and helped him inside. 'What, Whittle,' he said, 'and can ye really be such a poor fond fool as to care for such a wretch as I!' He was as wet as a sponge, and he seemed to have been wet for days.[13] Then I went on further, and some neighbourly woodmen lent me a bed, and a chair, and a few other traps, and we brought 'em here, and made him as comfortable as we could. But he didn't gain strength, for you see, ma'am, he couldn't eat – no, no appetite at all – and he got weaker; and to-day he died. One of the neighbours have gone to get a man to measure him."

"Dear me – is it so!" said Farfrae.

As for Elizabeth, she said nothing.

"Upon the head of his bed he pinned a piece of paper, with some writing upon it," continued Abel Whittle. "But not being a man of letters, I can't read writing; so I don't know what it is. I can get it and show ye."

They stood in silence while he ran into the cottage; returning in a moment with a crumpled scrap of paper. On it there was pencilled as follows: –

"MICHAEL HENCHARD'S WILL

"That Elizabeth-Jane Farfrae be not told of my death, or made to grieve on account of me.

"& that I be not bury'd in consecrated ground.

"& that no sexton be asked to toll the bell.

"& that nobody is wished to see my dead body.

"& that no murners walk behind me at my funeral.

"& that no flours be planted on my grave.

"& that no man remember me.

"To this I put my name.

"MICHAEL HENCHARD."

"What are we to do?" said Donald, when he had handed the paper to her.

She could not answer distinctly. "Oh, Donald," she said at last.[14] "What bitterness lies there! But there's no altering – so it must be."

What Henchard had written in the anguish of his dying was respected as far as practicable by Elizabeth-Jane, though less from a sense of the sacredness of last words, as such, than from her independent knowledge that the man who wrote them meant what he said. She knew the directions to be a piece of the same stuff that his whole life was made of, and hence were not to be tampered with to give herself a mournful pleasure, or her husband credit for large-heartedness.

All was over at last, even her regrets for not having searched him out sooner,[15] though these were deep and sharp for a good while. From this time forward Elizabeth-Jane found herself in a latitude of calm weather, kindly and grateful in itself, and doubly so after the Capharnaum[16] in which some of her preceding years had been spent. As the lively and sparkling emotions of her early married life cohered into an equable serenity, the finer movements of her nature found scope in discovering to the narrow-lived ones around her the secret (as she had once learnt it) of making limited opportunities endurable; which she deemed to consist in the cunning enlargement by a species of microscopic treatment, even to the magnitude of positive pleasure,[17] those minute forms of satisfaction that offer themselves to everybody not in positive pain; which, thus handled, have much of the same inspiriting effect upon life as wider interests cursorily embraced.

Her teaching had a reflex action upon herself, insomuch that she thought she could perceive no great personal difference between being respected in the nether parts of Casterbridge, and glorified at the uppermost end of the social world.

Her position was, indeed, to a marked degree one that, in the common phrase, afforded much to be thankful for. That she was not demonstratively thankful was no fault of hers. Her experience had been of a kind to teach her, rightly or wrongly, that the doubtful honour of a brief transit through a sorry world hardly called for effusiveness, even when the path was suddenly irradiated at some half-way point by daybeams rich as hers. But her strong sense that neither she nor any human being deserved less than was given, did not blind her to the fact that there were others receiving less who had deserved much more. And in being forced to class herself among the fortunate she did not cease to wonder at the persistence of the unforeseen, when the one to whom such unbroken tranquillity had been accorded in the adult stage was she whose youth had seemed to teach that happiness was but the occasional episode in a general drama of pain.

NOTES

These notes are designed to provide two complementary kinds of assistance: clarification of potential obscurities and documentation of significant textual variants between different versions of the novel. They do not include word definition or amplification, which may be found in the accompanying Glossary.

Where successive examples of a particular kind of variant – such as revision of conversational dialect – are not of great individual significance, although they will certainly have a cumulative effect on textual tone, notice of an early and representative example of the type will stand for fuller documentation. Change to the name of a person, locality, or building will be noted on the name's initial appearance only. While the scope of this edition is not that of a variorum, the notes include mention of all major changes and some minor ones. Readers can thus gain an informed sense of both the general attention Hardy paid to revision and the specific kinds of change he thought it worth making, in some instances nearly thirty years after the novel's composition. While one cannot with certainty know authorial motivation for revision, stylistic or situational context almost invariably suggests plausible explanations, which notes advance in full recognition of their speculative nature.

Since substantive changes made for the 1887 Sampson Low single-volume edition and the 1895 Osgood, McIlvaine Wessex Novels edition were in the main subsequently incorporated into Macmillan's 1912 Wessex and 1920 Mellstock editions, variants designated '87' and '95' apply also to those later editions unless otherwise indicated. Variants designated '12' are changes first made for the Wessex Edition and will also be found in the Mellstock Edition. For discussion of the novel's textual history, see A Note on the Text.

The following short-form designations are used for ease of reference.

Versions of *The Mayor of Casterbridge*

MS: Manuscript (Dorset County Museum, Dorchester). Deleted material is contained within angled brackets, and missing sections indicated by '(no MS)'

G: *The Graphic* (English weekly serial version, 2 January–15 May 1886)

HW: *Harper's Weekly* (US weekly serial version, 2 January–15 May 1886)

E86: English first edition, on which this Penguin edition is based (2 volumes; London: Smith, Elder, 1886)

A86: US first edition (1 volume; New York: Henry Holt, 1886)

87: First English 1-volume edition (London: Sampson Low, Marston, Searle & Rivington, 1887)

95: Wessex Novels collected edition (London: Osgood, McIlvaine, 1895)

12: Wessex Edition (London: Macmillan, 1912)

20: Mellstock Edition (2 volumes; London: Macmillan, 1920)

Other texts

Bullen: J. B. Bullen, *The Expressive Eye: Fiction and Perception in the Work of Thomas Hardy* (Oxford: Clarendon Press, 1986)

Firor: Ruth Firor, *Folkways in Thomas Hardy* (Philadelphia: University of Pennsylvania Press, 1931; reprinted New York: Russell & Russell, 1968)

Letters: The Collected Letters of Thomas Hardy, ed. Richard Little Purdy and Michael Millgate (7 volumes; Oxford: Clarendon Press, 1978–88)

Life and Work: The Life and Work of Thomas Hardy by Thomas Hardy, ed. Michael Millgate (London: Macmillan, 1985)

Literary Notebooks: The Literary Notebooks of Thomas Hardy, ed. Lennart A. Björk (2 volumes; London: Macmillan, 1985)

Millgate: Michael Millgate, *Thomas Hardy: His Career as a Novelist* (London: Bodley Head; reissued Basingstoke: Macmillan, 1994)

OED: Oxford English Dictionary

Personal Notebooks: The Personal Notebooks of Thomas Hardy, ed. Richard H. Taylor (London: Macmillan, 1979)

Personal Writings: Thomas Hardy's Personal Writings: Prefaces, Literary Opinions, Reminiscences, ed. Harold Orel (London: Macmillan, 1966)

Purdy: Richard Little Purdy, *Thomas Hardy: A Bibliographical Study* (Oxford: Oxford University Press, 1954, 1968)

Weber: Carl J. Weber, *Hardy of Wessex: His Life and Literary Career* (London: Routledge & Kegan Paul, 1965 [rev. ed.])

Materials designated DCM are to be found in the Dorset County Museum, Dorchester.

MS/G/HW *The Mayor of Casterbridge*
E86 *The Mayor of Casterbridge: The Life and Death of a Man of Character*

A86   *The Mayor of Casterbridge: A Novel*
87/95   *The Mayor of Casterbridge: A Story of a Man of Character*
12/20   *The Life and Death of the Mayor of Casterbridge: A Story of a Man of Character*

CHAPTER I

1. *Weydon-Priors*: Weyhill, a hamlet three miles north-west of Andover in Hampshire and situated on the old road to Amesbury, Stonehenge, and the West Country. Weyhill Fair, held in the second week of October, was one of the largest agricultural fairs in England. Granted its 1599 charter by Elizabeth I, it was of sufficient antiquity to be referred to familiarly in *Piers Plowman*. 95 adds 'in Upper Wessex' after 'Weydon-Priors'.

2. *from which protruded . . . in the aperture*: mention of specific implements replaces cancelled MS references to '<tools>' and '<a two-foot rule>', the latter indicating Henchard's original designation as a stonemason, woodman or sawyer (cf. n. 8 below). MS wording of his later exchange with the turnip-hoer has him seeking work in the building trade.

3. *domesticity*: 'stale familiarity' (95).

4. *steering off the rocks . . . into Maelstrom depths*: the image derives from the Greek myth of Scylla and Charybdis. Mariners negotiating the Strait of Messina were threatened by two monsters, on the one side Scylla, associated with a reef off the Italian coast, and on the other Charybdis, a whirlpool off the coast of Sicily.

5. *Jack Rag or Tom Straw*: familiar names for common fellows of little substance (i.e. anybody).

6. *She shall take the girl*: a cancelled MS passage, '<She shall take one of the girls, her favourite one>', indicates Hardy's original plan for two daughters. Cf. n. 14 below.

7. *simple as Scripture history*: presumably with the spareness in relation of motivation and event that distinguishes biblical narrative.

8. *trusser*: '<woodman>', '<sawyer>', and '<stone mason>' were all considered (MS). Cf. n. 2 above.

9. *a crisp piece of paper*: 'five crisp pieces of paper' (95). The dramatic gesture of clinking down coins on top of the note was made possible by an earlier MS change from pounds to guineas.

10. *Michael*: 'Giles' (MS). In MS Henchard's name progressed from Giles to James to Michael.

11. *and why not here?*: an MS deletion confirms precedents: '<Why, Jimmy Clay sold his wife, didn't he, for thirty shillings? And wasn't it done at Southampton the year before last?>'

12. *room*: 'booth' (95).

13. *a couple*: MS changed from '<five>'.

14. *for me and the child, both*: MS changed from '<Take care of the girl. I'll take care of this one>' (cf. n. 6 above). 12 gives the child's name as Elizabeth-Jane.

15. *and apparently . . . paid for her*: deleted from 95 on.

16. *not till the great trumpet*: i.e. not until Judgment Day.

17. *Mark me – I'll not go after her!*: 'Be cust <hanged> if I'll go after her!' (MS). Early editions frequently modified expletives. Original phrasing was sometimes later restored (although not in this case), particularly if a change had been made to avoid the exclamatory use of 'God'.

CHAPTER II

1. *Seven Sleepers*: seven Christian youths from Ephesus who, persecuted by the Roman Emperor Decius (A.D. 250), took refuge in a cave on Mount Coelian. The cave was discovered and its entrance blocked. The seven fell asleep, waking during the reign of Theodosius II (408–50) when a herdsman let light into the cave. Having given this apparent proof of resurrection, they died. Spread widely throughout Europe and the East, the story was incorporated into the Koran (Chapter 18), where the sleepers are protected by a dog lying at the cave's entrance.

2. *intellect*: 'intellect, which was far removed from strong, though not positively weak, as that word is usually understood in this connection' (G/HW; no MS). See Chapter IV, n. 2 for another example of the serial's greater emphasis on Susan's intellectual shortcomings.

3. *There may . . . placidity*: 'There may, too, have been enough recklessness and resentment beneath her ordinary placidity to make her stifle any momentary doubts' (95).

4. *fetichistic*: manifesting superstitious attachment to or reverence for something. The resonances of its application to Henchard may be positive, and related to Hardy's reading of Comte, most specifically his *Social Dynamics, or the General Theory of Human Progress*, from which 'Literary Notes I' quotes extensively (see *Literary Notebooks*, I: items 618–20, 640–42, 645–73, 675–769 [especially 754–62]). Distinguishing between 'the Fetichistic spirit which looks on all objects in nature as animate, and the Theological spirit which regards them as passively subject to supernatural powers', Comte suggests 'the first is superior to the second, not only in spontaneity but also in truth' (*Social Dynamics* [London, 1876], p. 68, cited in Björk, ed., *Literary Notebooks*, I, p. 324). Björk relates the Fetichistic spirit to both Tess Durbeyfield's responses and Hardy's own, as evidenced in a note of 10 February 1897: 'In spite of myself I cannot help noticing countenances & tempers in objects of scenery, e.g. trees, hills, houses' (*Life and Work*, p. 302). Henchard's impulse to read nature as animate is a source of both moral strength and practical weakness in his dealings with the supremely rational Farfrae.

5. *twenty*: 'twenty-one' (12). All subsequent references to the abstention were similarly changed.

6. *tantalizing*: 'perplexing' (95).

7. *southward*: 'westward' (G/HW/A86; no MS); 'south-westward' (95).

8. *pause till . . . more than a hundred miles off*: 'pause, except for nights' lodgings, till . . . in a far distant part of Wessex' (95).

CHAPTER III

1. *of eighteen*: 'about eighteen' (12).

2. *November*: Elizabeth-Jane later tells Henchard 'Father was lost last spring' (see Chapter x, n. 7).

3. *I suppose he never knew me?*: MS has neither Elizabeth-Jane's question nor Susan's answer. G/HW follow Susan's answer with 'Let judgment be reserved on Mrs. Henchard's morals for this negative till her hard circumstances are fairly recognized.'

4. *as she now called herself*: in this first mention in the extant MS (f. 29) of Susan's post-Henchard name, 'Newson' replaces '<Dawson>'. On f. 31, 'Newson' is used without correction.

5. *shameless*: 'thoughtless' (G/HW/A86); 'nameless' (MS).

6. *seize my life*: 'Lord's my life' (12). MS shows '<God's my life>' replaced by 'seize my life' here and by 'Lord's my life' a page later.

CHAPTER IV

1. *folly to think of making Elizabeth-Jane wise*: cf. the concluding lines of Thomas Gray's 'Ode on a Distant Prospect of Eton College': 'where ignorance is bliss, / 'Tis folly to be wise'.

2. *simplicity*: 'almost vacuous simplicity' (G/HW; no MS). Cf. Chapter II, n. 2.

3. *a real and binding right*: 'a morally real and justifiable right' (95). Also in 95, 'validity' in the next sentence became 'seriousness'.

4. *as too many rural records show*: Hardy found West Country examples of wife-sale in the *Dorset County Chronicle*, whose issues from the 1820s on he began exploring

327

in early 1884. He copied details of three sales into his 'Facts from Newspapers, Histories, Biographies, & other chronicles' notebook (DCM), kept with a view to using some of the unusual episodes it records in his fiction. Given the wife's price and the horse-trading mode of her delivery, one of these entries, dated 6 December 1827, is particularly relevant: '*Selling wife.* At Buckland, nr. Frome, a labring [*sic*] man named Charles Pearce sold wife to shoemaker named Elton for £5, & delivered her in a halter in the public street. She seemed very willing. Bells rang.' See Christine Winfield, 'Factual Sources of Two Episodes in *The Mayor of Casterbridge*' (*Nineteenth Century Fiction* 25 [1970], 224–31).

5. *sadness*: ', in which she told him her doubts if she could live with him longer' added in 95.

6. *England is a continent*: 'the England of those days was a continent' (95); i.e. those in quasi-feudal subjection to labour have little opportunity to travel.

7. *to see, to hear, and to understand*: cf. Isaiah 6:9–10.

8. *sailor was now lost to them*: 'sailor, drowned or no, was probably now lost to them' (12). MS shows '<dead & buried>' replaced by 'lost to them'.

9. *husband*: 'husband in principle' (95); '<in every moral sense>' deleted from MS.

10. *There were no hedges to the highway here . . . turf and sat down*: 'There were high-banked hedges to the coach-road here . . . turf within, and sat down' (95). Other minor changes to the subsequent description were necessitated by this addition of hedges.

11. *(as she may be called for the present)*: deleted in 95.

12. *thatch*: footnote added in 12: 'Most of these old houses have now been pulled down (1912).'

13. *corn-drills and winnowing-machines*: 'carts, wheel-barrows, and mill-gear' (95), a change probably made to avoid later contradiction in the supposed novelty of corn-drills.

14. *curfew*: originally rung to signal the time at which fires should be extinguished for the night (cf. Old French *cuevrefeu*), the curfew bell continued in use as a time-signal in many English towns until the early twentieth century. In Dorchester it rang from St Peter's Church, in front of which the women are standing.

15. *Sicilian Mariners' Hymn*: this traditional Sicilian tune provided the setting for a number of early-to-mid-nineteenth-century hymns. In 12 Hardy added the footnote: 'These chimes, like those of other country churches, have been silenced for many years.'

16. *manna-food*: the miraculous heaven-sent food said to have sustained the Israelites in the wilderness during their exodus from Egypt (see Exodus 16:14–36). A passage deleted from Chapter XIII in MS identifies the speaker here as Nance Mockridge.

17. *grown wheat*: 'growed wheat' (95), or wheat '[t]hat has sprouted in the ear after reaching maturity' (*OED*), a condition often brought about by late harvesting in wet summers. This untimely natural germination makes grain unsuited to the production of both bread and beer.

CHAPTER V

1. "*The Roast Beef of Old England*": a popular song from *The Grub-Street Opera* (1731): words by Henry Fielding, music by Richard Leveridge.

2. *The Golden Crown*: 'the King's Arms' (95). The eventual appropriation of the name of Dorchester's actual 'chief hotel' – the use of which, along with the Antelope and St Peter's Church, had been contemplated in MS, as can be seen from deletions and restorations – was part of Hardy's later attempt to give greater topographical cohesion and specificity to the presentation of Wessex. The hotel stands in the high street, a short distance down from St Peter's Church.

3. *approaching forty*: 'about forty' (95).

4. *Susan Henchard's*: MS deletion reads '<Elizabeth Jane's father, & the elder woman's>'. To avoid actual misrepresentation of Elizabeth-Jane's paternity the next sentence was modified in MS from 'Elizabeth<'s last view of him having been before> her <recollection, she>'.

5. *akin to a coach*: related to someone who maintains, or has official access to, a coach.

6. *banded teetotaller*: member of a temperance band, and therefore a teetotaller by sworn oath.

7. *jovial Jews*: see Exodus 32. Longways seems to be misremembering his scripture. God had threatened to punish those Israelites who, during Moses' absence on Mount Sinai, created and worshipped a golden calf and gave themselves over to feasting and play. He was dissuaded from doing so by Moses. But as soon as Moses saw the calf and the dancing, he enacted the punishment himself, bringing about the deaths of 3,000 of the ungodly.

8. *He and Casterbridge bank-folk are sworn brothers*: MS/G/HW continue '; and it's not every man that's hand in glove with a bank.' The sentence was deleted entirely from 87 on.

9. *Casterbridge Moor*: 'Durnover Moor' (95). In an MS deletion, the speaker's authority in the judgment of bread is established not by mere age but by his having been '<master dipper to Maister William Hood the taller [tallow]-chandler these five and forty-years>'.

10. *and though 'tis not my interest to spak against him*: deleted from 87 on.

11. *in which he had outwitted a sharper who had been bent upon outwitting him*: MS/G/HW tell the full story. Far from outwitting the business rival, Henchard is himself

bested, suggesting both lack of business acumen and inadequate knowledge of the hay in which he is dealing.

12. *face had grown*: 'face had become' (95). Hardy presumably noticed the obtrusive repetition of 'grown' in surrounding sentences.

CHAPTER VI

1. *fair and ruddy*: 'ruddy and of a fair countenance' (12). The expanded phrasing echoes the description of David in 1 Samuel 16:12 and 17:42.

2. *King of Prussia*: 'Three Mariners' (95).

3. *immutable*: 'ancient' (95). The change was presumably made because the inn proved far from immutable: a further modification in 95 adds ',now, unfortunately, pulled down' after 'man and beast'.

4. *others of that set*: 'others of a secondary set of worthies, of a grade somewhat below that of the diners at the King's Arms' (95).

5. *the King . . . a person . . . seated on a war-horse in a paralyzed prance. . . . both he and his charger*: 'the Mariners . . . persons . . . were standing in a row in paralyzed attitudes. . . . the three comrades' (95). In the next sentence, 'uniform of a man' became 'features of men'.

CHAPTER VII

1. *ceilings*: 'windows' (95). MS reads 'antique awkwardness, shabbiness, & obscurity of the passages, doors, walls, & windows'.

2. *twelve-bushel strength*: the weight refers to the quantity of barley in proportion to water used in the brewing, which governs the strength and quality of the ale.

3. *Donald Farfrae*: Hardy's original name for Donald Farfrae had been 'Alan Stansbie'. The page on which Farfrae first announces his name is missing from MS, but the original name appears as a deletion on surviving MS pages down to Chapter XXIII. Hardy experimented with various renderings of Farfrae's accent in early editions of the novel (e.g. 'corren' [87], 'advairrtisment' [95]), eventually accepting as authoritative the suggestions on both transcription and idiom made for 95 by his Scottish friend Sir George Douglas. These minor adjustments will not be noted unless they modify meaning or emphasis.

4. *ay, as Presbyterian cream*: deleted in 95. Presbyterian cream was cream laced with malt whisky, frequently served on Sunday to disguise the consumption of alcohol.

5. *I could drink a quarter-barrel to the pitching*: a quarter-barrel, whose joints would be sealed with pitch, holds nine gallons.

CHAPTER VIII

1. *It's hame . . . to my ain countree*: a song of Jacobite sentiment, collected by, and sometimes attributed to, Allan Cunningham (1784–1842), under whose name a version of it appears as entry No. 597 in Quiller-Couch's *Oxford Book of English Verse* (1900). Cunningham collected ballads for Robert Hartley Cromek's *Remains of Nithsdale and Galloway Song* (1810), but also submitted some of his own compositions. Cromek gave its source as Burns's Commonplace Book. Its equivocal authenticity fits well with Farfrae's armchair nostalgia.

2. *'Tis recorded in history . . . I can well believe it*: Buzzford's garbled history looks back to the Monmouth Rebellion against James II. Hardy may originally have intended the account to be even more confused: MS read '<helped kill>' before being changed to 'rebelled against', suggesting identification of the Monmouth Rebellion with the earlier Civil War and execution of Charles I (although Hardy may himself have momentarily confused them and then made a correction).

The rebellion was resoundingly crushed on 6 July 1685 in the last full battle to be fought on English soil, at Sedgemoor, near Bridgwater in Somerset. Monmouth himself was captured two days later and executed (15 July 1685) at Tower Hill. But more memorable in Dorset were the executions of rebels, many convicted on the flimsiest of evidence, after the setting up of one of Judge George Jeffreys's 'bloody assizes' in Dorchester on Friday, 4 September. By the following Monday, thirteen had already been hanged, and there were to be sixty-one more executions in Dorchester alone. The full total for the western assizes is unknown, but executions were in excess of 300, with hundreds more transported, many into slavery in the West Indies. Gallows Hill was at the intersection of South Walks Road and Icen Way. Treatment of victims confirms Buzzford's folk history. Most were cut down while still alive, disembowelled, and quartered, the quarters distributed for salutary exhibition throughout Dorset, the heads impaled on the railings of St Peter's Church. Buzzford's reference to 'the time of the Romans' may not be mere anachronistic nonsense but a reference to James II's Roman Catholicism.

3. *Botany Bay*: an inlet on the coast of New South Wales, Australia, and popular term for any Australian penal colony. Ironically, the area was found unsuitable by Commodore Arthur Phillip, who was commissioned to establish the original settlement in 1787, and the colony was relocated five miles to the north, on what became the site of Sydney. Coney's reference is already obsolete:

the transportation of convicted felons to New South Wales ceased in 1840.

4. "*Oh Nannie*": originally an English song, popular in Scotland (where its words underwent dialectal modification), and collected in Percy's *Reliques of Ancient English Poetry* (1765). Its rustic 'swain' asks, 'O Nanny, wilt thou gang with me, / Nor sigh to leave the flaunting town? / Can silent glens have charms for thee, / The lowly cot and russet gown?' The irony of its being sung by a forward-looking, scientifically inclined youth, who has himself deserted the 'silent glens' in favour of the promise of America and is about to become a successful businessman and municipal politician in a southern town, is presumably intentional.

5. *looking round upon them with tragic fixity*: 'showing his white teeth in a pitiful deprecating smile' (MS).

6. *Arthur's Seat*: a hill to the east of Edinburgh from which legend says King Arthur watched his army defeat the Picts.

7. *As I came in . . . bonnie Peg my dearie*: 'Bonnie Peg', a song by Robert Burns. MS/G/HW give the 'next verse' that Farfrae sings 'within the closed door of his room', and the song is described as 'a slightly modified version of an old ditty'. The modification occurs in the first stanza: in Burns's original, the speaker comes in by 'our gate end' and Peg comes 'tripping down the street'.

CHAPTER IX

1. *the churchyard wall*: 'St. Peter's churchyard wall' (12).

2. *two grains of corn*: 'two notes of admiration' (MS).

3. *Hintock*: 'The Hintocks' (95). While this was a conscious authorial revision, probably brought about by Hardy's refinement of his imaginative use of this area in *The Woodlanders* (1887), other variations in early versions of this list were clearly generated by compositorial confusion and error. In G/HW (no MS), Hintock was upgraded to 'Hintock-Abbas', presumably as a result of the accidental omission of 'Sherton-Abbas' from the list, while in A86 'Abbas' (a term appended to a place-name to indicate the presence of an abbey) is a village in its own right, along with 'Hintock' and 'Sherton'. In 95 'Stickleford' became 'Kingsbere'; 'villages round' also became 'towns and villages round', a change occasioned by scrupulosity about the presence in the list of Sherton-Abbas (Sherborne) and Kingsbere (Bere Regis, which was formerly a market-town and royal resort, though latterly a mere village).

4. *Cranstoun's Goblin Page*: in Scott's *Lay of the Last Minstrel*, Lord Cranstoun's wedding celebrations are disrupted by his malicious dwarf-page, who strives 'To rouse debate and jealousy' (see Canto VI, stanzas 7–9).

5. *stock*: in 12, Hardy added a footnote: 'The reader will scarcely need to be reminded that time and progress have obliterated from the town that suggested these descriptions many or most of the old-fashioned features here enumerated.'

6. *fronted with murrey-coloured old brick*: 'faced with dull red-and-grey old brick' (95). Hardy took the mid-eighteenth-century building at 10 South Street as the model for Henchard's house.

7. *by Flemish ladders*: G/HW (no MS) read 'short Flemish ladders', which may suggest that 'Flemish', otherwise unidentified, signifies size.

8. *New Walk*: 'Chalk Walk' (95). Chalk Walk, in actuality once called New Walk and later Colliton Walk (as it is still known), is the continuation of West Walks north of Top o' Town.

9. *for, hang it, Farfrae, I like thee well*: absent from G/HW (no MS).

10. *Surely there's destiny in it? Should a man turrun against fate?*: 'It's Providence! Should any one go against it?'(95).

11. *had*: 'has' (12). Hardy presumably finally noticed the temporal inconsistency.

CHAPTER X

1. *the quicker cripple at Bethesda*: the water at Bethesda, a pool by the sheep-market in Jerusalem, was periodically disturbed, supposedly by an angel. The first person then to step into it would be cured of any disease. Jesus cures a man whose infirmity has for thirty-eight years prevented his being the first in the pool (see John 5:2–9). Jopp's subsequent misfortune seems excessive punishment for his minor discourtesy to Elizabeth-Jane. Perhaps the implication is that, like the slow cripple, she has earned priority after waiting all her life for Henchard's attention.

2. *the master of the premises*: MS deletion shows '<her father>'.

3. *Pembroke tables*: the most elegant style of late-eighteenth-century drop-leaf table, probably named for the Countess of Pembroke (1737–1831), who supposedly first ordered them. Hardy invokes them rather approximately: distinguishing characteristics include extremely slender legs, very often on castors, and feet shaped not at all 'like those of an elephant', although they did occasionally take the form of elongated paws.

4. *a "Josephus"*: Flavius Josephus (*c.* A.D. 37–95), Jewish historian and soldier, wrote three main works: *The Jewish War*, a history of the revolt of Palestinian Jews against Rome (A.D. 67–73), in which Josephus himself took part; *The Jewish Antiquities*, a history of the Jews from the Creation to the war with Rome; and *Against Apion*, a defence of Jews against contemporary Roman misrepresentation. But more appropriate to Henchard is Josephus's *Life*, in which he absolves himself of any responsibility for the Jewish rebellion by remaking his past, claiming to have been an ally of Rome (and thus arguably a traitor against his own people and identity) from the outset.

5. "*Whole Duty of Man*": a devotional work, published anonymously in 1658, attributed to Richard Allestree. Its full title is *The Practice of Christian Graces, or The Whole Duty of Man*. It too has ironic application to Henchard's situation: much of its preoccupation with duty addresses the mutual responsibilities between husbands and wives. See Ecclesiastes 12:13: 'Fear God and keep his commandments: for this is the whole duty of man.'

6. *Chippendale and Sheraton*: Thomas Chippendale (1718–79) and Thomas Shera-ton (1751–1806), two of the most influential English furniture designers of the eighteenth century. Their books of furniture designs (Chippendale, *The Gentleman & Cabinet Maker's Director* [1754]; Sheraton, *The Cabinet-Maker and Upholsterer's Drawing Book* [1791–4] and *The Cabinet Dictionary* [1803]) were widely consulted and copied, and their names were attached generically to work in which they had no direct hand.

7. *Father was lost last spring*: see Chapter III, n. 2.

CHAPTER XI

1. *The Ring at Casterbridge*: Maumbury Rings is a Neolithic henge monument situated at the southern end of Dorchester. It was restructured by the Romans into an oval amphitheatre capable of accommodating more than 12,000 spec-tators, its arena area measuring about 200 by 160 feet. Enclosed by a high broad bank with a single main public entry-point at the north-east end (though Henchard himself enters by the smaller southern opening, over the rubble of the former animal dens), it still generates an eerie mood of muffled isolation, despite modern proximity to major roads and railway lines. Used in the Middle Ages and beyond for bull, bear, and badger baiting, it served in the Civil War as a gun emplacement, from which Parliamentary troops guarded the adjacent road to Weymouth. Its sanguinary associations were considerably heightened in the eighteenth century, when the town gallows were moved there (until 1767) from Gallows Hill. During a major excavation (1908–13), Hardy wrote an article about it for *The Times* (9 October 1908: see 'Maumbury Ring', *Personal Writings*, pp. 225–32).

2. *Casterbridge announced old Rome . . . as they passed by*: for Hardy's own experience of unearthing Roman remains during excavations for the construction of his new house, see 'Some Romano–British Relics Found at Max Gate, Dorchester' (*Personal Writings*, pp. 191–5).

3. *The Amphitheatre was a huge circular enclosure*: 'The Amphitheatre was in the form of a huge spittoon' (MS/G/HW). The next sentence was added in E86.

4. *It was to Casterbridge . . . same magnitude*: Maumbury Rings is an earthworks, not a stone building. Nor is it 'of the same magnitude' as the Colosseum which, before falling victim to earthquake and pillage, had walls rising to nearly 200 feet, an arena area half as big again as Maumbury, and room for about 50,000 spectators. Hardy first saw the Colosseum the year after *The Mayor of Casterbridge* was published.

5. *in 1705 a woman . . . hot roast after that*: Mary Channing's execution on 21 March 1705 held an almost obsessive interest for Hardy, in part because an ancestor witnessed it. Describing it at length in 'Maumbury Ring', he expresses doubt about Channing's guilt and asks, 'Was man ever "slaughtered by his fellow man" during the Roman or barbarian use of this place of games or of sacrifice in circumstances of greater atrocity?' (*Personal Writings*, p. 300). He recorded in his 'Memoranda, I' notebook (25 January 1919) a supposed eyewitness account whose details are even more horrific than those given here (see *Personal Notebooks*, p. 38), and returned to the subject in a late poem, 'The Mock Wife' (*Human Shows* [1925]), again implying that Channing may not have been guilty. The associative echoes of a marital crime that has dreadful consequences are contextually suited to Henchard's own domestic misfortunes. But Hardy's fascination with the awful fate of a convicted husband-murderer, whom (despite the absence of historical support) he recurrently figures as innocent, has even greater implications for *Tess of the d'Urbervilles* (1891), the novel that a few years later would be claiming most of his attention.

Hardy himself saw two public executions as a youth (*Life and Work*, pp. 32–3), the first that of a woman named Martha Browne who, like Mary Channing, had been condemned for murdering her husband. As with Channing, Hardy retained his interest in Browne into old age, as late as 1925 seeking out local information about her (see *Letters*, 7, p. 5 and Lady Hester Pinney, *Thomas Hardy and the Birdsmoorgate Murder 1856* [1966]).

6. *Hadrian's soldiery*: the Emperor Hadrian (A.D. 76–138, Emperor from 117) visited Britain in 122, where he inspected the construction, across the north of England from the Solway Firth to the Tyne, of the great defensive wall named after him.

7. *Æolian modulations*: the phrase is Shelley's (see *Prometheus Unbound*, IV, 188). Æolus was the Greek god of the winds. The sound of the wind brushing the bents is implicitly compared to the music created by wind passing through the strings of an Æolian harp.

8. *there's the rub o't*: an echo of Hamlet's 'ay, there's the rub' as he reviews the arguments against suicide (*Hamlet*, III.i.).

CHAPTER XII

1. *the education of Achilles*: the Greek hero Achilles received his early education from the centaur Chiron, primarily in sporting and military accomplishments, well suited to a child nourished on the marrowbones of bears and lions' entrails. Writing was not one of his more developed skills.

2. *leafy Laocoons*: Laocoon, a Trojan priest of Apollo, incurred Apollo's wrath by defiling his temple. Convinced that the wooden horse left by the Greeks contained armed men, he hurled a spear at its side. Shortly afterwards, while preparing to sacrifice a bull to Poseidon, Laocoon and his two sons were crushed to death by two sea-serpents sent by Apollo. King Priam mistakenly decided that Laocoon had been punished for attacking the wooden horse rather than for offending Apollo, and accepted the gift. The most famous representation of Laocoon is a statue of the first century B.C. (Vatican Museum, possibly the work of Agesander, Polydorus and Athenodorus) in which both serpentine coils and victims' limbs are splayed out like knotted espaliered branches.

3. *d—*: Henchard's expletives remained partly deleted, usually even in MS, until 95, and G reads 'hang'. The deletion has been retained, here as elsewhere, for the sake of period integrity.

4. *eighteen years ago*: 'nineteen years ago or so' (12).

5. *And it's not a small counterbalance . . . so much since!*: replaced in 95 by just 'Ay!'.

6. *keep at a distance*: 'keep mostly at a distance' (12). The original claim is immediately contradicted in Henchard's account of his relationship with Lucetta.

7. *Job*: see Job 3:3: 'Let the day perish wherein I was born, and the night in which it was said, There is a man child conceived.' The self-obliteration of Job's curse is echoed in Henchard's will, directed towards ensuring 'that no man remember me'. Job is again invoked in *Jude the Obscure* (1895): Jude's final words, delivered in isolation after Arabella has scuttled off to join the holiday crowds, are a death-bed recitation of eight verses from Job, beginning with the verse Henchard recalls here. For other associations of Henchard with Job, see Chapter XL, n. 6.

8. *of good family . . . the daughter of some harum-scarum military officer*: in MS/G/HW, Lucetta is the well-educated daughter of a merchant. Raffish refinement defines her now, not trade. Other changes between serial and book result from a major plot revision. Originally, just two weeks before Susan's return, Lucetta and Henchard had married, on a rash impulse that Henchard already regrets. A further significant change is that Lucetta now becomes involved with Henchard through ministering to a psychological illness; formerly she had rescued him from drowning. Thus she assumes the more emotionally charged and morally complex role of nurse and counsellor.

9. *I didn't encourage any such thing*: 'I wasn't worth it' (95).

10. *and her feelings warm,*: 95 continues 'we got naturally intimate. I won't go into particulars of what our relations were. It is enough to say that we honestly meant to marry. There arose a scandal . . .'

11. *I solemnly declare that I did her no wrong . . . careless of appearances*: 'I solemnly declare that philandering with womankind has neither been my vice nor my virtue. She was terribly careless of appearances' (95). The changed wording marked here and in n. 10 above makes explicit a sexual affair that in the first edition Henchard specifically denies.

12. *And I will*: in MS/G/HW, Farfrae performs a more laborious service, going to Budmouth to intercept Lucetta with Henchard's letter. Lucetta, suffering from seasickness, cannot see him, but accepts the letter by stretching her hand out from behind a curtain covering the cabin door.

13. *enable us to retain*: 'help us to keep' (95). Like Farfrae's speech, Henchard's too became less formal, notwithstanding his irritation at Elizabeth-Jane's occasional lapses into dialect. From 95 on his 'of' is often contracted to 'o'' and his 'ye' more consistently became ''ee'.

CHAPTER XIII

1. *western prospect*: 'past-marked prospect' (95)

2. *the flesh is weak*: see Christ's admonition to the disciples in Gethsemane: 'Watch and pray, that ye enter not into temptation: the spirit indeed is willing, but the flesh is weak' (Matthew 26:41).

3. *farmer Penny's sister*: 'farmer Shinar's sister' (95), later changed to 'aunt' (12). As well as changing place-names to give greater coherence to his imaginative Wessex, Hardy occasionally recast minor character references. For those who knew their Wessex novels, Mr Penny was an amiable Mellstock boot-maker and Mr. Shiner (formerly 'Shinar') a misanthropic Mellstock farmer (*Under the Greenwood Tree* [1872]). The change eliminates apparent intertextual contradiction. Regardless of whether Dame Ledlow was aunt or sister to Shinar, she was presumably wife to Farmer Ledlow, who lives in Mellstock in *Under the Greenwood Tree* and lies in Mellstock churchyard in the poem 'Friends Beyond' (*Wessex Poems* [1898]).

4. *small table ninepenny*: inferior weak beer (cf. 'small beer') sold at ninepence a gallon.

CHAPTER XIV

1. *Martinmas summer*: the feast of St. Martin falls on 11 November, around the time of the Henchard remarriage (see Appendix I, n. 1). A Martinmas summer lasts into November (cf. 'Indian' summer).

2. *Knowledge . . . had not*: the judgement of Elizabeth-Jane was formerly a little harsher: 'Knowledge, learning, accomplishments; those, alas, she had not' (MS/G/HW).

3. *to paraphrase . . . came there*: Hardy's source is Matthew Arnold's essay 'Wordsworth', as published in *Macmillan's Magazine*, 40 (July 1879); a slightly different version appeared as the Preface to Arnold's 1879 selected edition of Wordsworth's poetry, and was collected in *Essays in Criticism: Second Series* (1888). Hardy made eight entries of material from the essay in his 'Literary Notes I' (*Literary Notebooks*, 1, items 1102–1109), including a précis of Wordsworth's view of Goethe: 'Wordsworth said that Goethe's poetry was not inevitable enough. The remark is striking & true. No line in G., as G. said himself, but its maker knew well how it came there' (item 1108). MS/G/HW do not specify that the poet is 'recent'.

4. *unsophisticated*: 'uninstructed' in MS/G/HW, where the sentence ends at 'did it'.

5. *used to do*: this was originally followed by a paragraph in which Elizabeth-Jane displays at least one concession to fashion, the replacing of her old pattens with galoshes, 'an article of wear just then reaching the remoter towns' (MS/G/HW). In MS she splits the pattens up and burns them, while in G/HW she is tempted to do so but refrains.

6. *to which the future held the key*: absent from MS/G/HW/A86.

7. *she asked*: this obvious error was corrected in 95 with the substitution of 'she answered'. MS/G/HW/A86 read 'she said'.

8. *Dummerford*: 'Durnover' (95). Both stand for Fordington, the parish to the east of Dorchester containing Mill Street ('Mixen Lane') and St. George's Church, where the Revd. Henry Moule, father of Hardy's friend Horace Moule, was vicar from 1829 to 1880. The story 'A Changed Man' (1900; collected 1913) touches on Henry Moule's work in the parish during the cholera epidemics of 1849 and 1854. 'Durnover' derives from 'Durnovaria', the Roman name for Dorchester.

9. *When she was stepping out he added*: deleted in 87, perhaps because Hardy noticed Elizabeth-Jane stepping out again in the final paragraph. 87 makes other contractions in this exchange.

10. *"As I came down through Cannobie"*: Hardy could not remember his source for this song (see *Letters*, 5, 90). The suggestion (made in *Letters*, 5, 90 n.) that the line may be a variant in Burns's 'Bonnie Peg', which Farfrae is singing when he first meets Elizabeth-Jane (see Chapter VIII, n. 7), is plausible, although many Scottish songs of similar metre use the 'As I came' motif.

CHAPTER XV

1. *the prophet Baruch's . . . to go gay*: Baruch, not actually a prophet himself, was spokesperson for the prophet Jeremiah, whose words these are, as quoted in the Book of Baruch (6:9) in the Apocrypha: 'And taking gold, as it were for a virgin that loveth to go gay, they make crowns for the heads of their gods.'

2. *This particular virgin . . . constructed by art*: deleted in 87.

3. *In short, it was obvious . . . woman of correct education*: deleted in 87. In MS/G/ HW/A86 'correct' reads 'genteel'. Reduced emphasis on the response of Casterbridge youth to Elizabeth-Jane continues in the next paragraph, where 'young Casterbridge' became just 'Casterbridge' (87).

4. *Rochefoucauld*: the phrase is from Maxim 289 of *Réflexions ou Sentences et maximes morales* (1665) by François, Duc de la Rochefoucauld (1613–80): 'La simplicité affectée est une imposture délicate' ('Affected simplicity is a delicate imposture'). It does not appear in MS/G/HW.

5. *unfinished*: 'ignorant' (MS/G/HW/A86).

6. *Better sell . . . all the philosophies!*: in MS/G/HW, Elizabeth-Jane contemplates buying 'a copybook, and a dictionary, and a grammar of my native tongue!'; in A86 'grammar books and dictionaries and a history of my native country!'.

7. *Whittle*: '<Smallbone>Wringbone' (MS). Early deletions show '<Small-bone>' and '<Small>'.

8. *White Hart Vale*: 'Blackmoor Vale' (95). Blackmoor (or Blackmore) Vale, Hardy's 'Vale of the Little Dairies', lies south-east of Sherborne and south-west of Shaftesbury in north Dorset. It was formerly known as Forest of White Hart, hence the association of the two names in Hardy's mind. He describes the valley in detail in Chapter II of *Tess of the d'Urbervilles*, incorporating material from his review of William Barnes's *Poems of Rural Life in the Dorset Dialect* (*New Quarterly Magazine*, October 1879, pp. 469–73; see *Personal Writings*, pp. 94–6).

9. *Back Street*: South Back Street and West Back Street were former names of Dorchester's present Trinity Street and Princes Street respectively. But Whittle's Back Street is customarily identified with Charles Street, which runs behind South Street where Henchard's house is located.

10. *gibbered . . . smile*: 'replied . . . smile' (MS/G/HW/A86). MS shows '<of grief>' after 'smile', which in 95 became 'smile of terror'.

11. *laughing me to scorn*: 95 adds 'as a man 'ithout breeches!'.

12. *a chap o' wax*: a term of approval, possibly deriving from the notion that a figure modelled in wax would be faultless.

13. *by long chalks*: by a long way (deriving from the use of chalk for marking scores in games).

CHAPTER XVI

1. *just like him!*: 'just like a Scotchman!' (87). Neither phrase appears in MS/G/HW/A86. MS deletions specify a shilling as Farfrae's admission charge.

2. *a river*: 'the river Froom' (95). The earthwork is Poundbury, an Iron Age camp situated three-quarters of a mile north-west of Dorchester.

3. *Farfrae's erection*: 'in the West Walk' added in 95. The later reference to 'Chestnut Walk' was also changed to West Walk, and the avenue of chestnuts became sycamores, suggesting a change of location as well as name: Chestnut Walk was the former name of South Walks.

4. *the wind played . . . in Æolian improvisations*: not in MS/G/HW. A86 reads 'in Æolian modulations', but Hardy perhaps remembered an earlier use of this phrasing (see Chapter XI, n. 7).

5. *Correggio*: the familiar name of Antonio Allegri of Correggio (1489 [?] or 1494 [?]–1534), whose work is distinguished by particularly subtle chiaroscuro effects. In his early 'Schools of Painting' notebook (1863), Hardy notes against Correggio's name 'great knowlge. of lights & shades' (*Personal Notebooks*, p. 109).

6. *'Where would his business be . . . walked over it once'*: in all other editions these comments are given in direct speech, with corresponding adjustments in verb tenses. Hardy also tried other renderings of Farfrae's innovations ('smooth ciphering, and clockwork machines, and true circumference laws' [MS/G/HW]; 'smooth ciphering, and clock-work machines, and mensuration laws' [A86]). In 87, the phrasing became and stayed 'ciphering and mensuration'.

7. *"Miss McLeod of Ayr"*: Hardy remembered this, 'an old Scotch tune to which Burns may have danced' (*Life and Work*, p. 19), always moving him to tears as a child when he danced to his father's violin. The music is transcribed into Hardy's father's 'MS Music Book' (DCM).

8. *Port-Bredy*: 'Portwich' (MS/G/HW). Later MS deletions (Chapter XXVIII) show Hardy also considering '<Bridwich>' for Bridport.

CHAPTER XVII

1. *Old Walk*: 'West Walk' (95). Topography is ambiguous here since Bowling Alley Walk was itself once known as Old Walks. MS shows '<West>' before 'Old', '<South>' before 'Bowling'.

2. *honest*: deleted in 87.

3. *Like Jacob in Padan-Aram . . . multiply and prevail*: after serving his manipulative uncle, Laban, for seven years in order to marry his daughter Rachel, Jacob was tricked into marrying her older sister, Leah. He worked another seven years as payment for Rachel as well. Although then wanting to return to Canaan from Laban's home in Padan-Aram (Syria), he agreed to continue working for him in return for receiving all future spotted and speckled offspring born to Laban's flocks. Laban immediately rid himself of animals likely to produce such stock. But Jacob placed partly peeled chestnut, hazel and poplar rods by the animals' watering-troughs, which was also where they copulated. The rods' variegated colours caused conception of speckled lambs and kids, and Jacob became more prosperous than Laban (see Genesis 30:25–43).

Unlike Laban and Jacob's, Farfrae and Henchard's relationship is not governed only by mutual self-interest and duplicity. But the analogy with the Bible story goes beyond mere pastoral suggestiveness. Jacob builds up his riches in exile from his own land, and begins in quasi-filial subordination to an older man, in whose daughter he has a romantic interest. Laban's capacity to bring about the reverse of the outcome he intended and Jacob's greater canniness anticipate Farfrae's business ascendancy over his former employer.

4. *Novalis*: the pseudonym of Friedrich Leopold, Frieherr von Hardenberg (1772–1801), early German romantic poet and novelist, friend of Schiller and Schlegel. His chief prose work is an unfinished romance, *Heinrich von Ofterdingen*, which contains the observation 'Schicksal und Gemüt Namen Eines Begriffs sind' ('destiny and character name a single concept'). Hardy's probable source is Book 6, Chapter 6 of George Eliot's *The Mill on the Floss* (1860), in which Eliot uses Maggie Tulliver's history, as well as Hamlet's, to dispute what she sees as a facile claim: 'the tragedy of our lives is not created entirely from within. "Character," says Novalis, in one of his questionable aphorisms – "character is destiny." But not the whole of our destiny.'

In 1884–5, Hardy had been reading J. A. Froude's recently published *Thomas Carlyle: A History of his Life in England* (1884) and copied into his 'Literary Notes I' a check-list of names culled from a summary of Carlyle's lectures on modern German literature: Novalis is joined with his friend Tieck under the heading 'Romance'

(*Literary Notebooks*, 1, item 1338). None of the four brief references to Novalis in the notebooks comes from a source in primary works, which confirms the likelihood that Hardy, whose German was superficial, never read Novalis himself.

HW/A86 (no MS) lack this and the next three paragraphs.

5. *as Faust has been described*: the description comes from Carlyle's essay 'Goethe's Helena' (1828). Having typified Goethe's Faust as 'vehement' and 'gloomy', Carlyle concludes: 'Thus Faust is a man who has quitted the ways of vulgar men, without light to guide him on a better way.' There may have been associational reasons (other than Carlyle's description of Faust as being, like Henchard, 'the slave of impulses') for this essay's coming to Hardy's mind here: it begins with a judgement on Goethe by Novalis. For another Faustian echo, see Chapter XXXII, n. 4.

6. *the dirk against the cudgel*: 'the rapier against the bludgeon' (MS). MS also has 'Southern' for 'Southron', '<shrewdness>' and '<keenness>' before 'insight', and '<will>' before 'doggedness'.

7. *"Everdene," "Darton," and so on*: 'Shinar' (95)/ 'Shiner' (12) later added between 'Everdene' and 'Darton'. The names consolidate connections with Hardy's other fiction. James Everdene is the uncle from whom Bathsheba inherits Weatherbury Farm in *Far from the Madding Crowd* (1874) and Farmer Charles Darton is the central character of the short story 'Interlopers at the Knap' (1884; collected in *Wessex Tales* [1888]). For Shiner, see Chapter XIII, n. 3. Boldwood (see Chapter XXXI, n. 5) was also originally named here but deleted from the list in MS.

8. *Bellerophon*: with the aid of his winged horse, Pegasus, the Greek hero Bellerophon (Hipponous) triumphed in conflicts with the monstrous Chimaera and the savage tribes of the Solymia and the Amazons. But the gods ceased to favour him and killed his two children, Laodameia and Isandrus. Trying to reach Olympus on Pegasus, Bellerophon was thrown to earth by Zeus and crippled. He ended his days an outcast from both gods and men, wandering the earth and avoiding all human contact (see the *Lliad*, Book 6).

CHAPTER XVIII

1. *eighteen years*: 'fifteen or sixteen years' (12). Other rephrasing in this letter was necessitated by the removal of the marriage between Lucetta and Henchard (see Chapter XII, n. 8).

2. *my only relative*: in MS/G/HW, the relative is male, a merchant in MS, a rich banker in G/HW. Hardy made the change to avoid a later inconsistency. In Chapter XXII, Lucetta is revealed as having come into a legacy because of the death of her aunt, a banker's widow. Thus in the serial, both the banker Lucetta was visiting in Bristol and his wife have died with implausible rapidity.

3. *Stag*: 'Antelope' (95; '<Antelope> Stag' [MS]). The Antelope is, like the King's Arms, an actual hotel, located in Cornhill, just up from Henchard's house in South Street. In MS/G/HW Lucetta asks Henchard to 'direct some one to meet me' rather than indiscreetly suggesting that he meet her himself. Use of an intermediary complicates later plot developments (see also this chapter, n. 6 and Chapter XXXIV, n. 2).

4. *having them sent*: MS/G/HW continue 'since it would hinder dangerous inquiries in the house on what the bundle contained'.

5. *better you had not known me!*: 'better you had saved the devil's life than mine' (MS/G/HW). In MS this replaces '<six years of shilly shallying with me – engagement as she calls it!>'. Henchard's self-association with the devil, superseded though it was, is suggestive in the light of recurrent demonic imagery – particularly red and black colouring – attaching to him.

6. *As requested . . . not without a sense of relief*: these two paragraphs do not appear in MS/G/HW. In their place is an extended passage in which Lucetta passes through Casterbridge *en route* to Bristol. Strolling through the town while awaiting a coach connection, she engages Susan Henchard in conversation, as autumn leaves float down around them. Henchard sees them together and later questions Susan. She clearly knows nothing of Lucetta's connection with him, although he worries if 'Lucetta had aimed to see his wife, or whether the conjuncture were an accident'. When Lucetta is due back through Casterbridge, Henchard makes Elizabeth-Jane the letters-bearer, and she passes them on to Farfrae to deliver. But Lucetta is not on the expected coach, and Farfrae uses a coach guard as intermediary. A fortnight later he again sees the guard, who returns the parcel, having failed to find Lucetta. Farfrae guesses what the parcel contains and resolves to hand it back to Elizabeth-Jane, but Susan's illness and death intervene. Farfrae is thus left in possession of the letters (see also Chapter XXII, n.1, and Chapter XXXIV, n. 2).

7. *deprive life of fourpence*: 'rob life o' fourpence' (95). The pennies serve their funereal function remarkably rapidly. Susan's death has occurred 'that very hour'; yet already the pennies have been buried, dug up, spent, and turned into town-pump gossip. Use of coins to keep eyes closed until the onset of *rigor mortis* reflected a superstition that open eyes would be looking for the next corpse.

8. *I don't see harm in it*: MS/G/HW continue 'Baint we all lumps [MS "handfuls"] of one mixture, the dead and the living – say?' MS adds: 'Why, folks go to dust, & they grow & grow up in the shape of <ivy> <ivy leaves> ivy-thrum & such-like, & climb the church tower that they climbed in the flesh, & so there's no such terrible difference.'

CHAPTER XIX

1. *the avowal of Joseph*: sold into Egyptian slavery by his brothers, Joseph prospers and becomes second only to the pharaoh in power. When his brothers go to Egypt to buy corn, he recognizes them. He identifies himself and asks if his father, Jacob, is still alive: 'And his brethren could not answer him; for they were troubled at his presence' (Genesis 45:3). The analogy is limited to the response to discovery of unexpected, unwelcome but influential kinship. Elizabeth-Jane is troubled by the need to rethink her closest familial and emotional relationships, the brothers presumably by guilt for past actions and fear of possible consequences.

2. *better educated*: 'more patient' (95). In G/HW (no MS) the whole sentence reads only 'Mrs Henchard had been no practical scribe.'

3. *He remained unnerved . . . suddenly said*: absent from MS/G/HW.

4. *Like Prester John's . . . snatched up the food*: Prester (also known as 'presbyter' or priest) John was a fabled Christian ruler from the East, word of whom started emerging in Europe in the mid-twelfth century. Initially associated with India and Central Asia (Marco Polo makes him first ally and then enemy of Genghis Khan), he was by the fourteenth century usually identified with the King of Ethiopia. The specific legend mentioned here is found in Canto 33 of Ariosto's *Orlando Furioso* (1532). Having tried to add Paradise to his kingdom, Prester John is blinded by God and doomed to be plagued by monstrous harpies who steal his food and pollute his table. As with the earlier Bellerophon analogy (see Chapter XVII, n. 8), Henchard is associated with an exceptionally favoured and powerful figure brought low by aspirations that offend a divinity.

5. *Schwarzwasser*: black water (German). This general designation of the river as it flows through Casterbridge's bleakest area is to be distinguished from the actual name 'Blackwater' attached in 12 to the deep upstream stretch (see Chapter XXXII, n. 3, and Chapter XLI, n. 6).

6. *monopolized by a single gentleman*: 'monopolized over all England by a single gentleman' (95). The local hangman held a prominent position in nineteenth-century Dorchester's social and folk history. He was also responsible for public floggings, and Hardy's father witnessed one such event around 1830 (see *Life and Work*, p. 192). The hangman then, named Davis, figures (as Davies) in Hardy's story 'The Withered Arm' (*Wessex Tales* [1888]; in the same volume, see also 'The Three Strangers' [1883]). The cottage had a threatening fascination for local children, and the young Hardy himself allege4dly peered through its windows on an execution eve and saw the hangman eating his supper. Much enlarged and demystified, the cottage still exists.

7. *back lane into the town*: G/HW (MS incomplete) contain two extra paragraphs here. Initially Henchard resolves to say nothing of his discovery to Elizabeth-Jane: 'he would be to her a father, she should be to him a daughter, in sheer defiance of the untoward course of things. To make conditions, not accept them, was his customary conduct.' But his capacity to fulfil this intention is immediately questioned: 'a will that had worked powerfully in affairs of trade was not so operative in emotional relations. Henchard was a man of strong feeling, deprived of objects for its indulgence, though always seeking them; and it hit him hard that this child of his, as he had deemed her, upon whose ultimate attachment to himself as her father he had, as a final throw, staked all the sunshine of his future, should be revealed as spurious. After the heat of the wound had passed off came its inevitable ache and anguish.'

CHAPTER XX

1. *girl*: 'sensible unselfish girl' (G/HW: no MS).

2. *marks of the beast*: see Revelation 13:17: 'And that no man might buy or sell, save he that had the mark, or the name of the beast, or the number of his name.' In Revelation, those marked with the sign of the beast are its idolaters, and contrasted with those marked with 'the seal of God' (Revelation 7:2–3 and 9:4). This suggests a distinction between worship of temporal and divine authority. The purely secular application of the phrase is aided by its mercantile imagery, which invites facile identification between worship of false gods and trade. As Hardy later suggests, Henchard's irritation with Elizabeth-Jane's lapses into dialect only underlines his own tenuous hold on 'true' gentility, and its ironic dependence on buying and selling. For Hardy's view of Dorset dialect as 'a tongue, and not a corruption', see his Preface to *Select Poems of William Barnes* (1908; reprinted in *Personal Writings*, pp. 76–82).

3. *Minerva*: Roman goddess of wisdom, practical skills and war, identifiable with the Greek Athene. She was especially the protectress of commerce, which gives added point to her invocation here.

4. *Princess Ida*: in Tennyson's *The Princess* (1847) these lines (I, 233–4) do not describe the hand of Princess Ida herself, nor even that of a woman, but rather the style assumed by a man betrothed to the Princess in childhood and who, disguised as a woman, is attempting to infiltrate the women's university she has founded. The analogy underscores (perhaps unintentionally, given Hardy's misapplication of the quotation) not only the self-misrepresentation of which

Elizabeth-Jane would be guilty were she to write as Henchard wants, but also the misguidedness of the assumption that such a hand would define the genuinely feminine.

5. *Whenever she took . . . faults of breeding*: deleted in 87. Also in 87, 'and willing' was removed from the previous sentence, presumably because 'willing' occurs in the next. Hardy was very responsive to such repetitions when revising (see next note).

6. *so rough*: 'rough' (1912). This minor change was probably made because Hardy finally noticed that 'so rough' obtrusively echoed 'so visibly' (with the sound pattern maintained by the intervening first syllable of 'sorry') earlier in the sentence. MS deletion after 'rough' reads '<: at which she instantly forgave him. "Here's something to buy yourself a bonnet," he added, putting a couple of sovereigns into her hand.>'

7. *Nance Mockridge*: MS deletion shows '<Kezia Littlechild>' as her original name.

8. *men who held . . . and the Constantines*: the reference is to the custom of placing coins in the mouths of corpses at burial to pay the ferryman Charon for transportation across the River Styx. For Hadrian, see Chapter XI, n. 6. Marcus Cassianus Latinius Postumus was a usurper who, during the anarchy of the reign of the Emperor Gallienus (A.D. 253–68), took control of Gaul, received the allegiance of the governors of Spain and Britain, and established a provincial empire embracing most of western Europe. The first two Constantines, father and son, ruled as Emperor from A.D. 306–37 and 337–40 respectively. But Hardy probably also has in mind Flavius Claudius Constantinus, often misleadingly referred to as Constantine III. A common soldier who claimed descent from Constantine I, he ruled as usurper in Britain, Gaul, and Spain (A.D. 407–410) during the reign of the Emperor Honorius, on whose orders he was eventually killed.

9. *looked over the edge . . . the churchyard*: this replaces in MS a deletion in which Elizabeth-Jane '<thought of the shadowy beings she mentally designated as "Romans," who had laid out these square angles, & <roads> banks, & that earthen theatre hard by, & that <immense> stupendous fort which rose against the sky behind>.'

10. *stranger. And this was . . . simply pretty*: 'stranger, leaving her a plain human shell' (MS/G/HW).

11. *Henchard's Austerlitz*: Austerlitz, a town in central Czechoslovakia (Moravia), was the site of Napoleon's greatest victory, on 2 December 1805, over Austrian and Russian armies. But six weeks earlier, on 21 October, he had suffered the naval defeat at Trafalgar which would give the British control of the seas for the rest of the Napoleonic Wars, and guarantee – along with the later disastrous 1812 land campaign in Russia – his eventual downfall.

12. *Oh, I wish I was dead with dear mother*: in G/HW (no MS) this sentence is preceded by 'Why should I be called low, when my lowness is of other people's making?'

13. *dear madam*: deleted in 87. This is the first of a number of reductions in Elizabeth-Jane's courtesy addresses to Lucetta, suggesting somewhat greater equality in status between the two.

14. *High Street Hall . . . overlooking the Market*: 'High Place Hall . . . overlooking the Market' (95); 'High-Place Hall . . . looking down the lane to the Market' (12). In MS 'High-Street Hall' replaces '<Little-Park House>', although a deletion elsewhere (f. 214) suggests that Hardy may also have contemplated '<Little Paddock House>'. Though probably modelled on Colliton House (now part of the County Council offices) in Glyde Path Road, Lucetta's house is made to stand at the south-east corner of the High Street–Cornhill cross, adjacent to the town pump.

CHAPTER XXI

1. *studious*: 'simple' (G/HW/A86: no MS).

2. *like all architecture*: 'like most architecture' (95). The later qualification shows the caution of Hardy the erstwhile architect, as does the measured tone of the overall judgement. Deriving from the work of the Italian architect Andrea Palladio (1518–80) and the immense influence of his *I quattro libri dell' architettura* (1570), Palladianism became a force in English architecture after the example set by Inigo Jones, particularly in the Banqueting House at Whitehall Palace (1619–22). Its period of greatest dominance was the first half of the eighteenth century. It reflects the symmetry, simplicity, rationalism, and orthodoxy of classical forms. While 'its reasonableness made it impressive', for Hardy this clearly carried the attendant risk of derivativeness, resulting in 'a compilation rather than a design'. Hardy's implied preference for the greater energy of Gothic architecture has suggestive implications for both Henchard's problematic relationship with High Street Hall and Hardy's figuring of his two male protagonists. Lucetta's entry into this house marks the beginning of her separation from the passionate, unpredictable Henchard, and increasing involvement with the restrained, but finally less sympathetically rendered, Farfrae.

3. *up the alley*: 'down the alley' (12). The change removes the directional confusion caused in the next paragraph when Henchard is also described as coming 'up'. At the same time, Hardy removed references, in both this and the next chapter, to the alley's being 'blind', thereby suggesting possible accessibility from both directions.

4. *through the door. There is no other*: 'round by the gate. There is no other that I have noticed' (12). In MS 'door' replaced '<gates>'.

CHAPTER XXII

1. *imbecile*: MS/G/HW add 'I spoke to her once in passing through the town' (see Chapter XVIII, n. 6).

2. *I ought to endeavour . . . promise to me*: 'we ought to repair our former mistake as soon as we decently could' (MS/G/HW). The letter's concluding postscript is not in MS/G/HW.

3. *Lucetta is governess or housekeeper there*: 'Lucetta is related to her' (87).

4. *to settle among the* gentilhommerie *of Casterbridge*: 'to settle in Casterbridge' (87), later modified to 'reside' (95). Since earlier versions read only 'to be tenant of High Street Hall' (G/HW/A86: no MS), this is the only edition to contain the arch gallicism.

5. *given her time and attention*: 'given her time and heart' (95). MS/G/HW read 'given herself to him so unluckily at first', in reference to the original marriage (see Chapter XII, n. 8).

6. *he thought*: 95 adds " 'And considering what we –' ".

7. *somewhat older*: 'some years older' (95). G/HW/A86 (no MS) read 'not much older'. G/HW also read 'handsome' for 'pretty', and lack the reference to 'unmistakably French extraction'.

8. *well-known conception of Titian's*: Titian is the more familiar name of Tiziano Vecelli (*c*. 1487/90–1576), the greatest of Venetian painters, a number of whose paintings show this distinctive pose. Hardy's early 'Schools of Painting' notebook contains a thumbnail summary of Titian's style, mentioning other qualities suited to Lucetta's languid erotic appeal: 'deep & lustrous colouring in his wks. more than design – lucid clearness' (*Personal Notebooks*, p. 108). For suggestions of specific paintings Hardy could have had in mind, see Bullen, pp. 156–7.

9. *As a girl . . . wretched bit of Latin yet*: this differs substantially from MS/G/HW, where Lucetta owes her fashionableness to a post-legacy trip to a Paris '*magasin*': 'They half stripped me, and put on me what they chose. Four women hovered round me, fixed me on a pedestal like an image, and arranged me and pinned me and stitched me and padded me. When it was over I told them to send several more dresses of that same size, and so it was done.' Lucetta's caustic view of her own passivity in this transformation reflects Hardy's recurrent figuring of the fall into fashion as a quasi-sexual falling.

10. *Le Sueurs*: Lucetta's obvious pride in well-born Jersey ancestry, despite her immediate claim not to 'value such past matters', echoes Hardy's own. In *Life and Work* he claims descent for all south-western Hardys from the Jersey 'le Hardys', admitting an impulse towards self-elevation on the strength of the doubtful connection: he 'often thought he would like to restore the "le" to his name, and call himself "Thomas le Hardy"; but he never did so' (*Life and Work*, p. 9).

11. *been Henchard's attached comrade at a critical time . . . Thy speech bewrayeth thee!*: none of this appears in MS/G/HW, which read only 'saved Henchard's life'. When the extra material was added in A86, the partially retained sentence was completed as 'helped Henchard at a critical time', which gave way to the quoted phrasing before a final change of 'attached' into 'dear' (87). Peter's third denial of Christ is provoked by the accusation that his speech (i.e. accent) reveals him to be one of the disciples (see Matthew 26:73). In A86, the more familiar 'betrayeth' occurs, although 'bewrayeth' is the correct quotation.

12. *why their marriage should take place*: 'why their marriage should no longer continue void' (MS/G/HW; see Chapter XII, n. 8). In 87 the later 'comparative fortune' became just 'fortune'.

13. *Candlemas fair*: the main hiring-fair of the agricultural year. Although Candlemas was moved to 2 February after England accepted the Gregorian calendar (1752), the fair continued to be held on Old Candlemas Day, 14 February, which is still a chartered fair day in Dorchester. That it is also Valentine's Day has obvious ironic significance. Candlemas celebrates the Purification of the Virgin Mary and the Presentation of Christ in the Temple.

14. *in Jersey*: 'after their few days of union' (MS/G/HW; see Chapter XII, n. 8).

15. *The man before her was not Henchard*: in MS/G/HW/A86 this resounding concluding line was the opening sentence of the next chapter.

CHAPTER XXIII

1. *silver-topped switch*: 'switch' (MS/G/HW/A86). Farfrae's clothing has also been somewhat gentrified from earlier versions.

2. *wing-bonnets*: 'long bonnets' (95). Hardy perhaps noticed the awkward proliferation of alliterating 'w's and decided to dispense with one.

3. *Lady-day*: Lady Day (6 April O.S., 25 March N.S.) is the feast of the Annunciation of the Virgin Mary. Old Lady Day was the date on which all yearly agricultural labouring appointments began. For Hardy's fullest discussion of nineteenth-century rural labour, see his essay 'The Dorsetshire Labourer' (1883; *Personal Writings*, pp. 168–91), whose account of hiring-fairs contains some of this description of the old shepherd. The distance prospectively separating the son from his sweetheart was later changed to thirty-five miles (12).

4. *Thank you for staying*: in MS/G/HW this exchange is longer and more cryptically flirtatious. Lucetta continues: ' "What will you do when you get out?" "Something worse than I do here, no doubt," he replied recklessly. "For goodness sake don't say that – it is as if I were ruining you by inches." "I will not say it, but I may feel it. But no – maybe I'll get into my market-mind when I've been out a few minutes." As he went . . .'

5. *Lucetta as a young girl . . . so long as it was warm*: this paragraph does not appear in MS/G/HW. In A86, 'her ups-and-downs' reads 'her bereavements and impoverishments'.

6. *in the past*: G/HW (no MS) continue 'by his unpardonable ignorance of his wife's existence.'

VOLUME II

CHAPTER XXIV

1. *It was the node of all orbits*: G/HW (no MS) continue '; and there the movers paused, throwing themselves, as they conversed, into the form of capital K's, X's, and Y's to ease the stiffness of their joints, in the old, old Casterbridge fashion'.

2. *'Lass of Gowrie'*: a popular Scottish song set to the tune 'Loch Erroch Side', with words by Carolina Oliphant, Lady Nairne (1766–1845).

3. *No more sowers . . . and all that*: for Christ's parable of the sower, see Mark 4:3–20 and Matthew 13:3–9.

4. *'He that observeth the wind shall not sow,' so the Preacher said*: the Preacher is Koheleth, or Solomon: see Ecclesiastes 11:4. Elizabeth-Jane is misinterpreting the text, which is an injunction to action, regardless of meteorological circumstance. The Preacher's words will thus be all the more 'to the point', since sowing will now take place regardless of the wind, as the Preacher would seem to suggest it should.

5. *in her first excitement*: G/HW (no MS) continue 'after the discovery that their hasty marriage was void, and his method of rewarding her for saving his life by wedding her had proved itself to be a generosity altogether delusive. The only evidence of that marriage in existence were two – the register, and the letters alluding to the event. He had not returned her the letters, so that possibly they were destroyed; in which case there remained but one. She could have wished that there were none at all.' A86 is the same as E86 apart from the omission of 'in her first excitement'.

6. *gratitude*: 'reparation' (95). At the same time, 'They were intimate – rather' was added as the opening sentence of this paragraph.

7. "*Yes – fairly . . . I know*" not in MS/G/HW.

CHAPTER XXV

1. *curtly*: 'civilly' (MS), which may suggest 'curtly' is a compositorial misreading. 87 deleted 'homely' in the same sentence.

2. *H'm*: 12 adds ' "It looks as if you were living on capital." "O no, I am not." "So much the better. But the fact is . . ." '

3. "*Not at all!*" . . . "*I am English*": in MS/G/HW (MS partially missing) this whole exchange centres on mutual recriminations about the former marriage, Henchard maintaining that he and Lucetta are 'man and wife', Lucetta arguing that Susan's return made the marriage 'void'. The deleted section concludes with Henchard's observation 'It is very odd . . . that I, so little of a woman's man as I be, should find it necessary to marry two women twice over.'

4. *Yet having decided to . . . what fate offered*: not in G/HW (no MS).

5. *meaner beauties of the night*: from 'On His Mistress, the Queen of Bohemia' by Sir Henry Wotton (1568–1639). Its opening stanza reads: 'You meaner beauties of the night,/ That poorly satisfy our eyes/ More by your number than your light,/ You common people of the skies;/What are you when the moon shall rise?'

CHAPTER XXVI

1. *devotion to*: 'intimacy with' (95). In MS/G/HW, Henchard reminds Farfrae of 'my sending 'ee on the errand to that woman whose life was much mixed up with mine' (see Chapter XII, n. 12).

2. *nothing more now*: in MS/G/HW Farfrae precedes this with 'I think it shows no great sense of propriety in her – indeed, it shows very little'.

3. *like some Tuscan painting of the two disciples supping at Emmaus*: see Luke 24:13–35. Two of Christ's followers, one named Cleopas, are joined by a stranger while journeying to the village of Emmaus. On arrival, he dines with them and reveals himself as the risen Christ. In Hardy's invocation of the scene, Lucetta, 'the third and chief figure', is made ironically analogous to Christ, an identification underlined in 12 with the substitution of 'haloed' for 'chief'. At the same time, Elizabeth-Jane's role was made more marginal to the action itself (see next note). Given Hardy's frequent visits to the National Gallery during his early years in London (see *Life and Work*, p. 53), he may well have had in mind the version there of *The Supper at Emmaus*, one of two (the other is in the Brera Gallery, Milan) by Michelangelo Merisi da Caravaggio (1571–1610). Although this is not a 'Tuscan painting', it is the most famous rendering of the scene and a shadow cast by a serving man creates a dark haloed effect around the head of Christ. Hardy listed Caravaggio, under the name 'Morigi da Caravaggio' of the 'Roman School', in his 'Schools of Painting' notebook (*Personal Notebooks*, p. 107).

4. *could observe from afar all things*: 'could observe all from afar, like the evangelist who had to write it down' (12).

5. *Mixen Lane*: Dorchester's Mill Street, whose location is much as Hardy later describes it, although the cottages no longer exist.

6. *like Saul at his reception by Samuel*: unable to find his father's lost asses, Saul goes to consult Samuel, whom God has already prepared for Saul's arrival. When Samuel tells Saul that the asses are already found, intimates God's further purpose for him, and invites him to dine on food already prepared in anticipation of his arrival, Saul is deeply puzzled (see 1 Samuel 9). The biblical analogy does not appear in MS/G/HW.

7. *Cure the evil*: scrofula, or tuberculosis of the lymphatic glands, was formerly known as 'the king's evil' because it was supposedly curable by the touch of a king. Fall's toad cures for the same complaint were well known to Hardy, as an 1876 diary entry shows: ' "Toad Fair." An old man, a wizard, used to bring toads' legs in little bags to Bagber Bridge . . . where he was met by crowds of people who came in vehicles and on foot, and bought them as charms to cure scrofula by wearing them round the neck. These legs were supposed to twitch occasionally in the bag, and probably did, when it gave the wearer's blood a "turn", and changed the course of the disease' (*Life and Work*, p. 115; see also Firor, pp. 117–18).

8. *more like living in Revelations*: a general evocation of upheaval. Perhaps Fall has in mind the effects of the pouring out of the seventh angel's vial: 'And there were voices, and thunders, and lightnings; and there was a great earthquake, such as was not since men were upon the earth, so mighty an earthquake, and so great' (Revelation 16:18).

CHAPTER XXVII

1. *roasting a waxen image of me*: in *The Return of the Native* (1878) Susan Nunsuch makes and destroys such an image of Eustacia Vye, who subsequently drowns. Many Hardy plots fulfil superstitions while implying their absurdity and providing alternative rational explanations.

2. *the Capitol*: the hill in Rome on which stood the temple to Jupiter. Vanquished captives were paraded through the streets to the Capitol as a prelude to ceremonies celebrating victories.

3. *Bull Stake*: Bull Stake Square was the former name of Dorchester's present North Square. The practice of bull-baiting was made illegal in 1835.

4. *laden*: 'one laden' (95). The later 'as they were' was at the same time changed to 'as one was', to make it consistent with the reference to Farfrae's empty wagon.

5. *to the door and opened it*: 'to the street corner' (12).

6. *the giddying worm into the sheep's brain*: a type of burrowing worm causes sheep to become giddy, and ultimately die.

7. *staggering*: 'committing a nuisance' (95). 'Committing a nuisance' is euphemistic legalese for public urination. While the woman's conduct is indeed 'flagrant', the word is probably Stubberd's malapropism for 'vagrant'.

8. *All Saints' Lane southward*: 'a back lane westward' (95).

9. *proposed to marry me*: in MS/G/HW this and later references are to the preceding Jersey marriage (see Chapter XII, n. 8) and Lucetta's feeling that 'I ought to re-marry you'.

10. *in a fainting state*: a deleted MS chapter break indicates that Hardy contemplated ending the chapter here.

CHAPTER XXVIII

1. *Shallow and Silence*: two corrupt and bumbling country justices in Shakespeare's *Henry IV, Part 2*. Falstaff had known Shallow in their disreputable youth and addresses his elegiac comment 'We have heard the chimes at midnight' to him (III.ii).

2. *the country of the Psalmist where the clouds drop fatness*: see Psalm 65:11: 'Thou crownest the year with thy goodness; and thy paths drop fatness.' Referring to God's munificence, 'fatness' means natural richness here, though Hardy plays on its more mundane meaning of 'greasiness'.

3. *steeped*: while the connotation here is ambiguous, the context suggests an hauteur or loftiness indicative of urban rather than rural origins.

4. *of all the wrong places in the world for shouts and rolling*: 'of all the horrible places in the world!' (95). Other 95 changes suggest public indecency rather than mere drunken disorderliness.

5. *she insulted me*: 'she committed the nuisance, and insulted me' (12).

6. *a dee sight finer-looking than thee*: 'a dee sight finer-looking than a dee fool like thee, you son of a bee' (95). Henchard's later command to Stubberd to say the offensive word outright was also changed to 'we don't want to hear any more of them cust D's and B's!' ('dees and bees!' [12]).

7. *Twenty years ago*: 'or thereabout' added in 12.

8. *being a land smuggler*: the 'respectable station in life' attested to by being a receiver of smuggled goods may not be intended merely ironically, but indicate smuggling's exemption from community condemnation. In the early years of the century, Hardy's own grandfather stowed contraband rum in the Bockhampton cottage in which Hardy was later born (see 'Memoranda, I', *Personal Notebooks*, pp. 8–9). Hardy used local smuggling as a central plot element in his short story 'The Distracted Preacher' (1879; collected in *Wessex Tales* [1888]). In 95, 'in life' was changed to 'in the world', presumably because Hardy noticed his use of 'life' a few words earlier.

9. *to other places . . . nearly dusk*: MS deletes '<by chance or design a figure met her there>'.

CHAPTER XXIX

1. *Abrahamic success*: the success refers to Abraham's own generative patriarchal prowess as 'a father of many nations' (Genesis 17:4) whose seed is 'as the dust of the earth: so that if a man can number the dust of the earth, then shall thy seed also be numbered' (Genesis 13:16). As indicated above (see Chapter XVII, n. 3), animal husbandry was more associated with Jacob, Abraham's grandson. The reference to Abraham does not appear in MS/G/HW, where there are many minor differences in the description of the encounter with the bull.

2. *the Thames Tunnel*: one of the engineering marvels of the nineteenth century, the 1,300-foot double tunnel underneath the Thames, connecting Wapping on the north bank with Rotherhithe on the south, was engineered by Sir Marc Isambard Brunel and his son Isambard Kingdom Brunel. Nearly twenty years in the making, it opened on 25 March 1843.

3. *Gurth's collar of brass*: Gurth is a Saxon swineherd, serf to Cedric a Saxon noble, in Sir Walter Scott's *Ivanhoe* (1819). While Hardy's interest in Scott would guarantee his familiarity with *Ivanhoe* itself, Gurth was also invoked in Thomas Carlyle's *Past and Present* (1843: see particularly 'Democracy' [Book 3, Chapter 13]), entries from which occur in Hardy's '1867' notebook (*Literary Notebooks*, 2, items A165–7).

4. *What might have happened . . . a man appeared*: in MS/G/HW, this scene is considerably longer, with Elizabeth-Jane attempting to give Lucetta time to climb the clover-stack by taking hold of the leading-stick. When her strength gives out and she makes her own successful dash for the clover, she discovers that Lucetta, in her panic, has run to the other end of the barn. The bull is about to charge Lucetta when the man enters. The effect of this additional material is to make Elizabeth-Jane appear much stronger and more resourceful than Lucetta.

5. *to the floor*: MS/G/HW continue: ' "I thought you were up there!" she said. "But thank God, 'tis all right now. He always protects us when we don't expect Him [MS 'him'] to." '

6. *coals of fire on my head*: see Proverbs 25:22, where generosity to an enemy is recommended by Solomon, for thereby 'thou shalt heap coals of fire upon his head, and the Lord shall reward thee'. Lucetta's subsequent 'I am rich' became in 95 'I am a monied person now.'

7. *Grower*: '<Chalkridge> Grower' (MS).

8. *St. Jude's*: 'St <Peter's> Jude's' (MS); 'St. Peter's' (95). Despite Hardy's final choice of an actual Dorchester church name, St Jude's association with lost causes has more ironic point.

CHAPTER XXX

1. *John Gilpin*: a Cheapside linen-draper in William Cowper's poem 'The Diverting History of John Gilpin' (1782). About to leave for an inn to celebrate his twentieth wedding anniversary and first holiday, he delays when three customers arrive: 'for loss of time, / Although it griev'd him sore, / Yet loss of pence, full well he knew, / Would trouble him much more.' Gilpin's thrift is shared by his wife, who advocates taking their own wine to the inn. Like Lucetta, she goes ahead, accompanied by her sister and four children, in a light carriage designed for two. These economies destroy the celebration. Association with the meagre and comically ineffectual Gilpin implicitly judges Farfrae and his own privileging of business interest over romantic impulse.

2. *so that the good she would have done . . . like the Apostle Paul*: see Romans 7:19: 'For the good that I would I do not; but the evil which I would not, that I do.' In 12, the biblical analogy is replaced by a quotation from Ovid (*Metamorphoses*, VII, 20–21): 'Video meliora proboque, deteriora sequor' ('I see and approve better things, I follow the worse'). The change introduces a specifically romantic parallel (the context is Medea's unsuccessful resistance to her love for Jason) and also underlines Elizabeth-Jane's attempts at intellectual self-improvement: she has 'just been construing' the Ovid.

3. *were thrown together . . . had misrepresented us*: in MS/G/HW, Lucetta tells Elizabeth-Jane of her unintentionally illegal marriage to Henchard (see Chapter XII, n. 8).

4. *lack of respectability*: 'impropriety' (95). At the same time, 'correctness of environment' became 'correctness of procedure'.

5. *in Nathan tones*: see 2 Samuel 12:1–14. Having deliberately arranged the death of Uriah the Hittite in battle, David marries his widow Bathsheba, whom he has already made pregnant. Nathan the prophet constructs a parable to ask David how such a man should be treated, and when David condemns the conduct, Nathan responds 'Thou art the man.' Part of God's curse on David is the death of his and Bathsheba's child.

CHAPTER XXXI

1. *implicitly*: 'generously' (95).

2. *pinched, blasted, and smutted grains*: such grains are, respectively, shrivelled, blighted and infected with a black fungus.

3. *now you have all*: 'now you have all I've got in the world' (95). The details of Henchard's surrender of his watch, and the favourable impression created by his honesty, are taken from a bankruptcy report in the *Dorset County Chronicle* (27 April 1826). Hardy copied this account into his 'Facts' notebook, and the entry is printed in Millgate, pp. 238–9.

4. *Farmer James Everdene*: see Chapter XVII, n. 7; 'of Weatherbury' added in 12.

5. *Boldwood*: Farmer Boldwood remained reserved in maturity, when he was the introspective suitor of James Everdene's niece Bathsheba (see *Far from the Madding Crowd* [1874]).

CHAPTER XXXII

1. *Two bridges*: the first is Swan Bridge, the second Grey's Bridge. Both survive only in modern replacements, although Grey's Bridge still displays the date 1748 and a replica plaque threatening transportation as the penalty for damage.

2. *Abel Whittle*: 'John Wringbone' (MS).

3. *in the pool beneath out of reach of their troubles*: 'out of reach of their troubles, either here or in the deep pool called Blackwater, a little higher up the river' (12). See Chapter XIX, n. 5.

4. *Surely he'll buy my body and soul likewise*: the Faustian echoes are suggestive in the light of the earlier specific comparison of Henchard with Faust (see Chapter XVII, n. 5).

5. *on the bridge*: 'in the Chalk Walk' (95). Further minor modifications were made to Farfrae's phrasing throughout this exchange.

6. *the Prophet's chamber*: see 2 Kings 4:10. The prophet is Elisha, for whose use a woman of Shunem had a little chamber built, containing just a bed, table, stool, and candlestick. When she refuses payment, he rewards her with a son, whom he later restores to life when the boy dies.

7. *she was wise in her generation*: a reference to the parable of the unjust steward. A steward, threatened with dismissal and looking out for his future prospects, ingratiates himself with his master's debtors by discounting their debts and so cheating his master. Surprisingly, the master, or perhaps Christ (there is some linguistic ambiguity), praises the prudence that plans for the future, for in so planning, even 'the children of this world [i.e. the sinful and worldly] are in their generation wiser than the children of light [i.e. believers who follow Christ]' (see Luke 16:8). The parable, paradoxical as it is, has resonances relevant to all the main characters. Farfrae accepts lesser returns on investment and prospers as a result; Lucetta attempts to ensure her own future with Farfrae by calculating that Michael will keep quiet about the past when it is too late to separate them; Henchard's lack of forethought guarantees future disaster; and Elizabeth-Jane's literal-minded and rather self-serving rectitude generates qualified future contentment.

8. *intended wife*: 'what-you-may-call wife' (95). MS/G/HW have no adjective before 'wife'.

CHAPTER XXXIII

1. *choir*: church musicians rather than singers, as in *Under the Greenwood Tree* (1872). Hardy's grandfather, father, and uncle played for many years in the choir of St. Michael's, Stinsford.

2. *Stonehenge*: the most important and famous Bronze Age temple in Europe, situated on Salisbury Plain in Wiltshire. Built in a number of phases from *c.* 2200 to *c.* 1200 B.C., it comprises a ring of standing stones enclosing a U-shaped inner formation: hence its similarity to the circle of earthenware cups. It is the site of Tess's arrest in *Tess of the d'Urbervilles* (1891).

3. *Rogue's March*: the tune played when a soldier was dishonourably discharged and drummed out of his barracks (see *Life and Work*, p. 127).

4. *fourth Psa'am*: Psalm 4 proclaims 'the Lord will hear when I call unto him' and concludes with the comforting verse: 'I will both lay me down in peace, and sleep; for thou, Lord, only makest me dwell in safety.' Samuel Wakely is unidentified, and possibly fictitious.

5. *old Wiltshire*: one of Hardy's own favourite hymn tunes, Wiltshire was composed by Sir George Smart (1776–1867), and most frequently fitted to Psalm

34, a song of praise for God in the faith that 'none of them that trust in him shall be desolate'. But Henchard has the tune set to Psalm 109 (as rendered in Nahum Tate and Nicholas Brady's metrical *New Version of the Psalms* [1696]), in which God's 'Servant David', supposed author of the Psalms, curses his enemies.

6. *Rosalind's exclamation . . . a good man's love*': see Shakespeare, *As You Like It*, III.v. The lines form part of Rosalind's admonition to the shepherdess Phoebe, who has scorned declarations of love from the shepherd Silvius. Hardy's interest in Rosalind and memories of seeing *As You Like It* are reflected in two poems collected in *Time's Laughingstocks* (1909): 'To an Impersonator of Rosalind' (1867) and 'The Two Rosalinds' (1909).

7. *Abel Whittle's*: 'John Wringbone's' (MS).

CHAPTER XXXIV

1. *that funny song . . . one-and-forty wooers*: while the ballad 'Sir Patrick Spens' and Burns's 'Bonny Peg' (see Chapter VIII, n. 7) have both been suggested for this song, neither claim is supported by subject-matter and usual lyrics. The song remains unidentified.

2. *Why, bless the woman. . . . Had that safe been opened*: in MS(incomplete)/G/HW Henchard tells Lucetta that he had sent her the letters via Elizabeth-Jane, had assumed she had received them, and has no idea where they now are. Lucetta inquires of Elizabeth-Jane, and discovers that Farfrae has the packet (see Chapter XVIII, nn. 3 and 6).

3. *worm i' the bud*: the phrase is Viola's in Shakespeare's *Twelfth Night*. Disguised as the youth Cesario, she tells Duke Orsino of a sister (in fact herself) who pines in undeclared love: 'She never told her love, / But let concealment, like a worm i' the bud, / Feed on her damask cheek' (II.iv.).

4. *loud as Tamerlane's trumpet*: Tamerlane (or Tamburlaine, or Timur-the-Lame; 1336[?]–1405) was a Mongolian leader who conquered the area from Mongolia to the Mediterranean. His armies were distinguished for the large trumpets they carried. Hardy may have had in mind Nicholas Rowe's tragedy (1701) or Handel's opera (1724), both named *Tamerlane*, or possibly Christopher Marlowe's tragedy *Tamburlaine the Great* (c. 1587), in all of which the trumpets feature. In MS/ G/HW, two further sentences at the end of this paragraph reveal Henchard's discovery from Elizabeth-Jane that the packet had been passed on to Farfrae for delivery.

5. *that I may possibly have left . . . to sleep easy o' nights?*: in MS/G/HW, Henchard asks Farfrae what became of the packet, and is told Farfrae still has it at home.

6. *the letter went on*: 'Henchard read' (95). Hardy may have noticed the repetition of 'went on' at the beginning of the next paragraph. In G/HW (no MS) Lucetta's letter mentions her marriage to Henchard, the extract concluding: 'Thus I sit here a widow without the melancholy satisfaction of a husband's tomb' (see Chapter XII, n. 8).

CHAPTER XXXV

1. *"some day."*: MS adds 'Balaam's curse had <been unutterable> failed.' Called upon to curse the Israelites, Balaam blesses them instead (see Numbers 22–24).

2. *appearances and not her story*: 'that the episode was rather her fault than her misfortune' (95). In MS/G/HW, this sentence ends at 'was yet too bold' (MS shows the deletion '<for her, a woman in the wrong'), and in the next sentence Lucetta employs 'artifice' rather than 'persuasion'.

3. *She had not slept all the previous night*: in 12 Hardy added to the beginning of this sentence 'Beyond a natural reason for her slightly drawn look', intimating Lucetta's pregnancy (see Chapter XL, n. 4). In MS/G/HW, Lucetta's disfiguring toilette is much more deliberately deceitful, and aided by supplies from the local chemist. Her fear of ceasing to attract Farfrae is also emphasized: 'If her dear husband should meet her he would surely believe that this was her true aspect, and that her hitherto charming lineaments had been the counterfeit of art.'

4. *Lucetta waited breathlessly . . . her point was half gained*: the association of Lucetta with Susan, both here and in the later reference to her as 'the double of the first', does not appear in MS/G/HW: Henchard acts simply from sympathy for her physical decline and loss of sexual allure.

5. *lost all zest and desire to humiliate Lucetta*: in MS/G/HW this reads 'lost all zest and desire for Lucetta', a consequence of his now seeing her as only a 'poor, withered, worn-out woman'.

6. *I can keep my word*: in MS/G/HW this chapter continues with a substantial section in which Farfrae, looking for Henchard to tell him that he is proceeding with the original plan to buy him the seed business, comes upon Lucetta and Henchard in the Amphitheatre. Not recognizing Lucetta, whose arm Henchard draws through his own to help conceal her identity, Farfrae makes his offer, which Henchard is touched by but too proud to accept immediately. Farfrae departs, Lucetta and Henchard separate, and when Lucetta joins Farfrae at home, he tells her that he has just seen Henchard courting. See Plate XVI

CHAPTER XXXVI

1. *Saint Peter's Finger*: this had been 'Peter's Finger' in MS/G/HW, and became so again, permanently, in 95. The name is that of an inn at Lytchett Minster (near Poole in south-east Dorset), and derives from the church name St Peter ad Vincula – St Peter in Chains. The actual name of the long-since demolished Mill Street tavern was The King's Head.

2. *Adullam*: when David flees the wrath of Saul, he takes refuge in Adullam, the name for both a town and a nearby cave in Canaan: 'And every one that was in distress, and every one that was in debt, and every one that was discontented, gathered themselves unto him' (1 Samuel 22:2).

3. *"liviers," or lifeholders – copyholders*: these are very distinct categories. A lifehold lease was held for the lifetime of named individuals, usually, but not always, across three generations of a single family. While it could be renewed at the end of the last designated life, a landlord was under no legal obligation to do so. The loss of a home because of the last lifeholder's death is crucial in both *The Woodlanders* (1887) and *Tess of the d'Urbervilles* (1891). Copyhold, a much more secure form of tenancy, derived its name from a tenant's copy of the court-roll recording a manor's customary property holdings and rents. While the lord of the manor retained ownership of the property, copyhold gave protection against arbitrary eviction and could be passed down through a family, although economic necessity – such as the need to make expensive property repairs – often caused the surrender of permanent tenancy rights.

4. *blink like Ashton at the disappearance of Ravenswood*: in Sir Walter Scott's *The Bride of Lammermoor* (1819), Ravenswood, galloping along a seashore to meet Colonel Ashton in a duel, is suddenly swallowed up by quicksand: 'At once the figure became invisible, as if it had melted into the air. He [Ashton] rubbed his eyes, as if he had witnessed an apparition' (Chapter XXXIV).

5. *Horewood*: 'Yalbury Wood' (95), Hardy's name for Yellowham Wood between Dorchester and Puddletown.

6. *skimmity-ride*: primarily a rural practice, a skimmington was a procession, usually involving recognizable effigies or actual human impersonators, intended to mock and shame infidelity or spousal abuse. Skimmington was also the name for the effigy, often of a shrewish wife or a husband wearing cuckold's horns, probably derived from the image of a wife attacking her husband with a skimming-ladle. Under various names, the custom was widespread, and continued even after it was declared illegal (1882) under the Highway Act. See Firor, pp. 238–42.

7. *if a day*: in MS/G/HW, Mother Cuxsom continues to recall Casterbridge's last skimmington: '"Twer about Jane Criddle . . . that used to beat her husband with the mop-stem.'

8. *a bad bargain in any way*: 'not too particularly his own' (95). MS reads 'a scold, or a bad bargain in any way'. The successive changes put the emphasis more forthrightly on sexual offence. This may account for the removal of details of Casterbridge's last skimmington-ride (see n. 7 above), which seems to have lampooned shrewishness rather than sexual irregularity.

9. *no evidence remained*: MS/G/HW read 'no evidence, beyond the simple entry in a remote parish register, remained' (see Chapter XII, n. 8).

CHAPTER XXXVII

1. *Royal Personage*: in his 1895 Preface, Hardy invokes the visit of a 'Royal personage' in the 'real history' of Casterbridge (see Appendix II). The only such visit that fits the novel's approximate time scheme is that of Prince Albert in late July 1849. He was on his way to Weymouth to lay the foundation stone of the Portland Breakwater, and, unlike his fictional *alter ego*, arrived by railway, which had penetrated as far as Dorchester two years earlier.

2. *the third King George*: George III (reigned 1760–1820) made recurrent summer visits to Weymouth and would have passed through Dorchester on the way.

3. *by an artist*: in MS/G/HW/A86, the artist is named as 'one Miggs' and the sign-painter as 'Turpess'.

4. *advanced*: 'staggered' (12).

5. *Farfrae immediately rose*: 'Farfrae, with Mayoral authority, immediately rose' (95).

6. *Calphurnia's cheek was pale*: in Shakespeare's *Julius Caesar*, Brutus notices Calpurnia's pale cheek when her husband Caesar, having just refused the crown three times, suffers an epileptic seizure, shortly after being warned to 'Beware the Ides of March'. But more relevant to the novel's situation is Caesar's recent triumph over his rival and former ally, Pompey. His new eminence provokes hostility in the future conspirators, and Cassius, whom Brutus is addressing, is particularly indignant. Once having saved Caesar's life, he now bitterly typifies himself as a 'wretched creature' who 'must bend his body / If Caesar carelessly but nod on him' (I.ii). This parallel to Henchard's subordination to Farfrae and Lucetta is underscored by Mixen Lane's resentment of what it sees as Lucetta's haughtiness.

7. *rattled heavily as Pharaoh's chariots up the straight High Street and out upon the great open road*: 'rattled heavily as Pharaoh's chariots down Corn Street and out upon the Budmouth Road' (95). The change gives a more direct route out of Dorchester to Weymouth. The chariot reference (absent from MS/G/HW) derives from Exodus 14:25. Having parted the waters of the Red Sea, Moses leads the Israelites over dry ground between walls of water. The Egyptian army pursues them, but the Lord 'took off [bound] their chariot wheels, that they drave them heavily'. The chariots were inundated when the waters closed again.

8. *to go snacks with him*: 'to go snacks wi' en' (95), a change designed, like numerous other minor speech modifications, to heighten colloquialism. 'To go snacks with' means in a general sense to share something or divide profits, but more specifically to marry.

CHAPTER XXXVIII

1. *He can rub brine on a green wound*: salt water applied to a new wound can help prevent infection, but is also painful. The metaphor is not altogether apt since the motivation of someone doing this would presumably be a desire to heal rather than vindictiveness.

2. *And here's a hand . . . a hand o' thine*: the lines are from the fourth, penultimate, stanza of Robert Burns's version of the traditional 'Auld Lang Syne' (see Chapter VIII for Farfrae's singing of it at the King of Prussia).

3. *the forenoon*: 12 adds 'and his conviction that Henchard had been drinking'.

4. *Royalty be—*: 'Royalty be damned' (95).

5. *loft*: 'loosened his arm' added in 12.

6. *three or four miles*: 'one or two miles' (95).

CHAPTER XXXIX

1. *by main force*: in MS/G/HW the maid gives fuller details of the effigy, including a gold necklace and ear-drops 'like the pendulum of the clock that shows his inside in Facey's window'.

2. *rigid wildness . . . were growing*: the subject/verb disagreement was not noticed until 20, when 'were' became 'was'.

3. *cleavers*: 'tongs, tambourines' added here in 95, presumably to clarify Jopp's and the landlady's concealment of kitchen tongs and tambourine later in the chapter.

4. *Gover'ment staves*: in Hardy's short story 'The Three Strangers' (1883; collected in *Wessex Tales*, 1888), another bumbling constable excusing himself for inaction by claiming temporary separation from his staff gives a description of this cipher of office: 'there's the king's royal crown a painted on en in yaller and gold, and the lion and the unicorn, so as when I raise en up and hit my prisoner, 'tis made a lawful blow thereby'. Such truncheons were often highly decorated.

5. *Blowbody was one of the magistrates*: all other editions, including the serial versions, read '(Blowbody was the third of the three borough magistrates).'

6. *like the crew of* Comus: in Milton's masque *Comus* (1634), the pagan god Comus presides over 'a rout of Monsters', with human bodies and animal heads, who make 'a riotous and unruly noise, with Torches in their hands'. When a chaste Lady approaches, whom Comus intends to beguile with magic, he orders the monsters to disperse and hide lest 'Our number . . . affright'.

CHAPTER XL

1. *In a cutting on the summit of the last he listened*: 'In Yalbury Bottom, the plain at the foot of the hill, he listened' (95). In 12, the first part of this sentence was further revised to read 'In Yalbury Bottom, or Plain'. Also in 95, 'the moor' became 'Durnover moor', 'almost' was added before 'a third hill', and 'of Yalbury Wood' was added after 'spruce and larch'.

2. *Henchard thereupon descended the hill . . . foot of the incline*: 'Henchard thereupon retraced his steps along Yalbury Plain, the gig coming up with him as its driver slackened speed between two plantations' (12). This modification had been partially made in 95, but without reference to Yalbury Plain, and with the driver slackening speed 'at the foot of the decline'. In the next paragraph also, the by-road became specifically 'Cuckoo Lane' (95). All these changes evoke more precisely both the actual topography of the area east of Dorchester and the imaginative topography of Hardy's earlier novels, particularly *Under the Greenwood Tree* (1872).

3. *at a point where it plunged into a cutting . . . guarding himself from attack*: 'inviting him to come a particular way, where he [an assailant (12)] might have confederates, instead of [going (12)] his purposed way, where there might be a better opportunity of guarding himself from attack' (95).

4. *He had left his wife not long ago in perfect health*: 'He knew his wife was with child, but' added to the beginning of this sentence in 95 (see Chapter XXXV, n. 3).

5. *no joy in heaven*: see Luke 15:7: 'I say unto you, that likewise joy shall be in heaven over one sinner that repenteth, more than over ninety and nine just persons, which need no repentance.' This is Christ's conclusion to the parable of the lost sheep.

6. *a less scrupulous Job*: as has earlier been suggested of Henchard (see Chapter XII, n. 7), his temperamental volatility brings him rapidly to self-cursing. By contrast, Job is distinguished for righteousness and patience in adversity. He undergoes far greater tribulations than Henchard, none of them self-made, before his reduction to the comprehensive self-cursing of Job 3:1–10.

7. *dangerous illness*: 'and miscarriage' added in 95.

8. *bare facts of her peculiar intimacy with*: 'bare facts of her void marriage with' (MS/G/HW); 'bare facts of her early attachment to' (A86).

CHAPTER XLI

1. *I went through Casterbridge on my way to Weydon Priors*: 'I landed at Havenpool and went through Casterbridge on my way to Falmouth' (95). Havenpool (Poole) is a Dorset port to the east of Casterbridge, Falmouth the Cornish port where the Newsons lived on returning from Canada. The change makes the journey westward rather than north-eastward. Hardy presumably decided that the Falmouth friend, to whom Susan 'confided her history' (Chapter IV) before Newson's disappearance, would seem a more likely source for news of her present whereabouts than anyone at Weydon Priors. Hardy also contradicts the north-eastward direction later, when Newson mentions he has travelled through Casterbridge westward (see Chapter XLIII, n. 13).

2. *If she had known the truth she would never have left me*: 'If she had seen it as what it was, she would never have left me' (95). Henchard's self-justifying emphasis on Susan's naivety overstates itself. His later claim that 'She could write her own name, and no more' is disproved by the letter about Elizabeth-Jane she left for him.

3. *A year ago and more*: 'Two years ago next twenty-fourth of March' (MS/G/ HW/A86). MS also shows two deleted variants: '<The> twenty-fourth of March' and '<Three> years ago next twenty-fourth of March'.

4. *up the road*: 'up the road, crossing Bull-stake' (12).

5. *as they may be*: in MS/G/HW/A86 Henchard then inquires about the dream. Elizabeth-Jane responds evasively and 'remained in thought a long while'.

6. *the path leading to no place in particular*: 'the path leading only to a deep reach of the stream called Blackwater' (12; in HW/A86 the sentence ends at 'seldom found going that way'). Ten Hatches can still be seen, although with five of the actual hatches now removed.

7. *amongst the willows*: 12 adds 'at Blackwater', and also 'by the magistrates' after 'discovery'.

CHAPTER XLII

1. *Time, in his own grey style*: the quotation is from Shelley's *Epipsychidion* (1821). In the poem it is not 'Time' that teaches but 'Young Love' that would teach Time, but for the incapacity of the poet's muse: 'my moth-like muse has burnt its wings;/ Or, like a dying swan who soars and sings,/ Young Love should teach Time, in his own grey style,/ All that thou art' (ll. 53–6). 'Thou' is Emilia Viviani, with whom Shelley was infatuated and to whom the poem is addressed. Shelley's pursuit of an ideal love in the poem ironically contrasts Farfrae's pragmatic estimation of Lucetta.

2. *Juno's bird . . . Argus eyes*: when Jupiter fell in love with the mortal, Io, his wife Juno's suspicion caused him to turn Io into a white heifer. Juno, undeceived, requested the heifer as a gift. She set the giant Argus Panoptes, fifty of whose hundred eyes were always open even in sleep, to watch over the heifer. On Jupiter's orders, Mercury lulled all the eyes to sleep with his flute-playing and decapitated Argus. Juno distributed his eyes over the tail feathers of the peacock, her sacred bird.

3. *latterly been taking*: 95 adds[6], that the new books which had so surprised him,' (see n. 6 below).

4. *with an appraising, pondering gaze at her*: 'with a Scotchman's pondering, world-not-realised gaze at her' (MS/G/HW/A86).

5. *I have a reason for it*: 'I have no reason for it' (87); 'I have no great reason for it' (95). Also in 95, 'such as it is' was inserted after Elizabeth-Jane's later 'My reason, however'. Hardy may have made these minor adjustments because 'I have a reason for it', coming before any mention of an interest in the sea, risks sounding coyly flirtatious. This is certainly true in MS/G/HW/A86, where Elizabeth-Jane, after denying that she favours this direction, admits a secret reason for choosing it but makes no mention of the sea, thereby implying that her preference may have something to do with Farfrae's walking habits.

6. *a sailor's*: 1895 continues: ' "Thank you for those new books, Mr. Farfrae," she added shyly. "I wonder if I ought to accept so many!" "Ay! why not? It gives me more pleasure to get them for you, than you to have them!" "It cannot!" ' (see n. 3 above).

7. *Once he was standing . . . "Dearest Elizabeth-Jane"*: 'At last full proof was given him. He was standing behind a wall close to the place at which Farfrae encountered her. He heard the young man address her as "Dearest Elizabeth-Jane," and then kiss her, the girl looking quickly round to assure herself that nobody was near' (95). This change results from a conflation of two episodes in MS/G/HW/A86. One is the same wall scene as in E86; the other, deleted for E86, has Henchard spying on the couple through a telescope, and seeing them kiss. Hardy used components of both for the 95 emendation, but he did not notice that Henchard, concealed by a wall, would not see Elizabeth-Jane 'looking quickly round'. When the telescope scene was deleted in E86, parts were used for the description of Henchard seeing Newson's return (see Chapter XLIII, n. 3).

CHAPTER XLIII

1. *Mrs. Stannidge, having rolled . . . a tittle for Farfrae's domestic plans*: this entire section was dropped from both HW and A86.

2. *a lion in the path*: 'an irksome obstacle' (95). The image of a 'fangless lion' is used in the following relocated passage (see n. 3), so Hardy presumably made the change to avoid repetition.

3. *But what if he were mistaken . . . personal humiliation*: this section originally appeared in Chapter XLIV as part of Henchard's rumination after hearing of Elizabeth-Jane's forthcoming wedding from the driver of a road wagon (see Appendix I, n. 2). It retained its position in this present chapter in the 95 restoration. The next extended section ('Whether this were . . . immediately taking his measures') is an addition to E86 (see Chapter XLII, n. 7). It includes Henchard's spying on Elizabeth-Jane and Farfrae through a telescope, his sight of Newson returning to Casterbridge, and his learning from Elizabeth-Jane of the strange letter she has received.

4. *A quarter of a mile from the highway was a pre-historic earthen fort*: 'A quarter of a mile from the highway was the pre-historic fort called Mai Dun' (95); 'Two miles out, a quarter of a mile from the highway, was the pre-historic fort called Mai Dun' (12). Maiden Castle, one of the most spectacular prehistoric structures in Britain, was a Neolithic earthwork and long barrow, an Iron Age fortress, and site of a Romano-British temple. Hardy describes it more fully in his story 'A Tryst at an Ancient Earthwork' (1885; collected in *A Changed Man and Other Tales* [1913]).

5. *He stood in dark despair, obscured by "the shade from his own soul upthrown"*: the quotation is from Shelley's *The Revolt of Islam* (1818), Canto VIII, stanza vi. The image was originally used to define Henchard's response when he sees Newson dancing with Elizabeth-Jane at her wedding. When Henchard's return for the wedding was deleted in E86 (see Chapter XLIV, n. 7), it was transferred to this scene, itself an addition to E86. It was returned to its original place in 95.

6. *missed me*: 'a trick was played him, so that he did not' (95); 'see me' added in 12.

7. *difficult*: 'disciplined' (MS/G/HW/A86). Early versions of Elizabeth-Jane's response throughout this exchange show her with rather less emotion to master, for reasons given in the next note.

8. *for she could not urge. . . which could argue it away*: this is expanded from MS/G/HW/A86, which read, 'and it must be confessed that there was a leaven of half-heartedness in her deprecations, which after-events explained'. The after-events are the revelation that Elizabeth-Jane knows already of Newson's return and has been seeing him secretly. This explains her cooler response in the pre-E86 versions to Henchard's decision to leave.

9. *"It is because of Donald" . . . when Newson should come*: added in E86; 87 drops 'evasively'.

10. *with unfeigned wonder and sorrow. . . before finally letting him go*: 'with unfeigned regret – keeping him back a minute or two, as if she had something to explain, but finally letting him go without explaining it' (MS/G/HW/A86). In this early version, Henchard is leaving because of the prospective marriage between Elizabeth-Jane and Farfrae: unlike Elizabeth-Jane, he knows nothing of Newson's return (see n. 3 above). In 12, Henchard's 'straw' basket became 'rush', as in Chapters 1 and XLIV.

11. *I – Cain. . . not greater than I can bear*: after killing his brother Abel in a jealous rage, Cain is condemned by God to be 'a fugitive and a vagabond'. Unlike Henchard, 'Cain said unto the Lord, My punishment is greater than I can bear' (Genesis 4:12–13). MS shows '<a second>' and '<another>' deleted before 'Cain', and 'outcast' replacing '<fugitive>'.

12. *The meeting with the light-hearted man. . . wondered about my purchases*: 'light-hearted father' (95). In MS/G/HW/A86, Elizabeth-Jane, aware of Newson's reappearance for some time, has been meeting him two or three times a week on the Budmouth Road, under the guise of assignations with Farfrae. The passages in E86 revealing that Newson, not Farfrae, has financed Elizabeth-Jane's purchases were deleted in 95.

13. *nine or ten months before that day*: 95 adds 'last week'. Hardy must have forgotten that a few paragraphs earlier he had referred to Newson calling on Henchard 'between one and two years before this time'. The confusion may have resulted from the deletion of Elizabeth-Jane's prior knowledge of Newson's presence in Casterbridge (see n. 12 above). If her meetings with Newson on the Budmouth Road (MS/G/HW/A86) had been going on for some months, the discrepancy of 'nine or ten months' and 'between one and two years' is explained. Topography is also erratic in this paragraph: an initial journey to Weydon Priors would have taken Newson north-eastwards out of Casterbridge, not westward (see Chapter XLI, n. 1).

14. *Elizabeth sighed . . . forget him now*: ' "I never heard of such a thing!" said Elizabeth-Jane. "That's enough. He's a bad man. I can forget him now" ' (MS/ G/HW/A86).

15. *Thus they conversed. . . his own honour*: 'Thus they conversed; and there was nobody to set before Elizabeth any extenuation of the absent one's deceit' (95). The longer E86 reading incorporates material taken from the excised exchange between Henchard and Elizabeth-Jane at her wedding (see Chapter XLIV, n. 6, and Appendix I, n. 12). It was restored to its original position in 95.

CHAPTER XLIV

1. *two or three and twenty years before*: 'five and twenty years before' (12).

2. *path*: 'wandering' (12). The reference to the Canadian woodsman derives from a passage Hardy summarized in his 'Literary Notes I': 'Cruising in the woods of Canada – Without a compass the best woodsman cannot keep a straight line. Walks in circles, occupying him from ½ hour to 2 hrs. & an unobservant person will circumnavigate the same 100 acres of wood all day long' (*Literary Notebooks*, I, item 976 and note; the source is John Rowan, *The Emigrant and Sportsman in Canada* [1876], p. 273).

3. *no daughter of thine*: in all other editions except 87, there is a paragraph here revealing that Henchard took a hay-trussing job at 'a pastoral farm near the old western highway', proximity to the major road giving him the sense that, although fifty miles from Elizabeth-Jane, he was nearer to her 'than he would be at a roadless spot only half as remote'.

4. *painted scene to him*: MS shows the deletion '<He cared not even enough for life to take steps for putting himself out of it>', a claim contradicted by the next paragraph's final sentence.

5. *while I. . . if I try*: 'while I, <a blot &> an <sham> outcast, & an encumbrance <upon the ground>, wanted by nobody, live on, & can't die if I try' (MS); 'while I, an outcast, an encumberer of the ground, wanted by nobody, and despised by all, live on against my will!' (95).

6. *Had he been able to extend his vision. . . That happy form was Captain Newson's*: this whole passage replaces in E86 and 87 a much longer section deleted for E86 and later restored 'at the instance of some good judges across the Atlantic, who strongly represented that the home edition suffered from the omission' (see Hardy's Preface [Appendix II]). The deleted section appears in this volume as Appendix I. It describes Henchard's journey to Casterbridge for the wedding, his cold reception by Elizabeth-Jane, and his final departure. The American friends who advised restoration were the sisters Rebekah and Catherine Owen (see Weber, pp. 152–3).

CHAPTER XLV

1. *Crusoe*: the central character of Daniel Defoe's *Robinson Crusoe* (1719), who, having spent years on a desert island after being shipwrecked, is eventually rescued and returns home.

2. *Mrs. Elizabeth Farfrae. . . of his own accord*: other editions, excepting 87, have here an episode consequent upon Henchard's return to the wedding (see Chapter XLIV, n. 6). He had brought as a wedding present a caged goldfinch, later found dead in a concealed corner. A maid learns that the 'farmer's man who called on the evening of the wedding' was seen with it, and Elizabeth-Jane realizes its source. This causes her to soften, and initiate a search for Henchard.

3. *to extenuate nothing*: see Othello's final words to Lodovico before stabbing himself: 'I pray you, in your letters, / When you shall these unlucky deeds relate, / Speak of me as I am; nothing extenuate, / Nor set down aught in malice' (*Othello*, V.ii.).

4. *less than a month before*: E86/87 only. In the same paragraph, other editions have Henchard moving 'eastward . . . on the road by which he had come' rather than 'westward . . . on the road by which he had gone'. E86 is the first edition to specify the 'Melchester' highway.

5. *Minerva-eyes of one "whose gestures beamed with mind"*: for Minerva, see Chapter XX, n. 3. The quotation is from Shelley's *The Revolt of Islam* (1818) where the words describe the female members of a senate of immortals (Canto I, stanza liv).

6. *he had turned back. . . crossed Egdon Heath*: 'he had left the Melchester coach-road at Weatherbury by a forking highway which skirted the north of Egdon Heath' (95). A version of this had been the pre-E86 reading, but with no mention of Weatherbury and with the highway still crossing rather than skirting Egdon. These adjustments result from Hardy's deletion and restoration of Henchard's return to Casterbridge.

7. *Diana Multimammia*: Diana the many-breasted. Sometimes confused with her virginal namesake (goddess of the hunt and the moon), Diana of Ephesus was a goddess of fertility and represented in her temple by a statue with many breasts. MS shows '<of the Ephesians>'.

8. *some woodland to the east, the first outpost of which*: 'some extension of the heath to the north of Anglebury, a prominent feature of which' (95). Hardy's Anglebury is the actual Wareham, about seventeen miles east of Dorchester. Egdon and its environs figure most prominently in *The Return of the Native* (1878).

9. *for the night*: 87 adds ' "and that will make a hole in a sovereign," said Farfrae.'

10. *Whittle*: '<Lackday> <Lackstraw> Whittle' (MS).

11. *for the purpose*: 12 adds, 'The rafters were sunken, and the thatch of the roof in ragged holes.'

12. *I couldn't forget him . . . walking along in the rain*: 'I seed en go down street on the night of your worshipful's wedding to the lady at yer side' (95). This is a slightly modified restoration of the pre-E86 reading.

13. *He was as wet. . . wet for days*: deleted in 95. This and the previous sentence added in E86.

14. *she said at last*: 95 adds 'through her tears'. After 'What bitterness lies there!' 95 also restores from pre-E86, 'Oh I would not have minded so much if it had not been for that last parting!', which in 12 became 'for my unkindness at that last parting!'.

15. *for not having searched him out sooner*: this replaced 'for having misunderstood him on his final visit' (MS/G/HW/A86). In 95, both versions were included in the same sentence.

16. *Capharnaum*: the town, more usually called Capernaum, on the Sea of Galilee in which Jesus was living when he began preaching, performed a number of his miracles, and selected the disciples (see Matthew 4:13–23 and 8:5–27). Hardy invokes it to distinguish between periods of turmoil and peace in Elizabeth-Jane's life.

17. *even to the magnitude of positive pleasure*: deleted in 95.

APPENDIX I

Chapter XLIV: Henchard's Return to Casterbridge

The following is the text (taken from the American first edition) of the original later stages of Chapter XLIV, describing Henchard's return to Casterbridge for the marriage of Elizabeth-Jane and Farfrae. In 1895, it was restored, in somewhat modified form, to English editions. See A Note on the Text.

He often kept an eager ear upon the conversation of those who passed along the road, not from a general curiosity by any means, but in the hope that among these travelers to and from Casterbridge some would sooner or later speak of that place. The distance, however, was too great to lend much probability to his desire, and the highest result of his attention to way-side words was that he did, indeed, hear the name of "Casterbridge" uttered one day by the driver of a road wagon. Henchard ran to the gate of the field he worked in, and hailed the speaker, who was a stranger.

"Yes, I've come from there, maister," he said, in answer to Henchard's inquiry. "I trade up and down, ye know, though what with this traveling without horses, that's getting so common, my work will soon be done."

"Anything moving in the old place, may I ask?"

"All the same as usual."

"I've heard that Mr. Farfrae, the late mayor, is thinking of getting married. Now is that true or not?"

"I couldn't say for the life o' me. Oh no; I should think not."

"But, yes, John; you forget," said a woman inside the wagon tilt. "What were those packages we took there at the beginning of the week? Surely they said a wedding was coming off soon – on Martin's Day."[1]

The man declared he remembered nothing about it, and the wagon went on jangling over the hill.

Henchard was convinced that the woman's memory served her well.

The date was an extremely probable one, there being no reason for delay on either side. He might, for that matter, write and inquire of Elizabeth, but his instinct for sequestration had made the course difficult. Yet before he left her she had said that for him to be absent from her wedding was not as she wished it to be.

The remembrance would continually revive in him now that it was not Elizabeth and Farfrae who had driven him away from them, but his own haughty sense that his presence was no longer desired. What if he had been mistaken in his views? – if there had been no necessity that his own absolute separation from her should be involved in the incident of her marriage?

He proceeded to draw a picture of the alternative – himself living like a fangless lion about back rooms of a house in which his step-daughter was mistress: an inoffensive old man, tenderly smiled on by Elizabeth, and good-naturedly tolerated by her husband. It was terrible to his pride to descend so low; and yet, for the girl's sake, he might put up with any thing; even from Farfrae; even snubbings and masterful tongue-scourgings. The privilege of being in the house she occupied would almost outweigh the personal humiliation.[2]

But how to initiate this reversal of all his former resolves, without causing husband and wife to despise him for his inconsistency, was a question which made him tremble and brood.

He cut and cut his trusses two days more, and then he concluded his hesitancies by a sudden impassioned resolve to go to the wedding festivity. Neither writing nor message would be expected from him. She had regretted his determination to be absent – his unexpected presence would fill the little unsatisfied corner that would probably have place in her just heart without him.

To intrude as little of his personality as possible upon a gay event with which that personality could show nothing in keeping, he decided not to make his appearance till evening, when stiffness would have worn off, and the question who was or who was not present had become a matter of indifference.[3]

Not wishing to be in Casterbridge an hour earlier than the time planned, he started on foot two mornings before St. Martin's tide, allowing himself about sixteen miles to perform for each of the three days' journey, reckoning the wedding day as one. There was only one town[4] of any importance along his course, and here he stopped on the second night, not only to rest, but to prepare himself for the next evening.

Having no clothes but the working suit he stood in – now stained and distorted by their two months of hard usage – he entered a shop and made some purchases which should put him, externally at any rate, a little in harmony with the prevailing tone of the morrow. A rough yet respectable coat and hat, a new shirt and neck-cloth, were the chief of these; and having satisfied himself that in appearance at least he would not offend her, he proceeded to the more interesting particular of buying her some present.

What should that present be? He walked up and down the street, regarding dubiously the display in the shop-windows from a gloomy sense that what he might most like to give her would be beyond his miserable pocket. A caged gold-finch met his eyes; the cage was a plain small one, the shop humble, and he concluded that he could afford the modest sum asked – afford it or not, he would have it somehow. A sheet of newspaper was tied round the bird's wire prison, and with the wrapped-up cage in his hand Henchard sought a lodging for the night.

Next day he set out upon the last stage, and was soon within the district which had been his trading-ground in by-gone years. Part of the distance he traveled by carrier, seating himself in the darkest corner at the back of that trader's van; and as the other passengers, mainly women going short journeys, mounted and alighted in front of Henchard they talked over much local news, not the least portion of this being the wedding then in course of celebration at the town they were nearing. It appeared that the town band had been hired, and lest their convivial instincts should get the better of their skill, the further step had been taken of engaging the string band from Budmouth, so that there would be a reserve to fall back upon in case of need.

He heard, however, but few particulars beyond those known to him already, the incident of deepest interest in the ride being the soft pealing of the Casterbridge bells, which reached the traveler's ears while the van paused on top of a hill[5] to have the drag lowered. The time was just after twelve o'clock.

Those notes were a signal that all had gone well; that there had been no slip 'twixt cup and lip in this case; that Elizabeth Jane and Donald Farfrae were man and wife.

Henchard did not care to ride any further with his chattering companions after hearing this sound. Indeed, it quite unmanned him; and not wishing to arrive in Casterbridge till evening,[6] he alighted here with his bundle and bird-cage, and was soon left as a lonely figure on the broad white highway.

It was the hill on which he had waited to meet Farfrae, nearly two years earlier, to tell him of the serious illness of his wife Lucetta. The place was unchanged; the same larches sighed the same notes; but Farfrae had another wife, and, as Henchard knew, a better one. He only hoped that Elizabeth Jane had obtained a better home than had been hers at the former time.

He passed the remainder of the day in a curious high-strung condition, unable to do much but think of the approaching meeting with her, and sadly satirize himself for his emotions thereon, as a Samson shorn.[7] Such an innovation on Casterbridge customs as a flitting of bridegroom and bride from the town immediately after the ceremony was not likely; but if it should have taken place, he would wait till their return. To assure himself on this point, he asked a market-man when near the town if the newly married couple had gone away; and was promptly informed that they had not; they were at that hour, according to all accounts, entertaining a houseful of guests at their home in Corn Street.

Henchard dusted his boots, washed his hands at the river-side, and proceeded up the town. He need have made no inquiries beforehand, for, on drawing near Farfrae's residence, it was plain to the least observant that festivity prevailed within, and that Donald himself shared it, his voice being distinctly audible in the street, giving strong expression to a song of his native country.[8] Idlers were standing on the pavement in front; and, wishing to escape the notice of these Henchard passed quickly on to the door.

It was wide open; the hall was lighted extravagantly, and people were going up and down the stairs. His courage failed him; to enter, foot-sore, laden, and poorly dressed, into the midst of such resplendency was to bring needless humiliation upon her he loved, if not to court repulse from her husband. Accordingly he went round into the back street that he knew so well, entered the garden, and came quietly into the house through the kitchen, temporarily depositing the bird and cage under a bush outside to lessen the awkwardness of his arrival.

Solitude and sadness had so emolliated Henchard that he now feared circumstances he would formerly have scorned, and he began to wish that he had not taken upon himself to arrive at such a juncture. However, his progress was made unexpectedly easy by his discovering alone in the kitchen an elderly woman who seemed to be acting as provisional housekeeper during the convulsions from which Farfrae's establishment was just then suffering. She was one of those people whom nothing surprises, and though to her, a total stranger, his request must have seemed odd, she willingly volunteered to go up and inform the master and mistress of the house that he[9] had come.

On second thoughts she said that he had better not wait in the kitchen, but come up into the little back parlor, which was empty. He thereupon followed her thither, and she left him. Just as she got across the landing to the door of the best parlor, a dance was struck up, and she returned to say that she would wait till that was over before announcing him – Mr. and Mrs. Farfrae having both joined in the figure.

The door of the front room had been taken off its hinges to give more space, and that of the room Henchard sat in being ajar, he could see fractional parts of the dancers whenever their gyrations brought them near the doorway, chiefly in the shape of the skirts of dresses and streaming curls of hair; together with about three-fifths of the band in profile, including the restless shadow of a fiddler's elbow and the tip of the bass-viol bow.

The gayety jarred upon Henchard's spirits; and he could not quite understand why Farfrae, a much-sobered man and a widower, who had had his trials, should have cared for it all, notwithstanding the fact that he was quite a young man still, and quickly kindled to enthusiasm by dance and song. That the sober Elizabeth, who had long ago appraised life at a moderate value, and who knew, in spite of her maidenhood, that marriage was, as a rule, no dancing matter, should have had zest for this revelry surprised him still more. However, young people could not quite be old people, he concluded, and custom was omnipotent.

With the progress of the dance the performers spread out somewhat, and then for the first time he caught a glimpse of the once-despised daughter who had mastered him and made his heart ache. She was in a dress of white silk or satin – he was not near enough to say which – snowy white, without a tinge of milk or cream; and the expression of her face was one of nervous pleasure rather than of gayety. Presently Farfrae came round, his exuberant movement making him conspicuous in a moment. The pair were not dancing together, but Henchard could discern that whenever the interchanges of the figure made them the partners of a moment their emotions breathed a much subtler essence than at other times.

By degrees Henchard became aware that the measure was trod by some one who out-Farfraed Farfrae in saltatory intenseness. This was strange, and it was stranger to find that the eclipsing personage was Elizabeth Jane's partner.

The first time that Henchard saw him he was sweeping grandly round, his head quivering and low down, his legs in the form of an X, and his back toward the door. The next time he came round in the other direction, his white waist-coat preceding his face, and his toes preceding his white waist-coat. That face – Henchard lived a lifetime the moment that he saw it – that face was Newson's!

Henchard pushed to the door, and for some seconds made no other movement. He rose to his feet, and stood in dark despair, obscured by "the shade from his own soul upthrown."[10]

He was no longer the man to stand these reverses unmoved. His agitation was great, and he would fain have been gone; but before he could leave the dance had ended, the housekeeper had informed Elizabeth Jane of the stranger who awaited her, and she entered the room immediately.

"Oh – it is – Mr. Henchard!" she said, starting coldly back.

"What, Elizabeth," he cried, as he seized her hand – "what do you say? *Mr.* Henchard? Don't, don't scourge me like that; call me worthless old Henchard – any thing – but don't 'ee be so cold as this! Oh, my maid, I see you have another – a real father in my place; you know all, but don't give all your heart to him. Can not you save a little room for me?"

She flushed up, and pulled her hand away.[11] "I could have loved you always – I would have gladly," said she. "But how can I when I know you have deceived me so – bitterly deceived me? You persuaded me that my father was not my father, allowed me to live on in ignorance of the truth for years, and then, when he came to see me, cruelly sent him away with an account of my death. Oh, how can I do any thing but *hate* a man who has served me like this!"

Henchard's lips half parted to begin an explanation; but he shut them up like a vise, and uttered not a sound. How should he, there and then, set before her with any effect the palliatives of his great faults – that he had himself been deceived in her identity, till informed by her mother's letter that his own child had died; that, in the second accusation, his lie had been the last desperate throw of a gamester who loved her affection better than his own honor?[12] Among the many hinderances to such a pleading not the least was this – that he did not sufficiently value himself to lessen his sufferings by any active means.

Waiving, therefore, his privilege of self-defense, he regarded only her discomposure. "Don't distress yourself on my account," he said, with proud self-mastery. "I would not wish it – at such a time, too, as this! I have done wrong in coming to 'ee. I see my error; but it is only for once, so forgive it. I'll never, never trouble 'ee again, Elizabeth Jane – no, not to my dying day. Good-night. Good-by!"

Thus Henchard went out from her rooms,[13] and she saw him no more.

Notes

1. *Martin's Day*: St Martin's Day, 11 November. This places the marriage date close to that of Susan and Henchard's remarriage (see Chapter XIV, n. 1).
2. *He proceeded to draw . . . personal humiliation*: in E86 this section was transferred to Chapter XLIII (see Chapter XLIII, n. 3), a position it retained in the 95 restoration. It was replaced for 95 with 'To make one more attempt to be near

her: to go back; to see her, to plead his cause before her, to ask forgiveness for his fraud, to endeavour strenuously to hold his own in her love; it was worth the risk of repulse, ay, of life itself.'

3. *and the question . . . indifference*: 'and a gentle wish to let bygones be bygones would exercise its sway in all hearts' (95).

4. *one town*: in 95 the town is identified as 'Shottsford'; in 12 'Melchester' is added.

5. *a hill*: 'Yalbury Hill' (95).

6. *till evening*: 'lest he should mortify Farfrae and his bride' added in 95.

7. *a Samson shorn*: Samson is shorn by his Philistine mistress, Delilah, after revealing to her that the source of his great strength is his hair. He is then captured and blinded by the Philistines (see Judges 16).

8. *song of his native country*: 'song of his dear native country that he loved so well as never to have revisited it' (95).

9. *he*: ' "a humble old friend" ' (95).

10. *'the shade from his own soul upthrown'*: see Chapter XLIII, n. 5.

11. *pulled her hand away*: 'gently drew her hand away' (95). Elizabeth-Jane's subsequent speech was also modified in 95, in an attempt to soften and extenuate her response. She refers to Newson as 'my warm-hearted real father', and 'how can I do anything but *hate*' becomes 'how can I love as I once did'.

12. *the palliatives . . . own honor*: see Chapter XLIII, n. 15.

13. *Thus Henchard . . . rooms*: 'Then, before she could collect her thoughts, Henchard went out from her rooms, and departed from the house by the back way as he had come' (95).

PREFACE

Readers of the following story who have not yet arrived at middle age are asked to bear in mind that, in the days recalled by the tale, the home Corn Trade, on which so much of the action turns, had an importance that can hardly be realized by those accustomed to the sixpenny loaf of the present date,[1] and to the present indifference of the public to harvest weather.

The incidents narrated arise mainly out of three events, which chanced to range themselves in the order and at or about the intervals of time here given, in the real history of the town called Casterbridge and the neighbouring country. They were the sale of a wife by her husband,[2] the uncertain harvests which immediately preceded the repeal of the Corn Laws,[3] and the visit of a Royal personage[4] to the aforesaid part of England.

The present edition of the volume, like the previous one, contains nearly a chapter which did not at first appear in any English copy, though it was printed in the serial issue of the tale, and in the American edition. The restoration was made at the instance of some good judges across the Atlantic,[5] who strongly represented that the home edition suffered from the omission. Some shorter passages and names, omitted or altered for reasons which no longer exist, in the original printing of both English and American editions, have also been replaced or inserted.

The story is more particularly a study of one man's deeds and character than, perhaps, any other of those included in my Exhibition of Wessex life. Objections have been raised to the Scotch language of Mr. Farfrae, the second character; and one of his fellow-countrymen went so far as to declare that men beyond the Tweed did not and never could say "warrld," "cannet," "advairrtisment," and so on. As this gentleman's pronunciation in correcting me seemed to my Southron ear an exact repetition of what my spelling implied, I was not struck with the truth of his remark, and somehow we did not get any forwarder in the matter. It must be remembered that the Scotchman of the tale is represented not as he would appear to other Scotchmen, but as he would appear to people of outer regions. Moreover, no attempt is made herein to reproduce his entire pronunciation phonetically, any more than that of the Wessex speakers. I should add, however, that this new edition of the book has had the accidental advantage of a critical overlooking by a professor of the tongue in question[6] – one of undoubted authority: – in fact he is a gentleman who adopted it for urgent personal reasons in the first year of his existence.

Furthermore, a charming non-Scottish lady, of strict veracity and admitted penetration, the wife of a well-known Caledonian, came to the writer shortly after the story was first published, and inquired if Farfrae were not drawn from her husband, for he seemed to her to be the living portrait of that (doubtless) happy man. It happened that I had never thought of her husband in constructing Farfrae. I trust therefore that Farfrae may be allowed to pass, if not as a Scotchman to Scotchmen, as a Scotchman to Southerners.

The novel was first published complete, in two volumes, in May 1886.

T. H.
February 1895 – May 1912.[7]

Notes

1. *sixpenny loaf of the present date*: in the years immediately before the repeal of the Corn Laws (1846), the cost of a quartern (4 lb) loaf was 8½*d*., down from a high of 17*d*. in the years before Waterloo. By the 1890s the price had stabilized at 5*d*.

2. *sale of a wife by her husband*: see Chapter IV, n. 4.

3. *the repeal of the Corn Laws*: while laws governing the import and export of corn had existed in England since the fifteenth century, the law passed in 1804 was far more severe than any of its predecessors in the levels of duty it imposed on the import of foreign corn. For the next forty years, through fluctuating harvests, prices and tariff scales, it was a bone of contention between landed agricultural interests and urban mercantile and industrial interests. After Richard Cobden and John Bright's formation of the Anti-Corn Law League (1839), the push for repeal accelerated. The repeal act of Sir Robert Peel's Conservative government passed into law in 1846, slashing duties immediately and reducing them to merely nominal levels by February 1849. As Chapter XXVI reveals, *The Mayor of Casterbridge*'s main action is set 'in the years immediately before foreign competition had revolutionized the trade in grain'.

4. *visit of a Royal personage*: see Chapter XXXVII, n. 1.

5. *some good judges across the Atlantic*: see Chapter XLIV, n. 6, and A Note on the Text.

6. *a professor of the tongue in question*: Hardy's friend, Sir George Douglas (1856–1935). See A Note on the Text.

7. *February 1895–May 1912*: Hardy's Preface is taken from the 1912 Wessex Edition. It had formerly appeared, in essentially the same form but without the final information about the date of first publication, in Osgood, McIlvaine's 1895 Wessex Novels edition.

APPENDIX III

Robert Barnes's Illustrations for the Serial Issue

When *The Mayor of Casterbridge* made its first appearance in twenty weekly parts (2 January–15 May 1886) in the *Graphic*, every instalment of Hardy's text was accompanied by an illustration prepared by the artist Robert Barnes (1840–95). The serial was running simultaneously in the American journal *Harper's Weekly*, which also included the Barnes illustrations, with the exception of those for 17 April and 8 and 15 May. The illustrations were among the most accomplished, in both design and mood, ever prepared for a Hardy serial. All twenty are available together here for the first time since their original issue.

Unlike his fairly active attention to the preparation of illustrations for some of his earlier work, Hardy had virtually no involvement with illustrations for *The Mayor of Casterbridge*. Barnes was seemingly chosen because he was one of the staff illustrators for the *Graphic*. He had a well-established reputation, particularly for scenes involving children and rustic life. While his work was somewhat limited in range, it was a range well suited to Hardy's settings. As Forrest Reid observes, his subjects 'might nearly all be members of a single family – a family of the well-to-do farming class, healthy, sturdy, producing no disquieting variations from the sound yeoman stock that has reached back from generation to generation'.[1]

This may well account for the craggily handsome Henchard appearing rather more convincing as a self-confident and well-groomed mayor (see Plates VIII and IX) than he does as a far from desolate-looking hay-trusser (Plate I) or beaten-down *habitué* of Grey's Bridge (Plate XIV). But he seems most distinctively true to characterization in those pictures (Plates XV, XVII) where the Wellingtonian and rather demonic cut of his profile dominates. Farfrae looks by comparison distinctly unformed, not to say callow, particularly in the scene (Plate X) in which he surprises Lucetta on his first admission to High Street Hall. In the same scene, and even more so in Plate XI, Lucetta's own face has a full-lipped and rounded voluptuousness presumably designed to evoke vaguely Gallic exoticism, in contrast to the markedly more delicate-featured Elizabeth-Jane. Surprisingly Susan, 'the Ghost', has finer features and greater real presence than either of them (see Plates I, II, III, and V). Perhaps inevitably, the unashamedly proletarian faces are more characterful: the hag-faced furmity woman (Plate II), the androgynous Nance Mockridge (Plate IX), Fall's wizened querulousness (Plate XII), and Newson's chubby and weathered good humour (Plate XIX).

The choice of scenes for depiction is less predictable than the novel's full complement of cameo moments might have encouraged. While Henchard's murderous attack on Farfrae at the granary (Plate XVII) and Lucetta's sight of the skimmity-ride (Plate XVIII) are both represented, at many other points Barnes chose to explore the less volatile moment before or after the central drama: Susan and Michael on the road into Weydon-Priors (Plate I) and, twenty years later, Susan seeking news of Henchard from the furmity woman (Plate II) rather than the wife-sale itself; Elizabeth-Jane explaining the contretemps with the bull to Farfrae (Plate XIII) rather than the actual attack or rescue. In one instance the scene is sufficiently peripheral that it was subsequently excised from the book versions: Farfrae giving Lucetta the news that he has seen Henchard courting, not realizing that the woman with whom he saw him was the disguised Lucetta herself (Plate XVI: see Chapter XXXV, n. 6).

It is unwise to read too much into these decisions, especially since Barnes must have faced the illustrator's equivalent of what Hardy saw as the unsatisfactoriness of serial publication. If for the author the difficulty was over-eventfulness generated by the need 'to get an incident into almost every week's part' (*Life and Work*, p. 185), for the artist the matching problem was the need to have one, and only one, illustration per issue, regardless of how events fell in somewhat arbitrarily divided instalments (the division occurring on occasion in mid-chapter). The unity and subtlety of the whole group is testimony to the success with which Barnes fulfilled his demanding commission.[2]

Notes

1. Forrest Reid, *Illustrators of the Eighteen Sixties* (1928; repr. New York: Dover, 1975), p. 256.

2. For the fullest discussion of the illustrations in Hardy's novels, see Arlene M. Jackson, *Illustration and the Novels of Thomas Hardy* (London: Macmillan, 1982).

GLOSSARY

In the case of words that have various meanings, the definitions given here relate to the specific contexts in which the words are used in *The Mayor of Casterbridge*.

Abbreviations
a. adjective
advb. adverb
int. interjection
sb. substantive
sb. pl. substantive plural
vb. verb

Adonis sb.	a handsome young man (from the mythic Greek youth loved by Aphrodite)
Alastor sb.	avenging spirit, nemesis (Greek)
Aphrodite sb.	Greek goddess of sexual love and beauty
arch-labels sb.	mouldings above windows
ashlar sb.	straight-edged stone used to face a building
ballet sb.	ballad, or song generally
barge-board sb.	carved decorative board placed against the gable end of a roof to conceal projecting roof beams
barley-mow sb.	a stack or heap of barley
be jowned int.	euphemism for 'be damned'
bell-metal sb.	an alloy of copper and tin used to make bells
bents sb.	stalks of stiff rough grass or sedge
blathers sb.	bladders
bloody warriors sb.	dark wallflowers
blower sb.	a sheet of metal placed to increase air flow up

	a chimney, and hence improve the drawing of a fire
box-passenger sb.	a passenger who shares the driver's seat on a coach
brick-nogging sb.	brickwork fitted between the timbers of wood-framed constructions
brougham sb.	a closed one-horse carriage, named from Lord Brougham
bruckle a.	frail, and hence untrustworthy
butter-firkin sb.	a small barrel in which butter is stored
carrefour sb.	crossroads (French)
cat-head sb.	a projecting beam with pulley attachment for lifting heavy loads
chain-shot sb.	cannon shot composed of two balls or half-balls joined by a chain, particularly for use against rigging in naval battles
chassez-déchassez a.	a dance term signifying movement to the right followed by return to the left to rejoin one's original line of progress (French)
chine sb.	the rim at the end of a cask
clane advb.	clean (i.e. cleanly, completely)
clodhopper sb.	literally, one who hops over ploughed land; hence an awkward lout
clue line sb.	a line coming from a ball of thread (more usually 'clew'), used for finding the way through a labyrinth
cockle-snail sb.	the edible interior (as opposed to the 'cockle-shell') of the cockle mollusc
combe sb.	a hollow or valley on the side of a hill
comminatory a.	threatening with divine retribution
coulter sb.	a blade or sharpened disc at the front of a plough which cuts through earth vertically in advance of the ploughshare
cow-barton sb.	cow-yard
coxcomb sb.	a foolish, foppish or conceited person
croud sb.	(also crowd) a Celtic stringed instrument, like

	a combination fiddle and harp
crutch sb.	'A handle consisting of a cross-bar like the head of a crutch' (*OED*)
cyma recta sb.	a double curve in mouldings, with upper part concave, lower part convex
dimity sb.	a light but hard-wearing cotton fabric woven in stripes or squares
dog days sb.	the summer's hottest period, from early July to early September, when Sirius, the Dog Star, rises at the same time as the sun
doggery sb.	mischievous behaviour
doxology sb.	hymn, verse or liturgy praising God
éclat sb.	lustre (French)
enfilade vb.	to rake from end to end with fire (military)
entablature sb.	originally that part of an architectural order above the column; here the decorated top of a mirror-frame
espalier sb.	a fruit-tree or bush that has been trained to grow flat against a wall or fence
étourderie sb.	blunder (French)
fairing sb.	a gift or treat (such as cakes or sweets) bought at a fair
fall sb.	a veil hanging from the front of a bonnet
felloe sb.	rim or rim segment of a wooden wheel to which spokes are attached
felo de se sb.	suicide (Anglo-Latin; literally 'felon of one-self')
fête carillonnée sb.	high festival, marked by the ringing of bells (French)
fibula sb.	a decorative clasp or brooch resembling a safety pin
field-flagon sb.	a vessel for taking liquid refreshment, particularly beer, into the fields
fiere sb.	friend (Scottish)
finikin a.	paltry, trifling
fish-seines sb.	large fishing nets

flock sb.	cotton or wool waste used to stuff mattresses or upholstery
fly sb.	a light one-horse covered carriage, available for hire
foot-pace sb.	the raised floor beneath an altar
friable a.	crumbly
furmity sb.	one of several variants on 'frumenty', a porridge-like dish made from hulled wheat boiled in spiced milk
fustian sb.	hard-wearing dyed cotton fabric
gaberlunzie sb.	a wandering beggar (Scottish)
gawk-hammer sb.	a dull stupid fellow, a fool
gazebo sb.	a summerhouse, pavilion or other structure situated to command a view
gibbous a.	either potbellied or hunchbacked
gig sb.	a light two-wheeled one-horse carriage
hag-rid a.	literally, ridden by a witch; hence afflicted by nightmare, tormented, troubled
ha'p'orth sb.	halfpennyworth
hay-bond sb.	the binding for a bundle of hay
Heptarchy sb.	the seven kingdoms of Anglo-Saxon England from the seventh to the ninth centuries, *viz.* Kent, East Anglia, Essex, Sussex, Wessex, Mercia and Northumbria
hob-and-nob vb.	to drink to each other alternately, and hence to chat or socialize
holland sb.	a linen fabric of variable quality named for the original country of its production
honeycombed a.	undermined
horse-drill sb.	a horse-drawn machine for planting seeds
humstrum sb.	a crude musical instrument of the hurdy-gurdy kind
hurdle sb.	a portable rectangular frame used to make fences or pens. Constructed from interwoven sticks of hazel or willow, hurdles were sometimes thatched to provide additional wind-protection

at lambing-time

Hyperborean a. northern (from a race in Greek mythology that lived beyond the North Wind)

iron dogs sb. andirons (also known as fire-dogs), used to support burning logs in a fireplace

Jötuns sb. a race of mythic Norse giants

journeyman sb. a craftsman who has completed apprenticeship and is employed on a daily wage

jumps sb. an under-bodice used (by the nineteenth century usually only in rural areas) instead of stays

Karnac sb. a Nile village in eastern Egypt, site of part of the ruins of Thebes

keacorn sb. gullet, throat or windpipe

ken sb. awareness or knowledge

kerseymere sb. a fine twilled soft woollen cloth

kit sb. a small fiddle, used especially by dancing-masters from the seventeenth to the nineteenth century

knee-naps sb. pl. leather knee-protectors worn by thatchers

lammiger sb. cripple

larry sb. disturbance, commotion

leery a. empty, hungry

list sb. a thick border, here of unrisen dough

locus standi sb. place to stand (Latin)

Lucifer sb. the planet Venus, as the morning star

mandy a. saucy, insolent

mantle sb. a loose cloak or wrap

mattock sb. a pick-like implement used for loosening earth or grubbing up roots

misérables sb. wretches (French)

mixen sb. a dung-heap

modus vivendi sb. literally 'way of living' (Latin); working compromise

moment-hand sb. second-hand

murrey-coloured a. of a purplish-red colour, like that of the mulberry

netting vb. sb.	the process of making small network articles, such as purses, with needles
oven pyle sb.	a long-handled flattened shovel for getting bread and pies in and out of ovens
pari passu advb.	at an equal pace (Latin)
patten sb.	a wooden platform attached by an instep strap to an ordinary shoe to lift the foot out of mud
pier sb.	a load-bearing pillar or buttress
pier-glass sb.	a tall narrow mirror, designed to be hung between windows
pig chaps sb.	the edible lower part of the cheeks, often prepared by pickling
pis aller sb.	last resort (French: literally 'to go worse')
plim vb.	swell
poll sb.	head
pot-house sb.	ale-house or tavern
Protean a.	variable, capable of taking on various forms (from Greek sea god Proteus)
puffing sb.	deliberate padding or inflation in clothing
quarter sb.	a measure of grain, equivalent to eight bushels
quickset sb.	a hawthorn hedge
ram's-horn sb.	a primitive wind instrument, made of ram-horn
randy sb.	party, celebration
rantipole a.	wild, disorderly, rough
reap-hook sb.	a sickle-like implement used specifically for cutting grain
refluent a.	backward-flowing
reticulated a.	criss-crossed, like a net
roof-tree sb.	the main timber in a roof ridge, to which upper ends of rafters are attached (also known as a ridge-pole)
rummer sb.	a large drinking-glass, often used for heated wine or liquor, especially when drinking toasts
sacrarium sb.	the sanctuary area adjacent to an altar.
sallow sb.	any of several small species of willow
saltatory a.	relating to dance

sash-bars sb.	the bars dividing panes of glass in a sash window
scheme sb.	astrological chart or horoscope
schiedam sb.	strong gin (named from the Dutch city of origin)
seed-lip sb.	a basket in which seed for hand-sowing is carried
sequestrate vb.	to seize by law funds or property for non-payment of debt
serpent sb.	an ancient bass woodwind instrument, named for its coiling elongated shape, used in village church and secular music until the mid-nineteenth century
ship-coal sb.	coal imported by sea, as opposed to inferior locally made charcoal
shock sb.	a number of corn sheaves stacked on end against each other
smockfrock sb.	a loose overgarment worn by farm-workers
snack sb.	a share or portion (as in 'to go snacks with')
sniff and snaff sb.	superficial comment and response, trivial pleasantry
snuffers sb. pl.	a scissor-like instrument for trimming candle-wicks or extinguishing flames
sock vb.	sigh
solicitus timor sb.	anxious fear (Latin)
sotto voce advb.	in an undertone (Ital.)
sough vb.	to produce a sighing or moaning sound, particularly used of wind passing through trees
spencer sb.	a short fitted jacket or coat, named from the second Earl Spencer
springe sb.	snare or trap
staddle sb.	a raised support for hay or corn stacks
staylace sb.	lace used to tighten corsets
steelyard sb.	a portable suspension scale
stock sb.	a long, close-fitting neckcloth
stonecrop sb.	a yellow-flowered herb, commonly found growing on rocks and old walls
stunpoll sb.	blockhead or dunce

swingel sb.	(usually swingle) an instrument for beating or scraping flax; the striking part of a flail; a flail-like weapon or cudgel
swipes sb.	inferior weak beer
sylph sb.	a spirit of the air, hence young graceful woman
tailing sb.	inferior grain or flour, often the residue after milling
tenterhooks sb.	literally, hooks to hold cloth stretched on a frame (tenter); metaphorically, to be 'on tenter-hooks' is to be in a state of suspense
Terpsichorean a.	pertaining to dance, from Terpsichore, the Greek Muse of dance and choral song
thill sb.	shaft of a cart or waggon to which horse is attached, hence 'thill-horse'
thimble-rigger sb.	a trickster at the swindling game of thimblerig, in which bystanders are challenged to guess under which of three rapidly moved thimbles a pea has been concealed
tilt bonnet sb.	a large stiff bonnet in the form of a wagon-tilt
tittle sb.	jot, smallest amount
toppered a.	knocked on the head
top-sawyer sb.	one who occupies a higher, and hence more comfortable, position (the 'bottom-sawyer' in a saw-pit would be showered with sawdust)
toss-pot sb.	a habitual and heavy drinker
tumulus sb.	an ancient burial mound or barrow
turmit-head sb.	turnip-head
twanking a.	complaining
varden sb.	farthing
'vation sb.	salvation
via sb.	road (Latin)
victorine sb.	a tippet, cape or scarf, usually made of fur
vitrified a.	given glass-like appearance by exposure to heat
vivâ voce a.	by word of mouth, oral (Latin)
wagon-tilt sb.	a canvas awning for covering a wagon

wamble vb.	to totter or stagger
wash sb.	pig-swill
water-tights sb.	water-tight boots
welkin sb.	sky or heavens
Weltlust sb.	appetite for worldly things (German)
wimble sb.	technically a gimlet or auger for boring holes, here an implement for making hay-bonds
withy basket sb.	basket woven from flexible willow or osier
Yahoo sb.	a coarse brutish person (from a race of humanoid creatures in Jonathan Swift's *Gulliver's Travels* [1726])
yard of clay sb.	a long-stemmed clay pipe
zwailing vb.	swaying about, swaggering

READ MORE IN PENGUIN

In every corner of the world, on every subject under the sun, Penguin represents quality and variety – the very best in publishing today.

For complete information about books available from Penguin – including Puffins, Penguin Classics and Arkana – and how to order them, write to us at the appropriate address below. Please note that for copyright reasons the selection of books varies from country to country.

In the United Kingdom: Please write to *Dept. EP, Penguin Books Ltd, Bath Road, Harmondsworth, West Drayton, Middlesex UB7 0DA*

In the United States: Please write to *Consumer Sales, Penguin USA, P.O. Box 999, Dept. 17109, Bergenfield, New Jersey 07621-0120.* VISA and MasterCard holders call 1-800-253-6476 to order Penguin titles

In Canada: Please write to *Penguin Books Canada Ltd, 10 Alcorn Avenue, Suite 300, Toronto, Ontario M4V 3B2*

In Australia: Please write to *Penguin Books Australia Ltd, P.O. Box 257, Ringwood, Victoria 3134*

In New Zealand: Please write to *Penguin Books (NZ) Ltd, Private Bag 102902, North Shore Mail Centre, Auckland 10*

In India: Please write to *Penguin Books India Pvt Ltd, 706 Eros Apartments, 56 Nehru Place, New Delhi 110 019*

In the Netherlands: Please write to *Penguin Books Netherlands bv, Postbus 3507, NL-1001 AH Amsterdam*

In Germany: Please write to *Penguin Books Deutschland GmbH, Metzlerstrasse 26, 60594 Frankfurt am Main*

In Spain: Please write to *Penguin Books S. A., Bravo Murillo 19, 1° B, 28015 Madrid*

In Italy: Please write to *Penguin Italia s.r.l., Via Felice Casati 20, I–20124 Milano*

In France: Please write to *Penguin France S. A., 17 rue Lejeune, F–31000 Toulouse*

In Japan: Please write to *Penguin Books Japan, Ishikiribashi Building, 2–5–4, Suido, Bunkyo-ku, Tokyo 112*

In South Africa: Please write to *Longman Penguin Southern Africa (Pty) Ltd, Private Bag X08, Bertsham 2013*

READ MORE IN PENGUIN

D. H. LAWRENCE

NOVELS

Aaron's Rod
The Lost Girl
The Rainbow
The Trespasser
Women in Love
The First Lady Chatterley
The Boy in the Bush
(with M. L. Skinner)

Lady Chatterley's Lover
The Plumed Serpent
Sons and Lovers
The White Peacock
Kangaroo
John Thomas and Lady Jane
Mr Noon

SHORT STORIES

Three Novellas: The Fox/
  The Ladybird/The Captain's
  Doll
St Mawr *and* The Virgin and
  the Gipsy
Selected Short Stories
The Complete Short Novels

The Prussian Officer
Love among the Haystacks
The Princess
England, My England
The Woman Who Rode
  Away
The Mortal Coil

TRAVEL BOOKS AND OTHER WORKS

Mornings in Mexico
Studies in Classic
  American Literature
Apocalypse
Twilight in Italy

Fantasia of the Unconscious
  and Psychoanalysis and the
  Unconscious
D. H. Lawrence and Italy

POETRY

D. H. Lawrence: Selected Poetry
Edited and Introduced by Keith Sagar
Complete Poems

Penguin are now publishing the Cambridge editions of D. H. Lawrence's texts. These are as close as can be determined to those he would have intended.